DIGGING AROUND THE PANDEMIC
THE SWIFTPAD EXTINCTION

DIGGING AROUND THE PANDEMIC

THE SWIFTPAD EXTINCTION

BY

S. LEE BARCKMANN

BARCKWORDS
PUBLISHING

TABLE OF CONTENTS

CAST OF CHARACTERS

Aldane Blyden – Kip's partner in some outrageous adventures

Alice Hunt – Jim Hunt's mother, leader at Rehain Compound, and influential person in West Coast circles

Alison Aykroyd – Spence's former colleague at *Reigny Deigh Media*, assistant to Ben Cadez

Archimedes Moropolis (Arkie) – Operations manager of *SwiftPad*

Ben Cadez (Guy Jumano? Stewardo del Gente?) – Presidential candidate, former lover of Paula

Cynthia Oglethorpe (G, GG, Cindy) – Cofounder of *SwiftPad* – kidnap victim

Dashell Addison Sketerson – American rightwing radio personality

Dimitry – A technical lead at the St. Petersburg Dam

Elwood Taylor – Longtime friend of Nathan and Paula's

Erick Duke – Mercenary, ally of Real-Prez

Gary (Leone) Humpkin – Influential editor and TV personality

Gopesh Gupta – Billionaire inventor of C2B – kidnap and extortion victim

Gull – Native American, friend of Kip's father. Later fired from Rehain Compound.

Hadley – Programmer at *SwiftPad*

Hanata Yokashita – The President of *SwiftPad* Inc. (Japan)

Hank Ford – An outcast who floats on his Mississippi raft and helps Chubby

Heber Young – AWOL *SwiftPad* financial maven

Hester – Elwood's young girlfriend – good with a knife

Jerry – Arkie's assistant and manager when Arkie is absent

Kayla Holmes – Stanford Business School graduate, former manager at *Reigny Deigh Media*, assistant to Maybelle

Kendal – Real-Prez operative

Kip Rehain (Chubby, Cornelius Welles, K) – Cofounder of *SwiftPad*, Insurgency operative

Margaret Stromborn (Peggy, Maggie) – Hardened guerrilla fighter, Spence's wife, Nathan's former girlfriend

Maybelle – Spence and Gopesh's Texas supervisor

Milana Shikshavalli – Kip's girlfriend from the Republic of Georgia

Nathan Schuette – Legendary writer, former pothead Lothario

Nikoloz – Milana's Russian half-brother, indeterminate political reliability

Paula Flayer – Nathan's first love, a woman who seems to pass through time unchanged

Rodin Smersky – Manager at the Internet Research Institute in St. Petersburg

Sequoia – Former refugee, now master network designer and hacker

Spence Stromborn – Former creative force at *Reigny Deigh Media*, tech flunky for the Cadez campaign

Telly Haines – Businessman, Cadez's handler

Tiara Mason-Feldman – Behind-the-scenes leader of the Memphis Insurgency

Walter (Walt, Wally) Cherry – Longtime friend of Elwood, Nathan, and Paula

PROLOGUE

R EAL-PREZ WAS ON HIS WAY TO BE THE ARRGH NOM-
inee again, probably by acclamation at the Disneyland
convention, even though he had entered no primaries. His
dramatic return to power was portrayed in hushed, adoring tones
by his minions in the press, who conjured a tale of a fanciful midnight operation (organized by his son-in-law) that secreted him
out of the private NJ sanatorium, whereupon he simply walked
into the White House, reassuming power without a by-your-leave.
It was an illegal act of gall, upending his earlier removal by the
25th Amendment. But Temp-Prez was hated by everyone, and
after the failed (V)ICE invasion of Portland, something had to be
done. Real-Prez's chutzpah had worked, and even the displaced
Temp-Prez (who returned rather unconstitutionally to Veep) was
praising him by the end of the day. But the dramatic move was
all theater – Real-Prez was the power brokers' only hope, and
they preferred Real-Prez's unpredictable insanity to the charis-
matically challenged Temp-Prez. And since they had as yet not
found a new Veep, dumping Temp-Prez would have elevated the
Speaker, who was a Dee, and that would be infinitely worse. The
coup had all been planned and approved by the power brokers
and was accompanied by a great deal of back room maneuvering,
the details of which are still mostly secret.

The delegate vote leader, Doug Turdashian, had already

conceded and figured to be Real-Prez's new running mate, with Temp-Prez standing in the wings limply applauding. Ben Cadez, who was a close second to Turdashian in pledged delegates, refused to concede, claiming that Real-Prez was not really President anymore because he had illegally returned to power. Cadez's potential third-party candidacy picked up support from conservatives who could not stomach Real-Prez and was centered predominantly in Utah and parts of Texas (Dallas mostly), in the Dakotas, and in the suburbs of one or two southern cities. Even though Cadez was Tennessee's junior senator, he had been run out of his own "adopted" state and forced to close his Nashville office. He had moved his operation into Ross Perot's old Electronic Data Systems campus, now SMIRK (Social Media Internet Research Konsortium) headquarters, a bizarre fortress outside Plano, Texas.

Caroline appeared to be "winning" the nomination for the Dems, but a massive grassroots group refused to accept this. Rosie, the delegate leader, did not promote or endorse the splinter movement, but after a closed-door meeting with Caroline's team, agreed to a united front against Real-Prez. Her price for unity, however, was seemingly too high for the Dee power brokers. Rumors were rampant about what went down. Rosie at first refused to comment but soon announced that the platform changes she insisted on would be rejected, that Caroline's platform was completely inadequate to meet the national emergency, and it looked like the Dee super-delegates would override the unity front.

Rosie let out that she would allow her name to be placed on the ballot as the Green-Soc candidate for President. Millions of green socks were sold, orders for more poured in, and every major apparel company competed to win the market. The nascent "Golden Fungus Party" also threw their support behind her, but it was little more than a satiric grab for attention. There was no more

"Golden Fungus" to be found anywhere, and most mainstream commentators doubted it had ever existed in the first place.

So the two leading parties, the "ARRGHs" (rumored to stand for American Republican Righteous Going to Heaven) and the "Dees," each had splinter factions with significant support. The US was too big for only two parties, but the Constitution (i.e., Electoral College) wasn't really built for more than two. The congressional reps (with each state getting only one vote) might end up picking the next President, which boded badly for the Dees.

Congressional commissions were formed to look into the atomic bombing of the Hoover Dam as well as the "Disturbance in Portland," as it was called. However, both commissions were actually designed to "bury and forget," to paper over the truth rather than reveal it. "Do nothing until after the election" was sullenly accepted. Most doubted any of it would ever be investigated.

Along Big Muddy, from Cairo to Vicksburg, in Tennessee, Kentucky, and Mississippi, there were lawsuits galore, mostly involving the "Eastbank land transfers" (expropriations, a squatters' rights rebellion, made legal by Memphis-based eminent domain condemnations and redistribution). It was usually peaceful, with the vast majority of the squatting done on corporate land. Individuals were generally compensated fairly. However, there was some radical and violent opposition to the land transfer, and Real-Prez, of course, championed that group of rich whites who called themselves "The Dispossessed." If he won, he promised to reverse it all, by force if necessary.

In Portland, the long, difficult road to recovery from the (V) ICE invasion continued. Refugee camps for the million thirsty, dispossessed people from the water-deprived Southwest were built on the city's periphery, with an emphasis on protecting and educating children, as well as finding or building housing, and overall economic recovery. Portlanders took pride that almost everyone in the city shared in the sacrifices needed to help the refugees.

Finally, in a moment of moderation, a bipartisan bill passed both the House and Senate defunding (V)ICE, returning ICE to its original charter, and reducing it to about a tenth of its previous force. Real-Prez refused to sign the bill, but his veto was overridden and except in places where his support was overwhelming, the para-military group was disbanded. The vote was close, but passed when just enough of the congressional ARRGHs (led by Mormons and civil libertarians) voted against the legalization of what would have essentially been a military dictatorship. Scattered violence erupted throughout the country and many of the troops demanded revenge for their defeat in Portland. Former (V)ICE kept their guns, but the ringleaders in the Dee-controlled states were isolated or arrested. In ARRGH-controlled areas, there were reports of uncontested vigilante "rope" justice against opponents of Real-Prez.

The fly in the ointment that complicated everyone's political calculations was a strange and ever-mutating virus that was rampaging through the world, killing some and changing others in strange, terrible, and sometimes even beautiful ways. The closer scientists looked at it, the more elusive it became. The death toll was accelerating.

The civil war seemed to slowly simmer. With the election coming, no one knew what might lie ahead. By September, a cold peace settled on the country.

But then that cold peace crashed and was left smoldering. The nation held its breath.

First, though, a little more catching up…

CHAPTER 1

CADEZ AND HIS CAMPAIGN BRAINTRUST ESCAPE FROM PORTLAND

Late July

It was in the late spring that the first deaths from the bacto-virus were reported in Myanmar, in a village in the north, along the old Burma Road. The first victim was a 40-year-old man, a recluse, whom some called a devil and some a monk. He trapped snakes and monkeys out in the jungle, but had powerful family ties in Yangon (Rangoon). The first symptoms started as a brain fever, eventually filling the sinus cavities with a yellowish mucus. He was raving the whole time about Rama and Shiva coming alive in his head, bringing the entire universe in with them. It was unclear how long he had been sick when he showed up at a local clinic. He died within a day of arriving. At first the media took no notice, but ten days later there were hundreds of cases in the city of Nay Pyi Taw. At that point, the story of the first victim, Patient Zero, made world head-lines. About 10% of the cases were fatal. The majority of the other cases produced changes that at first were not believed possible.

From *The Fall of It All – A History of the Big Dump*

THEY LIFTED OFF FROM NORTHWEST PORTLAND'S Wallace Park during the very early morning hours while the ragtag Insurgency troops tightened the noose around the scattered and disorganized (V)ICE forces. As the heavy rain was starting, they skimmed low, just above the neighborhoods north of the city. The chopper aimed for the PDX airport. Alison unflinchingly watched out the side portal as tracer bullets zipped dangerously close. Senator Cadez leaned over and, in a weak and pleading voice, told her they "would do great things together."

She looked at him and saw that Cadez was scared. Scared of being shot down, or perhaps something even worse than a fiery death. At that moment Alison knew that if they didn't go down together now, she would do whatever it took to bring him down. Eventually.

Cadez had the face and the well-toned body of a fit young man approaching his middle thirties, but his eyes told a different story. Although clear and not rheumy, his eyes betrayed a fearful emptiness, eyes that had already seen a lifetime of eating a lab-grown version of the Golden Fungus. She now knew that what Nate Schuette had suspected about Cadez was true – the Fungus undoubtedly had retarded his aging processes. But as to the other effects – the lab version that Cadez had been eating for years had provided very little, if any, of the "enhanced consciousness" that the Golden Fungus was supposed to impart.

Whatever he had been before, now he was nothing more than a pathetic, hateful old man in the shell of a rising, handsome young politician. Whatever powers of "perception" Cadez might once have had must have decayed. His lab-manufactured artificial Golden Fungus, while outwardly keeping him "young," was actually poisoning him. She could see he was confused and needed Telly's help to understand what was happening.

Alison continued her charade. She gazed at Cadez with feigned compassion. She didn't remove his hand from hers. He was still dangerous; in fact he probably still had some of the residual mind-reading power of the Golden Fungus, and – even more frightening – had a decent chance of winning the coming Presidential election.

She tried to keep her mind blank, thinking only of the greatest basketball game she ever played, when she stole the ball in the last seconds and hit a long three to win the game. As she played the game over and over in her head, Cadez began to relax, although his hand oscillated between hot and cold. She had soothed him with her own thoughts, even though he didn't appear to realize it.

When they arrived, the chopper parked close to the Horizon West gate, downstairs on the tarmac. Spence still was a prisoner, a heavy canvas bag over his head, forced to squat in the middle of the waiting room. Alison controlled her anger. She remembered her afternoon of drinking beer with Spence; was it only two days ago? They had planned to attend the Jean Katon Haitian reggae concert together. She was angry that Telly had forced her to miss the concert. It turned out (although Alison didn't know it at the time) that the concert had serendipitously supplied the hundreds of street protesters who had hamstrung the (V)ICE militia downtown. She and Spence had secretly plotted to help Gordy keep control of *Reigny Deigh Media,* and not let it fall into Telly Haines's hands. Now those plans were for naught and their worst fears (considered absurd a mere three days ago) had materialized.

Gordy was dead, and Alison was being kidnapped, even though she was offering no resistance in word or deed. Telly made it clear before they left Gordy's condo that she was coming with them. But Alison "finessed" the situation by tacitly agreeing to help Telly consolidate his grip on the company, as well as his grip on Cadez, without actually being asked. Telly, a snake with no loyalty to anything or anyone, easily believed that Alison was the same kind of snake.

She knew she was being pimped out to the Senator, who, when he wasn't having micro-episodes of dementia, was probably a worse human being than Real-Prez, as preposterous as that seemed, if only for the reason that in his alternating moments of lucidity, Cadez was not terminally stupid. But some deteriorating change was slowly getting a grip on him.

Spence, sitting splay-legged on the floor, handcuffed, the canvas bag on his head, still occasionally screamed muffled profanities. And to the annoyance of all of them, Kayla, poor Gordy's last hire at *Reigny Deigh*, was sobbing like a pathetic prom queen whose date had left without her.

Alison kept trying to think about setting up that last shot to win the game because there was a real possibility that Cadez, demented or not, could read her mind.

"What's going to happen to Spence?" Alison kept her eyes on Cadez, who was lost in some kind of funk, his eyes empty, apparently unable to recognize what was going on around him. When it was clear he wouldn't respond, she looked at Telly.

Telly, who had been watching Cadez as well, shook his head, pointed at Spence, and said to the guard, "Take the hood off of his head." Telly then walked over and helped Spence stand up. "Take these off," he said, pointing at the handcuffs. "Listen up, everyone, Mr. Stromborn is to be treated decently, from this point on." Directly addressing Spence, he said, "We are flying you to Texas, where we are integrating C2B with internet social media. You are still a *Reigny Deigh* employee, only your salary as of right now is tripled. Gopesh Gupta's digital mental imaging technology is the greatest advance in social control and we are going to own it. Because if we don't, someone else will."

Telly did not specify *SwiftPad* as the social media, which struck Spence as odd. "You can decide then if you want to help us or not," Telly continued. "If not, if after seeing what we are doing and what your role is to be, you decide you don't want to do it, we will free you and see you get back here – to Portland."

Spence said nothing.

"We will join you in Texas in a few days," said Telly. "There will be no more handcuffs. You are free. I hope you will continue to work for RDM. But it's up to you, Spence."

Spence spat, just missing Telly's shoes. Telly, with absent-minded nonchalance, rubbed the spit into the concrete. Cadez seemed to wake up and walked over toward them.

"If you knew what kind of strings I had to pull to get you out of (V)ICE custody, you would be grateful, I think," said Cadez to Spence. "You are free to stay here if you want. Right?" He looked at Telly, who nodded. "But – but, I think it is a good possibility you will be re-arrested by (V)ICE if you don't get on that plane. If you decide to stay, they will probably shoot you out-of-hand as a spy and saboteur."

"Spy! I make corporate ads for social media. I had nothing to do with the fighting. I didn't even know anything about it until those goons picked me up yesterday morning! What the fuck!"

"Like I said, we know you had no part in all this. You are free. But these (V)ICE guys are pissed, and if you don't go to Texas now, (V)ICE will probably shoot you, because these Portland trai-tors, the so-called Insurgency, shoot their prisoners," lied Telly. "Our people have lost friends. So it is up to you. But if you stay, I wouldn't bet on you getting out of here alive."

"Alison! What's going on?" Then Spence caught himself, pulling back whatever he was about to say.

"We work for RDM, Spence," she said in a voice just loud enough to be overheard by the others. "Telly owns the company now. I am going to Salt Lake City, but I will join you later. You better do what he says."

Spence looked at her with a hurt expression, and she mocked and rejected him by reflecting his expression toward him. She gave him a bit of a twinkle with her eyes, though, hoping it might convey that she was still with him. And she was still with him; she was determined to fight Telly and Cadez from the inside. Could Spence do that though? She had a feeling that he might soon be gone for good, that he would go one way or the other, that he wasn't capable of playing both sides like she knew she was. She coldly rejected any silent entreaty of his with a mocking sneer. She hoped he would know she couldn't really do that…

"But if you take the flight to Texas," Telly said, trying to soothe Spence's anger, "in a few days, you will be free to decide if you want to stay with the company. Frankly, we need your skills, your *SwiftPad* scripting. Here is your new salary, which you will soon see has been directly deposited into your account."

Telly handed Spence a piece of paper.

"Where is my wife?" Spence, who was stiff and hadn't had a change of clothes in a couple of days, felt totally out of sorts, itchy, and hungry. He didn't look at the paper but did put it in his pocket.

Telly looked away.

"I saw Maggie earlier," said Alison. "She was fine. I'm sure she still is." Spence looked at the blank faces of Telly, Cadez, and Kayla. Alison knew that Maggie had probably joined forces with the Insurgents in Forest Park, but as to her fate, she really had no clue.

"Maggie?" Spence always called his wife Peggy; he never called her Maggie anymore, at least not since they had moved up to Portland from Eugene. But her old boyfriend, Nate Schuette, had called her Maggie. Spence shook his head, "OK, good." Alison calling her Maggie told Spence that Nate was around, and maybe…he would look after her.

"If you stay…," said Telly, shaking his head and shrugging. Two uniformed (V)ICE were watching them.

"We have to go," said the Lear pilot. "The Insurgency assholes are closing in. The airport won't stay open much longer."

Spence followed him quietly, looking back at Alison, who waved back. Then she, Telly, Cadez, and Kayla boarded their Beechcraft Premier, and the two business jets took off immediately, in succession.

Alison and Kayla sat in the front of the plane together but

didn't speak. Kayla continued to sporadically sob. The wind was from the west, and they took off into it. As they climbed, the city was clearly visible out the left side: Forest Park, on the west side of Portland, was burning in spots, and several spectacular flashes lit up the night around the city. The Beechcraft verged away toward the north then looped back east. Alison was exhausted and fell asleep, only to be awakened a little more than an hour later as they landed in Salt Lake.

CHAPTER 2
MAGGIE, NATE, AND SEQUOIA HEAD SOUTH TO THE REHAIN COMPOUND

Late July

The shock of the Portland Insurgency had everyone pulling back, including newly reinstalled Real-Prez. He was on TV every day, talking suddenly about "States' Rights." "I don't know anything about that, a lot of that reporting was phony," he said when asked about the ignominious defeat of his (V)ICE forces in Portland. "They tell me that the Portland traitors were animals, that they poisoned innocent people, sent hundreds of their own people to their death, just because I was trying to save them. Not smart. Not smart. But if they can do that, then so can others. We'll see what happens. We'll see what happens in other places."

From *The Fall of It All – A History of the Big Dump*

HEADING SOUTH ON I-5 IN THE RAIN, ALREADY 20 miles from Portland, no one was saying much in Aldane's old Ciera Cutlass. Nate Schuette was driving, Maggie was in the back seat, while Sequoia was playing with the radio, looking in vain for something good.

Because of the recent paramilitary attack on Portland, and its repulsion by Insurgency forces, the situation to the south in the nearby Willamette Valley hinterlands was unknown. Who was in control? Nate knew that off in the west, at Champoeg Park on the river north of Newberg, a huge refugee camp was being contested by the Insurgency and the (V)ICE forces. But there was no sign of trouble on I-5 itself. He didn't know the safest way to the coast. Nate looked back and saw Maggie was sleeping.

The rain was continuous.

He decided to get off at Keizer, drive through Salem, and get back on the freeway south of town. He had a feeling that they might put a roadblock on I-5, or some kind of wannabe commandos might be lurking with long guns behind the berm along the freeway. No reason or rationale for that feeling, but these were times when it was best to go with the gut.

Sequoia was playing with her fone now.

"Are we near Salem?"

"Almost. Why?"

"Because there's a *SwiftPad* S-Plog from somebody called 'Chemeketa Bighorn' who says there's a sniper shooting at the southbound traffic on I-5."

"Keep checking." Nate looked at the young refugee and smiled. He had had a good feeling about her. She was sharp, knew how to pay attention. Keep going with the gut (unless you actually know something!), he thought.

He looked back again at sleeping Maggie, who had hardly aged in a couple of decades. It was almost as if she was staying young to spite him for being the one to eat the Golden Fungus all those years ago. She had remained young the honest way, good living, exercise, and mostly a clear conscience. She was actually older than he had been when he quit the Fungus – just before they split and she had moved in with Spence. Still the same sweet

Maggie, his ethereal hippie princess. But now she was a hardened guerilla, a real life Sarah Connor, a Terminator hunter. It worked out the way it was supposed to, he thought. He checked the rearview mirror, not for cops but to see himself. Old as dirt.

They cruised through the streets of downtown Salem, almost nobody walking, one or two bicyclists, and not much traffic either. He wondered what people south of Portland thought of recent events in the city. Life seemed to be going on, but not too conspicuously. Nate realized he hadn't seen any trucks since leaving the Aurora Airport. Stores would be empty soon. He re-entered I-5 at Turner, just south of Salem.

"Who lives out where we are going?" Sequoia asked out of the blue.

"Hard to say. Alice, Jim's mom. I am thinking that Paula will be there. And some others."

"Paula was your girlfriend, right?" asked Sequoia. Maggie, sitting behind them, opened her eyes just as Nate looked at her in the rear view.

"Well, that's a long story."

"Oh," Sequoia said. Nate glanced at Maggie, who was smiling as she closed her eyes again.

"The interesting story is Alice. She was Walt Rehain's – I guess girlfriend is the right word to use. But they had a long history too, sometimes romantic, other times hostile. Walt was Kip's dad."

"Wasn't Alice a friend of your old girlfriend, Nate?" Maggie hadn't said anything up to that point, and Nate glanced back to see she had decided to be awake.

"I wouldn't exactly call Paula my girlfriend," he said.

"Oh," Maggie said in mock surprise. "Sounds like none of you geezers knew what your relationships were, did you? I mean, I would say you used to be my boyfriend. That is just a fact, right?"

"Yeah, facts are facts I suppose." Nate had more to say, but let that pass. He was emotionally spent after the last weekend, wondering if he, Paula, Maggie, or anyone would survive.

"So," said Sequoia, "Alice is Kip's dad's girlfriend. Kip started *SwiftPad* and is a billionaire, several times over. We just dropped off Kip at that little airport back there, and his father's girlfriend lives at this place in the woods where we are headed."

"Right. Kip's dad died earlier this year."

Sequoia waited about ten seconds before asking, "Who else lives there?"

"A bunch of people who work on *SwiftPad*. They are trying to set it up to be able to monitor and control the App from there. And some others, fighters, and back-to-the-land type people."

"Oh, OK. You mean like a disaster recovery site. Where big IT shops can relocate their business if their main location gets fucked up."

"Kinda. I guess so," said Nate.

"So how does this place out in the woods connect up to an App used by billions of people all over the world?"

"Well, I'm not real hip to the technical stuff, but Kip told me they hooked into a splice off of a trans-Pacific fiber cable that comes ashore near Newport," said Nate. "Satellites they lease still work, but they have no confidence they are secure, or stable. Cables can be tapped by subs, but there are telltale signs if that is happening, and none so far had been detected. It is wired up, a fast link to Asia, and hooks onto the main West Coast links just south of Newport. You really did study computer networking, right?"

"Yeah, and worked on the campus system. Why, did you think I was lying?"

Actually, yeah, thought Nate, I did think you were lying. Not now though. "I'll see if we can get you some experience helping with monitoring the computer traffic – with *SwiftPad* coming through, it is a nexus point that is one of the busiest in the world. Billions of terabytes of data pump through there every day."

"So what are these people like?" Sequoia laughed. "Is it just a bunch of survivalist computer geekazoids? Not a combination that gives me a lot of confidence. I mean after what we just went through, if you know what I mean."

"I know what you mean," said Nate. "They are pretty well armed, especially now. Real-Prez's (V)ICE got its ass kicked in Portland, so this might be the place they try to get back some. I'm interested to see, myself. The paranoia is appropriate. I assume everybody is doing double duty – tech and soldier. You ready for that?"

"Fuck yes!"

"Good. The Compound used to be a Christmas tree farm. I think it belongs to Kip, but I'm not sure of his relationship with Alice, other than that she's the mother of his best friend, Jim, the first guy killed in all the fighting this weekend." He looked at her and waited until she looked up from her fone. "You know how important Kip is, right?"

"Yeah, he invented *SwiftPad*."

"No, he didn't invent anything, but he...did the business to get it started. Cynthia Oglethorpe was the real inventor."

Sequoia looked blankly at Nate.

"The pregnant one who got kidnapped," said Maggie from the backseat.

"Oh yeah," said Sequoia. "GG, the one who left Kip for his best friend – oh! Jim's the guy who was killed at the party a couple of days ago! Shit, that's fucking – I don't know, weird or something."

"Yeah, yeah, the guy killed was Jim Hunt, Kip's childhood friend. Alice's son. Anyway..." Nate continued, agreeing in his head with Sequoia, it is weird. How many other tenuous threads looped through this strange tale? "Kip grew up out here. His father had a lot of land, deep in the middle of the woods, and made a fortune selling Christmas trees to Asia. High-end, perfectly shaped, six-foot spruce and fir flown over in refrigerated planes. While the old man was dying, Jim's mom, Alice Hunt, turned it into a retreat, built a bunch of underground houses, and well, now it's the monitoring center for *SwiftPad*."

They got off I-5 again at Albany, which was deserted, almost like a ghost town, and took Highway 20 south and east. Like Salem, Corvallis was nearly deserted. The grass on the Oregon State University common needed mowing. They continued on Highway 20 toward the coast, and six miles later the town of Philomath was buzzing, unlike the much bigger but sleepy Corvallis. It was lunchtime, and the coffee shops and diners were full. They had eaten breakfast in Sellwood only a couple of hours before, and besides, Philomath, an old mill and timber town (where Kip and Jim had gone to high school), was a hotbed of real-Prez supporters. So Nate didn't stop. The hard stares they got driving through town were disconcerting.

Forty minutes later, they turned off Highway 20, passed through Eddyville, then took the long, winding, narrow two-lane blacktop up toward the Rehain Compound. About six or seven miles up, the pavement ended and the road got steeper. A mile farther was a roadblock behind a small cutout, manned by a couple of guys, an Asian man and a taller white guy, in jeans and t-shirts with automatic rifles slung upside down on their shoulders.

"You gotta get out. No vehicles past here until we have them checked."

"Call up and tell Alice – Nate Schuette and a couple of friends are here."

A look of distaste, quickly contained. The two sentries were both in their mid-thirties with longish hair. They shifted the long-barreled guns low at their sides, acting casual yet alert. While unconcerned with unarmed Nate and his two female companions, they were simultaneously eyeballing the woods on the right, as if expecting an ambush. On the left, Bear Creek, which was running low even for late July, still gurgled audibly.

"Someone will be down to pick you up in a few. We'll get your car checked out, and send it up later."

After a few minutes, a crew cab pickup came down the hill.

Nate got in the back seat, and Maggie and Sequoia slid into the wide bench-like front seat.

"You only have two guys down below? They're kind of exposed, don't you think?"

The young woman driving looked back at Nate quickly with a hint of contempt.

"If they come for us it will most likely be through the air with choppers. If they send a battalion of Army Rangers, well, then of course we're fucked."

"They won't send regulars," said Maggie. "Maybe some kind of mercenaries." Maggie, who had spent the past weekend carrying an Uzi in the battle for Forest Park, had a newfound appreciation for the military implications of terrain.

"But those (V)ICE clowns will never be deployed again," said the driver. "So if they come..."

Nate hummed a few bars of "Send in the Clowns," then sang something about the clowns already being here.

Both Maggie and the driver ignored Nate. "If they send Army regulars," the driver continued, "we are Fucked, with a capital F. We ain't scared, but we ain't stupid either. But if that happens, we are at War with a capital W." Even though the road was winding and rocky, it took less than 10 minutes to climb the rest of the hill up to the Compound.

The big gravel parking area in front of the giant hangar-like barn was filled with trucks, ATVs, and well-armed people who could have been roadies in a grunge band. Some were working on various mini-construction projects on the periphery of the gravel square between the house and barn. Since last week, before the attack on Portland, when Nate and Paula had visited, things were much more frenetic, and now everybody carried a weapon. No little kids were visible either. They were met by a sharp-eyed, dark-complexioned Native American man with a slight smile and high cheekbones.

"I am Gull," he said. Pointing emphatically at Nate, he

continued, "I've seen you before, but – who are they?" A significant number of Native Americans were working around the yard.

Nate smiled at Gull, which seemed to surprise him. "This is Maggie and Sequoia."

The Siletz reservation bordered the northern edge of the Compound. When the old man was alive he always maintained excellent relations with the Native Americans. Gull had been his right-hand man during his last years. Walt had hired the Siletz people when he could, and essentially gave the tribe the run of his property. But since Walt died and Alice took over, the easy informality between the crew and the boss had changed.

"We assume that we are being watched now. Maybe by high-flying drones, but more likely by sneaky sons-o'-bitches creeping around the edge of the property. But we've got everybody down in the tunnel, playing video games or something. Alice and Arkie have no fucking idea what they are up against or how to deal with it. Walt knew how to deal with assholes who didn't like him – made friends with them, paid them off, or fucked them up – but he never just stuck his thumbs and head up his ass like we are doing now."

Nate and Gull stared at each other. "You work here long?"

"Work here long?" Gull turned his head, then back quickly, and looked at Nate more closely. "You know Kip, right?"

"Yeah, in fact..."

"That figures. Yeah. I've worked here long. I was born just over there." Gull pointed vaguely toward the north. "Where the fuck are you from? New Jersey?"

"Well, actually..." Nate stopped talking as Gull spat and looked away, and then at Maggie and Sequoia, and took a deep breath.

"What's his name, Archie, made a rule about who and how many people get close to Alice. Him and his fucking drones. So only one of you can go see her."

"Could I see your networking setup?" Sequoia asked.

"Yeah, could you show her where they are playing the video

games, as you call them? She has had some training, in systems and networking," said Nate, trying not to rise to Gull's bait. "Right?"

Sequoia nodded.

Gull looked askance at the young woman, but shrugged. "Go ahead over to the house, then. Someone will meet you. I'll show these two squaws around the hangar and if somebody says it's OK they can go down to the Comm bunker." Gull and Nate gave each other hard looks as they walked away.

Nate walked across the gravel square to the house. The three-story wooden structure was in the process of receiving a coat of dull paint that made it less visible. Inside smelled musty, and was dark and decrepit; in other words it had not changed much since Walt died. They walked through the kitchen, which had three huge pots of veggie stew steaming on the giant range, then over to the basement door. A young guy waiting there led Nate toward the back sitting room that overlooked the valley below.

"I manage the triage team. Jerry."

"Nice to meet you, Jerry. Nate."

"I know. Read your book. Didn't like it. I think you should write about this country. How can you write about China, being an American? Sounded like a fairy tale to me."

"You are right. Everything is a lie, including this sentence. There is no such thing as truth, because everything is always spinning. Everything ever written is all a lie."

"Yeah – well – that's not what I meant." Jerry looked thoughtful for a moment, then seemed to shake it all off. "We have a whole other command structure thirty feet down. We just finished wiring it this weekend. That was Chubby's idea actually," said Jerry. He shook his head in disagreement, as he listened in his earpiece, "OK, Alice wants to meet you up here."

Jerry, who had recently been promoted to Number Two Tech behind Arkie after a heroic 72-hours-without-sleep stint of manning the *SwiftPad* Comm board during the Insurgency, walked over to the other side of the parlor. The area had been converted to a site-system monitoring workspace and housed three women and two men intently working in front of laptops. A big screen divided into four quadrants was flipping from network maps overlaid on top of world maps, to problems and bottlenecks listed with descriptions, video from satellites, to changing scenes from around the Compound. With Arkie on a mission to the Midwest, Jerry was the Compound's de facto Ops Commander.

After a few minutes Alice, her long gray hair combed back into a ponytail, came in and sat in an old comfortable chair and waved him over.

"Thanks, Jerry. That will be all." Jerry looked over at Alice, shrugged, and left. "So you made it here safely, Nate, huh? I only got back last night myself. We took our time returning from Portland. They are deploying drones up above, probably with Hellfire missiles I'm afraid." Alice shrugged and smiled slightly, suggesting "Have a seat," as she gestured toward the couch under the window overlooking the little valley below. A bouquet of hydrangeas stood up in a blue Chinese vase on a round Queen Anne–style table next to the couch. The sun hit the opposite end of the couch from where he sat. "I never told you that I read your book back in the '80s. You should have continued writing fiction and stayed away from television and that Portland crowd at *Reigny Deigh Media*. You actually weren't a bad writer – until you prostituted your art."

"Thanks, that's nice of you to say," Nate deadpanned, then laughed to himself, wondering where all this literary criticism was coming from. He suddenly thought about his old friend Spence, Maggie's husband, now missing, maybe dead. Spence had funneled him paying work when he really needed it. He had been happy to "prostitute" his art then.

"I didn't mean to offend you," said Alice.

"You didn't. I am no longer the suffering, serious, lonely artist struggling for truth and beauty who lived in Eugene back in the last century. Art was a whole way of life – street politics, with paint splashed on the walls, impromptu poetic rants reverberating in the middle of parks, the street, or crowded bars. In the end, the whole scene sickened me."

"That was you, huh?" asked Alice. "I was trying to raise a kid, and keep from killing myself after my first husband's suicide. I missed the old Eugene 'scene' as you call it – I mean, I never got down there very much."

"Well, we were seeking the unification of nature, economics, love, and living as a new way to be, to exist." Nate smiled at Alice, making it clear he was almost kidding.

"Hmm, yeah, I suppose. I had real life to deal with. I didn't have much time for fun back then."

Och, there's a slap, Nate thought.

"So your old girlfriend came with you," Alice said a little too brightly. "I'm sorry about not having her come in with you. But if I don't follow the rules, protocols Jerry calls them, then it all goes to hell around here. I know Paula is excited to meet her. Well, actually I don't know that she is excited, per se, but...we can put Maggie up here at the house." Alice gave Nate a look that seemed to convey, you are going to have your hands full, with two women to juggle. Nate smiled an acknowledgment. He was abruptly very tired. Alice moved over and sat in a splotch of sun on the couch, next to Nate.

"I am so sorry about Jim. I never got the chance to meet him," Nate said.

"You didn't? So strange. You remind me of him, in a way. Thanks." Alice looked out the window and sat quietly for a minute or so. "I am still not ready to talk about it. It's like being at the bottom of a well. It is unbearable."

Nate said nothing, but took her hand.

"I have been pushing it away," she said, with tears welling, "I woke up yesterday, overwhelmed with grief. But – I realized this morning that we are in a war, and he was a casualty. I am not the first mother to lose her son in war. There just isn't time to grieve. He was my baby, and is always going to be here," Alice put her hand on her heart, then wiped her eyes. "His child, the child Cynthia is going to have, I don't even know if she is alive or not."

"I know she is alive," said Nate. "They have to care for her. They want something from her."

"Not a word. No ransom demand, nothing."

"Those fuckers! I have to – I can't surrender to it anymore." Nate, usually cold and detached from emotional scenes, leaned over and put his arms around Alice. They hugged for a while.

"Where is Paula now?"

"In her hobbit home at the bottom of the hill. We can go down later. She has been sleeping and reading by herself since she got here yesterday. She needs to heal. The wound is still pretty raw, but she is improving. On some strong antibiotics. We need to get her some Fungus soon, or I am afraid the withdrawal plus the wound might be too much for her." Alice stood up and gestured for him to lie down. Nate leaned back a little on the end of the cozy couch.

"I don't have any Fungus. I wish I did." Nate kicked his shoes off.

"Your friend Elwood might have found, or saved, a small batch he could share with us. He's in Illinois. Paula thinks he has been researching new strains of it, but who knows? Unfortunately it's pretty rare even there. Of course it's the wrong season for it now."

"I remember, vaguely, the day we found it. Over fifty some years ago in Vandalia, January, cold, below zero. Elwood just picked it off the tree and bit into it. Then Paula did. Fucking nuts!"

They were both quiet for a minute or two and Nate yawned. "Mind if I stretch out a little? This is the first time I have slowed down since flying to Portland last week. I must have ridden a bike 80 miles this weekend. Didn't sleep much. Still, I shouldn't be this tired."

"Can I get you a cup of herbal tea? A sandwich, or a muffin?"

"No, thanks."

Alice sat back down at the end of the couch, pulled off Nate's track shoes, and rubbed his feet. "Relax, you need to recharge."

"That feels good."

Alice smiled. "The Golden Fungus has become pretty rare, if not extinct. I guess it must be the weather. Paula knows quite a bit about it. She told me that it only grows where it gets very cold – in winter – along one specific Midwestern riverbank. When our people – Arkie and one other guy on our crew – contacted Elwood yesterday he said he would 'try' – I'm not sure what he meant, if he had a cache of it saved in a freezer...but he has not been exactly forthcoming about it."

"Is he still living in Vandalia?"

"In the general vicinity. Still a young stallion too, if what Arkie says is true. He has to change jobs and doctors every couple years so they don't get spooked by his perpetual youth. Doesn't need to work, and when he does, it is under assumed names of course. He tells people he's 32, but he looks younger. Has a teenage girlfriend from what I hear, he is..."

"What? He's not working for the RedHats, is he?"

"No, nothing like that, but we aren't too sure about his girl-friend. Local girl, you know, rural Illinois." Alice got up, peeled off Nate's socks, and put some lotion on her hands. "Anyway, he wasn't too forthcoming about her or even what he is doing."

"That feels so good, ah, almost too good! Elwood. It has been so long since I have seen him! Paula, Elwood, myself and Wally..."

"Wally?"

"Yeah – one of the originals. He's in Russia now..."

"Russia?"

"Yeah, he is a publisher, businessman or something. I think he has a place in Poland too. Moves around a lot, last time I heard from him he called himself 'a Baltic Bum.' But lately he never answers anybody, and seems to have gone completely to ground. Anyway, Elwood found the Fungus, or at least discovered its effects. When we found the Fungus growing on trees by that little river in Illinois, Elwood and Paula were the only ones who ate it – even though at the time, they didn't have a clue what it was. Wally and I just watched them, expecting them to keel over dead from eating the shit."

Alice smiled. "She is quite a woman. You should…"

"What?"

"Nothing," said Alice. "You thirsty? Let me get you a ginger ale."

Nate shook his head.

"So – you knew Cadez, right? Paula told me…"

"Yeah," Nate looked hard, and nodded. "Stewardo del Gente, PhD psychology; Guy Jumano, Nixon plumbers minion; Benjamín Cadez, junior senator from Tennessee. All the same guy. That fucker is at least 85 years old."

"Wow. Why doesn't somebody out him?" Alice stopped the foot massage and gestured with her finger emphatically. "Why don't we…?"

"Yeah, Paula and I talked about that a while ago. Should have done it when he was a nobody – or even just a Senate candidate. It's too late now, especially with Telly Haines' muscle behind him. Anyway, since he's against Real-Prez too…we just have to see how things play out, and not be stupid." Nate shook his head, with some exasperation. "They lived together for a while…" Nate looked at Alice intently, "when he was Jumano."

"Yeah, she told me. She could prove his life is a total lie, but they – Haines – would kill her. Still might, just because she is a threat."

"Events of this weekend in Portland have undoubtedly brought her back to his notice. He was there." Nate began to feel something strange. Alice went back to rubbing his feet. "Paula has been a flake all her life, did what she wanted, slept wherever and with whoever she wanted, when she wanted. I've known her since I was 18 and she was 25. Paula was my first…"

"What? I never knew that!"

"Yeah. Well, I certainly wasn't her first. But until three days ago, as you know, she was my housemate in San Francisco. I would get these jokes from neighbors that I was robbing the cradle. She is seven years *older* than I am! To be honest, and she would probably agree, we have been partners…mainly because I am so old, and she's still strutting around like a young goddess – or was. I don't know how to put it, but – she just never grew up, and…I liked that. So, yeah, I was robbing the cradle, going after perpetual youth, even though when I had the chance to have it, it disgusted me and I rejected it. If anyone should have eaten the Fungus, it was her. She exploited it for all it was worth. But, we – she and I – were leasing our love affair, we never really bought it."

"Leasing?"

"You know. There was always the possibility of a contract termination. For both of us."

"Speaking of termination, did you read about that…disease over in Asia – near Laos?"

"Myanmar. Used to be Burma. It's weird – they don't know if it is a bacterial infection or virus. Every time they try to isolate it, something goes wrong with the experiment. It attacks people in different ways. The worst way that people get sick sounds fucking horrible."

"That's all we need, rampaging disease to go along with a wannabe dictator."

"Yeah," Alice picked up her Pad and scrolled. "Says here in the *Times* that some people had life-altering revelations, that they met and talked to dead relatives, and now feel better than they have in years."

"Same disease?"

"Yeah, apparently, although as I said, it seems to be difficult to study."

Nate took out his fone. They sat there for about ten minutes looking at their devices.

"You meeting Maggie again – think it has something to do with this new feeling of impermanence?"

"No! No. It's not a new feeling at all! Anyway, Maggie has her own loss to deal with," said Nate. "We still have no idea where they took her husband. Or Alison, who worked with him. They might be casualties too, or they might be alive. We might have won the battle, but we lost a lot too. We need to figure out what happened to them."

"Protecting this Compound is job number one," said Alice. "But of course we will help find them. We do have an informal relationship with the Ishpeming group, and if Kip connects with Memphis, then...maybe we can link up our efforts better. (V)ICE teams are camping out in Newport. In civilian clothes, acting like tourists, but we think they are planning something against us – eventually. Do we stay and fight, or be ready to scatter? They can come at us from so many different directions. Or from all of them at once. I don't want us to be meaningless casualties."

"When Kip visited Paula and me in San Fran last spring, he said he remembered GG might have a way to blow up *SwiftPad* too. Kip seemed to believe GG left a Trojan horse in the program that can self-destroy the App, and all other versions on the net."

"No shit. That might be the place for us to start. We'll talk to Arkie when he gets back."

Nate lay down, closed his eyes, and took a deep breath.

"Getting back to Paula though..." he opened his eyes, and peeked at Alice as if waiting for news he didn't want to hear, and she looked back as she continued to rub his feet. "Until she was shot two nights ago, she had lived an endless summer of youth. She never experienced aging."

"Until now, and it's killing her," said Alice. She laughed. "But then, aging is killing all of us."

"I ate Fungus until I was in my forties, and I just couldn't keep it up," said Nate. "When you don't get old, you end up waiting to get old, looking forward to it. But once I stopped, it hit me. I was a basket case for three, four months, then I was fine, felt better than I had in years, even though I suddenly had aches and pains that I never knew existed."

"Unless you are Cadez."

"Who knows? Maybe Cadez just went further out? Maybe he is the ultimate Fungus voyager, dosing with all kinds of chemicals that mimic the Fungus, but don't quite – I don't know. But the guy ain't right."

"Is it true, though, that he kidnapped you and hooked you up to Howard Hughes's brain?"

"Paula tell you that?"

"Yeah," Alice slapped Nate's feet and he sat up and put on his socks and shoes. "She also said she had been kidnapped earlier, maybe by him too, she was never sure."

"And then she joined him, and helped kidnap me."

"So when you lived in Frisco, you ever talk about it?"

"No," Nate looked uncomfortable. "Yes. She went through a weird phase. Power, but mostly pissed off at the Weathermen who she had been living with before – rich kids playing revolutionaries – one of whom sold her out. She slipped into Nixonian fascism as if it's some kind of high-brow aesthetic. And of course she was still 'peaking' on the Fungus."

"You mean like she was fixating on some kind of sick fetish over the sharp uniforms the Nazis wore?"

"Did you ever read *Gravity's Rainbow*?"

"No. I have it on the shelf," Alice motioned with her head toward her bookshelf.

"Pynchon invented 'The Schwarzkommando,' German and African SS rocket engineers, who were in the process of deploying the next generation V-2 rocket, the 'super-secret' weapon – it had a missile navigation device that homed in on the psycho-sexual 'field disturbances' that are created by their targets. They were on the frontiers of the psychic wilderness, immune to Nazi race theories, erudite, kind of gay, seeking for themselves some kind of oblivion. I sometimes think that is where Paula was – and Cadez is."

CHAPTER 3

CHUBBY AND ALDANE FLY TO MEMPHIS

Late July

The disease was spreading into Bangladesh. The death throes were horrible, especially if the infected survived the initial onslaught to their body, and the virus got into their brain. In many it created a total dissociation from reality, amnesia, disconnection from themselves and the world around. Some assumed the identity of historical figures – including those outside of their own society – one Bengali peasant assumed the identity of Cotton Mather, quoting his obscure sayings about how the kingdom of witches had come down to earth. He spoke in Bengali of course, calling the doctors and nurses demons from hell there to destroy the work of God. As the sick recovered and continued their rants, they were often surrounded by Islamic mobs that beat them to death for blasphemy.

From *The Fall of It All – A History of the Big Dump*

THE SIX-HOUR FLIGHT FROM THE LITTLE AIRPORT

south of Portland to Memphis International was harrowing for Aldane and the rest of the Jean Katon Express, as they were followed at first by Air Force planes. Bernardo, their pilot, had filed the flight plan a couple of days before the Portland Insurgency, but had then ignored a general order issued later by the FAA grounding all flights. A vagabond cockpit jockey with small airlines around the Caribbean before signing on to fly the band around on Jean's leased G-5, Bernardo had no quibble with ignoring the rules. Once over the Cascade mountains, he kept the plane about six hundred feet, skimming over the desert floor, through the desolation of Eastern Oregon, before vectoring up to forty thousand feet over Utah. They were dogged by Air National Guard jets, but then left alone somewhere after Oklahoma. Chubby, however, slept through it all.

After a brief "who are you?" at the Memphis gate – FBI – Kip flashed his "Cornelius Welles" high-quality IDs and elicited no interest, but they held Aldane for over an hour, grilling him on what he did in Portland, why he was leaving, etc. The local Memphis government had not challenged federal control of the airport, but the FBI still seemed to have some level of independence from the Real-Prez junta, at least they posed as if. Aldane played it very low key, talking in a very non-Ebonic, gee-whiz, Wayne Brady-on-afternoon-TV patois. They still gave him a hard time, even after giving him back his totally legal, U.S. citizen–proving passport and St. Thomas driver's license.

Adele, the band's organist and wife of Leone Humpkin (the public face of the Ishpeming Resistance), had a driver wait for them in the main concourse, and he took them to the Lazy River Inn. Chubby took a suite overlooking the Mississippi River, cleaned up, came back down to the lobby, and picked up a couple of plain t-shirts and a pair of green heavy cotton pants and white low-cut tennis shoes at a shop next to the hotel. "Country club white boy," he thought, with a self-satisfied glance in the mirror. "It will piss off Aldane."

Over the next week, Chubby ate and drank, and tried to forget what happened in Portland, but as the details were reported, Chubby became morose. He couldn't stop blaming himself for the deaths of those he had convinced to march out of the Jean Katon concert and block I-84. About 80 people died, almost all of them under 30, many with young families. Some horrible injuries too. He moped around, avoiding Aldane and everyone else, and explored Memphis by himself for three days, walking and occasionally using public buses in the muggy heat.

He was trying to get a feel for the Memphis neighborhoods. The city's business core hugged the river. Tourists in bars and restaurants overflowed onto the sidewalks, just down the street from where the new rich had taken over the older mansions. He sat by himself at night listening to Blues on Beale Street. The outlying areas – the poor Black section in North Memphis (that had changed almost overnight in the sixties from a white neighborhood) seemed hollowed out, especially in the summer heat, where screen doors and opened windows revealed the squalor of poverty inside many of the homes. But some in the worst repair were the liveliest. Young salt-and-pepper construction crews, some all women, were putting on new roofs, painting, and landscaping, planting vegetable gardens. He saw quite a few automatic rifles leaning on sawhorses. This was Mayor Hassan Coleman's defense force.

Chubby rode public buses and hiked through South Memphis too, where he saw much of the same reclamation activity, the same old-school Israeli-style mix of weaponry and cultivation and construction tools lying casually about. Little kids were around too, but everyone looked very cool. Open lots were all under cultivation, with little greenhouses nearby and modern irrigation all set up with timers. South Memphis had been settled in the late 1860s by Black Civil War veterans living close to Fort Pickering. The houses were older, but the neighborhood seemed to have held up better. Still he saw much evidence of urban homesteading. Further out, East Memphis was a white enclave, and even there he saw Black and white teams refurbing some houses.

All this positive activity finally began to cheer him up. By this time he was seeing a theme to the place. Almost all of the residential neighborhoods, Black or white, seemed to have been built from the same set of blueprints – red brick, single-story, two (or three)-bedroom houses set back at least a hundred feet from the wide boulevards, sitting on relatively big pieces of property. It was a city that, from a real estate perspective, appeared fairly egalitarian. Now with all the urban homesteading going on, and the millennials integrating as a symbol of spite to the years of racial separation, it was becoming a new kind of American city. The alliance of white liberals and entrepreneurial and progressive Blacks was the story of Hassan Coleman's rise.

At a sandwich shop in the Edge District, Chubby was joined at the counter by a young white businessman who was eager to explain it to him. He introduced himself as Beau and ordered a sandwich and a beer. After some friendly chit-chat and personal history intros, Chubby (of course not mentioning his Kip Rehain identity) asked him how Memphis had suddenly become one of the most politically radical cities in the country.

"So," Chubby said at the end of a long preamble explaining what he had just seen in the city, and what he had heard about Memphis before, "Beau – what happened?"

"Real-Prez was a bridge too far for us," Beau took a bite of his barbecued pork sandwich as he thought about it. "You know, this is the South, and deep down things are pretty much the same as they have always been. White people, rightly or not, feel like they have a long-term relationship with – you know – the Civil War was pretty hot around here, and Black soldiers made a big difference in taking Memphis. Even though they got treated like shit, people still knew. I believe everyone understood we were tied together, but probably it's a relationship that – it is just not like we think.

"So hearing what you say, Chubby," Beau continued, "it is important, because living here, we can't really see it clearly. It goes way back and we never came to terms with the bad times, but we just wanted to skip all that of course. Can't skip it, gotta bring it out, let it air out in the sunshine. But it is beginning to feel good, to me anyway."

"What was the trigger for it?" Chubby signaled another round.

"Real-Prez is a psychotic racist trying to increase hatred between our communities. This town was just too volatile for that to stand. And then Hassan comes along. He's brilliant, a war hero, with limitless energy and is so gosh darn likable. He just came across like the West Point graduate that he is."

"I know. I met him. We – kind of worked together in Portland."

"He was first in his class. He talks crisp, clear, yet evocative and warm, although he will turn on the Afro-lingo like a crazed backwoods preacher invited up to speak at Ebenezer Baptist when he's in front of the right audience. Politically electing Coleman was a sudden decision by the whole city, just a realization, a communal 'aha' moment that everyone came to at the same time."

"When was that?"

"When? Election Day! The whites in Memphis, and people all talk about this as if we really had a single mind about it.

"I suddenly realized, I came to the realization that we have more in common with our Black neighbors than with the white trash out Nashville way, or worse, over in Arkansas. Tennessee is different. We have been trying to tell people that for a hundred years, but nobody listens! Hassan got elected, and convinced the city council to pass the Urban Homestead Act. Black and white kids, mostly working together, made it work. It spread to the outlying corporate farms, although the legality of all that is in the courts now. These kids wanted to be organic farmers, and break with the past." Beau ordered another beer. "Why are you in Memphis?"

"I'm with the Jean Katon band. Kind of a fan. Roadie, occasionally. Friend actually."

"I see they're playing down on Beale Street, huh? Tickets are hard to get."

"I'll see what I can do for you, Beau."

"Let me give you my contact," he took out his fone, to fone bump, but Chubby waved it off and found a light-colored beer coaster. "Got a pen? I can't bump with my fone."

"Oh?"

Chubby just smiled, but didn't explain his ultra-tight security regimen. As Beau wrote his email, Chubby asked him, "So how did they get so fucking tight militarily?"

"They organized," he said as he wrote out his name and contact info and passed it back to Chubby. "You know how they say young Jimmy Hoffa recruited almost each and every Teamster himself by jumping in their cab?"

Chubby shrugged acknowledgment.

"Well, Coleman almost did the same. Used the crazy gun laws to arm, and Coleman started training them. And they started training themselves. There are twenty thousand in the city militia, all broken down into companies and squads, with ranks, communications, the works. Nobody wants to challenge them. Anybody who abuses their position in this 'well-regulated militia' is drummed out, and turned over to law if they break it."

Kip wanted to tell him about Coleman's visit to his apartment over Ranjit's convenience store a week earlier, but forced himself to remain mum.

"Anyway," Beau continued, "There was some talk by Klan types, but their own people shut them down in a hurry. Coleman worked his ass off. Hard work – that is what won him the mayor's race, everybody knew him, because he was everywhere. He won 97% of the Black vote and almost the same of the under-30 vote white kids. They all open-carried as long as the Klan types did – every time two or more were on the street, they were followed and watched by ten of Coleman's people. Never was a shootout, by some miracle. They just faded back."

Chubby ordered them both another couple of beers.

"And Coleman's people occasionally got out of line, but were drummed out of Coleman's orbit, fast. He made some very strict personal behavior rules: any infractions and they are out."

"So he stopped the scary young Black men from frightening the solid citizens, huh?"

"Yeah, I guess you could say that," said Beau. "This back-to-the-land movement kept spreading around here; you know agricultural roots are deep around here. People who worked their own land were never bothered, although the movement had the effect of adding to the agricultural labor pool. But food is fresh, delicious, and cheap around here, and with all the greenhouses, popping up all year round. They are penetrating markets all over the South, and it is scaring corporate agriculture, especially since that is where the expropriations took place. Good beer too. It's like Israeli kibbutzim, with a different accent."

At that moment Chubby saw Aldane walking across the street and Chubby yelled and waved him over. They hadn't talked since they got off the G5 and walked through the airport. Chubby introduced him to Beau.

"You sound like you're from the Islands?"

"Yeah. So Chubby tell you where we come from, Beau?"

"Portland. I've been out there, great beer."

Aldane laughed. "Beer, huh?"

"Aldane plays in the band that opens for Katon, 'The Mane Shakers.'"

"Oh, shit, you guys are good."

Aldane shook his head.

"We need to get Beau tickets," said Chubby.

"Tonight. Pick 'em up at will-call," said Aldane. "I'll take care of it." Chubby handed Aldane Beau's info on the beer coaster.

"Thank you, Mr. Aldane! You know, I hear we all are in the 'Axis of Evil' together."

"The what?"

"That's what the Real-Prez's press bot said today. Portland and Memphis. Berlin, Rome, and Tokyo, 1939."

"What do you do?"

"Mr. Aldane, I'm glad you asked. I own a specialty import and export business. We sell high-quality foods, crafts, like cutlery, memorabilia, things like that."

"Get many Black customers?" Aldane asked as he seemed to casually glance at the menu.

"Some. Yes, more than some actually."

"Really?"

"Well, I was telling Chubby here, things usually don't change that fast, but that ain't right anymore, 'cause it really has down here, faster than anyone can believe. Not like it was two years ago, that's for sure. People still adhere to their tastes and habits, you know, but there is a lot of mixin', in every way you can think." Beau looked at Chubby.

"Aldane and I were barely in our twenties when we were almost killed together in Jamaica looking for King Solomon's treasure. Haile Selassie's loot."

"Really?"

"He's lying, you know," continued Aldane. "Chubby here's just a white boy trying to get away from Daddy's money. You understand what I'm saying, Mr. Beau?"

"I very much do, Mr. Aldane. I think you are running from the Islands because it cramped your style. Or do I misunderstand?"

Dane looked at Beau and wagged his head in a partial acknowledgment. "I don't know – I'm just a Black man living outside of Africa. What do you call that –"

"Part of the diaspora," said Beau.

"You mean like the Jews? You a Jew, Mr. Beau? Coming after us to get back King Solomon's jewels?"

"That is a complicated question, Aldane."

"Indeed it is! Diaspora," said Aldane, shaking his head, laughing. "Well, that was a long time ago, Mr. Beau, and..."

"All that was a long time ago," said Chubby.

"Yeah, it must have been."

"I like your scene down here, Beau," said Aldane. "The kids here in Bluestown are getting it together. It still ain't totally fixed though, and sometimes I just wonder – if it can be." Aldane laughed to himself at something that struck him as funny, apparently, and gave Chubby a look. "No offense to either of you mothafuckers. I need ta get the fuck out. You right, Beau, I still got unfinished business. I am headed back down Island. This country is fucked, and I ain't dying for it."

"Isn't 'down island' what the lesser Antilles are called? And you are actually from the Greater Antilles, right? So how are you going back down island?" Chubby asked.

"You the one with the lesser Antilly, not me."

Both Beau and Chubby were laughing.

"I go home and people say, 'where you been?' I don't know what to tell them anymore. 'Ain't you learned nothing yet?' they say. I been walking around this city all week, trying to figure it out, and I'm scared. The shit is going to come back – here – up in Portland – everywhere. In the end, whites own it all and will revert to the old playbook they always used. I'm just not feelin' all the love these children is. Sorry 'bout dat."

"It's different this time, brother," said Beau. "I just know it."

You could see Aldane pulling back just a bit at the "brother" remark. "Maybe," Aldane looked away. "Heard that before though."

"Things change, just too slow for people to notice," said Chubby.

"I hope so," said Beau. "I gotta go, fellows. Thanks so much for the music tickets. Nice meeting you both. Enjoy 'The People's Revolutionary Republic of Memphis'! And be sure to get over to Graceland too!"

They all shook hands, and Beau was on his way.

"You people!" Chubby shook his head with mock exasperation.

"You people!" They both started laughing at the joke that went back 30 years with them. "Well, let me tell you something, Chubby, about YOU people! If Real-Prez don't get shut down in November, they are coming in here and everywhere else shooting. Really shooting, not like in Portland. That was a picnic. And if you stand up and lose, it is all over. You people will kill everybody."

Kip looked away, and they were quiet for a few beats.

"I come from Down Island, or Up Island, whatever the fuck," Aldane looked hard at Chubby, waiting for a smart remark that never came. "And Island people be the hardest working, most responsible mothafuckers anywhere – hold three jobs, go to school, check the kids' homework, and play in the band too! But what is going on here is just bat shit! I just think we gotta have a plan, some kinda plan in case we lose. What we gonna do then? Die to the last man? Not me! These white people, they get together and engineer shit, draw up plans, pour foundations, set up railroads to make sure nobody escapes so they can kill everybody. Black people – shit. We get drunk on palm wine, go nuts with machetes for a few days, then sleep it off and lie and say it never happened. Maybe kill just as many, but somehow it's different. You see Black dictators in Africa being all crazy corrupt. Maybe that is Colonel Hassan Coleman too. I don't know. You know dem white moth-afuckers are thinking that all day! But we ain't got nothing on crazy whites when they get the blood in the eye."

"And another thing. I am tired of being everybody's magic Negro. You too. Specially you!"

They were quiet as a bourbon was poured.

"You mean like Morgan Freeman in every movie."

"Yeah, or Will Smith, the magic caddie who comes out of the fog and shows dat white boy how to play golf."

"My Magic Negro!"

Aldane stood up and made a fist and feinted throwing it. Then laughed. "I must be, 'cause you'd be dead by now if I wasn't. That shit is wicked." Aldane slammed the shot glass down. "There's a party tonight. I bring you. Maybe you get a little."

"Great. Another chance to fail in public."

CHAPTER 4

ALISON MEETS RIGHTWING WONKS IN SALT LAKE CITY

Late July

It was, in the view of most historians and political observers, a most dangerous moment. The country was on a knife's edge. No one knew which way the Army would fall. Most thought they would be with Real-Prez, but that wasn't necessarily true. Something needed to happen, and pretty quickly too.

Meanwhile, the bacto-virus had passed into Afghanistan and eastern Iran. No one was even trying to save the dying, only keeping them comfortable. Eating hashish seemed to help. Opium, plentiful as it was in that part of the world, did nothing to relieve the agony, but hashish seemed to calm people, and there were many cases where it appeared that it helped people recover, although there was no real medical evidence of a connection.

From *The Fall of It All – A History of the Big Dump*

UNIFORMED COPS WITH AUTOMATIC WEAPONS

stood at the ready every 50 feet or so along the airport corridor, while others held back growling dogs. Alison, Kayla, Telly, and Cadez walked briskly through the Salt Lake City terminal and piled into the back of a Lincoln Navigator waiting at the curb. The sun was nearly up when they arrived downtown near Temple Square at the Grand America Hotel. Telly checked them in, gave room key cards to Kayla and Alison, and briskly said, "Be down here in the lobby at 1:00 PM." Telly looked at Alison and frowned. "Please wear something decent; we are representing the next President!"

Alison didn't respond, but headed for her room. She tried but didn't sleep much. About 10:00 AM she got up, said to herself, "fuck it!" and decided to get some new clothes. But definitely not like what Kayla wore on the plane, and not brightly colored short skirts matched with low-cut monochromatic blouses, with sheer nylons or high platform shoes that pushed her ass up – she would not cover herself with FOX News Babe draperies.

She would placate Telly though, and find something a bit softer and conventional, and less like her grungy black sneakers, straight-legged loose fitting jeans, and black hoodie.

She went down to the lobby and walked over to Madewell's, which sold stylish casual clothes, mainstream, and hopefully acceptable enough to keep the Senator and Telly from harassing her. She bought a high-waisted black-and-white checked pair of slacks and a low-plunging green Lyric blouse. Not quite, but good enough. She picked up a few more similar ensembles and walked around Temple Square on her way back to the hotel.

Tourists from the Mormon diaspora were wandering around, looking at the Seagull Monument on Temple Square, quietly talking or listening respectfully to Temple guides dressed in cheap dark suits, second-day yellowish-white shirts, and dark ties. Alison overheard bits and pieces of conversations about the Portland Insurgency, and Real-Prez's threat to bomb it. Alison heard no glee or expressions of anger, and saw only head shaking and fearful shrugging. She was angry at herself – but reminded herself that she had joined Telly's little traveling vaudeville show to save Spence.

Alison caught the eye of a middle-aged man who muttered loud enough for her to hear, "Impeach the bastard!" His wife was pushing a baby carriage and herding three young boys in little jackets and ties while holding the hand of a little princess daughter. Alison nodded silently in agreement at his unexpected exclamation. The man saw her, then quickly looked away.

She headed back to the hotel and turned on the tube. General Steven Pak, a decorated fighter pilot from the first Gulf War, gave a fiery speech to some Air Force cadets, condemning any planned use of military assets against domestic opponents of the President. A brief interview in the parking lot of the Pentagon seemed to confirm the Chairman of the Joint Chiefs' agreement with Pak's comments. The Chairman also said that he had ordered air patrols over Portland to prevent any air attacks from anyone, "foreign or domestic." The military was laying down a marker. No "political" domestic action would be taken by any military units.

Since then, the Real-Prez Twitter account had been silent, except for retweeting a supporter's call for the firing of the Chairman of the JCS.

Alison got undressed, took a shower, and tried on one of her chic new outfits. She frizzed her hair out a little and stared at herself in the mirror, then turned away in disgust.

At least it looked like there would be no bombing of Portland by the US military. She collapsed on the bed and found a WNBA game to watch. She noticed one of the bench players, who had played against her in college. She watched until the end hoping her former rival would get into the game, but she never did.

High school had been smooth, but during her first year of college (in North Carolina) it got bumpy. At the time she was tired of living in the dorm, and during a particularly grueling practice she slightly tore her left meniscus, which kept her off the basketball court for a few months. She met a guy, left school, got married, and got a job at a call center in Raleigh.

One day she came back from work and decided that was it. She left a goodbye note, took the Greyhound back to Oregon, and found a job at *SwiftPad* tech support. Got her degree at night, along with a quick divorce, after which she got hired at *Reigny Deigh* by Gordy.

Poor Gordy, she thought. An asshole supreme, sure, but to be executed at that party? Shot down with no hesitation or warning? What – two days ago? Kayla, who was standing next to Gordy when it happened, was still freaked out about it. It seemed like years ago. Yet Alison swore she could still remember the smell of Gordy's frequent fragrance makeovers – mostly just different aftershaves – no matter what kind he wore, he still had stunk.

She got out of the elevator in the lobby, and even though she was five minutes early, Cadez and Kayla were waiting. Cadez had on a navy power suit and red tie, and Kayla a bright red skirt, extra high heels, and a white blouse with a plunging neckline. They were both smiling cheerfully and effusively complimented Alison on her new clothes.

"Let's go work the room," said Cadez. The Lincoln Navigator was waiting at the curb, and drove them the few blocks to the Salt Palace Convention Center.

The Utah ARRGH convocation was to the Beehive State what Politburo meetings were to the old Soviet Union. The Utah Dems were tolerated and unobtrusive, and won elections in Salt Lake City. But outlying areas in Utah looked at Salt Lake City as hopelessly liberal, and in most years overwhelmingly controlled the state. It was also a kind of a bellwether event for certain kinds of ARRGHs. Because southern Christian fundamentalists didn't like Mormons, there was a whiff of secularity to the convocation. Mormons had been demonized early in their history by the Bible Belt Protestants, and so had an ecumenical streak. The place was packed with rightward politicos from all over the country, all of whom were walking the floor hoping to be recognized, and the vibe felt somewhere between that of a gun show and a vitamin exposition. Alison stood silently on the edge of many conversations, where Mormon businessmen and women talked earnestly about finding a "third way" forward, that Real-Prez was not wholesome enough, as well as unhinged and dangerous.

"Ben Cadez is the only one with the integrity and discipline to take the country forward!"

Alison smiled. After a long and fulsome introduction, a famous Utah senator slow-walked Ben to the podium, and the crowd gave him full-throated and long applause.

Alison stood off to the side watching the crowd cheer, then looked toward the back and saw Telly talking animatedly to a tall dark-haired man in a power blue suit. She had a feeling she had seen him before; yeah, he was the chief financial officer of *SwiftPad*, the longtime Rehain Family consigliere Heber Young.

"Welcome everyone," effused Gideon Orton, the ageless wonder, a Congressional page during the Eisenhower years, five-term Utah congressman, political commentator, Barbershop Quartet Grammy winner (The Barn Raisers sang "Waiting to Cut the Pie" on the *Lawrence Welk Show* in 1965). In his trademark blue suit, red bow tie, smiling with giant capped teeth, Gideon looked out at the crowd of mostly young, mostly white men who had traveled to Salt Lake to gather and try and recreate the ARRGH Party from the dregs and flotsam that littered the political landscape in the wake of the Real-Prez regime. Orton had been a cable news fixture since the Reagan years, when he burst onto the national scene as a champion of supply-side economics. (He had a bachelor's degree in Theology from Brigham Young.) He often appeared with Arthur Laffer preaching a variety of tax plans (flat tax, national sales tax, VAT tax, negative child tax (tax rate falls to zero if you have four children – "legitimate" and from a traditional married family only – singles pay high rates regardless of income)). That these theories had either been proven disastrously wrong, or were regressive to the extreme, or pissed off large segments of the electorate, all this posed no barrier to him popping up regularly to applause in circles like the one now gathered in the Salt Palace.

But Real-Prez was too insane even for Gideon. Many in the crowd had been targets of Real-Prez attacks for insufficient loyalty, or some other perceived slight. The nuclear attack on the Hoover Dam had been a bitter economic blow to Utah, and how it happened and who did it were all vaguely and hesitantly answered by Real-Prez apologists. Asking too many questions, however, always carried the risk of being smeared as possible co-conspirators. Real-Prez had a go-to trope of accusing his accusers of what he was accused of, and it was so insane, and people were so used to it, that often it was just *SwiftPad*-bait, troll candy, wacko screeds that meant nothing other than a demographic checkpoint marking who still stood with him. That number never retreated far from 40 percent. The evidence that the Hoover Dam bombing was a "selfie" attack was swatted away by a rotating series of flacks and hacks, who while not Real-Prez supporters *per se,* still respected and feared his power. Everyone in attendance fell over one another in their bid for proximity to power regardless of from where it emanated. Alison wanted to scream.

But nothing came of it, and even though it was universally accepted that Real-Prez was deranged, and probably culpable of much worse, the country could only squat in the corner, averting its eyes and stopping its ears to the horrible noise coming out of Washington, DC. Alison watched Heber Young, until recently *SwiftPad*'s highly visible financial maven, navigate through the swarm of mostly young men, all of whom hovered around Young asking "whither *SwiftPad*?" Whither indeed. Although they had never met, he seemed to recognize her and approached.

"You worked for Gordon Lobetts, didn't you?"

"Yes, yes, I am Alison Aykroyd. I have wanted to meet you,

Mr. Young. I'm still with *Reigny Deigh*. Mr. Haines has acquired the company and convinced me to stay on."

"Excellent. I know Telly is around here somewhere. I just arrived in town myself."

They shook hands. Heber looked around for eavesdroppers. "What are your feelings?"

Alison didn't know what he was asking and gave him a quizzical look.

"About what just happened in Portland."

"I was just surprised at how well the Insurgency was organized." She had no intention of being drawn out by Heber until she knew where he stood, and standing in the middle of an ARRGH convention floor was no place to find that out.

"Oh, I know. I know. Our people – from *SwiftPad* Corp – are pretty much behind it, after what happened. I left town right after Jim Hunt died. I just didn't like the anti-government direction the company and city was taking. I knew something bad was going to happen." He looked up at Alison's poorly disguised shocked expression, and quickly said, "No, no, I didn't know – I just felt something was going to give."

Alison nodded in listless agreement.

"Everyone assumed the Prez was behind it," said Heber, "but he wasn't even in charge when it started. In some ways I trust him more than Temp-Prez. Something wasn't right. In any event, we needed to do something. Now I think we need to get behind Ben."

"Senator Cadez has been moving up in the polls."

"Portland has to do something about the refugees though. It can't absorb so many. That is not going away, and now the city is isolated, waiting for – Cynthia Oglethorpe and her husband are gone, and Kip Rehain – who knows what he's doing – I'm not sure who is running the company. I have no vision into the company anymore."

What was he saying, Alison wondered. He knows everything about *SwiftPad*, but now, no vision? Was he out, or was he like she was, pretending to be out?

"Until we find GG, it is not clear – and *SwiftPad* is still the main source of information for most of the world and not knowing who is in charge is a problem. To be honest, Alice Hunt doesn't like me, and she seems to be in charge now." Heber shrugged. "Old man Rehain would be turning over in his grave if he knew."

Who was running things at *SwiftPad*? Alison thought it must be Archimedes Moropolis, or Kip Rehain himself, wherever he was. "Who ordered the Hoover Dam bombing?" Alison looked closely at Heber, trying to get a read on him.

Heber shrugged. "I can't believe the things I am hearing – that it was the Prez or his people. I mean Portland – alone. Anyway, that will sort itself out in time. We need to get everyone off the ledge. If Prez retaliates, it is going to be a civil war. Alison, it's great meeting you. I'm glad you're on board, and that you're staying on at *Reigny Deigh*. Rest in Peace, Gordy."

"Not just him. Hundreds were killed."

Heber touched her shoulder and looked sad.

A well-dressed young man walked by, talking to Kayla, saying, "Portland is going through some difficulties. I have heard reports of militant leftwing dirtbags with automatic weapons roaming the streets, summarily executing people they dragged out of expensive cars."

"Really?" Kayla's eyes bugged out in shock.

"That is absolutely wrong!" Alison shot a daggered look at Kayla. "What reports?"

"Well, it was a post by someone who says he heard it."

"It is bullshit," said Alison. "Colonel Coleman and Harvey Grennell's troops that defended Portland from the President's (V) ICE militia were disciplined. Nothing like that happened!"

"Well," the well-groomed young man pulled back at her little outburst. But he smiled a bit, almost as if he were trying to needle her. "I heard the whole town has succumbed to drug-fueled murder and rape gangs roaming through neighborhoods, but if you say it is not true, then, OK. I wasn't there."

She hesitated, not really knowing exactly how to refer to the two days of fighting that resulted in over 800 dead and thousands of (V)ICE prisoners in the hands of the anti–Real-Prez Insurgency. He smiled at her condescendingly and they turned back to the podium to watch Cadez, who gave a short, but rousing speech that really said nothing. He left the rostrum to loud enthusiastic cheers. How much bullshit was she expected to accept?

Alison met Cadez and he nodded to her, his dark hair shining and pushed back, bright eyes flashing, acknowledging a long and extended standing ovation. Over 750 people, mostly white men, with perhaps a fourth of the audience middle-aged women, and a sprinkling of Blacks and Latinos, all enthusiastically cheering as Cadez smiled and waved. He waited for more from Alison, but she only pleasantly smiled and helped escort him to a green room, where he drank a glass of water and popped a couple of gel capsules, and seemed to shake as they went down.

"You rest, Ben, I'll be right outside," she said.

Hanging around outside the green room, young wonks who were all vying for a spot on Cadez's staff were buzzing and preening amongst themselves, each one dropping an assortment of rightwing *bon mots* to show their alpha dog potential.

"So, what is this, a (third) party planning committee?" Telly asked, acknowledging the unspoken fact that there was no way they could turn around Real-Prez at the Disneyland convention.

"With Rosie splitting off from Caroline's Dees, did that really make four?" A tall, buzz-cut, red-faced kid in a suit a half size too small tried to catch Telly's attention. "And if nobody gets 270, doesn't that throw it to the States, where at least we ARRGHs will be sure to win?"

"But if we don't coalesce," said another young wonk, who spoke up with obvious self-consciousness, "and the Dees do, we are in H-E double hockey sticks! And Real-Prez –"

"Look, Real-Prez is nuts," said Telly. "We can't say that publicly, but we have to face that fact. If we do, we will pull a large percent of the Dees to us and further isolate R-P. We either beat him, or he will hunt us down after the election. He hates us worse than he hates the Dees."

"Well, we are in it to win it," said Cadez, turning his back on Telly. "Alison, you lead the team and come up with a platform and strategy. We need to thread the needle."

~~~

So Alison took over the imaginary gavel, and they turned the wonks loose, and came up with a number of proposals in opposition to the Real-Prez platform.

They had position papers, pragmatic conservative stuff that mostly amounted to passing the buck on social issues to the states. But being in Utah, Mormons had suffered for their religion, so religious tolerance was strongly supported, even for atheists. Liberal on theological issues, a deal killer for much of the Bible Belt. While there were the usual protests against human services and assistance, there were also calls to radically defund the military. The Mormons were actually pretty flexible as long as they got some kind of equal respect "before the law" for their goofy theology. Most of them were descendants of polygamists, so they had a secret erotic sensibility that you didn't find in other American "Jesus" cults. Fine, thought Alison. Be what you want to be.

Of course she was there to sabotage all this shit.

How far should she go before she pulled the string? She smiled to herself with the thought that maybe she was just too good at helping these pasty-faced weasels. That was the easy part. Pull the string – the catch phrase from the cult film *Plan 9 from Outer Space* – she had no idea what that might mean.

Was it possible, she thought, that she was the only one who noticed that Cadez was rotting out?

The wonks latched onto her, clearly seeing her as the gateway to Cadez.

"You were there!" They begin to use her to deconstruct what happened in Portland and what it meant. Questions – "What political structure is left?" "What is the mood?" "How bad is the refugee crisis?"

She said, "We will not be responsible for the next holocaust! Even if it breaks us, we will take in our neighbors."

Silence. Many Mormons had left Arizona for Portland with nothing.

"Anger," "organizing," "arming," "fear," "a kind of martial law." Panic underlay every proposal and question.

There were Dem NeoCons in attendance too. They tried to overload the agenda with calls for an imperialistic foreign policy. Many had come over because Caroline had been forced to reject their positions, and everyone knew that Rosie was for a major demilitarization.

Alison recognized that while Cadez might be on the verge of a total mental and physical breakdown, he was still seen as the savior by this crowd. The big guns were beating the bushes, and many faces in the crowd were familiar to anyone who paid close attention to national politics. It was a who's who of radical conservative politicians from the past that hated Real-Prez for lots of reasons: personal slights, broken promises, and just a rational fear of having a lunatic in the White House, who was calling himself an "R."

All the conservatives who hated Real-Prez wanted a constitutional convention. They wanted to massively limit the federal government as well as the President's power.

All of this flew around the meeting that Alison tried to control, to pull some kind of policy together. In the end she knew it would be up to Cadez himself, and she knew, better than anyone, that he was even crazier than Real-Prez was.

"In the very beginning," Cadez told her, "the first few times you eat Golden Fungus it allows you to read the minds of everything around you, dogs, birds, trees, the whole world was vibrating, and you could tune into those vibrations and tune the other shit out. And you had an enhanced mental 'machine' for distinguishing and correlating everything."

Cadez's rare plunges into cogency and lucidity actually scared Alison more than his manic insanity. "The best theory is that it picked up on the alpha waves that everybody's brain broadcasts," Cadez continued. "But the power seems to fade with time. I can't read minds anymore, I'm sure you have noticed that. If you do it regularly, after about six months, you notice you have to work at it a little more to pick up on other people. And, more disturbingly, you start seeing people as bots, just machines designed to fill particular places in the larger ecosphere. Even people who you know."

She had no doubt he really saw all of life as "bots" with no value beyond what their component minerals would sell for.

CHAPTER 5

MAGGIE AND SEQUOIA WELCOMED TO COMPOUND, NATE MEETS ALICE

Early August

The virus seemed to avoid Europe, at first anyway. There was no explanation for it. As Doctors Without Borders was reporting from the rural areas of the Middle East, there were many cases, and sometimes as much as 30% of the local population died. People got very sick, but the majority recovered, after a fashion. Recovery manifested in delusions (or visions, as they seemed to be to the infected). It was inexplicably missing the cities, but hitting college students especially hard. Some argued that the "European genome" (whatever that was) protected the continent from large-scale infections. But that was refuted by the fact that the large Middle Eastern populations living in Europe also seemed to resist infection. Sicily was hit, as was Bosnia, and the regions of Russia east of the Volga, but by and large there were few cases from Gibraltar to the Bosporus, and regions directly north.

Ireland was an exception. The delusions manifested in uniquely Catholic religious experiences, including outbreaks of stigmata mostly among women. They were quickly quarantined. There were still no reported cases in North America.

From *The Fall of It All – A History of the Big Dump*

PAULA WAS UP, AND BREWING HERSELF TEA. ALICE had furnished the cabin with stacks of books, a couple of soft chairs, a sofa, and two perfect burners on a quarter-sized oven – it was cozy, it was heaven, she felt, a place to rest, which after a life of busy, active youth, she desperately craved. Perhaps a person's "spirit" or life force had an expiration date, just like our bodies do, she thought. Over the last few years, even though she had the physical strength and mental energy of a very young woman, the years had worn on her in some deeper way. But now she was feeling better. Nate knocked on the door.

She was very happy to see Nate. She invited him in, and they drank tea together and sat on her little patio that faced south and looked out onto the redwood grove that Walt, Kip's father, had planted more than 40 years ago. They talked about old times, and soon relaxed and almost seemed to fit right back into their old domestic ways. As the sun passed behind the trees, they retreated into her hobbit house.

"I understand Maggie is here." Paula sat back in her rocking chair and smiled.

"Yeah, after twenty-some years, we are...in the same place."

"Are you staying with her up at the house?"

"No. No. Alice gave her Kip's old room; I am on the couch for now. It's fine. We have no point to start from anymore. We start a serious conversation, but soon it sputters into laughter, at ourselves mostly, I guess. We both betrayed each other, and we can't hide from it. She isn't sorry, and neither am I. She couldn't do it, and neither can I."

"It?"

"You know, go back to the way it was 20 years ago."

"Oh, yeah. I can't wait to meet her," said Paula.

"She – I think fighting all night up in Forest Park above Portland with an Uzi has changed her outlook. I mean, I don't know. But she is a soldier now. An Amazon. Powerful, has a take-no-shit attitude. I am more sensitive than she is, which is a total role reversal. We don't mesh like before, and well, it is for the better. She used to be an elfin fairy queen. And I used to be a pompous ass – I mean even more than I am now. So – we smile at each other, but otherwise are at a loss. And, well, her husband, my old friend Spence – he is missing. Until that is sorted – I mean..."

"He stole your girlfriend. Was he really your friend?"

"What are you trying to say, Paula?"

"I don't know. I guess I am trying to keep you."

"You control the table, Paula, and you know it."

"Yeah, that's a laugh. So why was Spence your friend?"

"Spence found me paying work when I really needed it."

"Money?"

"We've talked about this, Paula. I had it all and lost it. He put me back in black. Anyway – with Maggie back then – I just couldn't do it anymore. Maggie was too timid then to act on it at first, but she really wanted something – someone – else. I knew that without the Fungus, I was just another lecherous old man. So I stopped eating it. She was grateful of course. Sometimes that's enough."

"Let's not talk about age, OK?" Paula closed her eyes, seeming to control some deep pain.

"Does it hurt much?" Nate moved closer to her and took her hand.

"Yes," said Paula. She smiled and fought back tears. "It really does. I don't want to be young anymore. But I don't want to get old like this either!"

"How is your wound?"

"Oddly, healed pretty well. See?" She lifted up her blouse and showed Nate her scar.

"Wow! Just some stitches around a small bruise. No other issues?" Nate looked closely at Paula, around her eyes, and neck.

"Nope. Just getting old too fast. If Elwood comes with more Fungus, I will take it. But maybe he won't come, or maybe he won't have any. If not, then that is over. I'll be 76 in a few months...and by then I will look it and feel it. Can I ask you something?"

Nate didn't answer right away. Then he smiled. "What?"

Paula shook her head.

"You were going to ask me, 'How old do I look?' Right?"

Paula looked away.

"Fifty. But a good fifty."

"A good fifty?" Paula put her head back and laughed. "I suppose I should be complimented."

"Fucking right you should! Your eyes are clear. You are sharp. You still have a killer bod. Still too young for me."

"Ha!" Paula clapped her hands and smiled. "So from appearances, I am the same age as Maggie, right?"

"Yeah, but she is a natural badass. She kept it together by working out every day. She can run forever," Nate shrugged, as if to say don't ask what you don't want to know.

"And she has had a child, and she has done the whole marriage thing. Stuff I have no conception of. You should leave me alone and..."

"Look, Paula," Nate said, "Let's just be. I'm here. Look at me? Do you think I care about age anymore?"

She smiled and touched his face.

"Still though," Nate said with a cruel glint in his eye, "I dream about tight pussy..."

Paula slapped him.

"Ouch! Elder abuse! That hurt!"

"Good," Paula said, her eyes flaring hot.

"Look, let's..." They stared at each other, both slowly coming to a smile. "Just let me be a servant. Wake up every morning and be alive. Give me a chance to be a good person for once in my life. Is that such a bad ambition?"

"No," she said.

"I know it sounds so trite, but monogamy – I've tried that. Several times."

"Me too," said Paula. "You want to take a walk? Down below here is an amazing cedar grove. So cool, and moist. There are two rocks covered with moss that are perfect chairs. The bubbling stream at their foot has the best tasting water. Then afterwards, let's cook something together."

"Yeah," said Nate. "Let's do that." Nate reached out to her with both hands.

"I don't need help getting up."

"I do," he said.

CHAPTER 6
CHUBBY MEETS TIARA, A LEADER OF THE MEMPHIS RESISTANCE

Mid-August

An unpublished but frequently referenced study by two Texas psychologists indicated no increase in emotion perception or in mutual cognition or any affective mentalizing when two people took the Golden Fungus together. However, the few people who experienced it back in the late '70s when the Fungus was still available on the street in limited quantities – Elwood Taylor was the only source – had no idea where it came from, because Taylor was extremely careful to hide his involvement, and also to hide the location where it grew. As for the Hughes study, those who experienced it knew that the study was a fraud, put out by the Hughes organization to tamp down demand.

The power of the Fungus wasn't just a myth. There were other psychologists who proved that the Golden Fungus mind-reading effect was real, and almost all had confirmed it. Their work was suppressed, however, and never published in any reputable journals. There was a fear that it could undermine the few traditional controls that still remained (such as the church, and some kind of low-culture understanding of "the way we all know it really is").

So there was scientific evidence that the shit really worked! But by the 1980s, the Golden Fungus had practically disappeared. Some said with little evidence that it was over-harvested, and others said the mild winters had wiped it out. By then Elwood had discovered he wasn't getting any older and had moved into southern Illinois to cultivate the few secret spots where the Fungus still flourished in the Kaskaskia River habitat.

From *The Fall of It All – A History of the Big Dump*

THEY WERE IN THE KITCHEN OF A THREE-STORY BRICK

home in Victoria Village, downtown Memphis, and Chubby was hanging around the chips and guacamole bowl. It was muggy, but the windows were open, the sun had been down for a couple of hours, and it was comfortable. He was talking with a pretty Black woman with freckles under her eyes, eyes which fired out a complex mix of messages that made Chubby realize they were about to hatch a conspiracy together. Her short, tight hair, her narrow yellow jeans, and her deep V-neck coral-colored floral blouse all accentuated her necklace of brown amber stones that were strung to be progressively larger as they plunged down her neckline. She was drinking white wine.

"You are a friend of Aldane, huh?"

"Yeah, uh…" As usual, Chubby stuttered and swallowed his words when talking to a beautiful woman.

"I know who you are – Kip, right? I am Tiara. You must have met the Colonel in Portland, right?"

"Um – yeah. I did." She was beautiful and getting more so by the second. "I guess you could say I worked – we worked together. The Colonel came to my apartment and he and Harvey Grennell worked out the strategy – for the battle."

"Really? You listened?"

"Well – yeah..." Kip didn't feel like talking about how he led several thousand people out to block the Banfield the night of the Portland Insurgency. "But actually, they just told me what to do."

"Oh my, well, I am going to want to hear all about that! But what do you think about Dash biting the big one?"

"I wouldn't want to have to carry the casket," said Kip.

Dashell Addison Sketerson was the second highest paid and rated AM jock in the country, the godfather of the rightwing tilt in talk radio. When the FCC eliminated "The Fairness Doctrine" in the late '80s, the hounds from fascist hell were released onto American radio airwaves, and Sketerson was the lead dog. Suddenly the Book of Revelation joined forces with the jabbering of demented, race-baiting Klansmen, with screeding spreaders of lies, vituperative fulminators of hate, and paranoid preachers of malicious propaganda. Led by Dash Sketerson, they delivered "the facts" of crazed liberal conspiracies being hatched by swarthy city-dwelling fiends right into your car radio.

Dash was not quite the vilest of the lot, but to some he was the most entertaining. As he got famous, he became "a thing," just by showing up at rallies and TV talk shows, and conventions. He started rubbing elbows with the new wave of unscrupulous pols, such as Real-Prez, and other similar scum, who themselves were trying to ride the rightwing radio wave the jocks had conjured up. To most of the folks outside RedHat country, he was no longer funny or taken seriously as a political maven. He had led his Dashoholics down too many easily disproved rat holes that even he now had disclaimed. His "fan base," the Dashoholics, totally bit into his daily shit sandwich rants, and were able to quickly forget what he told them if he changed his slant 180 degrees the next day. Analysis of his career showed that once he became famous he became a complete toady, and sycophant, who waited for the signals from the pols he helped elect. He basically created Real-Prez, but now he had to kiss his ass.

Dash, like Real-Prez and so many others of that ilk, was a

weakling who always sought Daddy's approval. His family had local prominence around southern Missouri. But Dash was a loser by most of his family measures. He dropped out of college and was a slob and a failure who lived on welfare through his 20s and early 30s while moving from radio station to radio station. Then the Fairness Doctrine went away and he discovered that hate sells.

Now he had an $80 million-a-year gig, plus innumerable side benefits. Dash wasn't stupid; he knew he was an entertainer, a circus monkey. His voice was everywhere. You could hear him yelling on loudspeakers into factory floors, dentist's offices, farmhouses, bars and lounges, dinners, and religious gatherings across middle and southern America. His voice was inescapable.

Much of the current situation, the Red-Blue shit, could be laid at his feet.

"Fuck, him, glad he's dead," said Kip. "How did he die?"

"He was pretty obese, and was in and out of the hospital for diabetes, and heart blockages. So, it was coming. Way over 300 pounds. One unattributed story is that he died on top of his skinny, young third wife. Can you imagine having to crawl out from under that hulking blob while he is leaking bodily fluids out of every orifice? I guess some think that is the manly way to go out. One of his admirers called it 'a curtain call at Rockefeller Center.'"

"Oh – right, Ford's VP went out that way too. So Dash pulled a Full Nelson," said Kip, waiting in vain for a laugh. "They will make a big deal of his funeral," Kip continued. "The so-called Real-Prez will probably speak."

"So-called! Who can speak his name without gagging? Fuck, it isn't anything to cheer about though. We have to be on guard. Some of their people will probably be looking for revenge."

"We didn't kill him," said Kip.

"No, but that doesn't matter. The fat fuck killed himself with junk food just to prove he wasn't liberal. He really is the prototype of Real-Prez."

"Not a decent bone in his carcass."

"Yeah," said Tiara. "But he was funny in a hateful way sometimes I suppose. If you see him as a dumb fool when he does his bits, they make a kind of satiric sense. But always, he has to hurt somebody, always in a cruel way."

"To junk food!" Kip held up his glass. "The great equalizer!"

"And third wives!" Tiara held her glass up too and they drank. "So, aside from that, what do you think?"

Kip thought – he stopped himself. Can't do it, he thought. Can't stop looking at her either. "You mean what do I think about Hassan Coleman?"

"Yes."

"He is the full deal, no doubt," said Kip. "I think if we can get past all this stuff now, he could be President."

"Oh, I don't know. I wouldn't go that far! Not yet anyway. He doesn't take himself very seriously. And with his reputation, as it is now, no. That is kind of a drawback in politics. In a small city like Memphis, you can practically meet everybody, or at least be seen. Anyway – who knows if we are going to get past this stuff, as you say." She took a long sip of wine, keeping her eyes on him the whole way. "I want to thank you for the money by the way. It came in handy. We needed to up our game. Know what we bought?"

"Uh, bourbon?"

She laughed. "No, we didn't really need that. Supplies are stocked! No, we used it to get some secure communications gear. Upgraded our whole system. Now we can put people in the field and keep in touch while keeping an eye on these bastards."

"Memphis helped save my city, so glad to help."

"Um huh! Well, five million is a nice thank-you! What do you think about the international situation?"

"It was short of five – more like four point eight. What do you mean, international situation?"

"Think the Russians are helping Real-Prez like they did the first time?"

"You mean are they exploiting *SwiftPad*, like they kind of did during the last election? I don't think so. I mean it is possible, but we, I mean *SwiftPad*, have thousands of people, all over the world, stomping out propaganda fires every day – all the time – I don't think it is a big problem."

"What about See-2-Bee? You know they picked up Gupta?"

"Shit? How do you know?"

"We got some antennas down here. You West Coast kiddies think you are on top of everything. We got some tricks down here too."

"Where is he?"

"Gupta? I heard outside Dallas. Cadez's outpost. In an old business campus that Big Ears Ross Perot built."

"How..."

"People are disappearing all over the country, and they ain't showing up in jail neither. We are setting up to strike back."

"Who are you?"

Tiara pulled her head back at his blunt question.

"I mean, when you say *we*..."

"Huh? You really don't know much, do you?" With a smile she couldn't contain, Tiara picked up the bottle of sauvignon blanc and filled her glass. She held it up. "That bourbon you're drinking is OK for sitting in on card games that you expect to lose." She held the bottle up, weaving to the funk coming out of the front of the house. "Are you expecting to lose, or are you going to keep your head in this game?"

Kip poured his drink in the sink and held out his empty glass.

"A dirty bourbon glass? This is good wine!"

Kip held his bourbon glass even closer, and she shrugged and filled it.

"Not bad."

Tiara put the bottle down and grabbed his hand and they did some shimmying to the music. She got real close to his face. "Nikoloz told me to say hi. And Milana sends her regards."

Kip didn't flinch or break his rhythm even a little. But his eyes did.

"Nikoloz, huh? Where is he?"

"Moscow."

"You know he works for…"

"Oh, I know who he works for!" She closed her eyes and moved closer with her hips. "What's the matter? Georgia on your mind?"

Yeah, Kip thought, Georgia was on his mind. He had left Tbilisi only a few months ago, yet it seemed like a lifetime. Milana! She had saved him at his low point, and made him happy, maybe happier than he had been with GG.

"That was rude of me. But I just wanted you to know – we really don't know – but – uh – Nikoloz seems to know something about it – and well – we think she is in Russia. Or maybe just on her way."

"Cynthia?"

"Yeah." Tiara looked at him quizzically for a couple of seconds. "Don't you call her GG?" Tiara gave him a look, with a hint of a smile that was both mocking and sympathetic.

"Not anymore. Too intimate. Is she OK?"

Tiara's countenance shifted and became more serious. She looked away, shrugged, and shook her head. "I don't know. Are you OK?"

Kip stared at her. "Nikoloz, huh?"

"Yeah."

Kip had told no one about his encounter with Milana's mysterious half-brother, whose theatrical deletion of the *SwiftPad* off of his fone had so shaken Kip six months ago. Kip had assumed he was GRU (KGB), and now he was in contact with the Memphis resistance?

Tiara gave him that look. He knew that look.

It might have all blown over, but what happened at the
Memphis airport shocked the nation. In some ways, we
have still not recovered from it.

From *The Fall of It All – A History of the Big Dump*

The next morning, Tiara and Kip were both having coffee in
bed, looking out of his eighth-floor hotel room, overlooking the
Mississippi.

"So…"

"Yeah…"

"Coleman's Chief of Staff, huh?"

"The political side, yeah. Lately, they have been ignoring me
because of all the military stuff going on. Which is fine with me,
because I see everything that comes across his desk anyway. But
I wrote the Urban Homestead Bill. My husband has brought in
the money – he knows everybody."

"Your left ring finger is bare."

"Didn't I mention that? Well, don't worry, he's not the jealous
type. I do this once in a while, and I think maybe he does too,
but I don't pry. He is even older and whiter than you are."

Kip laughed. "Don't take this the wrong way, but – I don't – I
have been a victim of infidelity – and it hit me pretty hard – I'm
sorry." Kip sat up and forced a smile. "I don't screw other men's
wives if I can help it."

"I thought Aldane would have…"

"Yeah, well – he enjoys seeing me…embarrass myself. I usually get him back…" He stopped talking and she kept looking at
him. "Tiara…when I was younger I could do this. But – it's just
too much anymore. Last night as I looked at you and we talked,
and then when you said…"

"…well I knew my husband was on his way home and…"

"That was your house?"

"Well…"

Suddenly, Chubby blurted out what had just come into his head, like he often did when he was trying to get under someone's skin, or when an idea popped into his consciousness. For some reason, no matter how many times his impulsive lack of a filter came back to clamp its jaws around his balls, he still persisted. "Have you ever slept with the Colonel?"

Tiara looked at him in shock, then with fierce anger. "What the fuck business is that of yours?"

He smiled. She had been so cool up to now.

"You didn't seem so high and mighty last night – Chubby!"

"And you didn't seem to mind prying into my business either."

"Your business?"

"Nikoloz."

"You think this is about your little sex vacation in Tbilisi? For someone who made as much money as you did, you sure are fucking naive!"

"You are right. How naive of me. I just can't get used to women who use sex to advance their own interests."

Tiara got up on the other side of the bed, dragging the sheet around her. "I don't know what the matter is with me. Maybe I should apologize, I just don't often seem to have the need to do that. But – you are a marked man now. Your performance in Portland – getting those people on the street – you can't go back to whatever it was you were before. So fuck you – yeah – I sometimes fuck the men I do business with. How else can I..."

"Control them?"

"I was going to say understand them. You are going to have to get used to the idea that your business is my business if you are actually going to find your – Cynthia."

"I don't have to get used to a goddamn thing!" Kip quickly sat up, then stood up and looked down at her. "You think you can wave that money maker of yours at me and own me?"

"I felt sorry for you. My mistake." She stormed toward the

bathroom. She stopped and turned toward him, dropped the sheet, and put her hand on her bare hip.

"Take a good look, Chubby. You'll not see this again!" She turned, went into the bathroom, and slammed the door.

Kip pulled on a pair of shorts, and went out and sat out on the balcony, wishing he had a bowl of weed to get whacked out on. So stupid! She's right: we are going to need each other. This war is just getting started.

She came out, not looking at him, wrapped in a towel, and began picking her clothes up off the floor. At first he thought to apologize, but then he thought better of it. Watching her, though, turned away from him, bending over, pulling her jeans on, he started thinking maybe...he should say he was sorry.

Then there was a flash, then a thundering, window-shaking boom from across the river.

CHAPTER 7

CHUBBY DRIVEN TO VANDALIA BY ILLINOIS RESISTANCE

Late August

Cadez met them long ago, in the hippie ghetto of Lawrence, Kansas, right after Cadez had "saved" Paula from the CIA-funded psycho-rapists and torturers in Latin America. She never figured out exactly where they imprisoned her. To escape, she allowed Cadez to seduce her.

Paula blamed the Weathermen for this period of her life. In fact, one of the Weathermen whom she spent a summer with in a tiny trailer in rural Michigan was a snitch, and had set her up at the Houston airport, where she was kidnapped and taken to South America.

She returned with Stewardo (Cadez), and then, in December of 1972, the two of them went to work on an assignment for the Huston Group, an off-the-books branch of the White House plumbers. Most historians, even today, thought that the Huston Plan had been disbanded because of an earlier agreement between the soon-to-die J. Edgar Hoover and Nixon. But Cadez had gotten a wink and a nod from Milhous himself, and believed in the Huston Plan's mission. With his new psycho-technical associate Paula Flayer, he had set upon Elwood and Nate to steal their electroencephalographic "mind-reading" machine.

There had been a black market in the Fungus in Law-rence, Kansas (Elwood was the source, although many dealers were selling it, or something they said was it). This was before it attained its very brief (first six months of 1979) cult-like attraction for the hippies of the Pacific Northwest. Although everyone knew of its "mind-reading" effect, at the time no one had any idea it could extend and main-tain youth. But its effect was especially powerful when two people ate the Fungus together. Paula taught Cadez how it worked.

That is how it all started, how the now 85-year-old former Nixon Watergate operative Guy Jumano (who later became CIA Latin American agent Stewardo del Gente) had finally morphed into Ben Cadez, who continued to seem perpetually youthful. With the Howard Hughes organiza-tion behind him, they had the Fungus components syn-thesized, or so they thought. It had worked after a fashion, except it made Cadez "unsound" (as a certain Colonel Kurtz had been described in another context). But still, Cadez saw its potential and understood it could be the engine to drive the C2B revolution that he wanted to control. When supplies of the native Fungus dried up in the early '80s, he came to depend on the shit that Howard Hughes had ordered to be made in his Houston labs. It slowly made him psychotic, but it seemed to him as if it had unleashed his true self (see *The SwiftPad Insurgency*).

From *The Fall of It All – A History of the Big Dump*

EIGHT IN THE EVENING, BUT IT WAS STILL HOT AND humid when Chubby jumped off of Hank's skiff on the Illi-nois side upriver a few miles from the Cape, and crossed a spit of wooded land. He walked up a dirt road in the middle of alfalfa fields and arrived at a paved county road a half-mile from a lonely farmhouse. In the other direction, he heard a car door slam. About a hundred yards up the road, a small Toyota pickup with a camper was parked in a cutout off the road. A man about

40, who looked like a semi-prosperous farmer, medium build in overalls, wearing a green "Marion Grange" baseball cap, made a furtive wave for him to hurry up, then got back in the truck and started it. Chubby, too tired to be cautious, ran to it and jumped in the back. The driver looked back, nodded, and took off.

From the little window in the back of the camper, Chubby saw cop cars with flashing lights hurry past them, but none stayed on their tail. A burner fone, powered off, was there to replace the "bomb igniter" he had thrown into the Mississippi. About an hour later they were in Centralia and wound through a tree-lined, Midwestern neighborhood, with well-kept, old two-story, mostly white-painted wooden houses. They pulled into a driveway, then into a garage. The nondescript middle-aged, middle-American farmer got out and Chubby heard a garage door close. His driver stuck to procedure, no conversation, simply pointed to a door, and then left the garage. Chubby opened the door to a small office in the back, with a couch and a mini-fridge with potato salad and mustard, butter, jam, mayonnaise, and one beer (Mich- elob). In the crisper were Kraft packaged deli ham and cheese. There was a loaf of whole wheat bread in the breadbox. The small bathroom with a shower felt luxurious after the long night and day of hiding in the brambles next to the riverbank on Hank's raft, and the final trip up to Ware.

Chubby tried not to think of the head attached to a half-torso he saw flying through the air from the other side of the brick building opposite the Hot Shots bar.

Oddly (or perhaps it was just a quirky joke of the extraction team), Nathan Schuette's novel *The Long Goodbye* (the book's cover picture – the once red-haired Schuette riding a dragon) was lying on a table. He had met Schuette earlier that spring in San Fran- cisco, and later in Portland during the short-lived battle with (V) ICE. Now Schuette was at his compound, with Alice and Paula. He knew that much, but little else. Why had Schuette become the key to so much? The Golden Fungus, the secret history of

Ben Cadez, and their complicated relationship with Paula Flayer, it all seemed to flow through Nathan Schuette? Chubby thought Schuette was a pompous ass, with questionable hygienic habits. He fell asleep after reading about 20 pages, the opened book on his chest, and dream-remembered the odor in his spacious apartment above Ranjit's Kwikie Mart, which stank like a third-tier assisted living home after Schuette had spent a night on his couch.

He slept late, made toast and jam, took another nap, and around 1:30 in the afternoon, Chubby heard a car pull into the garage. A woman, a bit on the chunky side, smartly but unobtrusively dressed, maybe 45, knocked on his door. They got into a Buick LeSabre and took off, this time with Kip sitting up front. The woman driving asked him nothing directly, but kept up the chatter, talking about the coming election and the low-level violent threats that she had seen and heard. Neighbors hating neighbors, each round getting worse.

"Don't they realize he is a monster?" she said without prompting or even seeming to direct it to him, but just a statement. "If I was younger, I'd move out of here, to the West Coast. But it is too late."

Chubby said nothing and wished she would shut up, because if he was captured and tortured, who knew what he might say? He couldn't believe how fearful Americans had become. But, he thought, we are a violent, vengeful people, less than a century from when lynch mobs were the final arbiter of "justice" in the American Midwest and South. Deep down no one has forgotten. And, to make it worse, we are talentless and horrible at maintaining conspiracies. Not like Eastern Europeans, or the Chinese, who have been using secret societies to fight oppression for centuries. Americans are blabbermouths; we just can't help it.

"As long as the Land of Lincoln votes Blue," Chubby said, "you are in the right place."

"Sure, but which one? Caroline is hopeless; Rosie – they will never go for her around here. Thanks to Chicago and vicinity,

Illinois is safely in the Blue column, whatever that means, but down here in the southern part of the state, it's pretty fucking Red."

For some reason Chubby was shocked and even a little disappointed to hear vulgarity from his Mary Poppins–like driver. Chubby looked down at a highway map on his fone. Couple hours to Vandalia.

"Nothing like those crazy RedHat people over in Missouri though," she reiterated, looking closely to see how he would react. Apparently, she has a lot more questions about me, Chubby thought, than I have about her. He could tell she was wondering if he was involved in the bombing. It had been on all the feeds, from eleven dead to seven, with only one *SwiftPad* post getting it right – two dead, and one with crippling injuries, some people with cuts from shattered glass, and some hearing issues from the blast. For a few hours, the big story said that the bomber – him, Chubby – had blown himself up. He looked down and patted himself on the stomach. No word on which ones died, but Chubby was sure he had lucked into hitting the right ones. And probably the Lollipop who followed Kendal and Jeff out on the street chasing him. Chubby was sure Lollipop was not collateral, but actually an unanticipated windfall. Anyway, apparently, one of those three must have survived.

On his new fone, Chubby saw a story about Hank – they had arrested him. Would he flip, give them a description of him? He knew a lot of people in Memphis too. He won't rat, at least not right away. But with all he knew, including where he let him off – north of the city and on the Illinois side rather than south of the bridge, on the Missouri side – that would make it a lot easier for them to catch him, or at least finger accomplices.

"Somebody was arrested in connection to the Cape bombing," he said.

"Fuck" was all she said. Chubby read her some of the particulars, unemotionally, as if it had nothing to do with him. His driver seemed to know differently, although she didn't ask him, and she said "Fuck" again. She looked at Chubby closely for an instant, while not slowing the car down. There was a picture on his fone that he turned toward her of Hank in handcuffs being led into some kind of inquisition.

He observed his new dimple-cheeked, permed-up, yet plain and down-home f-bomb–dropping Junior League conveyor over his personal River Styx. She was a cultural shift for Chubby. So wholesome, but not a bit naive. Probably his age or younger, but on another level so much older, steadier, really from another world – of bake sales, PTA meetings, and church socials. This was good, he thought. He would definitely be worried if a fuckup (like himself) was handling his transport. If people like her were volunteering to help an operation like this, it meant support must be deep. But then, he didn't really know her story. From looking around the slightly untidy Buick interior, he could see that she was a Presbyterian. A church bulletin was in the slot in back of the gear stick. As they were leaving Centralia, heading north, she got a call on her fone, and had a neighborly chat, planning a luncheon with some other women in two days, which had Chubby listening for any kind of coded signals. No, she just had friends outside the Insurgency.

"Did you see Real-Prez this morning?"

"No, what did he say?" asked Kip. He had seen the feed while lying in bed that morning but had deliberately swiped it away. He knew he had to keep a clear head.

"He announced a million-dollar reward for the capture of the – well..." She looked over at Kip.

"You don't have any idea what happened," said Kip. "You need to remember that."

"Well maybe not. But he said that the bombing had stained the memory of Dashell Sketerson, coming so soon after his funeral."

"The Fat man was the stain!"

"We don't call him that here in Centralia. We call him Dash."

Kip looked at his driver and shook his head. Yes, the Cape Girardeau bombing and Sketerson's funeral are connected, and no, I am not going to tell you anymore about it.

She knew she was helping "the Memphis operation," as she called it. What was her motivation? he wondered. She seemed very aware of the gravity of what she was doing, very matter-of-fact about the whole deal, a refreshing attitude, an attitude of competence. She pointed out two old farmers, walking next to each other on the downtown sidewalk, both in their seventies or late sixties, engaged in a serious conversation.

"They have known each other since childhood." She said they had started yelling about politics and were about to start punching each other while waiting in the checkout line of the Stop and Save just yesterday. "Everyone was talking about it. So embarrassed for them and themselves. We just don't do that here in Centralia. Everyone is looking for people to punish. It is insane. I am part of it," she said while giving Chubby a hard look, "yet – here I am, aren't I?"

"We weren't like this before him."

"Really? Are you sure? Maybe not as..." She looked at Chubby. "I know. But still, I am against violence. We were wrong to kill those men in Cape Girardeau. I don't care what they did. But done is done."

But, still, here you are, thought Chubby, not reacting, but staring straight ahead as he wondered exactly what she was saying. Don't explain, don't apologize, he thought. Did she know what he had done? Was this her way of speaking truth to power? Or was it a cover, a way of convincing herself that she was not involved? This was his country too, and yet there was so much Chubby didn't understand.

Suddenly they arrived, and she drove him through Vandalia's Main Street and let him off in front of the old Illinois Statehouse, where Lincoln had given his first public speech about the evils of slavery.

She leaned over, opened the glove box, and pointed to an eight-shot Tokarev 7.62 knockoff, a semi-auto pistol. "If you get in trouble, you might as well try shooting your way out, because if they pull you in, you will never get out, alive anyway," she said.

Kip looked at her and her deadpan changed ever so slightly to a resigned look of friendliness. She was just being nice, he realized. And if I am killed in a shoot-out, I won't be telling tales under torture about who drove me to Vandalia. He should have asked her to let him off further from town, but in a way this was best, the less they talked the better. Elwood's house was not too far. He powered on his new burner fone, pulled up a pre-downloaded Vandalia map, and walked a half a mile away from Elwood's to the west, then swung back, and then across a cemetery, looking to see if anyone was following him. He had a red St. Louis Cardinals baseball cap on, pulled down, partially hiding his face. He only saw two other people on the rural, unimproved streets of the poor side of town, and they seemed preoccupied. One of them also had on a red hat, embossed with the Real-Prez's campaign slogan.

CHAPTER 8

CHUBBY IN VANDALIA MEETS HESTER AND ELWOOD

Late August

In the [last] 150 years biologists have tried in vain to grow lichens in laboratories. Whenever they artificially united the fungus and the alga, the two partners would never fully recreate their natural structures. It was as if something was missing—and Spribille might have discovered it...that the largest and most species-rich group of lichens are not alliances between two organisms, as every scientist since Schwendener has claimed. Instead, they're alliances between *three*. All this time, a second type of fungus has been hiding in plain view.

"But really, we don't know what they [fungi] do...and given their existence, we don't really know what the asco- mycetes do, either." Everything that's been attributed to them might actually be due to the other fungus. Many of the fundamentals of lichenology will need to be checked, and perhaps rewritten.

From Ed Yong,
"How a Guy from a Montana Trailer Park
Overturned 150 Years of Biology,"
The Atlantic, July 21, 2016

CHUBBY STOOD IN FRONT OF THE HOUSE THAT THE

burner fone identified as Elwood Taylor's. There was no name on the mailbox, which was nailed precariously to the top of a rotting post. Over the last two days, Kip Rehain had been driven here from a rural road next to the Mississippi River in Illinois. He had never met Elwood.

The house was small, old, single story, maybe two small bedrooms, with the sweet odor of a septic tank that needed emptying. An unpaved, grassy driveway descended from the road to the house. There were no close neighboring dwellings. Chubby walked quickly down to the house and knocked. A broad-shouldered 6'8" man, early-thirties, or so he appeared, opened the door and grinned at him.

"Come in quickly." Elwood gave Kip a warm handshake, then a hug, and looked at him. A picture window faced the street, but its shades were drawn. It was kind of dark, with only a small shaded lamp in the corner emitting light. "You must be hungry; come on in, we'll eat in the back."

The kitchen was small and cluttered with fresh vegetables. A pantry door opened and a skinny, long-armed girl with a Reese Witherspoon–like narrow pointy chin, knock-knees, tight jeans, and stringy reddish-brown hair stared at Chubby. She was holding a thick chopping knife and slowly bringing it up to her waist.

Who is this hard-bitten, pointy-jawed, grange-hall debutante that was now secretively whispering to Elwood in the hallway? A local, from all evidence, a descendant of the pioneers. Behind her sunken, slightly pock-marked cheeks was a strong, practical, even gentle young woman, but with fierce eyes that missed nothing. Chubby felt she was a dangerous woman who didn't trust him. Elwood, 70 in years, yet still a kid from appearances, a young man looking for guidance, and some kind of approval, saw that Chubby saw that too.

"Just a minute!" She rushed past Kip into the kitchen to take a whistling teapot off its element. Chubby sneaked away from the doorway and waited in the living room, looking at the Escher print on the wall. Then she returned, walking as if in a procession, bringing Chubby a cup of Lipton tea. Tight jeans and work boots, flannel shirt. What looked like a Tokarev 7.62 in a black leather holster was strapped high on her left hip. Was this Romanian gun a sign of an alliance? Was it "standard issue" for all the Insurgents? Did somebody get a deal from the Romanians? His own "Tok" was stowed under his shirt and belt, just above his ass crack, and he was nearly used to the cold steel on his fleshy butt. Whose side was she on? Her reddish hair was combed back into a bushy ponytail that only came down to her shoulders. She had hard eyes experienced in making quick assessments of the threats they perceived.

"Hi, I am – er, Cornelius."

"Oh, you're Corny! Sorry about being so rude! Woody told me about you."

"Oh, really," Chubby gave her a tight-lipped nod of acknowledgement, with an expression that might have carried a smile – or something else. "What's your name?"

"Hester," she said.

"Oh."

"What do you mean 'Oh'?"

Chubby started to answer her, but Woody returned, holding two hot cups with Lipton tea bags hanging over the edges. Elwood handed a cup to Hester, then took a sip from the other. "Be right back – sit down, sit."

"What did I mean? You know, Hester from *The Scarlet Letter*?"

"What's that? Is that a book? I've heard something about that."

"A scorned woman, who silently carries on."

"No – no – Hester was the captive queen who saved her people and then got their oppressor killed."

"That was Esther."

"Not in my church."

Chubby nodded as nonjudgmentally as he could, but it felt

like he was smiling, and from the way Hester looked at him, he was afraid that he was. He suddenly began to feel *en garde*. He didn't know this woman, and had to consider her dangerous.

Elwood came back into the living room and pulled up the shade. Chubby sat facing the picture window that overlooked the front lawn and the narrow blacktop road. It was about 5:00 PM and still hot. His neighbor to the front (and south) was invisible, hidden by the leafy oak and maple trees, although you could see the driveway across the street. Elwood's backyard extended through the woods all the way down to the Kaskaskia River.

"There are only a couple of spots out there where you can see in here," said Elwood. "That was how Hester saw the two guys in the back sneaking up. When they jumped us, I was pretty sure they were alone, although no doubt their replacements will soon be arriving."

Kip didn't know what he was talking about, and he saw that Elwood and his girlfriend were in a state of distracted ecstasy. Elwood had the chairs and couch in his room arranged to face each other, rather than the television, which was customary. A dense curtain and a heavy windowless, brown wooden door behind the curtain divided the front from the back of the house. Elwood took pains to close both each time he came back from the kitchen. He was up and down, fidgeting, almost shaking.

A coffee table with old books piled on it, a stained brown rug, cream-colored walls, book shelves, a modest flatscreen TV, and an old couch gave the living room an air of lower-middle-class contentment with their lot in life. "I am telling you we are going to be hit with an avalanche soon. This fucking virus is off the charts. Have you been reading the literature?"

"No, I have not been thinking about it much, but I guess it will be here soon, right?"

"Oh, it is coming! How about in Memphis? Are they aware of it?" Again he was up looking out the window through a crack in the curtains.

"Oblivious," Kip said.

"Fuck! Same here. Same everywhere. Something is kind of strange about this virus. Started over in Asia, somewhere, and it's now in the Middle East," said Elwood. "I think it might actually be fungal related. The strange properties are similar to...like the fungus – the one we found here and that Paula and I have been eating for 50 years."

"No," Kip laughed. "You guys are so..."

"So what?"

"You three – the Vandalia Gang, you, Paula, and Nate." Kip shook his head. "I can't believe that other people didn't know about your Golden Fungus before you guys found it."

Elwood shook his head. "Oh, I'm sure they did. The native people must have. You know downstream, where the little river just down the hill, just behind us, runs into the Mississippi – there at the Kaskaskia-Mississippi river junction, there used to be one of the biggest cities in North America? Before the American Revolution I mean. The French were there, but not in a big way. Trappers, priests – I think it was some kind of trading city for the Fungus."

"Maybe so, but what has the Fungus got to do with this virus?"

"I don't know. I'm not an epidemiologist, but I understand biology. What I am reading and what I already know tell me something is connected. So," Elwood looked Kip all over, "Are you armed?"

Kip pulled the pistol out from the back of his pants and put it on the table between them.

"So tell me," said Kip. "You say two guys jumped you? What's going on?"

"Two men are lying under the air conditioner in my lab in the back, and are about to go ripe. Hester did the wet work. My only concern now is getting rid of the bodies and getting us the fuck out of southern Illinois. So – before we deal with that little chore – what the fuck is going on with you? I get a message to put you up, and then these hoods show up in my backyard…"

Chubby was a little dumbstruck. Wet work? Frying pan to fire, he thought.

The door to the back opened and a man pushed the curtain aside. "Chubby," he said. "I want to hear what's going on with you too." Kip turned around and holy shit, it was Archimedes Moropolis, techno-wiz of *SwiftPad*, cyber-czar of the Portland Insurgency.

"Arkie!" Kip stood up, walked over, and hugged the slight, short, nerdy cyber maven whose normally shoulder-length dark curly hair was cut down to half-inch nubs and who, other than GG, had more to do with *SwiftPad*'s technical success than anyone. GG had hired him over Kip's objections.

"I wasn't sure you would make it, boss." Arkie pulled up a chair. "We have to deal with those two guys tonight. Want to see them, Kip?"

"I've seen enough dead bodies recently. I'll take your word for it. So why are you here? What is going on back in Oregon?"

"You tell first – we have a couple of hours before dark. Can you still work the business end of a shovel, Chubby?"

"Sheet! I will outwork you easy!"

"Excellent! I'll watch then while you and Elwood bury those two guys."

"And I'll get dinner ready!" Hester did a quick *en garde* with her knife, pirouetted, and moved *en pointe* into the kitchen.

"Come on back before you start," said Arkie. "Let me show you what we have to move and bury."

"OK." Kip stood up and followed Arkie toward the back of the house, toward the lab. He stood for a half a minute looking at the two prone corpses, lying as if asleep on a plastic sheet, then walked back in with a look of shock. "Jesus, you knifed 'em!"

"Yes – I did," Hester said.

Kip turned toward Hester, who stuck her head in as Kip

returned from the "morgue." He wondered if he should be worried to be in the same room as her. Her eyes were fiery.

"I came out from hiding behind the dryer in the bathroom..." Her eyes shifted. "I cut the heavy one's throat while he was taking a piss..."

Kip was fascinated by her eyes as she talked about murdering two men with a knife. Her voice was cold, but her eyes were almost pulsating!

"The fat fuck dropped down to his knees and was kind enough to bleed to death into the toilet. Then the other guy burst in and saw his buddy on the floor. He didn't know I was behind the door."

"The fuck – Jesus!"

"...so I gutted him. Seppuku style."

Kip looked at Elwood. Nothing. Is it only women whose eyes give away their thoughts?

"He dropped his gun as he tried to keep his guts from falling out."

"That's my girl!" Elwood was grinning like an idiot.

"Frankly, I was relieved," said Arkie. "I mean it was us or them. These guys were going to kill us, I have no doubt. They jumped Elwood and me, just came up behind us out of the woods. The guy with the crewcut zip-tied both of us while the fat guy held a gun on us. I will never let anyone do that again."

"What?"

"Tie me up. I would rather take a chance bum-rushing the guy with the gun."

"Bull-rushing, not bum-rushing."

"What?"

"Bum-rushing is when you behave badly toward a bum, treat someone less fortunate than you unkindly."

"OK," said Arkie. "Thanks. Anyway, when crewcut heard the fat guy fall in the bathroom, he was about to shoot us, but fortunately he was taking his time about it. I think it might have been his first time to kill someone. He was sweating and nervous. Anyway, the fat guy in the bathroom was the boss. Crewcut didn't know what to do, at first, then he tried to – bull-rush – the bathroom. Did I get that right, Chubby?"

"How long ago did all this happen?"

"About an hour ago."

Chubby was stunned and speechless at what a close call it had been.

"You guys sit down and relax. I'm going to start cutting vegetables. Finish your story, Kip, and then when it's dark, go bury those guys down in the woods. Not too close to the river though," Hester directed.

"And then we get the fuck out of here," said Elwood. "The extraction team will get us to St. Louis by midnight." All three of them sat down and breathed an audible sigh of relief. "They will pick us up in about two hours. So what did you do, Kip?"

"I kind of filled them in on Portland, although I'm sure you have some stories," said Arkie. "Kip here was the main instigator. It all started when he convinced five thousand reggae fans to march out of a concert and face down the (V)ICE troops."

"I'm not proud of that at all. So many were shot down, killed. Sometimes it comes at me like a morbid darkness. I have to close my eyes against it and try and blank it out. I read about it, because I left the day after it was over."

"But…"

"…Yeah – I know, we stopped (V)ICE," said Kip, as he settled down into an easy chair in the living room. "As far as the rest of the fighting in Portland was concerned, that is another story, which you've probably heard a lot about."

"All I heard before Arkie got here was that Portland played dirty," said Elwood. "Poisoned the officers in restaurants, hacked the troop's night vision goggles and blinded them, used large unarmed crowds to prevent their troops from getting to the fighting. Executed prisoners."

"They were murderers who videoed themselves shooting unarmed kids. Harvey Grennell, the senator, ordered the worst of them shot. That is true. Battlefield justice. We were fighting for our lives. We were defending our city. And we did. Right, Arkie?"

"That's right."

"OK," said Elwood. "We are a little isolated out here. Please, Kip – continue."

"The Portland Insurgency was a sideshow compared to Memphis. Memphis built a movement around their mayor, a charismatic Black man, former Army Colonel Hassan Coleman. I stayed in Memphis for nearly a month. I didn't see much of my friend Aldane. He hooked up with a reggae blues project and was playing the marimba. I did have a brief flirtation with a Black woman, who turned out to be well connected. We talked all night once in somebody's kitchen. She convinced me that there was merit and basic fairness in the land expropriation they were doing.

"It left a lot of questions that we talked all night about. Was it theft? What if the practice spread? Everybody had a story, a personal story about how they had been ripped off or their grand-parents had lost farms to the Klan – and this was some kind of payback. It was a local issue. I mean – taking people's land is hardly a new wrinkle in politics. Ninety percent of the expropri-ations were corporate, which is almost secondhand theft if that.

"Memphis was hot and humid last month, and I was drinking and eating constantly. That's why I got a bit chunky again. But, more and more, I was obsessed with finding GG.

"And to that, I did find out one thing – last spring, when I was traveling through Asia, I met a guy – actually I met a woman, and she had a brother – half-brother – who I thought was KGB – or whatever the Russians are calling their secret police these days..."

"The GRU – Glavnoye Razvedyvatel'noye Upravleniye," said Arkie.

"Right..."

They all stopped and looked at Arkie.

"I study languages to take my mind off of code," he said.

"Anyway, this half-brother of – Milana – who I met in Georgia – the Georgia on the Black Sea – I thought he was – GRU," Chubby looked at Arkie, who nodded. "He – this half-brother – is in contact with the Memphis Insurgency. What does that mean? I don't know."

"We'll talk later, Kip," said Arkie. "But you are talking about Nikoloz, and yes – he is in play."

"You know too?" Chubby snapped. "He's Georgian, not Russian – right?"

"No – well – yes and no – we'll talk later," said Arkie. "But you didn't just happen to meet him in Georgia – he found you. The world can't wait for us to stop shitting ourselves. So – please – what happened to you in Memphis and after that?"

"But –"

"I said, I would tell you later!"

"OK, OK. So when I got to Bluestown, I dumped almost five million in cash into Comm-Sec gear, and helped them negotiate a relationship with the Ishpeming people and with Portland. We had to coordinate our efforts or we would be separately taken apart by Real-Prez. Anyway – the woman – the young Black woman I was flirting with asked me if I had ever heard of Nikoloz – she called him a 'Chechen' who worked for the Russians, but – it was something about connections to buy weapons, communication equipment. She described him down to a tee – and he told her I met him and that he must know me! The way we left things – in Georgia – well I wasn't sure what he was up to, but I see you know something about it. But the last thing he told me – or seemed to imply anyway – was that he wanted to shut down *SwiftPad*! He just deleted it from his fone and seemed to imply it would be that easy. Which I took as a threat at the time, but maybe it was an offer to help. He was right about that, even though at the time I didn't see it."

"Really?" Arkie said. He was frustrated because they were running out of daylight soon.

"Well, remember I didn't know whose side Nikoloz was on – and if he was on our side, he wasn't too interested in telling me that! But – my mind went through my experience in Georgia – with Milana and with Nikoloz. I just assumed that Nikoloz was part of the Russian government, and that anyone from the Russian government would be helping Real-Prez."

"This Russian woman must have been very seductive," said Hester.

Elwood laughed.

"She wasn't Russian..."

"Can we get back to this country and events that just happened please!" Arkie looked at his watch. "We don't have much time, and we have to figure out our next step and that depends on what just went down. We have people coming for us, and who knows if there is a second team of assassins?"

"Anyway, the good times in Memphis ended for me when Hassan Coleman was assassinated. I watched it happen. He was the real deal. So, at that point we decided we were going after them, that killing the people who killed Coleman was the most important thing we could do at that point. Otherwise – we were fucked. They would own us."

"How did you figure out who it was?" asked Elwood.

"Well, remember Dash's funeral?"

"How could we miss it? Real-Prez, Cadez, Turdashian, everybody came," said Hester. "They took turns praising Dash."

"And praising, in a roundabout way, the killing of Coleman," said Arkie.

"Yeah," said Hester. "I cracked up watching those poor soldiers pick up and carry the casket – that was the most entertaining part, they almost dropped him once."

"He grew up in Cape Girardeau," said Elwood. "That's why they had it there."

"Yep. The funeral drew thousands of people. Lots of famous ones too. Telly Haines looked like a player, even as he stood slightly behind Cadez. Two Supreme Court Justices, a third of the Senate, and Real-Prez's new mercenary buddy Erick Duke, along with his wacky sister, and – there were two other guys with him too."

"The guys who shot down Coleman, right?"

"Yeah, that's what we finally figured out," said Kip. "Tiara, Aldane, and I watched video of the speeches and the procession to the graveyard over and over. We saw two people there too, mingling with the crowd, up pretty close to the front row. They listened and took a lot of pictures too. You know – selfies, like the rest of them were doing."

"Do you think they assassinated Coleman so that people would be happy – you know triumphant – at Dash's funeral?"

"It had to be planned before he died. So it was a happy coincidence for them. Definitely was a money-shot for Real-Prez's re-election, no doubt. Even the images of Cadez being sternly lectured to by Telly Haines on the funeral platform worked to Real-Prez's advantage. Real-Prez understood imagery.

"We knew those two guys were the ones, Kendal Witcomb and Jeff Tash, both ex-naval air vets, with ties to Erick Duke. We had some long shots of the same two guys leaving the scene with a rocket launcher clearly visible over in Arkansas in the back of F-250 Super Duty truck. More CCTV at gas stations later. Same guys. They stood right up there at the funeral, not camera shy at all, shaking Real-Prez's hand, and Duke's. We were able to lip-read Real-Prez when he talked to them. 'Good job' was clearly decipherable. We figured out the rest – where they were staying, their bio, etc. Again, RedHat arrogant stupidity is our best friend."

"I don't understand why they were ordered to do this."

"This is how the rightwing in the US works – they kill the leaders. So I joined the team that went hunting for his killers. We infiltrated into Cape Girardeau, Missouri. And then I did it. I killed the assassins."

CHAPTER 9

ALISON FLIES INTO DALLAS, MEETS SPENCE, EXPERIENCES C2B

Late August

Was it a civil war? Did its origins extend back to the first one, in the 1860s, to slavery, and the regional differences in the country? This is still not a question that is completely decided, but more and more observers of that period are saying that the answer is "not really," at least not the way it had been defined by history. It wasn't a left-right ideological battle either. It had nothing to do with ancient ideas about economics, or even the Führer principle. No one believed in anything or anyone anymore, not capitalism, or socialism, or Real-Prez, and certainly not any of the Dee candidates. It was something much, much deeper than that, and it didn't matter what flag it all flew under. The divide was built in, innate. Just living here told you who the enemy was, by all the little things they said, and did, and what they wore, and how they smiled, how they walked, and what they smelled like, it was all there for all to see, yet, to an outsider, it was like nothing was amiss.

There were real differences among classes and regions for sure, but they were more and more becoming differences of the soul, that it was almost a struggle between two species, as the battle between the HomoSaps and Neanderthals probably played out. Except it was also teams that you could join or resign from, a "decision" that each person made. You weren't born into it, although stubbornly stable regional demographic patterns said in many ways you were. But still certain characteristics were very strong indicators, and from a 50,000-foot, statistical view, it was baked in. The Confederacy was still there, the border states were still there, and the Free states had not changed. In that way, it was a civil war. There were pockets of the enemy in each of their sections. And the split was worse than any historical example of a split – Catholic v Protestant, Army v Navy, Pepsi v Coke – and in some ways, it made less sense than any of it. Because it was all created by the stupidest, most unconscious buffoon in the country. By the time election season rolled around, conflict was inescapable.

From *The Fall of It All – A History of the Big Dump*

HER PLANE LANDED AT DALLAS–FORT WORTH IN A rainstorm, bouncing horribly on the descent, and worse on the landing. Alison put herself in a trance waiting until it was her row's turn to leave, grabbed her bag, and headed out the breezeway and onto the tram. It had been over a month since she had left Northwest Portland in Telly's helicopter and traveled to Salt Lake City, meeting the political wonks. The one thing she had liked about the nerdy ARRGHs in Salt Lake City– even though most of them were awkward and repressed men who had not yet psychologically left their mothers – at least they were able to listen to a woman's point of view. That, she figured, was a function of their closetedness.

The Salt Lake City ARRGHs also took the virus seriously, even though at the time there had only been a couple of cases in North America. Of course this was all theoretical then, but now it was getting serious. She just didn't want to get sick.

Having spent a great deal of time with Senator Cadez, she was convinced that his consciousness was rotting out, even while he was putting up repeatedly strong shows of cogency when speaking or meeting with other politicos. He still wielded a powerful intellect, but it quickly ran out of gas, and soon after would melt into delusion and paranoia. For brief moments, though, he could put on pyrotechnic displays of analysis that dazzled everyone who listened.

Alison had managed to repulse his sexual advances. On the night before she flew to Dallas, at her hotel room door, Cadez had made an awkward play to get Alison into bed, a pathetic suggestion that they "consummate." She easily parried it, saying she wasn't "ready," to let him off the hook. He pulled back into his shell and disappeared. She never thought of him as creepy, but something else, something much worse. She thought that someone or something was speaking through him, that there was no "there" there. He had gotten worse in the month since leaving Portland. Without any visible embarrassment, almost robotically, he told her that her rejection would not affect their "professional" relationship.

And what was that relationship? Cadez had told her that he had come to trust her political judgment, which she found funny. She was playing a role that was a parody of a serious right-wing apparatchik, but he saw no satire at all. Even early on, she talked about politics to Cadez as if she were the comic fall-gal in a political farce. She found it hard to believe anyone could not see through it. How could he take her over-the-top rants against "leftists" seriously? She certainly didn't. But Cadez did.

And so, with a small staff of well-groomed, sartorially resplendent young men as his team (most of whom projected an ambiguous sexual orientation), Cadez set off on a trip around the country, "campaigning," which meant controlled situations: no interviews; short, tightly scripted speeches; a wave; and goodbye.

Not caring in the least whether their awkward moment at her hotel room door had any bearing on her status on his team or not, she happily accepted being dispatched to the Social Media

Internet Research Konsortium (SMIRK) north of Dallas, in Plano, as its Special Projects coordinator and liaison with the Cadez campaign. But what was of particular interest – well more than just interest – was that Spence was there.

Alison and Spence had been colleagues at *Reigny Deigh* and – she thought – had been on the verge of something when the Insurgency in Portland broke out. They had kept it on ice for two years, partially successfully keeping their mutual feelings to themselves. So Alison was not completely surprised when she saw Spence waiting outside the gate to pick her up. He waved to her as she approached him. He wasn't wearing a mask. The virus had first shown up in North America in, of all places, Texas. She knew it was only going to spread. They awkwardly shook hands and they made their way to the baggage claim area. Spence was dressed like he did in Portland: a t-shirt, green Dockers work pants, running shoes, and baseball cap, this time though, a Texas Rangers hat. He had lost weight, and had his hair cut pretty short.

And he had new glasses. No more dark horn-rimmed frames, but thin, gold-tinted wire-frames. For Alison, this was the most disturbing change she saw, and she wasn't sure why. As they waited and watched the baggage carousel, he suddenly gave her a hug, and she hugged him back. She said, "There's my bag!" They broke off and he picked up her suitcase.

They chatted about the flight, and Spence asked her about their co-workers at *Reigny Deigh*, but avoided the unspoken herd of elephants lurking behind every word. Shrugged when asked if he worried about the virus. Alison let him drive the conversation, staying neutral but friendly. She had expected Spence would express in some way a feeling that he was a virtual prisoner. Shouldn't he think that she had come to free him? That was what she wanted to believe, but Spence gave no hint of the quiet desperation she expected from him.

As Spence drove her from the airport, Alison realized this was the first time they had been together alone since their flirty, half-drunken afternoon in the East Portland pub – only a little more than a month ago. If he hadn't left so hurriedly, and returned to his wife, she thought, who knows where it all might have led?

Then – two days later, when the guards took the hood off his head before putting him on the plane for Texas, Spence had looked at her as if she had sold him out. That look had hurt. He had been kidnapped and forced to work for the enemy. She fully realized that she had the same problem.

"You look so strange wearing that hospital mask," Spence said. "We don't do it down here. Still isolated, it won't spread down here. But I have to say – you look sexy. Mysterious."

"I don't care what anybody thinks. I don't want to get sick. I am wearing it."

"Suit yourself." He thought he had given her a compliment, but apparently not. He glanced quickly over at her, trying to find something to talk about. "You're worried about it?"

"It's a pandemic. Jesus, yes!"

Spence dropped it. He started rambling on about the changes just released in SP-Script program – mainly new functions that let you modify some of the media hooks into Gupta's C2B interface. She barely heard him, because she was thinking about what Telly had said before she left. She had asked Telly how he was getting Spence to work on the C2B *SwiftPad* interface after what happened to him in Portland. Like she was looking for hints on how to keep him under control.

Telly had said, check out Helmut Gröttrup.

Alison did a quick S-Plog search and discovered that Gröttrup had worked with Wernher von Braun on the German V-2 rockets that killed thousands of Londoners during the closing days of World War II. While von Braun led most of his staff into the Western Zone to surrender to the Americans (after which he would lead the US rocketry development that eventually sent astronauts to the moon), Gröttrup, a secret leftist, stayed in the

Eastern Zone, where the Russians held sway. At first he continued to work for his captors in Germany, but was eventually forced (with the remaining German rocket experts) to travel to Moscow to work on the Russian rockets. He was paid more than any Russian, his wife had a chauffeur, they lived in a mansion formerly occupied by a senior government minister, and they had freedom of movement, in Moscow anyway.

So it sounded as if Telly was telling her that they were bribing Spence with money and status. And, she wondered whether, perhaps like Gröttrup, he secretly agreed with the aims of his captors?

And wasn't that what they were doing to her? Or was she just bait in a bigger game?

Spence had an Audi sedan, not brand new, maybe a year or two old. She didn't know cars, but getting in, she began to know Spence a little better. Banana peels and apple cores were overflowing out of the plastic garbage bag, littering the floor of the front seat.

"You settled in pretty well," she said.

"Well, I feel better. I got a message from Maggie. I guess she is hanging out with the *SwiftPad* gang at Kip Rehain's place."

"Really?" Alison had heard that the *SwiftPad* braintrust had left Portland, moved down to Benton County to the Rehain Compound, but didn't know what had happened to Maggie.

"You know how someone sounds when they are breaking up with you? Kind of distant, but yet trying too hard not to hurt your feelings, to cheer you up?"

"Umm," said Alison. Actually, she didn't really know. She had always been the one who did the breaking up, and she had never sugar-coated it. Just ripped the Band-Aid off. Why leave any hope where there was none, she thought. No one had ever dumped her, but she still understood what he was saying.

"Anyway, Maggie and I – our marriage – was on the ropes for a long time. Our daughter is still in Boston and is OK, although

I'm sure she is out in the street demonstrating for Rosie. I don't know what to think."

"Me either," said Alison. She was not about to make any taxicab confessions (such as revealing what Maggie did during the Insurgency) or political statements.

"You know who is also down there at that Rehain place with her? Nate Schuette!"

"Oh."

"Yeah," said Spence. He looked over at her and saw she seemed to understand what that meant. He really didn't want to get into the whole story about how Maggie and Nate had lived together, and in fact, were living together when he – Spence – met her. Or the fact that he was Nate's best friend – or that was how they both played it.

Alison had heard part of the story from Gordy, who could be so bitchy and mean – he had slept with Spence's first wife, and made sure everybody at *Reigny Deigh* knew that too. They were quiet for a while driving across the flat plain north of Dallas toward Plano. She had never met Nate Schuette, but from all she had heard, it was pretty clear he was a typical Baby Boom hypocritical, self-involved jerk. A fucking great writer, sure, but that had nothing to do with his character or decency.

"I have to admit, you look – I mean – your eyes, that is all I can see of your face. I love them!"

"I just don't want to get sick" was all she said.

"Yeah, I hear ya. Maybe I – anyway, sorry about the mess. Hey! Did you get a room yet? You want to stay at my place?"

"Well, maybe later. I already booked a room, and..."

"It is huge, and right on a lake too. Well, not a real lake like in Minnesota or the mountains in Oregon – it doesn't have that much water right now, but – it's water! I was going to get a boat next week, but the dockside is all just mud right now. Anyway – I know it's a weird ask, but you don't want to stay in a hotel, do you?"

Alison didn't answer him. Spence looked over at her, and with her sunglasses and mask she looked like she was doing a feminist remake of *The Invisible Man.*

"OK, we'll talk about it later. Let's go right over to the campus then. You can meet the team. It is really pretty cool what we are doing."

"That's what I heard. Yeah, let's go."

The actual campus wasn't as big as she had imagined. It certainly didn't look imposing, more like a mid-sized shopping center.

"About half of the original Ross Perot EDS campus has been siphoned off as a business park. In fact most of our admin offices are in the Legacy – which is what they call it. You will have an office over there. Very upscale. I work down in the mausoleum with the hardware." Alison looked at him, but didn't ask him what he meant.

As they drove in, she began to understand the mausoleum comment. It did look like a half-filled cemetery surrounded by the reptile-den that was the Legacy business park. In fact it was hard to figure out which part was creepier, the sterile office buildings or the white concrete extrusions that looked like headstones.

"Come on, I will show you my office. Introduce you around."

Spence parked across from one of the white outcroppings of concrete that was set back about 30 meters from the circular driveway. The rest was grass. The white cement bunker was in the middle, completely surrounded by a patch of bent, unnaturally green grass the size of a soccer pitch. As they approached this odd little building on the flagstone path, Spence said, "I'm not supposed to park there, but so far nobody has given me any shit."

"Speaking of, what is that smell?"

"Oh, they water this grass with recycled sewage. Water shortage."

It was oppressively hot, and the sickeningly sweet smell of the half-processed toilet water made it worse. The bleached-white concrete shed, with a single steel door, had an antenna jutting above it twice as high as the edifice itself. Alison thought it had an insect-like appearance.

"It looks alien, doesn't it?" Spence gave Alison a goofy smile. She nodded. The door opened easier than expected, and they were immediately hit with an air conditioning blast that must have been 40 degrees cooler than outside.

"You all work here?" The outer space crypt looked like it was only big enough for an entrance and a small conference room.

Spence only smiled. It was a portal into an underground complex.

They entered and stood at an imposing stone counter, and were separated from the guards by a very heavy plate glass window, with a recessed slot on the counter for sliding in ID papers and the like.

"You can't park there, Mr. Stromborn." The CCTV inside the cage was focused right on Spence's Audi.

"Give him your driver's license, Alison. I am only going to be a few minutes, Victor."

"That's what you said last time. If Mr. Turner comes by and sees your German automobile, you know what he is going to say." Victor's short-sleeve blue-gray uniform shirt tightly covered his belly, which bulged way out above his thick black leather belt, on which hung a highly polished black holster cradling a .45 caliber Smith and Wesson revolver.

"Victor, this is Alison, she will have an office over at Legacy and will be here for a few weeks. Please make sure you get her a badge made up with all the authority. The paperwork should be in an email from Mr. Haines."

"Yep, I saw it. Miss – Ack-Road, is that it?"

"Aykroyd – like the guy who played Beldar on Coneheads."

"What?"

Alison thought this whole place might have been transported from Remulak.

"Aykroyd."

"OK, Ms. Ack-roy-ed." Victor nodded, slowly, as he carefully copied out her name on a roster sheet and then stamped a paper badge. "OK. Here is a temp-oh-rare-ee badge – I will have your perm-a-net badge ready when you leave today. I have your pic-ture on file. I can see it is you. Be sure," he looked at her meaningfully, "to pick up your badge – when you leave today." Victor intently looked up at her to make sure she understood. "Now. Do you want a clip or a lan-yard?"

Alison looked quizzically at Victor, but got nothing back.

"He wants to know if you want to attach your badge to your clothes or hang it around your neck."

Alison looked at Spence and nodded. "A lan-yard," she said, pitching her answer to Victor's tone and accent.

Victor shook his head slowly the way Joe Friday used to when talking to an LA hippie. "You will have a number of meetings and seminars to attend as well, Ms. Ack-Royed. They will be con-ducted by our Human Resources department. You must make sure you schedule them promptly or your card will stop working."

"When?"

"You will have to check the schedule."

"No. When will the badge stop working?"

Victor looked at Alison for a couple of beats without reaction. "Mr. Stromborn, please show her where the parking garage is – and where in the parking garage she can park. If in fact, she will be driving herself here." Victor had a sneer in his Texas twang, somehow implying his disapproval of Spence, or Alison, or both of them.

"I was going to ride a bike," she said cheerfully. "Do you have a place to latch it up?"

Victor just stared at her.

"She's kidding, Victor. Come on, Alison."

They took the elevator down. It opened up and in front of another security station, another guard, not as inquisitive as Victor, just did a badge check and a sign-in, and they turned left and walked down a long row of server racks. The pizza box–sized computers were putting out a humming heat that seemed counterpunctual to the dull, low-volume roar of the cool air blowing on them from every direction. A young server tech with a ponytail and red Real-Prez hat eyed Alison as they squeezed by.

"When are we getting those systems installed, Roy?"

Roy looked up at Spence. "Um, probably tomorrow. I think."

"Do you have them?"

"Yeah, yes, we –"

"I need them up today. I want to start the SP-Script patch install before I leave tonight."

"Yeah. OK, I'll make sure it's done." Alison could see fear and anger competing for attention on Roy's face.

"Thanks," said Spence.

"I kind of admire Roy," said Spence as they passed through an intersection of hallways. "He wears his Real-Prez hat, even though he knows Telly switched teams and is pushing Cadez. He's a decent tech, and knows it wouldn't take much for me to get him canned. I enjoy fucking with him."

Alison smiled, but something about how Spence was responding to all this worried her. He didn't seem the same guy he was at RDM, she thought.

Through another door, then into another section, this one fluorescently lit to the point of enforced squinting. Mostly staffed with clean-cut young techs including quite a few young women, all stuffed into double-occupant cubicles.

"Spence!" From across the office, the call shot right at them, only one word, but wrapped in a Texas accent as thick as a 72-ounce steak. A dark-haired, voluptuous woman, clearly in charge, flashed a smile, while summoning them both with her finger.

"Maybelle, this is Alison." Spence's attitude switched to serious on a dime. "We worked together in Portland." Maybelle was a big-boned white woman in her forties and, as with almost everyone else in the underground cavern, was not wearing a virus mask.

"Another one of them West Coast radicals, huh? Welcome, Alison, as you heard I am Maybelle, and this is my department.

We are building all of the supporting structures, the garland of flowers to wrap around the product we will be dropping in 27 days, if not sooner. Do I have that right, Spence?"

"Yes. Ma'am!"

"I understand you are here to help, Alison. You're not from the government, are you?" Maybelle gave Alison a mock serious look, then waved it all away with a laugh. "That got Ronald Reagan a big laugh once. Come on, I'll meet ya the real brains of this bowl of chili."

A dark-skinned, slight, older man was seated at a conference table large enough for about ten people all around. Of obvious south Asian origin, he was wearing a red, white, and blue face mask and was looking at a yellow pad filled with Devanagari script. In front of him were three electroencephalographic "helmets" with embedded EEG hygroscopic sponge electrodes, and a flat copper band that was apparently meant to anchor the headset around the skull.

"Hey, Gopee," said Spence as he sat down. "Are you sure we are ready to present the staff progress report?"

"Spence," Gopesh said. "Yes, but perhaps – it might be more illuminating to present – a demo?" He smiled and waggled his head. "Maybelle has wanted to know what we have accomplished, yes? Ms. Aykroyd, what do you think? It is very exciting that you have joined us."

"Alright, let's not get too touchy-feely now," said Maybelle. "A demo instead of a status report, huh? Well why not?"

"Your supreme patience up to now has been so appreciated by our team, Maybelle." Gopesh smiled and wobbled his head, again doing the "achha." "Since Ms. Aykroyd is joining us, I thought this would get her up to speed much more quickly than a dry report, with facts, figures, and projections, don't you think?"

"Laying it on thick today, aren't we?"

Gopesh smiled, and looked embarrassed. "Oh, no Maybelle, not at all!"

Gopesh Gupta is trying to say something, Alison thought, but what? How much does he know about me?

"OK," continued Maybelle. "I like your style, Gopee! Let's fire the sucker up!"

Gopesh then pulled a MacBook out of a brief-bag on the floor, plugged in a cable, and started it. He fit the mesh-like helmets on Maybelle and Alison's heads, adjusted the electrodes carefully, and calibrated each of the recessed, adjustable, touch-activated LED controllers. Spence fitted his helmet on himself, but Gopesh checked it. Then Gopesh placed his on his own head, and had Spence help him adjust it. Each helmet was connected with a cat-5 jack from the back, and then snaked into a five-slot Cisco switch, which had multiple connections into a three-foot-high, two-foot-square black, monitor-less and keyboard-less mid-sized computer.

"The wireless function works, but the signal is much stronger when hard-wired," said Spence. "When we fine-tune it, we'll go wireless, eventually."

"If not sooner – right, boys?"

Alison watched Spence nod and "yes ma'am" her. She noticed the MacBook was consoled in with a Linux Bash shell.

"Excuse me, I need to ensure the connections are all properly responding." Gopesh sat back away from the table and for almost five minutes was intently typing on his laptop, which he pulled up on his lap. No one spoke.

"OK, this first demo expresses how Americans, as a people, can overcome anything, and that we need to unite behind a strong leader, who will bring us out of our current troubles. There will be images that go with this – patriotic images of heroes, family, comradeship – all martial, masculine, uplifting, positive. It is perhaps crude, and of course the political team will need to redesign some of it. This is a mockup of a fictional TV awards show, with a C2B broadcast simultaneously tracking in, which matches the message. As you are transmitted the mental imagery, please notice how the impact is enhanced by the emotions projected into your head. Again, focus on the technique, not the message. This is only a demo of capabilities."

Gopesh turned off the lights with a handheld controller, and it became pitch-dark. Images began to flood her head – waving wheat, mountains, the ocean, and a fresh, outdoor smell, with a hint of horse shit? There was no sound – but what I am hearing, thought Alison. It was almost a low, deep humming. How is he doing this?

"Are you all ready? Relax, take a deep breath. Here we go."

A click, almost a grinding...

Alison, this different signal. me, Gopesh. genie loose. Tech flawed dirty seizures psychotic episodes braindumps I fix, do it all. Just you video0audio0brain00telio Cadez braindumps hopeless toxic schizophrenia sick Reading Question mark tap left pinkie once on table

Alison tapped her pinkie on the table once, as though she were impatient.

Reading reading

Brain dump data big space small C2B broadcast simple short data small Gopesh slowing down, inserting sabotages technology known stall lose

Trust Stromborn not not you question mark question mark

Understand question mark tap left forefinger

Alison tapped

only you

again **She tapped** *good*

Spence Maybelle now echoes of Lysergic alkaloid like intoxication elevated endorphins uplift time-released match telio all feeling no content you get content slow project Spence speeding.

Stop Cadez No Natural Fungus stop Cadez

*Delete SwiftPad everywhere Natural Fungus Cadez trouble agents
sent stop integration C2B Natural Fungus Cadez control mania.*

*Delete SwiftPad lose Spence close No Script C2B SwiftPad
Portland control C2BTube transport C2B flawed SP-Script
SwiftPad Future bad*

*People Desperate normal auto C2B lies normal hero Sheep
graze wolf feasts.*

Suddenly, a feeling of immense relief rushed over Alison, the scenes of nature returned, and she began to regain control of her thoughts. She looked and Gopesh was narrating the re-entry, in his modest sing-song voice, soothingly addressing his remarks to Maybelle. Maybelle and Spence acted stoned and dreamy, with a sense of amazement.

"That was really – something!" Maybelle started to remove her headset, then stopped, as if the effort was overwhelming.

"We will intersperse short Seed-a-Bee blips that, while slow and clunky to access even with the newest, most expensive C2B boxes, still should be quite impressive."

"Have we overcome the problem of some receivers getting headaches?"

Gopesh shook his head, perhaps in the negative; it wasn't clear.

Maybelle put her hand on her head, and looked groggy.

"Are you OK?" Spence got up and looked hard at Gopesh. "Gopee, did you soften the D channel like we talked about?"

"Yes, I did, Spence, it was a very good idea, very good."

"I am all right," said Maybelle. "I just, ohhh. Maybe we still need to work on it some more. But – I received it. Yes. It was amazing. Clear as a bell, at least, at first." She took a deep breath and smiled. "I'm OK. Continue."

"We are also experiencing some difficulties with S-Plogging," said Spence. "I'll take a look at that and see if we can de-couple that channel."

"We'll need to figure out how to combine them somehow,"

said Gopesh. "*SwiftPad Central* in Oregon is blocking most C2B uploads, claiming it is a health and safety issue. So we need to provide proof that is fixed quickly. We are working on that."

"That is your issue, Spence," said Maybelle. "This is not ready. I understand it is – Spence, are you feeling sick?"

"No. Well, a little."

"Alison?"

"I am – it is like a mild hangover. I feel – carefree but not in a real good way."

"Yeah – hear that, Gopesh? We need to fix that!"

"I am so sorry, we will work to fix this."

"Still, I have to say I am impressed!" Maybelle stood up and regained her composure. "Don't get down, it ain't all bad! I blame the jamming! In spite of the jamming coming from the *SwiftPad* shits in Oregon, revenue remains strong, as long as we keep it light and fluffy. Public political statements should remain muted until we can properly control them, and direct them with precision."

"And we need more computing power, much more," said Spence.

"Whatever you need, just order it, I'll sign for it."

"Roy has promised that another bay of pizza boxes will be mounted and online by this afternoon," said Spence.

Gopesh nodded. He looked just an extra second longer than necessary at Alison.

"Sounds like we are making progress," said Maybelle." Don't worry about the *SwiftPad* links. We have irons in the fire." She smiled, but waved away any questions as the other three looked at her.

"We should have a 15-second 'American pride' broadcast ready to test with a sample audience by the end of the week," said Spence.

"Well, you know what they say about work estimates," said Gopesh. "Double it, and multiply by a fudge factor. But we will do our best."

"What is the fudge factor?"

"Much less than the over-promise penalty," said Gopesh. "But

I think we can have the overwhelming emotion ready to deliver at the end of your candidate's convention speech."

"Candidate? You mean Senator Cadez? It will be specific to him, won't it?"

Gopesh smiled and let his head wobble with what Maybelle took to mean yes.

CHAPTER 10

KIP TELLS ELWOOD, ARKIE, AND HESTER HOW HE KILLED ASSASSINS

Late August

The assassination of Hassan Coleman pushed the situation as far as it could go short of war. Behind the scenes, two missions with similar aims for opposite purposes were set in motion. The quickly unifying Insurgent resistance groups based in Memphis, in Ishpeming, and in Portland were communicating constantly, putting grudges and doubt behind them, and were working on a plan. 1) Kill the assassins of Hassan Coleman. 2) Find and rescue Cynthia Oglethorpe.

On the other side was fragmentation and disunity. Utah and the Intermountain West were quickly coalescing around Ben Cadez, seeing him as a young, thoughtful "conservative" who might challenge the increasing insanity of Real-Prez. But many pockets were holding out. Turdashian had his own supporters, mainly in the gated communities of SoCal, while in deep Dixie and in various armed pockets around the country they held fast to Real-Prez. The propaganda from the Insurgency increased in volume and frequency, and appeared to be winning the war for hearts and minds.

Rumors began to spread about Cadez – was he ill? Still, no one suspected that Cadez himself was addicted to the synthesized Fungus made by the Howard Hughes Foundation.

Meanwhile, reports were circulating that GG was alive and working under duress – but where and for whom?

From *The Fall of It All – A History of the Big Dump*

"LET'S EAT," SAID HESTER. ELWOOD WAS PULLING
the barbecued onions and eggplant off the grill and piling them on a platter while Hester laid out the tomatoes, peppers, and corn.

Kip and Arkie walked up from the woods below and joined them, and they sat around outside in the back, with their plates on their laps.

"Did you dig the hole?"

"I'm not sure it's deep enough," said Arkie.

"I've got two bags of lime in the garage," said Elwood. "We'll throw those in the hole. Then – we're out of here tonight after we bury them."

"It was self-defense," said Hester.

"Absolutely," said Arkie.

"So I guess we are all in this – together," said Kip. "OK, you want to know what happened and how I got here?"

"Sure," said Arkie. "We'll be dropping you off in St. Louis, and we can't really talk in front of our driver. So what happened?"

"OK. Here's how it went."

So, after they shot down Coleman's plane, things were serious, and we got serious. The Memphis people didn't object when I insisted I be part of the team that went after his killers. Because of my age and appearance we all decided that I was the one who should do them. I mean, I had as much motivation as anyone else. I knew Coleman, worked with him, and as I said, it made sense tactically.

After Dashell Sketerson's funeral, all the big shots got on helicopters and headed out of town fast, mostly up to the St. Louis airport. But our boys stayed around. We tracked them to the Marriott, set up, and found out they planned to meet some women in a downtown bar about 6:00 PM.

I walked into the Hot Shots and didn't avoid the stares of people who looked up and then turned away quickly. I think looking back hard discouraged them from studying my face. I was older, tending to fat, as you can see, and trashy looking even for southern Missouri, deliberately downright unattractive.

A sad song about a broken heart disguised as an old pickup truck that won't start was casting a gloomy pall over the half-crowded saloon.

Behind the bar, a pretty blonde in her thirties stared at her fone and not only ignored me but also my spotters, a man and woman, both watching and occasionally reacting to a preseason NFL game on the TV behind the bar. There was an occasional whoop or shout of raw approval from the back, but no one looked up to see what the excitement was about. I walked by the bar and sat at an empty table, back near the wall, facing the door.

"Wait, wait," said Hester. "I am not glued to *SwiftPad* all day like the rest of the world. I have too much work to do. What the fuck is going on – I mean I heard about the plane crash in Memphis, but what is this really all about? What the fuck is really going on?"

Nate looked at Elwood, who shrugged and smiled a little.

Arkie, looking at his fone, said without looking up, "It is hard to understand history when it is current events. I don't know that anyone can answer that question. Go ahead, Kip, but we got to get going in about 40 minutes. Our ride is on the way from St. Louis."

OK, Hester, here's the story. A little more than a month ago, my best friend from kindergarten, Jim Hunt, was murdered in his own kitchen, and his pregnant wife, Cynthia Oglethorpe, was kidnapped. You heard about that, right? Well, I was there, helpless to do anything as she was led away at gunpoint by masked men. I am still not totally clear who did it, but I know they had some link to the Real-Prez junta.

Then, more than seven thousand (V)ICE wannabe storm troopers invaded Portland. They were quickly routed and expelled by a ragtag group of determined high-tech volunteers, assembled by the Insurgency. In the weeks following, almost the entire West Coast was taken over by a loosely organized, mostly nonviolent amalgamation of groups whose unifying factor was extreme opposition to Real-Prez.

In Los Angeles, (V)ICE and the LA Insurgency had a weeklong running freeway battle, with sudden "flash" traffic jams, at exactly the right place and time to bottle up any large-scale movement by Real-Prez forces. In Seattle, it was a bloodless walkover. They read a manifesto in San Francisco that declared Real-Prez a traitor who was fraudulently elected and therefore illegitimate. Local and state governments stepped up, and purged or isolated the Real-Prez movement. Most of the northeast, from Richmond, Virginia, north followed suit, but here in the heartland and South they held out for Real-Prez. Except for Memphis and its east bank surroundings.

"Illinois is still probably resisting," said Elwood.

"Yeah, I hope so."

"Shit," said Hester. "That's Chicago. Down here we ain't much different than Kentucky."

For three weeks after the Portland Insurgency, nothing happened, just waiting, hoping life would return to normal. Then the other shoe dropped. Coleman, the charismatic mayor of Memphis, was shot out of the sky as his plane came in for a landing at the Memphis International Airport. I was standing on a balcony in my hotel room, looking out at the Mississippi, and I felt the blast, saw the mid-air explosion and the fiery crash. Former Army Ranger Colonel Hassan Coleman, along with eleven others, died as they returned from co-leading fewer than a thousand military specialists of the Portland Insurgency to a complete victory over seven thousand (V) ICE storm troopers. Wild rumors about who did it and why quickly spread on *SwiftPad*, fueling the shock and anger among Coleman's supporters, galvanizing support for the Insurgency. The assassination united the city, in fact united the nationwide resistance to Real-Prez and his minions.

But it also unleashed something on the other side as well. Two days later, six people at a Lawrence, Kansas, rally that was mourning Coleman were killed by drive-by shooters. Then that night, seventeen of Real-Prez's most prominent Kansas opponents, the core of the Kansas Insurgency, were dragged out of their houses and apartments and shot in the streets of Lawrence. Two days after that, Austin, Texas, was declared a "lib-free zone" by militant Evangelicals, and there were scattered reports of severe fighting and atrocities, mainly among students at the University. Similar actions took place in several Midwest college towns. RedHats were striking back sporadically, with proclamations that they were establishing "faith-based" governments.

"OK, I'm caught up," said Hester. "So how did you kill them?"

It was late afternoon, and the mood in the Cape Girardeau, Missouri, country-western bar was restrained and even somber. They had all been in the crowd at Dash's funeral, and he was a local boy. There was no rejoicing. The winds of war were blowing, and no one was happy; everyone knew it would be horrible, maybe worse than the first US Civil War.

I had arrived in Memphis right after the Portland uprising, meeting and then working with Hassan Coleman's Memphis staff, eventually including his charismatic chief-of-staff Tiara Mason-Feldman. We looked for ways to consolidate the two cities' victories into a national movement. Since I technically still owned what was left (after our sale to Amazon) of the ubiquitous social media software app *SwiftPad*, most of my work in Memphis was coordinating an online response, looking for a common message to unite the forces, and building a cross-Insurgency communications network, especially after Coleman's murder.

But RedHats, who took over the entire national party of ARRGHs (as in the pirate "arrgh matey!") were now in the throes of Real-Prez's tantrums and struggled (and failed) to argue their case with any logic or policy other than hatred of Dees. Even with *SwiftPad*'s powerful algorithms designed to force dialog, it was becoming obvious there was little to talk about.

I knew we were working on some unification of *Swift-Pad*-C2B (Computer-to-Brain) technology with GuptaTech, but frankly, that scared me even more than Real-Prez, if that was possible. Then we heard of the kidnapping of Mr. Gupta himself, and the rise of the splinter group within the ARRGHs, centered around Senator Ben Cadez. I told everyone that our goal should be to stop the RedHats, whether from Cadez or Real-Prez. But Coleman's murder made me realize that talk was cheap, and when it got down to it, political talk was the cheapest of all.

I slipped in over the bridge into Cape Girardeau from the Illinois side, having come up through Kentucky. I stayed at a hideous, stinky dive filled with bedbugs in the outer regions of "The Cape," as the locals called their town. The others set up closer to the targets, or planted themselves in advance in the bar, where our newly deployed Comm interception gear eavesdropped on a conversation about a celebratory drink with one of their political contacts. Since they were staying in the Old Town Marriott, we found they were surprisingly over-confident and careless. Aldane Blyden took over the planning of my escape and recruited a local river rat, who had a small boat and a nearby raft hidden in an estuary. The targets had texted someone to meet them at this cowboy/ country bar for a drink, and we decided that it was a go.

I had shaved my head before I left Memphis, but now, with five days' worth of stubble-growth, I had a low-class, maybe crazy, possibly dangerous appearance. Since I arrived in Memphis, I had gained at least 15 pounds. For three weeks, I had been eating and drinking because, well, I can't blame Memphis for having great barbecue. The Memphis team had a dentist remove my upper front tooth, which was an implant anyway, so they just had to unscrew it. It made me sound slushy, but again, dangerous, like an old, white, fattish Mike Tyson. I had patchy, brownish-gray facial hair that passed for an unkempt side beard, which connected to a long gray mustache that made a "U" around my eyes and nose. An old guy (I'll be 50 next year), a weird pogonophile, clearly not in disguise but just another vain self-promoting Real-Prez fanatic. Hiding in plain sight.

I didn't argue about it with the Memphis intel team, because they said the disguise worked. I thought it made me too memorable. But they said that was what made me unsuspected, that it was a steganographic masterpiece (if I could pull it off), that I was too outlandish to be dangerous. Only a sad, probably lonely exhibitionist would spend so much time grooming such an ugly facial ensemble. A low-rent, angry white guy with a familiar and politically trustworthy appearance for a RedHat, yet still with a sinister, semi-intellectual libertarian-conspirator vibe going, that stuck out enough to seem believable. I really wasn't so sure about all that; I thought I might look like an out-of-work "fat-love" porn actor, or a barista at a second-tier corporate conclave, or even a philosophic psycho-killer. But whatever image I projected, it was a part I knew how to play, and so far it had worked. Nobody even looked at me funny, just a few quick glances and then they always looked away, in some mixture of disgust and embarrassment.

As you might know, I was reared among the hard-drinking dwellers of the Oregon Coast Range, aging, scarred, insanely independent loggers, who were further to the right than Attila the Hun...

"You cannot apply modern Western political labels to a nation of raiders and herders in a pre-industrial state," said Elwood. "The parallel does not make sense."

"OK, I looked like a deranged American neo-Nazi."

"Not so much, anymore. I'll take your word for it. How did you fix your tooth?"

"It screwed in. It took me an hour, but I managed it. I have these little tools and used a mirror at my last safe house. You want me to finish or do we need to get rid of those bodies in your lab?"

"I want to wait until it's darker – finish your story, while we eat."

So, I am still going to call the loggers I grew up with "Attilas," even if the "parallels" don't fit. You have a problem with that, Elwood?

I can remember we used to laugh together and at each other. Me and all those Attilas, who topped Doug firs in raging wind gusts, or scrambled up steep hillsides to set the choker cables around precariously unstable four-ton logs. We could drink together until we were blind. The Attilas used to worship my dad, but in the end, he ruined most of our neighbors, and ended up owning their businesses and logging equipment. Dad would, of course, say that they ruined themselves.

I left all that as soon as I could. I certainly didn't want to live with the Attilas anymore, in their bitterness and regressive anger – by now, most of those guys I knew back in the woods have slipped off the edge. I just couldn't be around them anymore. Self-preservation instinct, I guess. If you told them that the old-growth trees wouldn't last another generation, they would get angry. They didn't want to hear about trees making oxygen for the planet.

Real-Prez told them he would get it all back, just like before, that he would let them do what they wanted, to cut the last forest, frack the last well, net the last fish, and then it would all come back like before.

Maybe I felt guilty about leaving the woods and becoming a Portland hipster and helping spin up a mega-software company, particularly since I jump-started it from Dad's ill-gotten fortune, a fortune he largely stole – took advantage of anyway – from those crazy Attila-loggers.

Didn't my software company help make this mess worse? you ask. Yeah, it did, I can see that now.

"It's not what we wanted – not at all how we planned it," said Arkie. "Admittedly, speaking for myself, it was a game, designing, redesigning, enhancing the app, but I couldn't see what it would mean once we released it into the wild. People are only designed to communicate to others one at a time or at most in small groups. Once technology allows us to 'broadcast,' well –"

"The problem," said Elwood. "It can be a good thing ten times, but then one bad thing and all of the good no longer matters."

"Yeah, well, at the time, I thought the total, instant democracy it promised would be a good thing. But it's a nightmare. Millions are crying fire in the crowded theaters of their own minds. I just want to stop people from staring at their fones, stop taking their cues from a manipulative computer program.

"But to do that, I need to find GG, because she knows how to make it stop."

"If she did set a sleeper bot inside the app, she sure hid it well," said Arkie. "She never mentioned anything about it to me."

"The bot would have to broadcast the self-destruct signal, and listen for one at the same time, right?"

"Yeah," said Arkie. "Yeah, and still so small, so tight that it escapes detection from the best programmers at Amazon. It doesn't seem possible. Except I have never met a programmer like GG. I can't even begin to tell you how brilliant she was with her code."

"When Hassan died, the Memphis Pillow Fighters (so-named after the Confederate massacre of 300 disarmed Black soldiers in nearby Fort Pillow during the first Civil War) were shaken to the core. But I was just visiting. How they sorted out their own leadership issues was no concern to me, but now it appears they were being led by a Black woman, Tiara Mason-Feldman, a beautiful intellectual with deep ties to the white power structure of the city. I met her, and uh – she is a force to reckon with."

"So did you reckon with her, Chubby?"

Kip looked at Arkie, but was briefly lost for words. "We had some conversation, if that is what you mean."

"Ah, the plot thickens," said Hester. Elwood laughed.

"Tiara and I worked together well together after our...initial encounter and the subsequent murder of Hassan. We both felt a great deal of grief over it. I didn't know Coleman long, but even from that short time, I knew he was special. Tiara – I think she had even a deeper connection. Anyway, we found we were perfectly in sync with each other on aim and means: find and kill the killers, by very public means. She opened the whole Memphis Insurgency Command team to me. We worked together for almost two days straight, following the Dash funeral and going over recon video. We worked well together. She brought me in, and we figured out a lot of shit we could consolidate, mostly with Ishpeming, AKA the Great Lake Group, along with the online domination by the *SwiftPad* team, plus with our little brothers and sisters in Silicon Valley and Seattle. Our aim was to find the people directly responsible for bringing down Coleman's plane, and our means was to do it as publicly as possible. We were going to make sure everyone knew what we did and why. I only had one demand – that I be on the team that went after Hassan's killers."

"And she submitted to your demand, huh?" Arkie chortled.

So here I was in this Missouri river-town cowboy dive, Hot Shots Bar, on Main Street in Cape Girardeau, drinking vodka and lime soda. It was getting dark outside, twilight, and I knew I had to move quickly if I didn't want to miss the ride that Aldane had arranged for me. I sat at a side table by the wall hanging around like a good old boy with nothing to do but drink. I had a bit more than a pound of C4 in my camo rucksack, fused and ready: electronic hair trigger linked to my burner fone.

An old cowboy, my age, in the back of the bar slammed his glass down, shouted "Goddammit!" to no one in particular, and stormed out. No idea who he was or why he was pissed off, but I knew how he felt. People looked up and watched him, but they went back to staring at their fones, no one talking very much, but some just staring off.

I used the Marlboro Man's hasty, unexplained exit as a cover to look around, and try to catch someone's eye to see how they were handling it. I rakishly raised my eyebrows and got probing looks from a sluttily dressed big country girl, who then smiled and turned to her similarly dressed friend and laughed.

Suddenly, the very disturbing vision of these two women being blown to bits by my C4 popped into my head. Dressed like Branson backup singers, they were sitting across from me. I scanned the bottles displayed, trying to guess the brands from just the images on the labels. But what I was really doing was watching the front window, looking for two guys in jeans and workshirts. I had seen them enough in video and pictures before I even left Memphis. They were under 30, fit, both about six foot and last time I saw them they had on plain, blue baseball hats. Not projecting any kind of fanatic vibe. Smart, good-looking white boys, probably college grad engineers. Memphis intel said both had some recent connection to the Real-Prez NatSec.

I looked around at the faces. A few conversations picked up; perhaps the Marlboro Man's sudden departure shocked them out of their stupor. The news was bad, but no one seemed overly dismayed, but maybe just a bit worried. Shooting down Coleman's plane was terrorism, plain and simple, and most of them knew it, and it didn't set well with them. The other news was the murder of 23 people in Lawrence, Kansas, 17 of them taken out of their apartments and shot in a campus neighborhood, and their bodies left in the street with signs saying this is the fate of all "libtard traidors."

That raid, out of Missouri and patterned after Quantrill's Raid on Lawrence during the first Civil War, was my cover of last resort. I had all the details down cold, where the raid started from, how many of "us" there were, where we stayed, and how we got out. I had the names of some of the participants and a bio. We had advance intel on the whole operation, but unfortunately we didn't act on it. Still training and recruiting, and frankly, being cautious. Anyway, I had no intention of getting into any conversations about it, but it was a "just in case" precaution we were taking. Always have a story ready, and you are never out of the game.

There were about eight of us here for this operation, and we knew our roles.

As I looked around Hot Shots, I suddenly came to the

flesh-and-blood realization that if things went as planned, most of them would be dead in a few minutes. I would be lying if I said that I did not start having second thoughts.

Our two spotters were acting like a young jock couple, neither looking at me. They had worked the Dash funeral as a couple, and had been seen enough to fit into Hot Shots society easily. "Bethany," not skinny or real femmy, wore an old St. Louis Rams jersey, number 73. They played it out as if on a tentative date. "John," tightly trim in a body shirt, jeans, and loosely tied red Pumas, talked close to her, occasionally snuggling close, only to be briskly shrugged away, as they nursed their drinks at the bar.

Our targets passed the window, walked in, and after they sat down and were ordering drinks, John and Bethany, with what seemed like haste to get to a bedroom, got up and hurried out. I got up and moved to the bar, carrying my camo backpack. The Memphis team had hacked our targets' fones, and was coordinating with Aldane, who was remotely controlling our Op from across town. We only had about 30 minutes to put this together. I was hoping the getaway bike and boat would be waiting for me. We knew it was unlikely it would all pan out exactly as we hoped, but I figured I could improvise. My throat was tight and dry.

The targets: Jeff, shorter, darker, muscular, and Kendal, lanky with close-cropped blond hair. Both had on baseball hats without logos, and tight monochrome t-shirts. They stuck out in this place, which was filled with seedy, hairy, slightly overweight, 30-something men, mullets, and long scraggly "biker hair." The women were a mix of over-dressed bottle blondes and "country girls," some pigtails, or boofoo hairdos, along with the usual unpretentious middle length, middle-parted, and streaked style. A few plaid shirts open to the cleavage, and tied around the ribs as a halter top. Butts squeezed into tight, torn jeans that were stuffed into shiny, pointy high-heeled boots. Overall it was a heavy crowd, but not morbidly obese – this was a singles bar, after all, not Walmart.

People were slowly nursing drinks, as if on a very tight budget, or worried it might not be a good day to drink too much. Jeff and Kendal did exactly what we wanted, sat at the bar on the stools next to me as I stood, trying to get the attention of the pretty bartender. And even though I had arrived first, the cute barkeep asked them what they wanted, ignoring me. They were young and handsome, and clearly, I was neither. They ordered some local craft beers that I had never heard of. Well-spoken, upscale killers, with engineering degrees.

Taking out the skilled and educated people is often a strategic aim in war. The Insurgency has not yet gotten to the point where we are doing that systematically; we don't have the manpower yet to do that, and as a rule, we were not targeting classes of people, professions, to wreak economic or strategic damage. We were after the trigger men, regardless of their background.

Meanwhile, these two assassins got into some aggressive flirting with two permed-up bottle blondes in tight skirts and butt-thrusting heels on their ankle length booties. They had been sitting quietly on the other side of the bar, as if waiting – or watching. They could have been mistaken for the wives of mega-church pastors – dolled up, push-up colored bras that were visible at certain angles or through semi-translucent blouses. At first, I thought they might be working girls. I laughed to myself and kept leaning on the bar, when the barkeep blonde (whose hair appeared natural) finally noticed me, and I ordered another vodka and lime soda and she made me a redneck gimlet.

"Howdee?" asked Kendal, the nearest assassin, with a radiant and warm smile, which I tried to return as best I could.

"Hey partner! Me, I'm as giddy as a pig in the corn crib!"

"Why you say?" he asked. His buddy was talking to both women.

"Well, first off, it's a sad, sad thing about Dash. But ya know – if he went out like they said he did, that ain't bad."

"I guess," he said. "He shoulda taken better care of himself. We're going to miss him."

Don't lay it on too thick, Chubby, I told myself.

"Well, yeah. His work though – it will live forever. He is going to be remembered with all the big boys – Washington, Jackson, Teddy Roosevelt."

Kendal laughed knowingly, and silently shook his head to himself.

My fone had two icons – on the second panel – the top one set a timer – two minutes then ignite. The bottom, a clown face, would make the C4 go boom right then and there.

Behind the bar, the natural blonde, whose name I overheard as Trudy, switched the TV to baseball. It was getting down to it; most teams were already out of the playoff picture. The Cards were still in it, and they were playing Milwaukee, which was not.

"You a Cards fan?"

"No, I like KC."

"You from around there? Trudy, can I have another?"

"Um-hmm, but not anymore," I said, nodding slightly to myself.

Kendal took his drink and put down a $20 tip for Trudy. She picked it up and returned his leer with one of her own.

"Some shit over in Kansas, huh?" Kendal seemed to say that to himself, although he said it loud enough for me to hear.

"Yeah." I looked at him. "So what do you guys do? You look military."

He made a face of mock surprise, then said, "Used to be."

"Yeah, a lot of guys used to be. Once this election is over, maybe Prez can get control of his own people. Hang some of those generals who won't follow direct orders."

My new friend didn't say anything. Too much?

"But we are getting it done, in spite of," I plunged on. "Somebody took care of that Black bastard Memphis A-Rab. And then Quantrill Two! We're on a roll! I think things are starting to get straightened out."

"What if we lose the election?" Kendal asked darkly. "Florida ain't even for sure. Can't lose Florida."

"Jews," I said, looking to get a rise out of him. He shrugged with an affirmative nod. Good, another reason to tap the clown on my fone. "But I'm not worried," I continued. "Prez just needs to say that they stole all that time bitching and keeping the country from moving. We just have to extend his term to make it fair. What are they gonna do? We have guns."

"Guns mounted on the back of F-150s are not going to decide this one. The battle is gonna be in our heads."

"What do you mean?" I said. Hmm, might be more to this guy than just a pretty boy who shoots down unarmed planes.

"You still do the *SwiftPad*?"

"Some. Don't you?" I looked at him carefully. Kendal was staring at me with the same attentiveness.

"Once you put on that electrode Gooroo hat, I hear it's like heroin," said his friend Jeff, leaning into our conversation. "Plug in and you are done. Hooked. It is over and they have you. That's what Cadez is pushing, I hear."

"Cadez ain't shit. Something about him ain't right. Anyway – the real question is, why don't we control that shit?" Kendal asked.

Well, he is asking the right person, I thought. Smart. Another reason to blow this motherfucker up.

"Fuck if I know," I said. Jeff is looking at me real funny, as if he had seen me someplace before, but isn't sure.

A coiffed-up little guy, strutting like a Munchkin Lollipop Guilder, came in wearing a white tie on a dark shirt. He motioned with his finger to my two new friends at the bar.

"Excuse us," Kendal said as he picked up his beer and he and Jeff moved to the same table toward the back where I had been sitting. They looked concerned as they talked. I turned my back to them and pulled out my fone and pretended to scroll.

Since it was well known that Portland was associated with *SwiftPad*, RedHat Country was making an effort to wean itself off Social Media. The *SwiftPad* feeds went back up nationally after going semi-black for a week, during the Insurgency. There was social pressure down here in RedHat country to unplug, and to some extent it was working. A few days previously FOX announced it was starting its own app, followed conveniently by a story about some startup trying to build a C2B broadcastable link into the FOX app.

A chyron, a TV news crawler, scrolled under the Cards-Brewers game – "Real-Prez refuses to condemn the attacks in Lawrence."

Anyway, other than a thin newsfeed, I only had an encrypted Comm program on this fone (a one-time-pad app), and of course my C4 bomb igniter, so I put my fone away.

I was partially able to watch my two targets and the new guy through a reflection in the mirror behind all the whiskey and gin bottles. I could see Kendal surreptitiously glancing at me a couple of times.

I didn't really want to kill everybody in the bar, just these two guys, with extreme prejudice, although considering that they took out a small plane full of people, maybe taking out everyone in this bar would even things. I wouldn't mind if the Lollipop boy got it too. Yet, the more I thought about it, the worse I felt. I wondered if it made sense to kill these people, even if most of them assuredly were Real-Prez supporters.

I certainly didn't want to kill myself.

Something was up. Were they on to me? They might have been talking about baseball. Then they all laughed, and Kendal stood up and came back over.

"Can I ask you a question?" he said. "Were you involved with Lawrence?"

I looked at him. "Can I buy you another drink?"

He looked at me and didn't answer my offer.

I laughed. "No, of course not! Why would you think that? Anyway," I looked down and let show a tiny micro-smile, "do you think I would tell you if I were?"

"It doesn't matter," said Kendal, smiling and nodding like he got it. "We all have a job to do. I am Kendal by the way." (I know, I thought.) "Me and Jeff, my friend over there – well – I'll just say – we all have a job to do. But you ever wonder what it is we are fighting for?"

"All the time," I said. Trudy poured him a bourbon and actually smiled at me as she got me another vodka and lime soda. I was almost drunk enough to do what I came to do.

"Yeah. Look around. Everyone's having a good time."

Toby Keith was singing "American Soldier." Jeff had got up and was slow dancing with one of the wannabee-FOX news-babes, and nearly everyone was mouthing the words to the song.

It's kind of a slow song and the bottle blonde was leaning on Jeff, swaying with her eyes closed.

"When I was serving, we had all kinds of people, and we ate together, slept together, and I saw all kinds of shit, but I never thought about who we really are and all that," Kendal continued. "But, now, looking here..." He scanned the room. "You can see this..." he waved his arm around, gesturing at the bar full of people, "...everywhere, if you look. Iowa, Kansas, North Carolina, doesn't matter – damn, even California if you get out of Los Angeles or..."

"You mean, our culture," I said, "music, church, small-town stuff…"

"Yeah! Look, I have been around, all over the world, and it's clear to me that people like to be with their own. You can come together, kumbaya and all that, United Nations and shit, or whatever, and we all agree that yeah, we are all made of the same shit. But not really. No, I don't believe that, not for a minute. If you ask anybody here deep down, they don't really think they are the same as…"

He stopped and looked at me, and I think that is where I fucked up, because I didn't really give him the "Amen" he was looking for with my look back.

"Now I am not saying we're better," he continued, a little defensively. "Hell, we dance like rusty robots, and dress awful, but that doesn't matter. When you are with your own you can relax, feel at home. And they are taking that away from us. You know?" His pleading look was slowly changing to something else.

Here we go. I gotta recover, I thought.

"I just wanna big-assed wife," I said, "and a job I can do without too much lyin' or cheatin' or havin' to drive 100 miles every day. I don't know about you but I hate being stuck in traffic. Or fucking on a skinny-assed bitch either, if truth be told."

He toasted me with his beer. "To Dash! To Real-Prez!" he said, but I saw the doubt in his eyes.

"To Dash and Real-Prez," I replied.

They called him Real-Prez. They almost never said his name. I didn't either, because it leaves a bad taste in my mouth. But for the RedHats, I think not saying it is some kind of respect, like Kabbalists who don't say the secret name of God. Well, I am sure they would look at me funny if I pointed that out.

The other guy, Jeff, was still sitting at the table with

Lollipop. The FOX-Tart walked over to their table but got the brush-off, and she seemed a bit miffed, and looked back at me, came over to the empty stool next to me, and made a you-can-fuck-me-if-you-ask-nice smile, and I told her I was from out West, in case they caught any fakery in my accent, but I said I had a hell of a story to tell 'em.

Well, I overdid it somehow, 'cause the FOX-Tarts looked at each other, obviously discussing something about me. They looked over to the table and nodded to Kendal and he got up, while at the same time the other bottle blonde, Jeff's dancing partner, walked over, leaned down, and whispered something to Jeff. I was getting a bit edgy. Maybe the two bottle blondes were on to me? The one next to me flashed her eyelids at me like a flapping manta ray, adjusting her short skirt, and leaning in low so her cut-tight pullover pushed her too-symmetrical tits out and up right under my chin.

I looked in the mirror behind the bar. Something was up because I know I'm not the type; they didn't get all dolled up for a guy who looks like me.

When she asked me what I had been doing I just gave her a smile and said, "Quantrill 2 baby!"

"Wow! You got away!"

SwiftPad had put up a big feed on details, but not much had come out on FOX about it. I told a tale to the bleached honey like I really wanted to impress her. I bullshitted my way through the story about how I had been one of the bad boys. I knew how to do that. There is a way to be believable when you are lying through your teeth, and I am one of the few who has the gift.

Kendal came back like he was jealous that I was getting too tight with her. Kendal had classically chiseled features and acted a bit aloof, tending to use a wan smile as an answer for anything that might tend to reveal something about him. His eyes kept shifting to me. Jeff, his partner, was still talking to the little guy at the table.

"After that horror show in Portland, it looks like we are finally turning things around," I said.

"What do you think is going to happen?" she asked.

"What do you mean?"

"Well, you know about that plane in Memphis, and now what you all did in Kansas. What do we do next?"

"We just gotta keep taking out the trash, if you follow me." I kept my eyes on her.

She just smiled at me. I smiled back, but was suddenly terrified.

Maybe I had overplayed it.

"What's your name?"

"I don't want to tell you," she said.

"OK," I smiled with understanding. "I won't tell you mine."

I could feel her checking me out now, and while I didn't turn around, I had a feeling the guys at the table were doing the same thing. Her instincts were right – I was not her friend. I looked over next to me and Kendal was staring at me.

I threw a twenty down on the bar, said, "Have one on me," picked up my camo backpack, and headed out the door. I had no plan, but I knew I just couldn't go through with it. They were watching me too closely now to pull it off and get away. I had fucked things up royally.

It was dusk, and getting dark fast. Main Street was two blocks from the Mississippi River, and if things had gone to plan, a bike was waiting for me on the other side of the block in front of the levee.

"Hey." I was in the middle of the street and I turned and looked. Kendal and Jeff, followed by Lollipop, were fanning out and slowly coming toward me. I turned and started to walk fast – between two cars. Kendal sprinted around the car, while Jeff leaped over the hood of another. I was running now, and dropped my backpack on the sidewalk next to a car before I reached the corner of the block and sprinted around the building. My bike was there. I looked at my fone, switched to the screen with the clown face, and hit the boom-boom clown icon.

CHAPTER 11

ARKIE, ELWOOD, AND HESTER LEAVE VANDALIA AND CHUBBY HEADS FOR THE UNKNOWN

Late August

The virus continued to spread throughout the Middle East. In Syria, enemies who had been fighting for decades suddenly came out of their trenches and from behind rubble, and dropped their guns. Both sides had been seen surrendering to each other. It appeared to be making half of the people who get it sick, while the other half seemed to be under the spell of a powerful hallucinogen. Some said the dead were the lucky ones, but their deaths were seen by themselves as a revelation, a moment of rejoicing, a liberation. The dying felt bad for the living. The death throes were celebrations, and the living forgot their anger. This, of course, was a source of worry for intelligence agencies, corporations, and governments in the West. Business relationships were being torn up, troops were invited to leave, and self-sacrifice was the watchword on all lips.

Then, the first cases began to show up in North America. Texas first, then it began moving north.

From *The Fall of It All – A History of the Big Dump*

THE DULL, DEAD "THUMP" OF THE SECOND BODY HIT-
ting the first body six feet below gave both Chubby and
Elwood a start. Neither reacted, although they both glanced
at each other and just as quickly looked away. They were murderers – well, killers anyway – burying the bodies of their victims:
it seemed to hit all of them at once. Archimedes tipped the first
bag of lime over the edge of the hole and dumped it in until it
was light enough for him to pick up and spread around. Chubby
opened the second bag by hitting it with the blade of his shovel,
cutting a gash across the bag.

"Let's try to get it in the hole and not all over, huh," said
Arkie, as he helped by picking up one end as Kip picked up the
other, and they carefully carted it over and poured it out.

"Just throw both bags in too," said Elwood, who watched,
leaning on his shovel. Then Kip picked up his shovel and he and
Elwood quietly and intently filled the hole with the loose dirt.
As they got close, Arkie raked as much as he could into the hole,
which soon became a little mound. The three of them did a war
dance on the mound, packing the dirt as tightly as possible. They
spread loose twigs and leaves around, trying to get it to blend in
with the ground around them. It was pretty secluded, and not
likely to be discovered by casual traffic. But they had no doubt
someone would find the grave, eventually. What that might mean
for them in some future courtroom, they didn't think about.

They walked back to Elwood's house, sat down in the living
room, Hester poured out the last of Elwood's Irish whiskey into
four glasses, and they sipped. The sound of a car driving slowly .
out on the road roused them from their semi-stupor.

"That's them," said Elwood.

They each had a small backpack, with toiletries, underwear,
socks, IDs, etc. Elwood, Hester, and Arkie carried Fungus spores
in small sealed jam jars.

"This is the last of it unless we get the spores to kick in – but that would be a couple months away at least." Elwood held out some partially dried Fungus buds, but only Chubby took any.

"This is probably a mistake, considering I am going to be traveling for a while." He chewed the Fungus. "It doesn't taste very good. Have you tried sautéing it? As a side dish? Does cooking affect its efficacy?"

"Oh, yeah, it's great with a nice red wine sauce. Problem is, finding enough to make it a worthwhile side dish. And if you have that much, it is a lot more than you need if you are on a maintenance diet."

"How long will it last?"

"A few days," said Elwood. You'll have superpowers for a few days, and great clarity for a month after that."

"I'll wait until the Oregon crop comes in, if it does," said Kip. "Save the rest for Paula back home. She needs it."

"I have been grooming this blend for the last 20 years. I think we can restart the strain in Oregon – maybe. Climate is always the tricky part. It's worth a shot."

Kip and Arkie both shook their heads.

"You need it to function, right?" asked Arkie.

"Yeah, I guess so," Elwood said. "I cut my dose to less than a gram a day. Keeps me together for the trip back." He looked at Chubby. "It is an interesting experiment. I know – I feel – that it can't last forever, but how does it end? It could be real bad, but I'm curious. I'm beginning to tire. Even though – I am young – I look young, and seem to be 30 or so, I know and feel – my memory won't let me forget I am 70. I suppose I still have a young man's strength, but it is hard to get up to use it. You know, I learned how to play baseball back in the '90s. Never played as a kid, but I have been playing – 25 years? Pitching actually for an adult hardball league in East St. Louis. We beat a minor league club in an exhibition a few years ago. I struck out 8 of them."

"Nate told me you were not much of an athlete."

Elwood nodded. "I hated sports."

"It sounds too good to be true."

"You're right. It's hard to understand, much less explain. But I'm tired of it. I think our consciousness has an expiration date. I don't think Fungus helps with that."

"Once – I tried it with Jim, when we were kids. Nothing happened. We were experienced pot smokers then, and I think Paula left some for Jim's mom when we were in high school. I liked psilocybin much more."

"Yeah – Fungus is 'REAL' real life," said Elwood. "It was boring for kids, no kick."

"I wouldn't eat that shit with your mouth," said Hester.

"Where did you learn to talk like that, Hester?"

"You friend here, Woody, who's from New York."

"Long Island. It's not the same New York that you're thinking of," said Elwood.

"I wanted a circus when I was young. Lights and crazy sounds, visions. You know, the crazy shit that happens to your head when you do 'shrooms or acid." Kip glanced at Elwood's jar. "Will you have enough left for Paula?" Kip looked at the large orange-blackish Fungus ear, along with two or three smaller ones at the bottom of the jar.

"Yeah, I guess so, but," he pinched off a little bit, put it in his mouth, sucked on it, and made a face. "It's not going to be enough in the long run. I plan to wean off it when we get to Oregon, if I can't get them to grow this fall. It will give her a little longer if we make it in time."

Elwood washed the spongy, dry fungus down with the final sip of his Irish whiskey.

"Are you going to be old, Woody?" Kip looked at Hester, as she sheathed her double-edged dagger with an elk horn handle. She sounded so innocent. "I'm not sure how I feel about that."

"I am not either. But at some point – I'm thinking about it, stopping eating it and just letting nature take its course. It's going to take a while though; otherwise it will kill me. Probably a couple of months, if Nate's experience is any guide. So – think about –"

"You both should stay in Oregon with us. I mean long term. Coming back might not be a good idea." Arkie nodded his head toward the woods and the two assassins they just buried.

"I've never been to Oregon," said Hester. "Does it rain all the time there?"

Kip smiled. "Sometimes it seems like that. But July and August are perfect."

"Are you going back?" asked Hester.

"No," Kip said. "Not now. They are letting me off at the St. Louis airport. I have a connection to make."

They left the TV on, the door opened, and a note on the kitchen table saying "Gone fishing, be back soon."

"The way people in this town are, it will be a week before they discover we are gone," said Hester.

"No, we probably have a few hours," said Arkie. "Those guys we left down near the river have friends who will be looking for them."

The driver of the Silverado crew cab didn't look at them as Hester, Elwood, and Arkie climbed in the back. The truck had a "Re-Elect the Real-Prez" bumper sticker on the back, and a 30-06 hunting rifle in the cab window.

"Everybody on the floor until we get down the highway away from town." They all squeezed down, closed their eyes, and tried to drift off into their own world.

CHAPTER 12

ALISON GETS TO CAPE GIRARDEAU AND IS INTRODUCED TO THE ASSISTANT DA

Early September

There is no such thing as the "Golden Fungus." It's New Age nonsense. The effects reported have never been verified scientifically. Even those who claim to have taken it are mocked by others who seem to "believe" in it. Those who believe in its existence are delusional, perhaps under the influence of the frightening virus that is spreading near the Holy Land. That is a scary situation, if true. Perhaps those who are suspected of using this dangerous ergot should be forcibly quarantined.

From Dr. Cumagoo McKenzie, TV appearance
on a late-night FOX-like chat show

BOUNCING ON TRACK SHOES THAT MATCHED HER tightly tailored powder-blue pants suit, her hard-shell backpack slung casually off of her left shoulder, Alison walked into the lobby of the Cape Girardeau Marriott. Her bosses, Cadez and Telly, had been in Cape Girardeau for the Dash funeral. She had been slightly perturbed that Cadez hadn't asked her to attend the festivities with him. She was pretty sure Telly was not letting her get too close to the candidate.

She had let her spiky hair grow softer since working in Portland, but she was still caught in the glare of the eyes of nearly everyone in the lobby. Alison was too fit, too confident, and just too plain sharp in every way to be a Real-Prez supporter. But then she was too sharply dressed to be pro-Rosie (who dressed with a style that could only be categorized as "Early Depression"), so that could only mean she was from the Cadez camp. It was interesting, she thought, how quickly little decisions you made became emblems. She knew what kind of signals she was sending. She had only just begun to settle into her new job and apartment north of Dallas when she was dispatched to Cape Girardeau by Telly to find out what was going on and "help him decide the next move." He also wanted her to represent the Cadez camp on the investigation of the Cape Girardeau bombing.

Here in this historic southeast Missouri town, a terrorist bomb detonated outside a crowded bar had killed two and maimed another. Although nothing had been released, she knew the "victims" were Real-Prez assassins who had blown Colonel Coleman's plane out of the sky. The retaliation showed that the Insurgency's capabilities were growing, and that murder would bring the death penalty – applied professionally, with speed, discretion, and finesse.

It was very hot and muggy, even for early September. The virus was in the Midwest, and from what she had read, it had arrived here in Cape Girardeau. Alison was wearing a mask, but she saw that very few were. She was moving a bit too deliberately and unapologetically for someone in an enemy camp. The first rule is don't stand out, and that was what she was doing. The few people who were wearing virus masks seemed ominous, like vampires, or the hooded figure with a scythe. She felt onlookers' eyeballs, and at first thought she should dial it back, not strut so brassy, and stay off the radar, but then again, she was fronting for a Presidential candidate and needed to project a confident demeanor.

Because of Cadez's addiction to the synthetic Fungus, Ishpeming had encouraged Alison to continue propping up Cadez, thinking his weakness could be exposed later. Alison wondered, though, what if he wins it all? That might actually be worse. She knew Cadez was severely manic and could blow a gasket at any time – hopefully before he was elected – and very publicly.

The ARRGH Convention in Disneyland was finally just getting under way, after a number of delays, and Telly was still managing the Cadez campaign. In spite of the "Molotov-Ribbentrop" alliance, there was bad blood between the two camps, although neither Real-Prez nor Cadez hinted at any acrimony in their numerous joint appearances. These dueling press conferences were a big hit, because it forced a degree of decorum on the Convention. Real-Prez read haltingly from a script prepared by his family and sycophantic staff, and occasionally Cadez had flashes of human-like spontaneity. Both sides pretended that it was understood that they would head the ticket. For once the press could bait neither candidate into a blusteringly dumb moronic pronouncement, as one would expect. There was still no clue as to who would head a "united" ticket, but the movement of the polls suggested Cadez was leading slightly, as he was seen as the "sane" one. They had another night of "unity" with another gaudy memorial to Dashell A. Sketerson.

Alison had known Senator Cadez for about six weeks and she already had his ear. She twice had avoided sleeping with him, while allowing him to hold out hope that she eventually would. She had thought about cashing that chip in, because it would be a surprisingly meaningless act, and might pay dividends, but she pushed that idea back out of her mind.

Spence was safe at least. She allowed herself to believe that his act of submission to Telly was partially faked, even to himself, and that he really was working to undermine Cadez. But she just could not trust him enough to make the first move, and apparently, neither could he, if in fact…he had to know that she had saved him by her own duplicity, and like Scheherazade, she had kept the balls in the air with her distracting stories (while never letting on to him or anyone else that she was working for the Insurgency).

Something was up, a deal perhaps, maybe even Telly convincing Cadez to be VP. Everyone knew that the former Temp-Prez, now Veep-Toast, was on his way out as Real-Prez's running mate. Telly Haines had sent her down here while he managed the Senator's negotiations with Real-Prez. So here she was, amidst the RedHat camp in southern Missouri, on a mission she didn't know how best to undertake.

RedHats had taken over the Marriott in Cape Girardeau. She had an email to show the front desk, and she stood impassively waiting for the front desk person, "Anton," from Rēzekne, Latvia (his badge said), tall, clean-shaven, wearing a mask, to check her reservation. Do they have Mormons in Latvia, she wondered.

"We have you on the fifth floor; elevators are down the hall to your left. Enjoy your stay, Ms. Aykroyd."

"Alison?" She turned around and a maskless square-jawed man with dark hair and an ingratiating smile extended his hand. "I am glad you are here. Can you meet us in the Maple Room in about 20 minutes? We have a pretty full agenda."

"Excellent," she said, shaking his hand. "I'll be there." He walked away without introducing himself. She had no idea who he was.

The meeting was long, and procedural, and for Alison, who was desperately struggling not to seem tense or in a hurry, a boring waste of time. She noticed the square-jawed man (who still had not introduced himself to her) sat near the back and also kept quiet. The DA, a bald, fat, white man in an expensive suit that fit too tightly, said that the bombing proved they needed to impose martial law, but no one spoke up to support that.

They took a five-minute break and she made a beeline to her mystery man in the back, catching him just outside the men's bathroom. He saw her coming and spoke first.

"Alison, Bart Jones, Assistant DA. Hi – I am glad to see you!" He went in awkwardly to shake, and she blocked with her elbow. "Oh, yeah – sorry. Let me…" Bart pulled a mask out of his jacket pocket and put it on. "There. It's hard to remember that here. Anyway, I am going to be questioning the suspect, and I understand that you have requested to be there?"

"Yeah, I would appreciate that." She had made no request, but didn't mention that. "I am part of Senator Cadez's staff."

"Yes, so I heard. I welcome you here, because there is some – how to say – ugliness afoot."

"How do you mean?"

"Well, as you might have heard, there are prominent citizens who have made it known they would not be against certain – say – extra-judicial actions taken against the prisoner."

"Doesn't Ford have a lawyer?"

"Umm – yes and no. His grandfather has provided an attorney, but so far, well – I think the attorey is there mainly to protect his grandfather."

"Who is his –?"

"His grandfather? Robert Sketerson Cadish owns the local FOX station, as well as half the real estate around here. He is somewhat of a friend of the President."

"Oh. And his middle name? Is he related to…"

"Yes. That's the other problem. Ford – Henry Ford, just Hank to almost everybody in town – is well, to speak bluntly, Priscilla's son. Priscilla is Mr. Cadish's daughter and was a bit indiscreet as a teenager and her son, Henry, is the one suspected – not suspected, he has admitted it – of helping the bomber escape."

"I see."

"Henry – Hank – well – his father is – was Black – well, we are not sure, but the rumors are he was killed in Texas over something – many different versions of the story. This fact of his grandson's paternity has not sat well with Mr. Cadish, nor his friends and many followers. Hank is thought by many to be – touched in the head, perhaps not an idiot, he takes care of himself, and mostly stays away from town. But 'off' if you get my meaning. That is the general understanding in the community. He lives on a raft that he parks up river a bit."

"Really?" Alison knew Ford was no idiot. She had not heard his origin story though, and the laws of inheritance being what they were, Hank could well be the old man's principal heir. Alison knew that Hank's mother was currently in rehab, and had some state drug charges hanging over her. "If Hank is generally understood to be an idiot, how could he have helped the killer escape?"

"Ha! I wonder if Tommy Thockwall will use that as a defense. Tommy works for Mr. Cadish, and I am not sure how that sits with Hank. Yeah, huh. Maybe he's actually pretty smart. Hmm. I don't really know. He makes a living on the river, which is not an easy thing to do."

Hmm – Mr. Bart Jones, Assistant DA! He's the guy! He's the one who was to contact me, she thought. Jones was smiling slightly. According to what the Ishpeming Center told her, Henry ("Hank") Ford, 25, was a well-known local who lived on a tiny houseboat that he moved around the various creeks and inlets north of the city. His houseboat was actually a log raft with a tin "wigwam" where he slept. He moved frequently to avoid the Marine Patrol, who didn't seem to believe that he never used the river as a bathroom. He towed his raft from place to place with a flat-bottom skiff powered by a 20-horsepower Evinrude.

Alison was told by Ishpeming to always maintain deniability, to "play-act" her support for Cadez even when she was nearly sure she was talking to a friend. She was given one critical piece of information, though. The Assistant County DA, Bart Jones, was a secret supporter of the Insurgency. When he contacted a friend who attended the Convocation of the Ishpeming Fifty and tried to volunteer himself, he was told to "shelter in place" as he might be needed for a future operation. There were many officials in the field in his position, hiding their sympathies, waiting for an opportune time to execute an action.

His position, however, was so precarious that she was only told about him as a possible "friend" but to maintain a distance, if possible, so as not to endanger either of them. In some ways, that made sense, because her talking openly to him was so innocent seeming that no one looked at them twice. Jones didn't know what Alison's real mission was of course; as far as he knew she was Cadez's emissary, who might be "persuadable," but nothing about her real role. Since he did not know her real status, there was no danger of him giving her away – it was up to her. He was the main investigator, the DA having recused himself because of his close friendship with the defendant's grandfather. So Jones had to seem to be working to condemn Hank.

Hank had helped the sheriff look for missing bodies on a couple of occasions, and sold beer to big boats passing through, and ran errands for the barge captains. He was considered harmless, a character who came in to have a drink in town every once in a while. The town was mostly shocked and angry, and there had even been talk of lynching him. They questioned him after the bomber escaped, and he didn't try to hide anything, even the fact that the explosion had hurt his eardrums, it had been so close. He said the man had a gun and told him to take him up the river, but that he had also given him money.

Alison attended the first interview with him, along with her new friend, Bart Jones, Assistant DA, and several others, including a reporter who was not allowed to record it or even take notes. Hank was housed in a bare, whitewashed cinder block, 100-square-foot cell.

CHAPTER 13

HANK TESTIFIES HOW HE MET CHUBBY AND HELPED HIM ESCAPE

Early September

The most difficult thing to explain was the support that continued for the ARRGHs in general and Real-Prez in particular. Many people with long, successful careers and great academic credentials still supported Real-Prez and the other Rs who stayed loyal. But as the year went on, each time they spoke, it looked more and more like a hostage video. Rosie was at best bet only a 50-50 tossup to win the coming Presidential election. The electoral college gave a lot of weight to the states where she wasn't very popular. But Caroline, despite – or maybe because of – her family history, seemed to have lost her enthusiasm for the race, and all the major Dees were behind Rosie. The ARRGHs were split, with Cadez ahead of Real-Prez by nearly 20 points among likely RedHat voters. But rumors abounded of them joining together in a Unity ticket. Everyone agreed there was still time for a realignment of their ticket.

From *The Fall of It All – A History of the Big Dump*

HANK

HE'S IN THE CROWD, WHEN THEY BRING me in. We looks at each other, but he pretends; nothing to see, or remember. These masks sure do change things. I think I can recognize most people, mostly by their clothes, some just wear the same thing day after day. Eyes. You gotta look a lot closer now, 'cause you just see their eyes. But – him? His walk alone tells you it's him, long, striding with a little bop in it, some kind of internal rhythm generated flex, and he is sure as black as black can be, even through his hat, mega-mask, and wrap-around sunglasses. I turn away, look again, and he is gone. Well, this fast-talking Island brother – so black, you'd think he was African – he told me Bart knows, but is pretending he doesn't, at least not in the way he really knows. Of course, I know Bart and he knows me – he and Granddad had a go-around a few years back. I suppose he is wondering if I am gonna let on. Easy Peasy. I let my eyes dart around, about – five people watching me. Well, I guess I caused quite a stir. There is no way out. How much more time have I left? That Island blood told me that Bart is counting on me, I'll not let him down, no matter. Point of pride, he understands it, although I am sure in the back of his mind he wonders what will make me break and call him out. But I won't, no matter. They might think I am slow, but I know what's going on. I am never getting out of here. I can't. Nothing's gonna change that.

I know this sounds funny, but there is a lot of strange stuff I really wanted to do. I mean when I am out on my raft, I think about a lot of things. On a hot summer day, when the river isn't really running high or fast, it is so easy to float out there, and I wonder about the stars, and ancient stuff, like who built the pyramids? Maybe we have done all this before? Maybe somebody like me thought all this before. Nothing's new, I know that. I know this stuff with Real-Prez – it's old hat, everybody knows that. This ain't the first time somebody like him took over. I read about how the Romans just gave up and let Caesar run things. Or maybe it was the other guy? Anyway, I know we have all been here before, and will again too. Probably. Maybe – if we even get that far.

But now things are getting really strange. Mind-reading machines. I hear about them and I want to try it myself. I thought about that whole deal once, and had it all figured out. If we could really see what was in people's mind, wouldn't that fix so much? We would see what really bad people was thinking, even if they seemed to be acting good, and the other way too. I hear people are "hooking up" – that's what they say – with that C2B, or See-to-Be, whatever it's called, advertisements for it all over, everywhere. People just lettin' it take over their mind. Supposed to be those guys in turbans playing the flute for cobra snakes that do it, combined with some techno gizmo. Well, now that I think about it, it might be bad too – 'cause what if what you think is good is what is against the bad people? And they find out that I'm against 'em? 'Cause I am.

They say they're gonna hook me up, to find out what I know, who helped me. Still, C2B sounds pretty interesting, gotta admit I am curious. Oh I am not afraid neither, my mind is my own, they can't take it. But I'll probably never get to find out. It's supposed to let you learn a whole college book in a couple of hours, or so they say. Learn a foreign language in a week – parley voo fransay, hab low esplanada – at least that is what they say. I saw people up in St Loo last week toting a box around in a backpack, connected to one of those sticky hats of criss-crossed plastic on their heads, staring off in their own world, barely able to avoid running into people. I'd like to try it.

But they're talking about hooking me up, to see if the gizmo can tell if I am lying. Shit, if they beat me, I'll tell something, but I ain't gonna really say nothing. They is looking at me as if I was a catfish, stinkin' in the sun.

I see a lot of other faces too, a woman dressed nice, a couple others mostly angry and ugly. That's just the audience. Well whatever they are gonna do to me, they probably won't do it here, at least. Might as well enjoy what time I got left.

"How did you know when to be there?"

"Be where? You mean with my boat? I don't got no fone no more, but I still get messages and check them once or twice a week on the pooter in the library. Lots of people seen me there. I still need to pay my fone bill, and I will, and get my fone back, because after 90 days they take away your messages, and I need that. That is how I get business. I get the messages to pick up guys, stuff, do shit around the river. I could make a lot more money than I do, you know. I turn down a lot of work."

"We checked your messages, Hank, and there was no message from anyone named 'Chubby' or anybody else who wanted to hire you to take them up the river."

"I know. I delete my messages as soon as I hear them. I am really sorry I did pick him up."

"Why?"

"Why do I delete them? 'Cause I don't want the phone company to know I am getting messages I ain't paying for. I always delete 'em permanent too. Gone."

"It's not permanent, Hank. But regardless – why are you sorry you picked him up?"

"Why? What am I gonna do? I left my raft docked upriver by the Randall bend. I am gonna lose it for sure. Who is gonna pay for that?"

I know, I know, you all are wondering why I worry 'bout that? Who gives a floating turd about the raft with a tin wigwam right? Yeah, maybe, but I don't want these people thinking they have me figured out, 'cause, see, I'm "touched" a bit. Sometimes it pays to be misunder-estimated.

Somebody in the back said, "We don't have time for this."

"Hank, why don't you just tell us in your own words what happened."

I just stared at him, like I didn't hear him correctly.

"We will make sure you get your raft back, when this is over, if, as you say, you are innocent."

"My boat and my raft. That's all I wanted to hear. OK?"

"And your boat too."

They look at me all sad like I don't even know what is going on.

"I had been pushed up on the beach there for about an hour when I heard the shouting. I was scared to bejeezus, because I wasn't at all sure if I was doing something right or not. I mean, maybe I am not – I mean, I didn't mean anything bad to happen. I lived around the Cape all my life, and I knew how people think. Not everybody, but most of them. Mostly good people. Right? I just thought this guy was like everybody else."

"So who told you to wait there?"

"Who told me? Nobody actually, I mean, I have been talking to people for quite a while about this Real-Prez business, and then I get a message saying they need my help, so I said I would do what I can..."

"Who gave you the message?"

Who? You did, Bart, you sneaky bastard. That's how that Island dude who never told me his name got me in on it! You, Bart – you who tried to shut my granddad down for putting that Klan bastard on his show. Is that why Granddaddy don't talk to Momma no more? Bart was sweet on Momma when they was in high school, she said. Granddaddy liked him too much though, so she and my real daddy made me. Bart went away then comes back all lawyer-like, but he don't like Granddaddy no more. Granddaddy don't like him. Don't like me neither. Twice he offered me money to leave town for good. I try not to smile. Momma is his only child and I am hers. He told Momma he is giving everything to the church.

Bart, not even smiling a little – this was kinda fun, 'cause I knows he knows and him knowing I knows, but nobody else knowing we both know – my Island buddy said never, ever tell anyone who or how or what.

"I shoulda suspected then," *I says out loud,* "I know. I had no notion about this thing happen outside Hot Shots."

"This thing?"

"You know, the toorrist bombing." *I look around at their blank stares.* "I didn't know."

"Uh huh," said his interrogator, who stopped and just stared at Hank.

"What are we doing?" *Alvin Hinkle, who owns a shitty landscape company I worked for years ago, and who accused me of stealing a lawn mower, when I didn't, is talking now.* "This is a waste of time. I got a rope in my truck." *It don't matter now, he said it, and everyone heard it. A rope. That Island black dude, who I never seen before and who set this up, said Bart would be there to help, and now, he's leading the investigation. So, I figure I have to be scared and sorry about it all, but really, I ain't. If they is that good, maybe I got a chance! Or maybe I get sacrificed. Like Abraham was fixing to do, when the Lord stayed his hand. Maybe this time, I'm just like Abraham's son, only maybe God don't call it off at the last minute. I just gotta lie here like Eye-zac. What if I slip up or get really scared? It's all on me. But, then, Bart is in as much danger as I am. Stick together – I hope we are together – and hope for a sign – that's my ticket! Lay it on Hanky boy!*

"Oh, no, no, Oh God, please don't, I am telling you the truth!" *Got dem tears coming!*

I see Bart look at Dumphy, and point at Hinkle. Deputy Dumphy walks over and touches him on the shoulder and signals him to leave. He does, shaking his head 'bout "wasting county money on a half-breed parasite." I do admit after he accused me of stealing his lawnmower, I sugared the tank of his backhoe. He never mentioned it that I know of, but I heard he sold it to Matt Honeycutt's outfit and they had a ruckus about it.

"Well, we aren't going to hang you, Hank. Or torture you." *He signals for the other deputy (who I don't know, but his name tag says "Black") to remove my handcuffs. I do know that he is the only black working for Sheriff Garrett.* "Would you like something to eat, Hank?"

I shake my head. I was playing a game with myself, gotta make me forget what I know. Keep control, stay in my own mind. Sob a little, Hank. "On second thought, yee-ah, maybe a cheeseburger. You got any of that good catsup?"

"Sure, Hank." *He looks around and I see him signal Dumphy to take care of it. Everybody around here knows what the good catsup is!*

"The more you tell us about this guy you say gave you the message the – know what I am saying, Hank?"

"I don't know who it was."

"Was he white?"

"I don't know – he sounded foreign. I never seen him – never seen his face I mean."

"What?"

"Long brown pants, long-sleeve bright green shirt with flowers on it. Looked nylon or something flimsy. Wore a hat and a big white hospital mask, I mean it covered almost everything. And sunglasses. Just glanced at him, and he was gone. Listen, some of you, you know me. I do a little independent business, you all know that. I move up and down the river, sometimes up above St. Loo…"

"How about Minneapolis?"

"Naw, that be up a tributary. I stay on the main river. My raft's been to Kansas City. Maybe someday, I go to Montana." There was laughter in the room.

"And sometimes down to Memphis too, right?" Bart snapped as the laughter subsided.

"Not lately."

"What do you mean, when were you last in Memphis?"

"Well, you know, since the trouble down there, not much traffic going down or coming up, and you know how the – I don't want to say who asked me, but I brought back a few cases of that good, that real good bourbon, and up and sold it. Couple months ago. Before all that hecka-booloo out in Or-ee-gon I mean."

"Meet anybody there about this thing here? About meeting this 'Chubby,' as you call him?"

"Hell no! Just some man at that distillery on the river from, what's it called, 'Blue Note'?"

"How long it take you?"

"Going down river, about two days. Coming back, almost a week. River was running high last June. I had a breakdown too."

"So you take ten days to float down the river, and back, to pick up a couple cases of whiskey, to sell? How much did you make?"

"Maybe fifty bucks. That covered my gas, which was almost that much, I guess it's hard to get good bourbon. Anyways, you know I just like being on the river."

"OK. So you met nobody in Memphis except some guy at the bourbon distiller. Did you go out, drink, eat?"

"No. I ate on the raft." *I can't do more than shrug. They don't believe me. Maybe one or two do, but I need mo'! I just know they gonna beat me later.*

"Well, Hank, you think about it. We will come back to talk about your Memphis business more thoroughly later."

Oh, later! I doubt there will be a later.

"So you say you get this call to meet a guy near the Shawnee Bridge?"

"Yeah, he said he give me fifty bucks."

"Again, fifty bucks. Is that your going rate?" *This gets a laugh. I smile too, at first.*

"At least it ain't thirty pieces of silver!" *A bunch of 'em laugh even more. Maybe I shouldn't a said that.*

"Where were you supposed to take him?"

"Down the river, that is what he seemed to mean. Just a short trip."

"Down the river – you mean across, to Illinois. And this was right near the bridge?"

I give them all a dumb look, like that was the first time I had thought it odd. I shake my head. "He never said across. I took him down to Gray's Point. Let him out by that bit of beach near Nash Road. He seen some headlights flash and run to it."

"OK. What happened next?"

"I head back up the river to my raft parked up by Bainbridge Creek."

"About 8 miles upriver from the Cape here, right?"

"That's right. I been parking the raft there for years. Sometimes I go across to Illinois, but I stay there mostly."

"Bart, he is stalling!" *I look over at Deputy Dumphy. He's been riding me since grammar school.*

"Darryl, where's that hamburger I asked about?" *Bart, he looks hard at Dumphy.*

"Cheeseburger," *I say quietly. I was gonna say something about the catsup too, but the good lord mercifully put a stop in my mouth.*

"Yes, cheeseburger," *says Bart, and everybody laughs quiet-like. Darryl leaves the room, shakin' his head.* "How did you know to pick him up, Hank?"

"So I gets this call," *I says,* "he said his name was Chubby. That he would pay $50 to pick him up just before sundown at the base of Morgan Oaks Street, where the levee breaks off, and you can walk from Water Street to the beach. Just upriver from the Shawnee Bridge."

"It was getting dark about then, right?"

"Nearly."

"Did you hear the explosion?"

"I sure did. I expect everybody in town did."

"And when did this 'Chubby' fellow..."

"That's what he said – to call him, 'Chubby.' He was pretty – pretty big, as they say. Every part of him was pretty thick. Not exactly fat though."

"What else?"

"His hair was real short, like he shaved his head not too long ago. Missing a tooth. Weird beard, long stash – sideburns – old-timey looking."

"OK."

Bart is writing something down, and there is a murmur and a bunch of whispering. A guy I don't know whispers something to Bart, and Bart nods.

"Right, that fits with other descriptions we have. So how long after the explosion did he show up?"

"Five minutes. Maybe less."

"Did you see him on a bicycle?"

"Bicycle? No."

"Where did you go?"

"He said he wanted to go down a ways, down past town. He had one of them picture maps, a photo from high up in a plane and I recognize Gray's Point."

"You mean the big bend in the river south of town?"

"Well – yeah. It was just 'bout dark by then, but I knew the way. I let him off, and he gave me a hundred bucks. Five twenties. I wasn't unhappy, I do say that, even though I sure am now."

"You helped a terrorist escape. You know what that makes you?"

"Stupid, I suppose."

No one answers that. Actually, we did go down to Gray's Point, then we turned around and he pulled the tarp on his self and I crossed over and hugged the Illinois shore and took him about 8 miles up and I was fixin' to let him off on the Illinois side. But he changed his mind, so we crossed back over and hid out inside my raft. Waited all night and all day, then the next night, I took him over to Illinois near Ware. And he was gone. If they catch him, they will put it together, and I will get the needle for sure. People been talking about hanging though, probably so they can all watch. Probably will anyway. Al Hinkle has a bunch of friends who would help hoist me up. So it don't matter anymore. Probably pulled Momma in for it too, but Granddaddy will help her, at least I hope he will. Anyway, how did he – he did call his self? Dean, Dane? That Island blood did actually say his name real fast, but I could hardly understand him when he talked. Had all the cool – like a slick city brother, but more like a hippie, and then the Island too – Bob Marley but unplugged. He's the one I met in Memphis and figured out somehow I was secretly for Colonel Coleman and the whole Memphis thing. Al Den. Albert Dennis? I really can't remember, which is good, I guess. It was something like that. I suppose he looked at my skin tone. Or else he got a message from Bart here. I just gotta let it ride. Don't wish for nothing, keep my mouth shut, see how it plays. Probably – I am dead. Nothing to be done. No point squealing, won't help, besides. I have never tried to pass for white, even though I think I could, better than Michael Jackson anyway. Fuck, the older I get, the more happy I ain't white! If anybody asks – I am glad to tell them my black daddy was Ezekial Moncrief, who everybody around here knows, or at least heard him play the saxophone a few times. And they also know my momma was the daughter of the owner of the local FOX station, as well as a number of other businesses, mostly to do with real estate and construction, and he was mayor some years back. When she went to the hospital, she said Jack Ford was my daddy. Jack's a white man of course, or at least was. But Momma never married him, and he drowned when I was a baby. So everybody knows me, and they think I am touched, and I may well be. My granddaddy tried to get me to work for him, but he refuses to forgive Momma for making me the way she did. So I'll be damned to hell and back if I am gonna work for him! Anyway, I know everything about that river, and have been from one end up in Minny-soda too, and yeah way up the Mizzoo too, down to Big Easy. I figured what else do I need? My dream – what I always thought maybe I could do someday is work on one of them barges, maybe be captain someday, but I know this stuff – this thing I did – well, I ain't ever gonna get a job like that now. At least not the way things are now.

"Anyway, this guy, Chubby, the same man said for me to be at the levee directly by Morgan Oaks Street, before sundown, so I was. All Chubby said was, 'Be ready,' and I was. There was another man talked to me about it earlier, it's true. He must of told Chubby, as good as I can figure."

I looked out at all the faces, and they didn't look too happy at all.

"Other man?"

"Yeah. A couple days ago. Said I could make some fast money if I want, take a guy down river some. A Black come up to me outside the Quick Mart, over on Townsend Street. I come in there mostly on Wednesday night to check on the Powerball numbers. And buy a ticket for next week."

"Never seen this Black guy before?"

"Never in my life!"

"And that's where you met this Chubby?"

"Yeah – told me to come back the next night. That's where I first seen this Chubby."

"So what were you doing when it happened, Hank? Didn't it make you suspicious it being a rush job. And a secret?"

"Well I was there, expecting to make a little money, as I said. I thought maybe – I don't really know what I think, except about the money. Anyway, I was waiting there on the beach near Morgan Oaks. I was dabbing some glue onto a patch of fiberglass I put on the bottom of my skiff when I heard the loudest explosion I ever known, felt real close too. Hurt my eardrums for a minute or two. Then, I don't know – five minutes, maybe longer, I turn and this Chubby is walking real fast, right at me. Nobody behind him at least. He looked kind of funny, at the time anyway."

"What did he say to you?"

"He said something that I couldn't make out 'cause I think the explosion made my ears a little deef, just a little, you know, 'cause I was a good – well not a half mile away, if that, if it happened by Hot Shots, as I hear it happened. This Chubby fella, he just jumped into my boat and stared at me. "Let's go!" he yelled, pointing downstream. I pulled the cord on my outboard and we took off headin' down river. I decided to ride nice and slow. I stayed real close to the shore, riding under the bridge, right along the edge. Pretty soon sirens were going off and people were screaming, you could hear it all because sound travels really clear on the river. Nobody was paying any attention to me though. I just kept going."

"Then what happened?"

"We got to the bend in 30–40 minutes or so. He paid me and runned off toward some flashing headlights."

"It was pitch dark out."

"Yeah, I know. No moon, neither. He was gone before I could say boo."

"Then what?"

"Then I turned around, rode up past town. Sirens still going off as I passed town. I started wondering if I done a bad thing. I got to the raft and stayed there. I started thinking maybe I done a bad thing, like I said, so I stayed on the boat for a day, looking at my money, wondering if it really was like them thirty pieces of silver. I always wondered what they meant by pieces? Like little rocks or something? Anyhoo, I stayed on my raft all the next day, doing little chores. More and more though, I known I done wrong. So I came back to town, figuring I would tell somebody. Pulled into the Red Star ramp and then Darryl picked me up real quick. He threw me around hard, like I was trash. I suppose somebody seen me."

"Did this Chubby say anything when you were on the boat?"

"He said some guys were looking for him 'cause he was lovin' on one of their girlfriends."

"You believe him?"

"Yeah, at first, 'cause I was – you know – I sure didn't think he sploded that bomb and kilt people!"

"What'd you think the big noise was?"

"I asked him. He shook his head, said it sounded like a propane tank getting too close to a welding arc. I remember the McKee boys was putting up some iron struts in the warehouse up the block they was fixing to make into expensive apartments. I seen them work, and I knew they was foolish hiring them, so, yeah, I thought it might be that."

"You really thought it was a propane tank?"

"More likely acetylene or one of them other arc-welding gases. Why not? How it make sense other-hoo? Who think somebody gonna do that? It kinda made sense – I figured a really ugly girl with a mean boyfriend mighta let him do some lovin', 'cause he was pretty disturbing to see."

"So you didn't even consider the possibility that this Chubby, who you describe almost exactly like the other witnesses described the bomber – you didn't even suspect he might have something to do with the bomb?"

"What bomb? How did I know it was a bomb when it went off? When this Chubby get on my boat, after he gave me fifty, he said the splosion must of been some kind of a gas leak or a maybe a gas tank, real casual. He acted like he had no idea either.

Yeah, I believed him. Him being in a hurry and all, that did concern me, it's true, but only later. He paid upfront in cash – and then after we got going he gave me another fifty, double what we agreed. That made me pretty happy. I really didn't think he done something bad. What else could it be? He seemed a nice guy, funny. He said he was sorry about Coleman dying down in Memphis, I suppose 'cause he thought – I don't know."

"Because you're Black."

"I ain't Black, I am cream, with a touch of coffee." No one laughed. "Or the other way. No, I didn't say nothing one way or the other about Coleman. When he paid me double, I admit I was pretty happy and didn't think more about it. Hundred dollars a lot of money."

Actually, me and Chubby spent the night in my tin wigwam on the raft and settle in for the night. Up north by Bainbridge Creek. He had some real good mara-jew-wanna, so we sparked up and that made sleep easier. That's when he told me about killing those guys that killed Colonel Coleman. Boom! I knowd it was something like that. I knowd he did the bombing, sure, but not why he did it. They ran right next to his bomb and he fired it off with his fone. Showed me how it worked. He wanted me to come with him, and get out of the Cape. Leave my raft and boat? I suppose I should of listened to him. But since I knowd that Bart Jones, sitting right in front of me, introduced me to the Island brother, Adean, or whatever his name is, I figured I wouldn't have no trouble. Now he is pretending to be against me. Maybe he can get me out of this. But I didn't think it would be like this.

CHAPTER 14

ELWOOD AND ARKIE ARRIVE AT REHAIN COMPOUND

Early September

Neither Temp-Prez nor Real-Prez had been seen for days. In fact, in those waning days of summer, almost no major leaders made public appearances or gave out pronouncements. The virus had arrived in North America, and was hitting like a million sledgehammers. It was killing people across the Southwest and into Southern California and moving north.

The mechanics of its spread were still unknown. It was at first thought to spread via micro-spray from people breathing, but when they conducted experiments to prove it, there was almost but not quite enough correlation to say that was the source. So some time after the first wave, a majority of people began to wear protective masks. The spread continued, but it seemed to help, and then it didn't. Mask enforcers started to show up. There were loud arguments, fights, and finally a lot of killing. Masked gun fights popped up all over. Real-Prez took up the cause of the people who didn't wear masks at first, but then, only a week later, he had his little mobs attacking people who didn't wear a mask, or people who wore it wrong, by not following strict rules to only buy his brand of colorful (and some said slightly toxic) masks. There still was no agreement in the medical establishment as to how it was transmitted, when in the infection cycle it was transmitted, or even how to identify infected people.

Because of the refugee crisis, the Insurgency, and the terrorism, the "Persian virus," as Real-Prez called it, still seemed unimportant and far away, in spite of the reality that it threatened the human species. But every day more people were being infected.

That psychological factors might have triggered infections was first proposed by a Seattle doctor who noticed a similar biographical profile in the victims, apparently people with a history of repressed anger and a fear of strangers, a form of xenophobia that manifests itself not just in rejection of foreigners but also the rejection of anyone outside a circle defined by race, or even political ideology. Which is to say it seemed to attack irrational extremists. When a gated community famous for its near unanimous support for Real-Prez in Florida was devastated by virus fatalities, some epidemiologists took notice. But the data, again, was mixed, and similar trends were not noticed in South Asia.

Whether it was the virus or not, people were behaving more strangely than normal, and what constituted "normal" was becoming more and more strange. Suddenly, normal was very weird. People started acting hyper-normally. Scenes out of *Twilight Zone* were occurring all around, where the good townspeople were the monsters and the marginalized were the saviors. The reality being told in the media, a reality that was bright, primary colored, sharp, snappy, and perfectly framed, seemed out of sync with life as it appeared to everyone. It took many forms, but suddenly no one recognized the "shared" reality anymore.

For the survivors of the virus, in the beginning, there were few hospital cases, and most were diagnosed with something else. It was generally just strange behavior, people saying strange things, acting without fear or caution as if suddenly released from some form of captivity, from a prison they could no longer remember or comprehend. What was strange was its overwhelming unfiltered, unedited normality. There was an utter disregard for the catastrophic political and natural events that were occurring every day. Was it some form of mass psychosis?

The first cases in the US were confirmed in August. That virus was identical with cases identified in Bahrain. But when the DNA sequencing was performed on samples from the earlier Myanmar case, it was found to be identical to it too. *However* – when Myanmar and Bahrain were compared, they were not identical! The differences were not explained by any normal mutation process. More testing only confounded previous results.

From *The Fall of It All – A History of the Big Dump*

N EARLY EVERYONE AT THE OLD REHAIN COMPOUND, about 150 people, gathered together in the gravel square below the two-acre solar energy farm. Behind them was the huge barn (and workshop, lab, and central office), and on the other side stood the three-story Rehain homestead. Further out, near the horizon, the Pacific Ocean reflected giant pillars of sunlight that filtered through the white fluffy clouds. The crowd was welcoming Arkie back. He had returned, along with extremely tall, youthful, sandy-haired Elwood Taylor and a young red-haired woman in tight jeans and no bra under a form-fitting body shirt. She also had a big knife on her belt.

"All right, we don't want to be drone bait," said Jerry, after hugging his boss Arkie like a long-lost brother. "Spread out! Also, I repeat this for any of the new people – we are under siege here from a disease that is spread through the air, so everybody, wear a fucking mask everywhere, so you keep your spittle to yourself!"

"How do you know it's spread that way?" somebody shouted.

Jerry looked down at the dirt for a few seconds. "I don't. But it's the best guess I have heard. So we wear masks because if it starts spreading up here we are fucked. Any more questions?"

Jerry looked around and met everyone in the eye. They had all been quarantined for the last month up on the Compound, except now they had two strangers and Arkie, just back from the dead zone – the corridor of death. St. Louis to Indianapolis had been hit like a sledgehammer; it was almost medieval how whole towns had lost as much as 70% of their population.

Alice had exiled three people last week, including Gull, who made a big ruckus as he left. Gull had been working on the Compound for decades, and had been pretty close with Walt; in fact, he had even gone on a business trip with him once. Alice had threatened him before, but this time he called her a stupid old white cunt, and that was it. Nobody called Alice stupid. Although Alice and Gull had known each other for decades, they had never cared for each other. Alice had a lot of friends on the coast; her family had lived here for generations. Same with Gull. The other two exiles were just dumb fucks who could not handle the responsibilities they were given.

The two dumb fucks were staying down in Newport, at the Shilo, the RedHat hotel, they called it. The Shilo franchise hotels were armed camps, definitely Real-Prez friendly, the owner being a friend. The two numbskulls were spreading rumors about the Compound: they were hiding criminals and were having group sex, according to the disgruntled former colleagues.

Jerry knew there had been a spy living on the Compound. Too many new people had come up, refugees from Portland for the most part. Vetting was necessarily sketchy. Jerry had watched Gull leave, patching out, spitting gravel in a couple of directions as he slalomed his Tesla pickup off the mountain.

"Come on, Arkie, let's go down in the bunker," he said. "We have been screwing with all your code! Man, you are going to hate us!"

Arkie rolled his eyes and shook his head with a slight smile.

"You must be hungry," Jerry said.

"Where's Nate?" asked Elwood.

"Visiting his old flame," said Maggie. Maggie had lived with Nate for almost three years in the early '90s, when she was still floating through the garden of life, as the last true flowerchild, and Nate was riding out his final days as a "promising" young writer. Now she was a hardened guerilla fighter, and her new best friend, young Sequoia, laughed at the irony of Maggie's comment. But it went over the head of everyone else.

"I can wait to eat," said Arkie.

"His old flame?" Elwood looked at Maggie with vague recognition. They had once met, very briefly, a quarter of a century ago. "You mean Paula? Is she OK?" Elwood continued to stare at Maggie, but still couldn't place her.

"Let me take Elwood down the hill," said Maggie, who was getting a strange look from Hester.

"Sequoia, take Arkie to the command center and explain how and why we redirected traffic coming from the Bay Area out to Asia," Jerry said.

"You what?"

"Come on, Mr. Moropolis. I'll explain," said Sequoia.

"You'll explain? Who are you?"

Jerry and Maggie laughed. "She's Sequoia. She is redesigning the network. It made too much sense to me not to do it, but I think she can explain it better," said Jerry. "If she got it wrong..." He drew his finger theatrically across his neck.

"Why did you change it?"

"Faster," said Jerry. "More secure."

"Really," said Arkie in a tone dripping with doubt, looking at Sequoia, who shrugged. Jerry shrugged too.

"Come on," said Maggie. "I'll bet Alice is down there too. Something will be on the stove. I'll take these two down to Paula's hobbit hole," Maggie was pointing at Elwood and Hester.

"I'll stay up here, look around that barn up there," said Hester.

"Sequoia – tell Arkie..." Maggie directed.

Sequoia nodded. She had found a backdoor into the Texas headquarters of Cadez. Into Gupta's C2B project.

Arkie saw their furtive exchange.

"It's just like you predicted, Arkie," Maggie said.

"If it is like I predicted, then that's not good," said Arkie. He looked at Sequoia again, but she ignored him.

Earlier that morning, Paula had been up and brewing herself tea. She was moving slowly, her rapid aging more and more apparent. Her hair was turning grayer by the day, her wrinkles seeming to deepen by the hour. She was already in the first stages of menopause, which had hit her suddenly with a week of hot flashes nearly every hour while she was recovering from the gunshot. In spite of all that, for some strange reason she was feeling better. She had her hair back in a ponytail, and wore jeans and a thin cashmere sweater.

It was early and the sun would not arrive overhead for another two or three hours, and she liked to stay warm. She had just walked around outside her hobbit burrow at the bottom of the hill, below the Rehain homestead. The former Christmas tree farm was overwhelmed with new, chaotic growth. The possible pathways through it created a wild labyrinth. Behind her burrow, the woods were thick in Douglas firs, and there was even a redwood grove a short walk away. And down below that was the cedar grove, in the damp mossy flat ground that served as the headwaters for Kataka Creek, which flowed down to Big Creek, which emptied into the Pacific. It was her favorite spot, so moist and cool and fragrant! Looking up, toward the top half of the little valley of spruce and fir that had gone to seed, she could see the slow building-up of a natural ground cover. The offshoots, irregular even for nature, formed an underlying pattern of dispersal. The birds were singing; the squirrels were romping and tumbling all around. Sometimes the birds made a racket worse than the city at quitting time. It smelled so fresh, Paula was sure the air itself was the main agent of her recovery.

She was still eating mostly soup, but was beginning to feel the pangs of real hunger again. Still weak, and so much older in every way than she was two months ago, Paula was finally feeling better. As she sat thinking about it, she felt more alive than she had in years. She took a nap after a light lunch, and was just waking up when Nate and Elwood knocked on the door.

Paula saw Maggie, who waved, quickly put on her mask, and then tried to sneak away. Nate had told her about Maggie during their brief SanFran HaightStreet romance. That they (Nate and Paula as college students) had done exactly the same thing 50 years previously was irrelevant. Both had tried to forget it, and had just about succeeded in doing so by the time they got close to their seventies – well Nate's seventies anyway. Paula was still in her early thirties until she got shot at GG's party.

Paula knew Maggie was about 50, but was now so unlike the flowerchild that Nate had described to her. After a quarter century of marriage to Spence Stromborn, a brilliant but weak man who helped found *Reigny Deigh Media*, she was now currently a veteran of the fiercest fighting of the Insurgency. Gray streaks ran through her short dark hair. She wore a monochrome green t-shirt, cut-off jeans, thick socks, and light-weight hiking shoes, and had an Uzi slung casually over her shoulder. They both knew they had had significant "past lives" with Nate, but until now had avoided each other at the Compound.

Paula invited them all in.

They sat around her in her small living room. Maggie stood back and watched as the three old friends awkwardly made small talk. Paula slid over on the couch for Maggie and signaled her to sit next to her, and they smiled at each other.

Nate at first had been shocked by the changes he saw in Paula, even though he had known it was coming, and had himself experienced the rapid aging that went along with being deprived of the Fungus.

Paula thought his discomfort at seeing her as an older woman was hilarious.

Now she showed Elwood and Maggie a picture of herself, Nate, and Kip taken in Frisco three months ago. As she passed her fone around, Nate pretended to glance at it, but could not look at how much she had changed. In the picture she had a ponytail, and was wearing pajama bottoms and an oversized sweatshirt. A cutie just out of college, ready to sow her oats. Kip's face seemed blurry, with two weeks' beard growth and a pack on his back, as if he was about to leave.

Maggie was also enjoying Nate's discomfort. She showed them a picture of Nate and herself in Eugene from the '90s. Nate looked almost 30 when she was a 20-year-old hippie fairy queen. He was really in his forties then.

"We are a fucking weird bunch," said Elwood. "Maggie looks best of all, and in some way, if you pardon me for saying – I mean the change in you," he said to Maggie, "...from that," he pointed at her picture on Paula's fone, "to..."

Paula and Nate silently stared at Maggie.

"You never ate Fungus, did you?" Paula said.

"A couple of times, but not every day like Nate did," Maggie said. "It didn't do anything for me that I could tell." She looked at Elwood. It took her aback a bit. She didn't mention it, but there was a fuzziness about him that wasn't caused by the light or any blurriness in her eyes. It didn't seem real. Nate and Paula both looked tired and old.

"You three need to catch up," said Maggie. She smiled at Nate. "I am going to head up the hill. We had some intrusions last night near the solar farm that I need to check out. I'll talk to you all later. Elwood, I noticed the big knife on Hester's leg – is she..."

"Yes, crazy as a rabid wolverine. She saved Arkie and me with that knife. Sliced open two men."

"Seriously?"

Elwood just looked at her.

"I gotta figure out what to do about Spence," she said and left.

Maggie knew Spence was stuck in Texas, working on integrating C2B with *SwiftPad*. That was what he had wanted to do at *Reigny Deigh*. Did it matter to him where and for whom he worked? She really didn't know. She wanted to get a message to him, but that might put him in danger, and anyway, she thought, it was on him not her. She wondered if he had contacted their daughter in Boston. She would send her a message. She was emphatic with herself about it. Up until now, just knowing her daughter was OK was enough. As for Spence, well she just didn't know.

Maggie said, "See you all later," and walked up the hill toward the barn.

All the reminiscing with the photos got Nate and Elwood laughing, remembering their trip across the Midwest fifty years earlier. They were kids, especially the two men. Paula, who was on that trip with them, listened impassively. Elwood described the Vandalia of today. It had not changed very much. He explained his plans to try and spread spores of the fungus at the Compound. Paula told him about the perfect spot, down below where it was wet, among the cedar trees. His experiments had slowly led him to think he had a strain that would take to the Northwest climate. Nate listened impassively, without making any comments.

"Here," said Elwood, pulling out a small jar from his fanny pack. "Paula, here is a six-month supply. Hopefully, when it runs out, we will have some growing around here."

Paula looked at it, nodded, and put it on the table next to her. "I don't know," she said. She looked at Nate, who had lost weight, and looked less healthy since they had last seen each other just before the events in Portland earlier in the summer. He shrugged.

Elwood asked when Nate had quit eating Fungus. "That was when you and…" he added, pointing with his thumb at the door, "Maggie split, right?"

"Right." Nate laughed to himself. "She and Spence were dying to fuck each other. I could see that. So…" He thought about it for a minute. "That's what I tell myself. That is the reason I quit eating it." Paula took his hand and smiled. The both knew, even if they never acknowledged it, that things would never go back to the way they were. She had changed, and as hard as it was for him to admit it, so had he.

Paula tired soon, and her mind drifted a bit. How much older looking was she than before? Twenty years? In one month! It made her dizzy thinking about it, but actually, she felt OK. Not hurting. She looked fairly old now, but her lethargy made her seem even older.

"I'm going to explore this place," said Elwood. "It is fucking amazing!"

"You have your PhD in fungus, and you have never been to the Northwest?"

"Mycology, a PhD in mycology. Yes, but I was never here for long. I stayed around the mid-Mississippi valley. Unbelievable diversity, enough for five lifetimes of study."

"You mean our lifetimes or a normal person's?" said Paula.

"Normal. We still don't know how long ours will be."

"Yeah, but with no Fungus, we'll never know," Paula said.

"That's why I think it will be perfect – perfect for us, I mean – to start another Fungus colony here. Of course I know the Pacific Northwest is the Garden of Eden for 'shrooms and fungus. But it is also overcrowded with scholars. You think Alice will let me stay here?"

"I think so," said Paula. Paula knew the reason he hadn't been to the Northwest. His last delivery of Fungus had not gone well. "I'll vouch for you, and your girlfriend."

"I'd hold off on all the vouching until you meet her. She is – different."

"Then you'll have to vouch for her," said Paula.

~~~

Nate was still sleeping on the couch in Alice's living room. It didn't bother him. He didn't need privacy, and he had all of the other amenities required: shower, stove, washing machine. He slept better being closer to the door anyway. He always did. Alice had told him to stay away from Paula during the early days of her recovery. "You are irritating," she told him, without further explanation. So Nate tried not to be irritating.

Paula had healed amazingly fast out in the Oregon woods. The Compound's doctor, Pierre Nivel, did nothing but clean the wound every day. She had no more Fungus, having given her very last piece to Kip just before the shootout. She did have a short drink every afternoon with the doctor, a splash of Seagram's Canadian rye, just a wee bit, with ginger ale. She had been sleeping about 15–16 hours a day since being shot.

So when Nate had been allowed to visit, she stepped out and they sat in the sun, just outside her door, catching the last of the afternoon sun before it hid behind the hill. They were finally comfortable again.

"Tell me a story, Nate."

"About what?"

"What happened after China? Did you really chase down Dagmar like it said in your book?"

"I wouldn't say chase," said Nate slowly. He adjusted his virus mask and told her all the things they never spoke of during their strange six-month attempt to live together in San Francisco.

"We have been together off and on, for so long, do you think we need to wear a face covering?"

"I might have picked it up," he said. "Let's be careful for a while."

"I guess we aren't really…"

"What?"

"Nothing. You're right, we have to be careful. We have to fight through this."

Over the last 50 years she had been to Nate almost everything a woman could be to a man. Her smooth, alabaster skin was turning weather-beaten, and dull, and he was fascinated by her and what she was going through. He would have thought the process would be worse for her than for him, because she had so much more aging to do in a shorter time, without any Fungus to aid her withdrawal. Such a shock to the body – and the mind – especially the mind. But other than aches and pains that she ignored, she got through it, day by day. She had known serious hardship before; in a way, this was nothing. Was it the strength inherent in women, or was it her, just her? Probably both, he decided.

"They have been wandering around the perimeter." Sequoia came into the Comm office in the big barn on the Compound. Alice and Nate sat in the corner. Off to the side, Hester was getting familiar with the Comm Center and was checking the feeds from the cameras around the perimeter.

"Yeah, they have been probing for the last two days. They destroyed a couple of our cameras, and mostly just watched for a while, moved a few hundred yards, then watched again."

"How many?" Nate asked.

"Six, ten, but a battalion might be out there and we could miss it," said Hester.

"Do you think this is Feds?" Nate was checking out Hester, trying to figure out what it was she and Elwood saw in each other.

"Couldn't he just order the Army in? He's nuts," said Elwood.

"As that Welsh sorcerer said in one of Shakespeare's plays," said Alice, 'I can call demons from the briny deep!' And his buddy replied, 'Yes, but will they come when you call them?' Real-Prez can order the Army to attack domestic opponents, but it would be illegal. Would the Army do what he says?"

It was early in the morning, and Nate sat in a stuffed chair, not looking at his fone, just staring off. Paula slowly ambled in, and didn't say much, her newly trimmed hair combed back, and it appeared she wore a hint of blush on her cheeks, an improvement that Nate noticed. She was thin, almost athletic looking, and she had her old lope in her walk as she came in. Paula carefully propped herself up on an ancient couch in the antechamber to the *SwiftPad* command center.

Deep in the Oregon coast range, the nearly thousand-acre Compound was bordered on the north by a Siletz Indian reservation, and on the south by a steep mountain, with an old logging road as the only approach. At the highest point on the property, Kip Rehain's dad had long ago built the house and massive barn. The barn had been refurbed like a high-tech fortress. A deep concrete bunker housed their Comm Center, all built with *SwiftPad* money. There was almost an insect-like quality to the activity in the big gravel square, people walking with unhesitating directness to accomplish their tasks. It was military-like – but the discipline was on a different level than anything generated by a hierarchical reporting structure. Everyone was totally dedicated to "success," which they all knew was another word for survival. They all understood that there was a bull's eye on the Compound. About ten techs watched and modified the metrics of their monitors from around the globe. *SwiftPad* still provided most of the news – well – most of the information connectivity for much of the world.

Alice continued to maintain and to run the Compound. Her word was law. Most problems got settled before she heard about them, although most of the time she knew anyway, and just let things ride.

Arkie came in, his mini coffee thermos in one hand, his fone in the other. "We have some up-to-date info on Spence, Maggie's husband," he said.

"Spence is still working for the Cadez campaign at their headquarters in Plano, Texas," continued Arkie, "at Ross Perot's old EDS campus."

"EDS? What is that?" asked Alice.

"You remember Ross Perot?"

"Of course," said Alice. "A jug-eared little fruitcake who thought aliens were after him, and who split enough of the vote in the '92 election to put the big Hound Dog in the White House."

"Right. It is ironic that his old headquarters is being used again for the ARRGHs, even if it is sort of a third party," said Arkie. "Perot built a weird, post-apocalyptic campus for Electronic Data Systems back in the '80s, where the entrances to 'buildings' were concrete outcroppings that mainly consisted of an office for the security guards and elevators down to oppressive air-conditioned offices and rows and rows of computers."

"I actually worked there once," said Nate.

They all looked at him, but he waved them off.

"Anyway," said Arkie, rolling his eyes, "he has established contact with Alison Aykroyd."

"They were kidnapped together, right?"

"I am not sure how it went down, but they disappeared at about the same time," said Nate. "Maggie and I met with Alison, just before the fighting started in Portland. She planned to infiltrate the Cadez group. She somehow ended up in Salt Lake and Spence went to Texas. We made contact with Alison, and she finally was able to figure out where Spence ended up."

"Maggie is working on it with Sequoia," said Arkie. "They are trying to get a read on exactly what is going on now."

Alice shook her head. The description of Perot's "weird

post-apocalyptic campus" brought to mind their own forest compound here. Weird could certainly describe the hobbit houses at the bottom of the hill. But she had to admit to herself if no one else, she had a good crew now.

Maggie and Sequoia carried out her plans and ideas with indefatigable energy. No one could deny they had brought a renewed spirit to the Compound. The two were inseparable, and they seemed to work 20 hours a day keeping the place shipshape, alert, and ready.

But hard work and efficiency were one thing; personal chemistry was a whole other matter. Neither Paula nor Alice liked Maggie and Sequoia very much. Nate had convinced them that the new blood was essential to keep the place humming, and both of them hated admitting he had been right. The fact that he had lived with Maggie for two years probably didn't make it easier for Paula and Alice to admit it.

"So what is his situation?" Alice asked with a sharp impersonal tone.

"Spencer Stromborn is OK," said Maggie, "and is inside their operation."

"That's great news! Maggie, you must be so relieved to hear that!" said Paula.

"Yeah. He is supposed to be working on integrating Gupta's C2B with *SwiftPad*. They've got Gupta too. I contacted Alison through the NAVSTAR system on the Denali we procured for her. One time, it's virtually untraceable, it was part of the "welcome to your new Denali" message. Anyway, Alison said my husband is OK, up to now anyway. She seemed to hint that – anyway, it seemed from talking to her that she thought Spence might be looking to avenge his kidnapping by ratfucking their operation. But she wasn't sure about that."

"I think she fucked him," said Nate, "and is covering for him." Maggie spun around and started to say something, but then seemed to change her mind. Paula smiled at her.

CHAPTER 15

ALISON MEETS ALDANE IN CAPE GIRARDEAU; ISHPEMING GETS INVOLVED

Early September

The Theory of the Mind had been overturned, apparently. Cadez was ready to win over the highly connected people with his telepathic implanting power that Gopee seemed to have perfected. Telly Haines had found Gupta's sister, and had hired Indian thugs to kidnap and hold her. So Gupta surrendered, promising to really upgrade his C2B interface.

"Real-Prez is a moron – Cadez knows that, believe me, he tells me that every day. We have to start shifting our line of attack, gotta get ready to go after him, and stay on him until he is down for good. We can dump him when his stock is at its peak so we can lock in our gains," Telly said.

Cadez had been slowly corralling the oligarchs and now had the keys to a number of business empires. All good shops to have as allies, with lots of off-the-books resources. Get the entities that will still be around at the end; fight it out in the final round.

But the real question – again – was what did it do to the Theory of the Mind? What is it that we perceive with C2B? And how is it different from doing the same thing with Fungus?

What is it – what is the mind when projected with a C2B-induced, hardwired invasion of its consciousness? Well one person who really knew was Alison Aykroyd. Alison knew, or at least had experienced it. After her experience of Gupta's demonstration, right in front of Spence – and his nightmare boss Maybelle – after losing control of her own thoughts to Gupta, things were never the same. She had been having horrible dreams, dreams she couldn't shake. Even though she was sure that Gupta had meant her no harm, she could not shake the persistent feeling that her mind could be invaded and controlled by something else. Every stray thought, every strange feeling was suddenly a potential harbinger of an invasion. Nothing helped. She had a feeling that it was getting worse every day. Sleep was elusive. Each day brought her closer to the realization that she had to do something to stop it.

From *The Fall of It All – A History of the Big Dump*

ALISON LAY PRONE IN THE MIDDLE OF HER CALI-

fornia King bed, on the third floor of the Cape Girardeau Marriott. Her orders were observe, report, and wait. She had spent the afternoon in a foul-smelling interrogation room watching the kid dance away from all the questions that really mattered. Alison truly admired Hank. Was it indeed Kip "Chubby" Rehain he had been working with? It sounded like it. None of the Missouri cops or lawyers had put it together. She stared at the ceiling, hungry, but resisting the minibar's $10 Toblerone stick of Swiss chocolate, or the $12 salted nuts. She glanced over at the clock. It was just after midnight. She had closed the lobby bar two hours ago and was still under the influence of the three Old Fashioneds she had drunk by herself while staring at her fone.

She had wanted to text Spence. But the C2B telepathic message from Gupta in Texas still bothered her, to say the least. She had reported it the best she could, but the nature of the experience was difficult to describe.

After the initial introduction to Spence and the team he worked with, led by Maybelline Johnson (see appendix for personal observations about the staff at the (NAME??) Plano Campus), I believe I was more prepared than most people for C2B neural transmissions. I experienced the internal "visuals" and accompanying emotional bombardment in earlier tests we have done in Portland at RDM, before the Insurgency. However – the experience of actual specific "internal dialog," of specific narration from Gupta, was beyond what I thought possible. Gupta is hiding this advance from the rest of his team at (NAME). There were still weaknesses to his syntax, verbs were weak and sometimes missing, but it was clear that those were truly only "technical details." It seemed as though Gupta was commenting using what seemed to be words, in English, directly with my right frontal lobe (I am left-handed). It is very seldom that I "think" in words. Sometimes I narrate my thoughts to myself if I am rehearsing what I intend to tell someone about something. It was like that, only "involuntary." Once it was over, it faded back into other thoughts, and I am sure I could not repeat the "message" word for word now. But it was something like this:

Alison [he made me think] – I am taking a chance speaking to you this way. I have made advances – this is direct access to your brain. Move your finger if you understand. Yes, I see. First I don't trust Spence. I am not even sure about you. He doesn't know I can do this. We both acted as if we were advancing the technology, seeking to be the first ones to achieve safe, reliable telepathic messaging. The political nature of our work is not discussed. No one here in Texas knows I have succeeded yet. But they will soon begin to discover it, as Spence's research is on the same path as mine, only a bit

behind. I am doing what I can to mislead and mis-
direct him, without arousing suspicions.
We must not allow Cadez to get natural
fungus. We must stop Real-Prez.

As a result of Gupta's telepathic message, I did not break my
cover with Spence. This was very difficult because we had worked
very closely before. If he really is working with us, I have no way of
knowing, because he did not break his cover with me.

But Alison left out any allusion to the hotel room doorway encounter, sudden embrace, and dash to her hotel room bed for furious sex with Spence. It had been a long time in the works, and she wasn't sure who moved first. If it was him, she went with it instantly, she knew that. There were no languid post-coital confessions afterward.

He did ask me why I was working with Cadez and I said it was
either him or Real-Prez and that Cadez was the lesser evil of the two,
especially since Rosie and Caroline seemed hopeless. He agreed, and
that was it, no winking or guilty hesitations from either of us. It is
possible that we were both lying, but most likely that only I was. But
Gupta's warning that he did not trust Spence was enough for me to
not reveal my true mission.

What was her true mission, she wondered. To support Rosie? Would she actually be allowed to take power? Caroline was still a basket case, yet standing at 40% of the Dees, only a little bit behind Rosie.

No chinks in the armor. Ishpeming's reach was expanding. That's me, she thought, accountable to no one, but dedicated to bringing down Real-Prez. She was taking orders, but until now it seemed technical. But more and more, she felt a will, an ego at work for the Ishpeming group. Their agents were everywhere, even down here. Look in the mirror, bitch! But still no leader, at least none she knew of. Rosie was a placeholder. Caroline wasn't even that, more of a cute knick-knack for the coffee table. Stop Real-Prez and figure it out later. Mensheviks to Bolsheviks. The worst people end up at the top of heaps created by aimlessness. She was getting in deeper and deeper and was wondering why.

A knock at her hotel door. She got up, peeked out, with the chain-latch still attached. A woman, about 30, wearing a red football jersey that made her look big. She seemed drunk and pulled her arm away from a man, who seemed to be whining, just out of sight. "I'm sorry, I must have the wrong room. I am looking for Margaret."

"I told you it was the wrong room," she heard the whiny man. "We are on the wrong floor, Cindy!"

Alison stared at her for five seconds, then reflexively remembered her code-phrase. "Maggie's not here."

The woman slipped her a book of matches through the crack. "My fault. Sorry to bother you," she said and left.

The matches were from a bar on King's Highway on the other side of Cape Girardeau – The Blue Lagoon. Her code word left a bad taste in her mouth. She was sure it was deliberate. It had been given to her on the way here from the St. Louis airport. Then told to use that name – Maggie – as a recognition code. Was she jealous? She could have been the one who went into Forest Park back in Portland instead of Maggie. Or Peggy, depending on who was talking to her. Was she responsible for fucking up Spence? Was it Spence's wife's fault for his weird behavior in Texas? Had he been pining for his wife? Was she jealous? Maggie made it out alive from the Insurgency. Did Spence know? Did he care? After Gupta invaded her mind, and Spence pretended that he had not sold out – and she pretended with him – her mind blanked in self-defense. She refused to rewind and watch it again; she just pushed it out. Gupta had proved that her mind wasn't her own anymore anyway, so what difference did it make?

She walked down to the garage, toward her rental, and opened the door with her remote key. Alison had rented a Chevy Malibu at the St. Louis airport's Amazon Car Rentals "Pick Your Own Car" lot. It was an inconspicuous everyday kind of car, which was the only criterion that mattered to her, but it was blowing smoke five miles away from the airport, as she was heading south on I-270. She got on the fone, and within fifteen minutes a tow truck and replacement arrived. They brought her a 2021 armored Denali SUV. It was a monster, 420-horsepower, bullet-proof, satellite linkup, heads-up display, cameras front and back, blinding spotlights, external speakers loud enough to break plate glass, and other features only found in drug cartel kingpin or Secret Service vehicles. The Amazon delivery people apologized for the Malibu, showed her the online manual on the video display on the dash, and left in spite of her muted protests.

She sat by the side of the road, looking at the myriad features of the SUV, when a woman with short dark hair, maybe between 35 and 50, popped up on the car's video screen.

"You OK? Like the ride?"

Alison looked at the screen. Maggie, Spence's wife, her old partner. They had killed two men together with Nate back in Couch Park during the Portland Insurgency. They last saw each other in Northwest Portland, when she was on her way up to Gordy's condo, while Maggie headed up to Forest Park on her bike to join the Insurgency. She stared at Maggie, who looked back with placid, languid, yet alert eyes, and a wan smile. A look of benign tolerance. "No, not really," she said.

"Read the manual. There is some other stuff in the car too. Sending you a list. Read and delete."

"A little ostentatious."

"You represent the candidate – the next President of the United States!" Her smile turned sardonic. "Don't worry, it won't show up on your expense report. If anybody asks, just tell 'em what happened. I mean that the shitmobile you first rented broke. Amazon rental threw you a bone."

"Yeah, but...

"I sure as hell don't know what to do with this Monster Truck you foisted on me."

"Just park it. You can walk to the Courthouse until you need it. Great report on Gupta's C2B progress. We are reviewing options, so stay focused. Get to know Cape Girardeau. So – how was Spence?"

The back of Alison's legs hurt from where she had them up around and over Spence's shoulders. "Until I need it?" It took her a few seconds to catch Maggie's drift.

"I don't know."

"Yeah. What did he say? How is he?"

"He's – fine. We – didn't talk at all about Portland."

"Nothing?"

"Cover," Alison said.

"Really? Are you sure?"

"No. No, I am not sure."

They looked at each other – digitally.

"Instructions to follow," said Maggie. "Good luck." She blinked off.

She had read the Denali manual while drinking at the hotel bar and found out she had a true armored car, big, fast, able to stop high-powered rifle shots, fire-resistant, self-healing tires, powerful incandescent spotlights. In addition there was a compartment under the seat and a key. It was labeled "personal protection kit." She put the key in her bag. "Until I need it?"

Her mission, as far as she knew, was to observe and report. She wasn't trained for anything like what this armored vehicle was suggesting. And now she was meeting some mystery man at a sleazy bar on the shitty side of town in Cape Girardeau, Missouri.

She arrived at the Blue Lagoon at three in the afternoon, and the air conditioning hit her like it was a refrigerated vault in a morgue; however, the faint odor of formaldehyde was overpowered by stale cigarette smoke, sweet, sweaty B.O., and urine. She slid her hospital mask on. A couple of drunks sat at the end, pointedly ignoring her and each other. She sat at the other end and ordered a Tom Collins. She played with her fone until the drink came, with an umbrella, and she gulped it and ordered another before the maskless barkeep with a rattlesnake tat across her bare chest could walk away.

After making the drink, the barkeep turned on the TV. The ARRGH National Convention was on, "live" from Disneyland. Actually it wasn't clear that anyone was in Disneyland, just remote shots of crowds lined up for rides from years past. She looked at Alison, who shrugged, put down the remote, and walked to the other end of the bar to closely ignore the two drunks.

The Convention was remote this year. The virus had moved fast, and scared the crap out of Real-Prez. The pundits were split as to whom the sudden change in format would favor.

The screen on FOX suddenly shifted to headshots, split twelve ways, three on top, four down. The upper right was reserved for the anchor (most of the time unless there was a compelling speaker – that didn't happen much). Real-Prez was middle top, sitting like a late Ottoman Turkish pasha, eating and ordering minions or otherwise sitting in his baggy suit, splay-legged, only paying attention when his name was mentioned. Temp-Prez sat behind to his side, and occasionally came into view.

Cadez was in the left top, and sat stone-faced through the proceedings.

The bottom nine boxes were the best though, rotating shots of the delegates in various stages of embarrassment. Whoever was running the control room was having a good time showing the famous and unknown alike flashing strange reaction shots. Since it was often timed with speeches, the results were hilarious. If someone was praising Cadez, five or six of the squares would be booing. Or sometimes picking their nose.

Cadez was actually leading in the delegate count, 31% to Real-Prez 29%. Although 21% were still pledged to Turdashian, he had dropped out – but was holding onto the votes to angle for a cabinet post. The rest were controlled by "superdelegates" – governors, senators, CEOs, and religious leaders, and it was generally understood that Real-Prez had a lock on them, so Cadez's chances were diminishing. Temp-Prez was still begging to stay on the ticket, playing the sniveling lapdog role he was assigned.

The TV showed it was all just a fucking game show. Alison nursed her second TC and scrolled her fone when a Black dude – between 30 and 50, a bit of a 'fro, nice smile, not muscular – showed up. He wore a long-sleeve blue shirt, green work pants, and like-new white Stan Smith Adidas tennis shoes. He ordered Jameson neat at the bar and retreated to the pool table. As he was racking the table, she looked over at him as he looked up at her.

"You play?"

She looked and saw he had racked up for 8-ball. She turned and sipped her drink. "Sure." She got up and grabbed a stick. "What's your name?"

"Dane."

"Dane?" Alison lifted an eyebrow and smiled.

"Yeah. As in Hamlet."

"Huh. OK. You break," she said.

"What are we playing for?" Dane gave her a quizzical look. He laughed and looked away when she stared him down.

A couple of white men came in wearing collared golf shirts and Dockers, laughing as if they had just shared a joke. The laughter stopped as they looked at Alison and Dane, and they gave each other a look and one of them seemed to whisper something because they laughed again as they sat at the bar.

Dane got down to one ball left and missed an easy shot.

Alison ran six in a row and left herself a tight kiss down the rail for the win, which she made with a behind-the-back shot. She walked to the cue rack, put up her stick and sat down at the booth. Dane sat across from her and they just stared at each other as they finished their drinks. Another couple came in and sat in the next booth.

"Let's go," she said.

Outside the sun and heat hit them like a blast furnace. "Take your car?"

"Where is yours?" she asked.

"I got dropped off."

They drove off in the Denali.

"I saw you play in Portland once. I mean with the Mane Shakers. You guys were really good."

"Yeah, we had our moments. You know Chubby?"

"Kip Rehain? Not really." Alison side-eyed him. "I've seen him around, but not in the last year. Wasn't he off on some kind of trip? It was him who did the bomb, right?"

Dane laughed. "We ain't supposed to be talkin' bout this. But yeah. He messed it up and then, as always, it worked out."

"How much does Hank really know?"

"I met him down in Memphis last month. He's hard to figure out, but he knows what is going on. How's he playing it?"

"Dumb," Alison said.

"Smart."

It was hot and there was not a cloud in the sky. They drove north, weaving back and forth, west, across the Interstate highway, then back under it again, heading northeast toward the river. The old two-lane blacktop passed between gently rolling hills, along stretches of rich bottomland. It was close to harvest time and the corn was high. They passed through little towns, Pocahontas, Appleton, headed toward Perryville. It was then that Alison noticed the signs that said North Kings Highway was really Highway 61.

"Highway 61," she mused.

"Ha!" Dane nodded his head in time to some internal rhythm. "Where God said something to Abraham about killing him a son!"

"Wow, we are really out there, out here, aren't we?"

"This is the edge, indeed!"

"It looks kind of idyllic though, if you didn't know where you were."

"Exactly where dis killin' to be done?"

Alison looked at Dane, trying to figure him out. She had seen him play once at a beer garden at PSU out along Park Street. Dane was the star of the Mane Shakers, even though he only played the vibes and marimba. Every eye (at least the eyes of all the women) was on him. "So, what's the plan, Dane, as in Hamlet?"

"Have you looked in the back of this big rental?"

"No – it looks locked with a digital key."

"I got the key too. We gonna light 'em up and get Hank out of jail."

"What?" Alison really wasn't that surprised, but to actually hear it was still a shock.

"Plan A. Grab him, fly him out."

"Where?"

"Not my problem. Definitely not yours. You have to keep your cover and stay out of it. Orders. Nothing personal. You just a delivery girl. But keep the ride until I need it. Then I'm gonna steal dis here rental from you. Maybe kidnap you, tie you up, leave you by the roadside, watched by rattlesnake eyes! Maybe muss up your clothes a little, for appearance sake, you understand. We'll see."

"Sounds easy. What's the escape route?"

"We on it."

They were quiet for a bit. Things were suddenly beginning to make sense to Alison.

"So you say you saw me play. You mean with Jean?" he asked.

"No, I never could get tickets to see her. I missed your last performance at the Moda Center."

"Didn't miss much," Dane said laconically.

"Yeah, sure," Alison remembered she had been stuck that night in poor dead Gordy's penthouse with Telly Haines's crew. "No, I saw you with the Mane Shakers."

"I miss those days," he said. "Seems so long ago."

"Where are we going?"

"Take a left, stay on this road. Head north," he said. They remained on King's Highway, Highway 61. "So, Hank. You think he'll hold up under pressure?"

"I can't tell. He's – so – you know he is – aware of –"

"Oh, he is aware, I just wonder how he is going to react when it goes down. I know him pretty good, but where he is now is a bit concerning. He's an outdoor guy – jail might be messin' with him. We had no time to test or train him."

"He's not breaking. Yet. I don't think anybody thinks he's playing them," Alison said. "They all think they know him." She didn't mention the Assistant DA was with them.

They continued to drive in silence. It was hot and there wasn't a cloud in the sky. They drove north, still weaving, west, then back toward the river, gradually straightened out and headed north between gently rolling hills, then along long stretches of rich farmland. They passed little towns, then came into Perryville, still driving on Highway 61.

Alison drove through Perryville in silence. The quiet air conditioning in the Denali kept them cool, but the pedestrians on the sidewalk in Perryville looked pained – 101 degrees in the shade. A woman in shorts carrying a baby crossed the highway in front of them as they stopped at the only light in town. She looked in at Alison and Dane and her face wrinkled up in what appeared to be anger, or maybe just discomfort.

"That baby needs to get out of the sun," said Alison.

Dane looked at the woman, and nodded. "Plan A," he said.

"How do we get him up here? Where do we take him?"

"Not our problem."

Alison looked at Dane and shook her head.

"Not yours, anyway. Nothing personal, but you aren't coming. You gotta maintain your cover. They didn't want me to even tell you this was going down, so you would be cool."

"Who's they?"

Dane shook his head. "No matter what, it will be dangerous, so I am telling you. They say you cool, so I am telling you. But you have to stay out, and if they're gonna shoot me or Hank right in front of you, you gotta cheer. You feel me?"

"You need a better plan than that."

"We'll have to tie you up or something. Maybe tear your clothes a little. Gag you. That will piss them off."

"Hmm," she said. Piss me off, she thought.

"You not liking Plan A?"

"I didn't say that. How would you tear my clothes?"

"I need to kidnap you and him, and dump you before we fly. White girl kidnapped by black man. You know the drill. Dump you alive, but – maybe we get 'em riled a bit, know what I am sayin'? If at all possible."

"Sounds easy," she said with only a tiny trace of sarcasm.

"Or, leave you out of it altogether and just take him."

"Or let me go with you."

"No," he said. He shook his head. "Definitely not. You are more important than Hank. Definitely more important than me."

"What's the escape route?"

"I told you, we on it! We close to the end. Up there – see the sign with the airplane on it. Turn there."

"So you are going to snatch him away from the best cops in Cape Girardeau, maybe a bunch of State cops too, somehow drive him 60 miles north on the most God-forsaken highway in the American songbook, and somehow get him into an airplane that is going to appear magically out of the sky on a desolate country airstrip?"

Dane didn't answer her.

They drove past green pastures, surrounded by well-tended, sturdy fences. It smelled sweet, horse shit sweet. Within a couple of miles, they came to a quaint bed and breakfast. Behind it were several barns. The sign said, "Ride on Inn."

Beyond that was the end of a runway. The road ran on across a flat field, toward a doublewide trailer painted bright red and a parking lot. There was nothing that could be called a control tower.

"Turn right there – let's drive down the treeline here. Check it out."

On the same day that Alison and Aldane were scoping out the little airstrip north of Cape Girardeau, Gary "Leone" Humpkin sat on a folding chair at the end of the pier behind his estate on the southern shore of Lake Superior. He heard footsteps, turned, and saw Adele, his wife, walking toward him. She was wearing a gray sweater, snug jeans, and big sunglasses. Gary waved to her listlessly. To his right, facing in opposite directions, two men stood, one with a long gun, the other watching him.

Gary lived outside the town of Ishpeming, but within the township of Ishpeming, on the empty windswept shoreline. It was an odd place for a "revolutionary outpost." Although Michigan's Upper Peninsula had gone "strongly" for Real-Prez in the last election, Ishpeming and nearby Marquette had voted overwhelmingly for Caroline's mother. Somewhat isolated, windy, rocky, and now, in early September, it was beginning to get cold, especially at night. In other years, the fall colors drew many tourists, but this year, with the virus, and the danger of political violence, the UP had very few tourists. Marquette and the surrounding area benefited from the movement's several hundred staffers, volunteers who had rented vacant homes and apartments through November.

Gary was embarrassed that his lakefront home was the center of the so-called Insurgency. He had totally plowed his life savings into the home, imagining a quiet retirement from his media personality livelihood: fishing, sailing, and mostly just sitting around with Adele. But the meeting at his home the previous January had taken hold of the nation's imagination. The Ishpeming Statement had been reaffirmed in many cities and towns. "Ishpeming" was a watchword nearly everywhere, and it told anyone listening where you stood and why. Some had died with it on their lips as lynch mobs hoisted them up.

"Hi, love," he said as she sat down. "How is she?"

"Awake. Eating."

"Hope he gets here soon," Gary said. "I need him to talk to her."

They heard a buzzing sound coming from out over the lake. Gary looked out toward the Keweenaw Peninsula and glimpsed a glint, a silver speck that appeared out of the blue. As the speck grew brighter and more distinct, the buzzing got louder. It was aimed right at Gary and Adele, who sat in folding chairs impassively watching.

Down, dropping down, then sliding across the water on skinny pontoons, a little two-seater Icon A10, the latest model of the lightweight low-altitude sport plane (with a range of nearly 800 miles), settled on the water. Gary stood up. The pilot turned off the engine and slowly coasted up to the pier. The canopy opened and Nathan Schuette stepped out onto the wing, and then up to the dock. Wearing shorts and a long t-shirt, and a hospital mask, he was lugging a small bag, but was otherwise unencumbered.

Gary and Adele quickly put their masks on as Nathan approached. Nate and "Leone" (Gary's nickname at school for reasons lost to both of them) stared at each other with faux-cold stares.

"Adele!" Nate looked at her and she came and gave him an elbow bump.

"Wish I could hug you. Long trip?"

"Just overnight, Amtrak to Minneapolis. Had a sleeper. Tony picked me up and we took off in his little bug there."

"Tony," Gary yelled. "Want to come up and have some lunch?"

Tony flashed a big smile and shook his head back and forth. "I'm staying in Marquette. Be back tomorrow, right?"

"Yeah," yelled Nate.

Tony restarted his engine and slowly brought it around and headed out to open water. He was soon in the air, headed east toward Marquette.

"Leone, it's good to see you," Nate said as they faked a high five. "You've lost weight! You getting back on air doing the Sunday shows? Maybe run for something?"

"No!"

Nate was taken aback at Leone's vehemence. He really had only been joking.

They three of them headed back up to the house.

"Are you hungry, Nathan?" Adele asked.

"A sandwich would be nice."

They came up the bank and slid the door open to the walkway between the kitchen and the living room. Five others were there, grabbing a snack. An older man was busy taking orders and working on various nibbles and noshes. Two of the people fetching food for themselves had big automatics strapped to their hips, while the other three looked like Ivy League campaign staffers: young, good looking, and well dressed. Leone just went ahead and grabbed bread and some sliced ham wrapped in butcher's paper. Condiments were spread all over the counters.

They took their sandwiches into the living room, where Nate recognized a couple of people from the political news reports but the room was mostly filled with people like those in the kitchen. Everyone had a hospital mask, and nobody crowded anyone.

Nathan had been here at the original Ishpeming Meeting, eight months ago, when they issued the Ishpeming Statement.

The now famous document had been hammered out in this room. Other than Leone, none of those original attendees were here.

Nate ate his ham sandwich and watched Leone work the room. Leone had an ability to turn on some kind of public charm that revealed a completely different person than the one that Nate had known off and on for the last fifty years. The "real" Leone was shy, taciturn, seemingly easy to bully or persuade. But he wasn't like that with others. His personality was almost completely elastic; it could bend in any way depending on the audience, yet he never seemed to lose his balance. Of all his friends, he had been the most successful. He made money, everyone thought he was great, and he had a beautiful, talented and famous wife – the organist for the Jean Katon Express.

Before though, through the '80's, '90s, and through the Mesopotamian Wars, Gary Humpkin had been the unofficial spokesman for the nation. Crooks and sleazeballs came and went through the White House and Congress, but Gary's voice and powerful editorials remained. His articles, and later his appearances on TV at critical times during the last forty or so years, occurred at "turning points," and to many, he had been the person who directed the "turning." He always had an instinct (which went back to his college days) for exactly when the popular tide was about to flood an issue to the top, and he always put the "finishing spin" on it.

His most recent rants had been about tariffs, of all things. He had never particularly cared about trade economics before, at least not until Real-Prez made them a point of national honor, and claimed that money collected came from the other countries rather than Americans who bought the products. That kind of ignorance, combined with dishonesty, enraged Gary. He railed against Real-Prez's rationale, if you could even call it that, and carried on fascinating discussions on international trade theory that economists praised, but few actually understood. Lately he had been pushed aside somewhat as newer and younger faces had taken his place on the national opinion stage.

But ratings inevitably spiked whenever he was a guest. His articles, now down to about one a month, were widely read, and vigorously commented on. Gary's "aw-shucks modesty" is what endeared him to nearly everyone. Although most cynical commentators thought his shy act was put on, in Nathan's opinion, even if it was an "act" that he could turn on and off at will, it was the most genuine part of Gary – of Leone.

In college Leone had been his rival in nearly all things, as well as his drinking buddy. Nate had always thought that Leone looked up to him, but that might have been all part of his act too. During senior year, they had shared a girlfriend, or had been mutually shared by a woman, depending on how you looked at such things. A part of their friendship, the part that included the total trust they had in each other (as well as the woman), was lost after that.

"You should never have retired, Leone."

"Finish your sandwich? Want anything else?"

"No, it was good."

"Come on," Leone said. "Let's talk. Follow me."

They walked out, then down the hallway toward the office and the bedrooms. The second bedroom door was closed. Gary knocked.

A woman in full quarantine gear, PPE from head to toe, answered. Behind her was a sealed-off plastic barrier separating them from the inside. She took off her plastic shield, and pulled her mask down.

"It's alright. We have finished running the infectiousness tests. She is no longer transmissible. I am quite certain you are in no danger of being infected by her. I think, for her mental well-being anyway – it actually will be better if you take your masks off. I will be right in the next room."

The doctor had set up the large bathroom as a lab, and she went in there.

Sitting up in the hospital bed, Rose Silverman was sipping

through a straw from a plastic bottle. She was not wearing her trademarked big dark glasses, but still she recognized Gary right away and smiled, and lifted her water bottle.

Gary and Nate pulled up chairs and sat next to her.

"I don't remember any of it, but my daughter over there says I am a raving lunatic. I have to drop out, Gary."

Nate looked over in the corner and saw a woman of about 40, with bloodshot eyes and tangled dark hair, who merely nodded to him. Gary looked over, smiled and waved. "Hi, Rachael," he said.

"Who's this?"

"Oh, sorry, Rosie." Gary said. "This is Nathan Schuette."

"Oh! The writer. Nice to meet you. Sorry for my somewhat disheveled appearance."

"Mrs. Silverman, I am deeply honored. I am so sorry to disturb you like this. I hope you are –"

"Stop babbling! I am sick. I am finished, and I know it. So, while I am not a 'raving lunatic' NOW, tell me – how are we going to fix this, Gary? Are you bringing in this guy to write something? I thought you could handle that?"

"I don't know yet, Rosie. We are hoping you will recover."

Rachael over in the corner let out an audible gasp that sounded disgusted, angry and discouraged, all at once.

"Well, maybe I will try again in four years. Or maybe I'll run for the senate. But the doctor told me the score: I am off the field for a while, at least."

"Mrs. Silverman, you have changed the country, no matter what. No one is going to forget what you have done. You have made the idea of government palatable again. You have revitalized political discussion. You are a great woman. We just have to find someone worthy of you, but it's not easy," said Nate.

"Where did you get this guy, Gary? I'm beginning to like him."

"That's because you don't know him."

Nathan shrugged his shoulders, acknowledging that it was probably true.

"You are from Oregon, right?"

"Well, not originally, but yeah."

"Yeah," said Rosie, mocking his accent. "I can hear it. Jersey, right?"

Nate nodded.

"Well, this is a fine fix I've got us in. Is Caroline here?"

"She's coming."

Rosie shook her head.

"Five more minutes," said the doctor from the bathroom. Nate looked closer and saw she had a little computer terminal set up to the side.

"She insisted on setting up there because I had so many 'hush hush' talks with people like you. Lydia, I told you I have no secrets from you!"

"Rose, I can see your heart from here. Just take it easy, ok?"

"Nathan," Rosie said. "That's a nice name. You're not Jewish, are you?"

"No," he said.

Rosie waited for him to continue.

"Actually, I was named after Nathan Bedford Forrest."

"You mean the schmuck who founded the Ku Klux Klan?"

Nate looked away. "Yeah. Him. He was a pretty good general, they say. Never lost a battle."

"Well, that's comforting, anyway." Rosie rolled her eyes, vaudeville style.

Gary was just rising to leave when Rosie groaned.

"Oh, Lydia." Rosie's face went almost gray at that point.

Her doctor was already standing over them. "You have to leave now. Remember, put on your masks, and keep distant from everyone as much as possible. Wash your hands. We have a lot of new people around. This is probably the safest room in this house."

Nate looked over at Rachael as they walked out. She had her eyes closed and seemed to be praying.

Gary led Nate to his office and they sat down. Gary poured them both a couple of neat fingers of scotch without asking.

"Leone, how long has she had the virus?"

"I don't know. A month maybe. She wasn't symptomatic until about ten days ago. Her daughter brought her here for some reason."

"What do you mean some reason? We are two months away from the most important presidential election – ever – and she is out. How have you kept it secret?"

"Bullshit press releases, we have a double – that is standard procedure for all campaigns – and in long shots you really can't tell them apart. But of course the story is getting too thin. There are already lots of rumors about her."

"What did she mean, 'raving lunatic'?"

"Well she is OK – usually by late morning. Stays up and is her old self for two, sometimes as much as four hours at a time. But then she slips into delirium."

"Does she lose consciousness?"

"Consciousness? That's a good question, actually. But you need to define your terms."

Nate knitted his brow. "Well, you know – the usual kind. Where you are self-aware and can remember what happened?"

"Oh, she remembers. Just not when she quote wakes up unquote. But later, in her 'delirium,' she remembers."

"Will she live?"

"Maybe – 50-50. Maybe worse than that considering her age."

"If she lives, will she recover?"

"Again – some do, some don't. But never very quickly. She is done, regardless, for this election."

"So me saying I am named after the founder of the Ku Klux Klan didn't send her over the edge?"

"No, Nate. This is how she is, or has been since last week at least."

"Fuck," said Nate. "This is like finding Santa's body stuck in the chimney in summertime."

"I never believed in Santa Claus," said Leone.

"Is – Caroline really coming?"

"Her people said she was. But I'm not sure. She's not answering text messages. Maybe she will join us by *SwiftPad* Meet."

"*SwiftPad* Meet?"

"It's like Zoom, but private and secure. I think they just rolled it out. With this virus – I mean…"

"You are a fucking beta tester. What are you going to do?"

"I don't know, Nate."

"Ya know, Leone, I was in the San Francisco Airport in the '70s sometime, probably holding, and undoubtedly hoping I could get a lid of shitty Mexican onto the plane so I could actually know – I mean so I could be sure – that I could get stoned right after I landed. That was my main concern at the time. I have no idea where I was actually headed but that is not the point. The point is while I was rushing from the street – remember back then it was a – nobody gave a fuck what you were taking onto the plane. No fucking lines to let some perv run his hands over your butt looking for a bomb. So I was hurrying to my gate, and I am not shitting you – this really happened! I ran straight into, smack dab against, like right up on him, two inches from his face – Joe Fucking DiMaggio! I ran smack into him chest to chest in the middle of the old SFO. He was just as much at fault as I was. He wasn't looking where he was going either. Mid-'70s mind you – he's like 60. It was like hitting a fucking brick wall. Bang! No give at all! He was stacked!

"Anyway – I was wondering – you know – since he left the scene – you know – where is he? Where did he go? Shit, we all have to go. I mean you know – nothing lasts forever. We only have so much time, and we have to do it during our time. It's a tiny window, Leone, because – in reality most people – most people never…"

"What the fuck are you talking about?" Leone shook his head.

"I am just saying, the country really needed him…and he left. When everyone was looking for something."

"Life isn't a Simon and Garfunkel song, Nate. No! Listen – look, Nate, I brought you here because, you know, I have always looked up to you. And – I have always listened to you. I need you to set me right. I don't have a lot of people who I trust. Outside of Adele."

"You have never listened to me."

Gary looked at Nate for a beat, then away, clenching his jaw. "You heard about what happened in Cape Girardeau?"

"Yeah," Nate said.

"Do you really know?"

"Kip Rehain blew up the men who shot down Hassan Coleman's plane."

"Right. Most people think it was something to do with Dash Sketerson's funeral, which happened a couple of days before," said Leone. He held up the scotch bottle and refilled both glasses. "But that was just because the assassins were stupid enough to be seen there, and that is how we found them."

"Memphis told us that."

"Right. Well, we have a problem. We recruited a local guy there and he helped Kip escape. He got caught, and we have it on good authority that they will hang him – publicly, the first public execution in the United States since – shit, I don't know when. It will be a big hit. Real-Prez is planning on attending."

"We can't let that happen."

"Excellent. Good, we just have to figure out how to not let it happen." Leone smiled. "Not everybody thinks we should try and rescue him. I do, and now I know I'm right. See? I do listen to you."

"You just want me to confirm what you already think."

"You like that scotch? Let's go meet the crew." They finished their drinks and walked back toward the living room. As they passed Rosie's room they heard a high-pitched outburst that sounded feral, or maybe what angry cursing would sound like in an extraterrestrial language.

〜〜

About 15 people were sitting and standing around a large video screen positioned in front of the big fireplace. Adele was sitting on the couch near the front, and Gary sat next to her. Nate stayed toward the back. On the screen, the upper three squares were occupied by Caroline, Alice, and the Speaker of the House. The people on the TV screen were the only ones not wearing masks as protection against the virus.

"Madam Speaker, it is your call."

"It's not my call! There has been an election. Primary elections. If Rosie can't run, then we run the next candidate. Next person up. That is how it should be done."

She should be here, Nate thought. Chicago is a short flight. But everybody is scared, with good reason.

"I've been around politics my whole life. I was born in a governor's mansion and raised in the White House," said Caroline. "I've seen what it does. I thought I could do it but I was wrong. I got out for a reason. I can't do it." She sniffed back a tear. "Are you sure Rosie can't do it?"

"Caroline, I don't understand. Why did you run in the first place? Didn't you think about this then?" asked the Speaker.

Of course everyone knew why. Her mother told her she had to. Her father got teary-eyed and asked her to. Everyone in the country watched that poor girl grow up and have to live the daily drama in her father's White House. And anyway, they had a whole campaign team all cocked and loaded for her. If she didn't run, it would all be for nothing.

"I never thought anyone would vote for me!"

Gary spoke up quickly and loudly. "What about your duty to the country?"

Caroline's sobs grew louder.

"Caroline, you need to step up," said Senator (and General) Harvey Grennell.

"No! You do it, Harvey! You are the perfect person, a military man who saved us from becoming a military dictatorship. Senator Grennell, you have to do it."

"Half the country thinks I am a war criminal. They have footage of the firing squads I ordered. I don't think I am a good candidate. Caroline, you got almost as many primary votes as Rosie. How can you back out now?"

"No!"

"You are leaving us at the altar."

"Well, thank you for reminding me of that!" The room went stone silent. "It was better that than a disastrous marriage. A marriage of convenience! I know something about that! I am not being talked into anything anymore. By anyone! Goodbye!"

Her square in the screen went blank.

"Fuck me," said Grennell.

"OK," said the Speaker, who was currently third in line of succession. "Well, Gary."

"Yes, Madam Speaker."

There was an awkward silence.

"You have some technical things to discuss, I understand," the Speaker said finally. "I am dropping off, have a lot of calls to make. I'll be in touch. We need to make an announcement – tomorrow morning. I think we can combine the sad news about Rosie along with Caroline's sudden unavailability. I will reach out to Caroline one more time and encourage her to make her own announcement of withdrawal. She owes us that at least."

"We could talk to her mother," said Senator McCarron.

"No, I'll handle it. Rosie is more important."

"We could maybe get a bedside announcement from her. When she is – awake."

"No it's too complicated. People don't understand this disease yet. They will think she is – anyway, we do this early tomorrow." The Speaker dropped off.

They moved on to the plan to snatch Hank. Nate watched Gary sitting on the couch, saying nothing through the staff presentation of the options. Nate had no doubt that Leone would make a grab at the ring. He had been preparing for it his whole life. Nate knew he was just lying back, knowing a premature lunge at the prize would lose it. He was pretty sure his college roommate was going to be the next President.

The screen now hosted some people he didn't know, along with Alice and an enlarged map of the middle Mississippi between Memphis and St. Louis.

"What if we fail?" asked Alice. "What if we can't get him into the car at the courthouse?"

"We have three people assigned to the snatch. One is a uniformed officer, who lost his brother to a lynching in Alabama. The other is the Assistant DA. They are in reserve. If it goes south, they are pledged to start shooting. If it is going so bad there is no hope of getting away, the Assistant DA will kill Hank. That of course is worst case. But we think with surprise, which we believe we can deliver, no one will resist. We know what their plan is perfectly. The Assistant DA has been in all of their meetings. How many they have, who, when. We are pretty sure none will be willing to die. It is going down in a parking garage. We can control the environment," Grennell explained.

"So we are willing to sacrifice a sitting DA for this?" asked McCarron.

"Assistant DA. Yes. More to the point, he is willing to do it. But it is very unlikely he will have to. If he fails, he knows we will remember. If he succeeds, we think we can get him out.

"So they get Hank into the Denali, head toward the bridge,

where they stop here – and pretend to do a swap. Then the two cars go in different directions. If they see it, they will have to follow both. If they don't, they go after the Denali. It doesn't matter, because neither will have Hank in it.

"So far, if the plan holds, and nobody is dead, then Hank and his handler, who he knows, Aldane, will have him. It's a short walk to the beach and they will get on the *Bat Masterson*, the fastest cigarette boat on the Mississippi. They board here," Grennell pointed at the map.

"That spot is exactly," said Tiara Mason-Feldman, "where Hank picked up Kip."

"Yep."

"Isn't that a little obvious?"

"Yep," Grennell answered once again, with a loud, proud voice. He smiled and looked around. People were nodding.

"Then the *Bat Masterson* makes a run upriver – maybe 60 miles, just south of Kaskaskia. Here. Our other operative picks them up with an Audi – here – and then makes a run to the airport. Then we have a Lear in a low holding pattern over here, comes in and lands on this airstrip. The team – Aldane, the other operative, and Hank – run over to the plane and board. Then it takes off."

"I see so many problems," said Gary. "We could end up with no Hank and everyone else dead."

No one said anything.

"Anything else, Harvey," asked Gary.

"Yes, there is something else," Grennell said. "It's you, Gary. You have to step up and be the candidate. The Speaker is polling the virtual convention delegates now. She just texted me. It is going to be you."

Gary looked around at Nate. Nate nodded and mouthed the word "yes."

"Let's uh," said Gary Humpkin, candidate for President,

"let's hope – hope and pray – they get Hank Ford out of Cape Girardeau safely."

Nate breathed a sigh of relief.

Alison continued driving down the dirt road along the treeline just off the end of the airstrip. Aldane was reading off his fone. About half a mile in they came to a little clearing and pulled in. Alison parked under a tree and turned off the Denali. They got out and walked back a little. A large oak had fallen near the path they were on, and they both sat down. It was shady and cool, and Alison noticed a grassy patch behind the log.

"Looks like we do it tomorrow."

"Really? Me too?"

"Yeah. It's nuts. We will come up the river in the *Bat Masterson* – it's a fast boat. They are bringing it up tonight, along with another one filled with a full tank of nitro fuel. This boat can go almost 100 miles an hour. We get Hank in the courthouse parking garage – with this monster truck. Pretend to switch him off to another car in case we are seen – then up the river. You pick me up, John is picking up an Audi in Carbondale tonight. Once we get past that point, we need to drive across that field, and meet the plane. It will all be about timing. If we are followed, our team can cover. This is a perfect place to block any cars following."

"What about the other side – over there?"

"That's Kaskaskia – it's in Illinois."

"It's on this side of the river!"

Dane laughed and shook his head. "Yes – but it's still Illinois."

Alison shook her head.

"It's on this side of the river, but it's Illinois. About some long-ago flood, I suppose. But it's a different jurisdiction. Not a big deal, but maybe enough delay to matter."

"So from the Cape up to the Kaskaskia airstrip is about 60 miles."

"Right – 45–50 minutes in the boat."

"You pick him up off the beach near town, like they said. And you are dropping him off here – with you?"

"Yes," said Aldane, suddenly looking concerned.

"What if they see the boat and follow you by chopper?"

"They only have only one nearby. We are spiking the motor."

Alison nodded and looked carefully at the chart.

"Why not just go part of the way to the airstrip. Pick him up – here? Not as close to the airstrip."

Aldane slowly shook his head. "We could have two cars take off from there in different directions. One could head for the freeway."

"Right! Not as close to the airstrip, but this depends on stealth, not speed and firepower. Less time on the river, less chance of being seen."

Dane thought briefly, then started texting. They sat there for a while.

"Yeah," said Dane. "They like that. Maybe throw them off the airstrip. Think we are heading up 61 to St. Louis."

"You want to have sex with me, Dane? I think it might clear your head."

He smiled, sat up, and put his arm around her. He looked at her and she kissed him. After a while, they both fell back into the grass.

CHAPTER 16
ESCAPE ON HIGHWAY 61

Early September

Latest polls put Rosie Silverman in the mid-forties. A few reports noted it was odd that she was not doing more media events to take advantage of her lead. But then Real-Prez and Cadez, who were almost tied, both in the high twenties, had announced an alliance. The photo of them shaking hands dominated the news cycle. They were all smiles, announcing a "United Front" against socialism, with a promise to come out of the Convention "very strongly" in the Real-Prez's words. The ARRGH Convention at Disney-land was just getting under way.

From *The Fall of It All – A History of the Big Dump*

ALDANE LOOKED AROUND. THE SIRENS WERE GET-ting closer. He looked up and the Lear was on its final approach. They had to start running in the next minute if they were going to get to the plane and get on it. Hank, squatting behind Dane, was shaking his head, but had already been told to shut up about this not being worth it. There was no way out now. The two patrol cars were headed for the taxiway and that was a short hop to the middle of the runway. This was it, their ruse had worked, but time was up and now it was a sprint to get on the plane before the cops could stop it. But they had too much runway to cover. It was a little too late.

Alison's real mission had been to get him out, spring him, or silence him, because she knew that Hank knew too much. It was about a propaganda coup too, and no one knew its importance more than she did. After all, she (and Spence, who somehow had lost his way) had been first-line associates at *Reigny Deigh Media*.

No one had told her exactly what her mission was down here. She was to define her mission as she saw it; she had operational freedom to make whatever call in the field she thought would best serve the movement, whatever that was. Was she more valuable than Hank? Of course she was! She was on the inside of the Cadez campaign. Why was she anywhere near here? She had no business getting near physical danger, and getting her hands dirty, much less bloody.

On the other hand...just before she left Dallas, she had been to a shooting range with an old man with droopy eyelids, and had practiced for hours. So it was clearly understood, by her handlers and herself, that something like this was a contingency.

Alison was afraid that Rosie just couldn't match Real-Prez's sick charisma. But if Real-Prez faltered, Cadez was even more likely to beat her in a head-to-head match. Alison had a plan, a – vision of taking them both down in one move, but now she had to clear that out of her head. Not her problem, as Aldane said.

No – we had to get Hank out.

"You can still get out," said Dane. "Run toward them crying, say I raped you, they will believe you. Go now!"

"Yeah, good idea." She smiled at Dane. "Raped?" They both laughed. Even Hank smiled, although he had no idea at what.

"OK," she said. She smiled and tore her blouse open, exposing her blue bra.

Both Dane and Hank looked stunned and even a little embarrassed. She answered to no one now, but was out beyond the buoys, where, sink or swim, few would ever know who she was or what she was doing. She could have disappeared and no one would know. No, she was with Dane now.

She took a deep breath – the time had come. She turned and saw the Lear touch down. She checked her Beretta 9 one more time. Fifteen shots. She could handle this gun, she was confident.

Dane was going to get Hank out, and she was going to give him time to do it. Now was the time. She just wished she had a successor, someone who knew what she knew. Something was up, a deal perhaps, maybe even Cadez agreeing to be VP. Everyone knew that the former Temp-Prez, now Veep-Toast, as he was jokingly called, was on his way out as Real-Prez's running mate.

She missed riding her bike to work in Portland, drinking beer and hanging out with Spence, and even the work, which had been challenging in a fun way. She missed the Oregon rain. Life didn't need to be like it had become. She had been hoping to convince RedHats to just chill. Step back from this entrance to hell we are in, using Cadez. Surely a holy mission. But – maybe societies have to go through this every couple hundred years just to be reminded how bad it is. We need a warrior now, she thought. She thought about all the basketball games she had won in the last minute. This was to be her finest run.

She was not a killer, but right now, that looked like her best chance: just wait for the opportunity and kill them all – just keep shooting until they were all down.

"I can give us time," she said. Dane was squatting behind the Denali and Hank was behind him. "They will recognize me. You can get him across the field. I'll stop that first car. They will let me approach."

She was thinking about this, and how she was giving it all

up, giving up a chance to change history by being on the bridge instead of down here in the bilges. All this passed through her mind in a matter of a few seconds. She tore her blouse further, from the shoulder down to her ribs, exposing the left side of her bra and her skin. The cop car had just turned onto the access road. It would be on top of them in the next 30 seconds.

Dane peeked over the hood at the fast-approaching car. If the patrol car made it to the runway, it was over.

"Who knows, maybe I'll get them all and we can all fly back together."

With her Beretta tucked snugly behind her in her jeans and her blue bra exposed to the world, she ran out across the taxiway waving and screaming. The first cop car slowed, then stopped. One of the cops got out and yelled "Wait" to either her or to his partner, drew his gun, and ordered her on the ground, but she ignored him and kept running, somehow knowing they wouldn't shoot a white woman in torn clothes who was running from Black men. When she got close enough, she pulled out her gun and shot the two cops while running at them, then kept going toward the second car and somehow shot the cop on the passenger side through the windshield, and then was hit. But she hardly felt it, kept running and somehow wounded the driver before falling. The third patrol car was just skidding into the parking lot and was fast approaching the runway.

Hank and Dane began running across the tarmac as soon as Alison exposed herself. The plane's door opened and Dane pulled Hank in front of himself and pushed him up as the crew on the plane pulled him into the fuselage. As he had one foot on the edge of the entrance, a bullet exploded Dane's head, and he fell. With only a few seconds of sad hesitation, the plane started taxiing away and just made it barely off the ground at the end of the runway, then rose agonizingly slowly and steeply, just over the trees that lined the Mississippi River. The plane climbed away, soaring into the beautiful late summer sunshine.

CHAPTER 17

THE ELECTION BECOMES MORE – OR MAYBE LESS – COMPLICATED

Mid-September

Because elections are held in early November, American politics has always been full of October surprises. Introduction of changes in "the state of play" a month before the votes were to be cast was a standard part of every election mechanic's toolbox. In 2020, partly because of fears about the virus, the October surprises started early.

Traditionally the surprise could be a mistress coming forward; a "Peace Deal" with an intractable enemy might suddenly be announced; bribes might be paid to foreign countries to keep peace deals from happening; indictments for previously unknown crimes might be filed; evidence of ignored evidence might be discovered; old soldiers might have suddenly clear recollections of decades-old cowardice or heroism; shady audio-video showing a "compromised" opponent could be promoted; announcements that "charges were being dropped" where no charges had previously existed – all standard stuff, meant to cause a shakeup in confidence in the process, or in the character of your opponent.

But this election was different. The virus played a role, as did the unhinged behavior of the Incumbent, along with the shaky shifts in political orientation by the challenging party. Continuity was gone, and the electorate was ripe for manipulation.

From *The Fall of It All – A History of the Big Dump*

"*M*R. PRESIDENT, DO YOU HAVE ANY *comment on the recent withdrawal from the race by the two leading Dee candidates for your job on the same day?*"

"Well, there should be an investigation. Can you imagine what they would be saying if we did something like that? The two winners, the two who won forced out, driven out, who knows what they are doing? And this – guy – I don't even know him – Larry – Harry – what's his name...Gary. Gary Humpkin? Who has even heard of him? He wasn't elected to anything but now he is running for President? Obviously this is political, a purely political hoax. They knew Rosie couldn't beat me. I like Caroline, but I feel sorry for her. But at least she ran in the primaries. People are saying it's a coup. Some kind of coup. You know this is all being controlled, because they are all puppets. They knew neither of those women could beat me. Rosie, the Frog, I call her the frog, because she is from the swamp. All corrupt. She knew she could not win so she caught a convenient cold. Well, I wish her a speedy recovery. I am going to miss her, because beating her would have been fun. So much fun."

"*Mr. President, Gary Humpkin called on you to stop pandering to and encouraging local militias that have taken over local governments in many places, and that have not prevented a number of extrajudicial murders...*"

"Well, he has a number of problems, as I am sure you know. First of all his wife is a citizen of a foreign country. You know that, right? I think somebody should look into that."

"*Mr. President, there was recently a heart-wrenching interview with*

Rachael Silverman where she describes how the virus has affected her mother. She released a short video showing the former union leader's endorsement of Humpkin. Do you…"

"That video was a total disgrace. People are saying that Rosie was drugged and being held against her will. I don't know – is it all faked? You should do your jobs. This is a disgrace! Why? Because they know I was going to clean her clock. It's all fake. Same with poor Caroline. I know Caroline, she is a – or was – a friend of my daughter, until these nasty people took over the Dees. It's a total coup, and the American people won't stand for it."

"Mr. President…"

"I'll tell you something else. After this election we are going to clean this up. It is going to be clean like you have never seen. These corrupt cities are going to change. I promise, the chaos is going to stop. You are not going to believe what we will do in Portland. You won't believe it. Six more weeks, and it's over."

～～～

The only journalist to get both Osama bin Laden *and* John Gotti on record, intrepid journalist Jim Barry sat down with Gary Humpkin to talk about the sudden change in the election landscape.

"Mr. Humpkin, thanks for talking with us. You heard the President recently disparaging your candidacy. Do you have any comments?"

"The Federal Election Commission approved the process. We are going through with the election, one way or another, in a few weeks. The virtual convention delegates were duly elected in the primaries and they voted. I admit I was reluctant, but now I am not. Rosie went down, and she is sick, although we know she is going to get better. But the calendar rules. We need an alternative to what we have. I am embracing this. It is a duty and I will do my best to win and try and put the country back together."

"Only a few months ago this virus was not even acknowledged as a

serious threat. Now it has disabled a major candidate for office. How will you deal with it if elected?"

"It is the greatest threat we face as a species. A post-virus landscape might be one none of us recognize. We have to prepare for it. Look, I don't have a crystal ball. I don't know what is going to happen, much less what we are going to do about it. But I know this. The only – the only thing that matters is people. Human beings need an environment to live and thrive in. I am not promising I can fix this quickly. This is going to be a long and sometimes discouraging struggle. In the end, we are all just hanging on. We are going to focus totally on saving people. I recognize no group other than people, human beings. It is that simple once we set ourselves to understanding all the old rules of 'constituencies' are over, that 'blocs' that are controlling things rather than people – we are not going to recognize them anymore. I know that sounds like old-style Communism, and that speaking for the 'people' has often been a cover for dictatorships. I promise, that is not what I mean. You know my commitment to democracy. I have spent my life talking about it, and that is not going to change at this late stage of my life.

"We have to think. The only thing we have going for ourselves is our ability to think, to understand, to communicate with each other in many ways. But then – to act. How do we put our ideas into action that is humane yet effective? I have been around for a long time. I have never held office. But I have a paper trail longer than the lifetime of most people living. Fixing this is going to take sacrifice. I promise I will do everything I can to make sure this sacrifice will not fall disproportionately on those who have already suffered disproportionately. We might need to dismantle some institutions, and do things differently. We have a democracy that allows all voices an opportunity to be heard. And argue. I am good at that, if nothing else. But I promise, we will do more than argue."

"So you are not committing to any of the reforms that Mrs. Silverman was advocating?"

"I think we need to be careful about projecting too far ahead. We were surprised when the current... we were surprised four years ago by the results of that election. We were surprised by the pandemic. There will likely be more surprises coming. We need to take it slow, to think. To me, that means we follow the science and learn how to live in this new world we that we now live in. The virus – so far – almost seems like an entity with its own plans. The research into its behavior and how it affects its victims is – well, it will likely overturn many ideas we have about nature, and the universe. We can't reject these findings because they are scary. It is all bigger than us. This world which we used to think was so awesome and large...is really tiny and could disappear in an instant. We have to learn and to commit to keep learning. We are going to make research – real research and science – relevant again. We need to understand, to plan and understand this disease's strengths and weaknesses and come to terms with them. This will not be the last microscopic enemy we face, and probably won't be the most threatening. We need to save ourselves, all of us. We will share the burdens and benefits of the future together. But every child, any child, everywhere is our child."

CHAPTER 18

ERICK DUKE, MERCENARY, MEETS HIS TROOPS IN NEWPORT, OREGON

Early October

Erick Duke's father, Parnell, had made a fortune in direct marketing. When Erick was born, his family lived in a single-story, three-bedroom red brick house in St. Louis. Parnell was an Army helicopter mechanic, but he left the service under a cloud after the failed Iranian hostage rescue during the Carter years. Erick was only an infant then. Parnell joined the first Pentecostal Fellowship Council and started a multi-tiered direct marketing company called NewLife with a partner who later died under mysterious circumstances. NewLife sold ammunition, handgun components, and various other combat paraphernalia. It also sold women's make-up and "survivalist feminine hygiene" products plus self-help books (*How to NOT be a Homosexual, Clean and Sexy Makeovers, The Psychiatry Cult, Jesus in 30 Days*, etc.).

It took almost eight months for Parnell to cull through all of his potential business partners, who were promoted as an exclusive group, and he was very public in his sermons at his growing church about the need to be very selective (as well as the sacredness of the number 12). He sold the lifestyle to the associates. He made them feel special and exclusive. It was the lifestyle of the committed evangelical. Lots of meetings, deep regret about nothing, deep amnesia about the really bad shit. But that was just theatrics, the "small talk" before the short strokes. Parnell instinctively knew he needed to convince them to be "slaves" (to the spirit of Jesus), and make them believe their business served a higher cause. For the first six months they war-gamed their plans. They were to burn through family, grade school buddies, buddies' parents, plus anyone else they could guilt into paying 5–10 times more than they would pay at Target, or Cabela's or even online for stuff they didn't need.

Maybe 1 out of 20 people had the willpower to go outside their own "circle" and find strangers to buy the shit. They had to be determined not to end up with boxes of the shit in their garage. That's the trick. Find those people, the 1 out of 20. Parnell taught them to be their own cult leader. They had to be as careful in finding their first "12" as Parnell had been. Once they learn the trick of lying, the rest is easy; there are an unlimited number of suckers out there. Those people who shamelessly promote the shit are your "bottom bitches." You just need to find some good bottom bitches. Everyone has those people in their lives. They depend on you for their self-worth. So do them a favor, and put them to work. It's what they want anyway. They understand what's going on, but what they get out of it – self-worth, a reason for getting up every day – THAT is all the payment they need or expect. Just teach your bottom bitches to feel like royalty, better than royalty, and for them to do the same to their bottom bitches. There is an end-less supply of BBs. And once you show them how you did it for (to) them, they will know how to do it themselves, and they will all believe that they are going to get rich too. Erick watched his father carefully through his youth and early teenage years as he grew his business.

In actual fact, 98% of all "associates" in all multi-level marketing schemes (pyramid selling), regardless of the products, lose money. The math proving it is simple. And

this always ends up the same. You need the maniacal qualities of a psychotic narcissist to be a leader in multi-level
marketing. It is Cult Leading 101.

Erick, or ED (not Ed as in Edward), understood his dad's
business and knew he could do it better. He thought his
dad was lame and declared loudly that he didn't need his
fucking money or his bullshit company (or his evangelical religion for that matter!). He left home after finishing
his homeschooling and getting an approved Missouri
GED, joined the Navy, then quit that and with the secret
help of his dad's money got into Virginia Military Institute
(VMI). Graduated with a degree in Geopolitics. Joined the
Navy (again) via Officer Candidate School. He got very fit
and made it onto SEALs and within a year, on his second
deployment, was charged with machine-gunning 19 Arab
villagers. He spent six months "under house arrest" but was
never brought to trial. He was thrown out of the SEALs, but
the murder case disappeared. Rumors said a lot of money
flowed for a little silence. Congressional investigations
circled all around his "honorable discharge" but again,
crickets. Nobody would talk.

Meanwhile his younger sister Martha became a Christian Internet sensation. Little innocent sister – caught in
the maelstrom of our perverted culture! She was shrewd,
built her image as a cult slut – long bizarre rants about how
rap music and vaccines had stolen her sense of right and
wrong – called out over fifty celebrities for "psychically"
raping her as a child, had actual sex with three rich, local
notables, all older men, one after the other, over a single
week, videoed it all, and then outed them. She started an
S-Plog that morphed into a high-production popular show
on RFD network about the Satanic influence in popular
culture along with cooking tips. She dressed in white, and
wore daisies in her hair.

On Sundays she delivered screeching video sermons
in tight t-shirts and often would spin around when deliv-
ering a punchline, to show off her tramp stamp of Jesus
on the cross just above her low-slung, cut-off jeans. She
claimed prominent Dees were recruiting young girls into a

sex cult and she had nearly been caught in it herself! They came for her, but she had fought them off, attacks which she described in graphic detail, attacks that nearly lost her newly restored virginity! No place or person was safe!

On her show Martha interviewed another young woman who claimed to have been violated in her own bed by demons ("They told me that Black-Prez had sent them and that he was laughing and jizzin' all over me!"). The woman gave tearful, long detailed descriptions of being raped repeatedly by big men – white men, "Chinamen," and bringing up the rear, a Black man batting clean-up with a huge dick! How big? asked Martha. How is that possible? she asked, looking at how far her hands were spread apart.

Martha talked about the power of her visions, and how those visions told more truth than anything – they told her the future, and most importantly, they told her what was in the hearts of people. Millions of views.

She soon was preaching at her father's mega-church, and quickly became the star attraction, driving attendance and collections too of course, higher and higher. And then – ED's little sister was asked to be the Official Chaplain of the White House.

Erick, a civilian again, hiding from his SEAL fuckup, had taken over his father's business. His father had died on the pulpit while preaching. Some say he was trying too hard, competing with his daughter, who watched in what appeared to be fascinated horror as he flopped around on the stage like a walrus trying to get off the beach into the water. For the first 30 seconds of his death throes, the congregation clapped in unison to the strange rhythm of his convulsions. But when the true nature of his moribund condition was finally evident, they all burst into "Nearer My God to Thee." When he died, Parnell was worth nearly a billion dollars.

The autopsy found strychnine. The church had had recent infestations of rats, and the theory was he had accidentally eaten some of the poison left out. An investigation failed to find any evidence of foul play.

ED sold his shares of his dad's pyramid marketing company, NewLife, to Amway for $16 billion. He immediately kickstarted a domestic protection force, based on the SEAL model. It was all white men (except for Echo Devious) and came to a certain kind of fame during the rise of Hassan Coleman. There were kidnappings of squatters, shootings, and social media campaigns against Hassan. Some of his guys got caught and begged for forgiveness. But there was no extrajudicial action; trials were judged fair by all accounts. After the (V)ICE debacle in Portland, when it was slowly revealed how Coleman had been closely involved in the defeat of the (V)ICE forces, the battle for Memphis's soul was over and a warrant was issued for Erick Duke in Memphis.

From *The Fall of It All – A History of the Big Dump*

"MR. DUKE, THERE'S A GUY DOWNSTAIRS IN THE restaurant."

Erick was sitting at the kitchen counter drinking coffee with his back to the picture window that overlooked the Pacific Ocean in the Presidential Suite of the Shilo Inn in Newport. He looked quickly at the messenger and nodded. The jacked, square-jawed burr-head turned and seemed to take the casual nod as a dismissal.

Ten guys, most of whom had driven in the night before, were loafing around the suite. The parking lot was filled with Harleys, Jeeps, and RVs, as well as a few high-end foreign sedans.

The Compound knew they were there, and had a fair idea what they were planning. But the details – how, when, where, how many – they never had a handle on that kind of information. A number of people working at the Shilo Inn in housekeeping and even a night clerk at the front desk all listened, and spied, and pulled shit out of the trash, and even planted bugs. But they never uncovered definite plans.

As for Duke's guests, most looked like they were ex-WWF "wrestlers" coming off a steroid recovery program. Two ultra-tanned women bodybuilders were also in the suite, in metallic make-up.

There was a lot of huffing and puffing, and jocularity as they stood in line getting seconds from the buffet table. Most were dressed in khaki or jungle camo, most were packing, and all were lounging or standing around, talking with basso-profondo voices, in twos and threes. Erick Duke had an Austrian 9 mm on his hip, and was dressed in a white shirt and some brown military-esque cargo pants. Everyone had their eye on ED (as Erick Duke insisted his team call him) even as they pretended to look anywhere else.

"Echo Devious, get over here," Duke said, using a call signal for a dumbshit former worker at the Rehain Compound known only as Ed (as in Edward), loud enough for those nearby to hear but nobody else. He left it to them to find Ed, and give him his summons.

"What's the scoop?"

"They watch," Ed said. Ed's mom was Siletz Indian. He had grown up on the reservation and had hunted around the north side of the Rehain Compound as a kid. He had gotten his ass kicked by Kip when they were in grammar school. Kip had started it, and nobody from the Rez stuck up for Ed, because most of them knew and liked Kip (even though they also thought he was goofy). Ed left the area when he was 18 or so, and moved to LA for about ten years. High-water mark of his time in SoCal was a walk-on fuck role in a Simi Valley porno movie. No dialogue – just came in for sloppy seconds and he got paid scale. Big tits and a shaved cooch, he could describe every inch of her body. He got paid for fucking her! It was his go-to story and he could talk about it for an hour if he could find somebody to listen. Ed had made his mark. He had a video of his moment made and kept it on his fone. Didn't get any better than that.

Ed met up with the real ED, Erick Duke, through a friend of a friend who introduced them in a darkweb Soldier of Fortune chatroom. ED was smart and he seemed to remember everything about everybody he ever talked to – and he remembered Ed (just Ed – never Edward or Eddy). Ed always made a point of that. And when ED started calling Ed "Echo Devious," he loved it. He loved the way ED had quizzed him too!

Skills? "Tracker, wilderness, sniper."

Where? "Oregon coast range."

When the Rehain Compound showed up on ED's radar, he remembered Echo Devious. Made him a captain. Duke's teams only had two ranks – Captains and Bosses. Bosses do the dirty work. Captains clean it up if required. "Can we beat it?"

"Oh, sure. Will they be warned though? Probably."

"Well that's what I mean – can we get in without being seen or heard?"

"Not that way. Wood's too thick. They've got the holes covered."

ED only had 25 guys, but they were all high quality mercs. No pussies like those dumb fools who tried to take Portland.

"Let's go, Ed," ED said. Ed put on his "The One and Only Real-Prez" red baseball hat and followed ED out. Erick Duke never wore a hat unless he was about to go into combat. His hair was his best feature, blond, short, but not too short. He looked around, prowling like a cat, weaving around the Presidential Suite, checking out his team, looking for the disgruntled. He knew they didn't like Ed's rise up in the hierarchy but they were pros, at least they better be, or they would end up dead. ED had no room for slackers or the disgruntled.

When they entered the restaurant, Ed said, "ED, this is my brother – Gull."

"Gull, nice to meet you," ED said. He was looking at a full-blooded Siletz, with a curled-up black cowboy hat and a big blue feather stuck in the side.

Gull nodded.

"How did you get the name Gull?"

Gull looked at Ed. "What is this? You told him we were brothers?"

"Mr. Duke, you don't want to ask that – names are a very private thing with our people."

"Our people?"

"Fine," said ED. "I just wondered why somebody would name their kid after a scavenger bird. Maybe you people look at it differently." The waitress came over and gave ED a big smile.

"You people?"

"Oatmeal, raisins, and an English muffin. Coffee," said ED. "Thanks."

"Three eggs, sunny side up, bacon, toast," said Ed.

"I don't want anything," said Gull.

"Excuse me, Sweetheart!" ED waved at the waitress. "We'll just have coffee." Ed looked crestfallen, but nodded. "So, Ed tells me you used to be part of that traitor group that took over Walter Rehain's tree farm. Is that true, Gull?"

"I thought it was just work, but it turned into a cult."

"It is happening all over. Real-Prez calls it the 'Portland Rot.'"

"I used to work for Walt – the old man, he was a good guy. I know every inch of that piece of property. It's beautiful land, clean, clear streams, stands of ancient old growth. Walt took care of the place. Used to be a money maker. Lots of work. It was one of the few places you could count on getting some work between October and January. Walt worked your ass, but he was fair. His son though, he turned it into shit – a hippie place. And that bitch Alice Hunt. She's a fucking whore. Moved on the old man when he was about to die." Gull looked out at the ocean. "But I don't blame her. It was Kip who I blame. Fucking Kipling Rehain – he fucked it up."

ED nodded his head. Even smiled, just a tiny bit. "It's not right. Everyone says the old man was a right-thinking man. But I can tell you from experience, inheritance is tricky."

"Walt understood business," Gull said. "And yes, that is my point. Eventually it's going to come back to business. This whole deal, including the coming election. I can't see a full-bore Leninist revolution. We won't go that way."

"Thank the second amendment."

"Maybe. That's what the fucking liberals don't understand. All this bullshit – give up your guns, you give up the God-given right to enjoy the fruits of your labor! Making money is hard enough."

"OK, I think we understand each other," said Erick Duke. "We're on the same side – right?"

"I'll vote for a moron who promises to let me run my business and not have to put up with everyone trying to take my money."

Gull paused. Erick started to say something, then changed the subject.

"Walt Rehain gave the Rs money," said Erick. "Going back to Nixon at least. Maybe Goldwater, I don't know. Hell, I know he gave ten thou to Reagan's campaign. Now his life's work is being turned against everything he stood for."

"I went with him to Washington once."

"What for?"

"It had to do with tribal rights."

"Really? Was Walt contesting anything?"

"He owned land on both sides of Skookum Creek. He wanted to rent it out to us for fishing. A dollar a year, it was the principle of the thing with him."

"How'd that work out?"

"It was denied. Even though he owned both sides of the creek, plus its source, the BLM said they controlled fishing rights."

Erick nodded as if he had heard it all before, and stirred his coffee.

"So how do we get them?"

"I don't know," said Gull. "I don't know what we can do. What do you want to do, ED?"

"Kill them. All of them," said Ed.

ED took a sip of coffee and rolled his eyes at Ed's comment.

"I mean, that is what I want to do," said Ed. ED looked at Ed and Ed smiled, and shook his head.

"Well, the easy way is just to capture or kill Alice Hunt," said

Gull. "She runs the place. She used to fuck Walt, so Walt's kid kind of gave her the place."

"Where is he?"

"Who, Kip?" Gull looked disturbed about not knowing something. "I don't know – he's AWOL."

"That fuck," said Ed, looking up from his breakfast. "I will kill him myself if I ever meet him again."

"Oh," Gull smiled. "You are so full of shit, Ed. You had a chance once and it didn't work out too well."

Ed glowered at Gull, who smiled.

"Well, I don't give a shit," said Ed. "I want to shut that fucking place down. They have been disrespecting the President, and some of the criminals from the Portland bullshit are on the lam there. So, we should hit them hard and quick and leave it smoking."

"Only two easy ways in – up the road and through the air," said Gull. "They watch the road and it would be bloody."

"I want simple," said Erick. "Bang, boom, bing. It's over. Look – no offense, Gull –" ED let a little disrespect slip into his pronunciation of Gull, "but I know how to assault a compound. All I need from you is something about the place – a weakness – a habit I can exploit. Describe the place."

Gull turned to Ed. "Is he kidding?"

Erick looked perplexed.

"He wants money, Mr. Duke."

"Oh, Oh – OK. How much?

"Fifty K."

"You are out of your mind."

"Good luck," said Gull. He got up and walked out. Erick Duke went back to eating as if nothing had happened.

"Don't worry, he's just negotiating," said Ed. "He'll do it for ten."

CHAPTER 19
CHUBBY HEADS FOR ASIA

Early October

When the virus arrived in North America, it suddenly attacked on several fronts. Canada moved quickly to take steps to identify and isolate cases but was just as quickly stymied by the pathogen's bizarre behavior. In spite of ample warning from its spread through South Asia and the Middle East, it was not unexpected that it caught the U.S. by surprise. The politically inspired refugee crisis in the U.S., and the political instability surrounding it, drowned out almost all discussion of the virus until it arrived. Within the span of two weeks, infections popped up in Los Angeles, New York, Kansas City, and Dallas. Death, as it was overseas, sometimes came hours after the first symptoms were noticed. But other times it took a week. It appeared that most infections produced a kind of euphoria not seen by the medical world before. For most of the victims who survived, the experience exceeded their vocabulary to describe it. For those infected who had previously experienced psychoactive drugs, the experience was reported to be much deeper. Most spoke about it eschatologically, invoking visions of worldwide renewal and the ending of the rule of man.

The virologists investigating the microbe reported behavior never before encountered. The virus changed its configuration as it approached a cell, from a smooth ball of protein to something that looked like a 1960s lunar landing craft. But then it behaved in a way totally different from anything previously reported. The same virion morphed back to a protein ball to one observer, while another saw it quickly invade and go critical and explode into thousands of infected cells. It appeared to have an affinity to quantum behavior by subatomic particles, as though it evolved to avoid detection. An experiment was performed by two microbiologists in Canada, with both observers using separate photographic eyepieces on an electronic micro-scope. They were able to mark specific virions and watch them. The two observers reported different behaviors by the same virion, yet recordings of the behavior showed no difference. The experiment was repeated multiple times at multiple labs and the same result was found.

But the most frightening aspect of this experiment was in spite of ultra-secure precautions, all the experimental observers later tested positive. Some died and some experienced visions and recovered. Further experiments to follow this anomaly were terminated.

From *The Fall of It All – A History of the Big Dump*

CHUBBY HAD HIS AVIATOR SHADES ON, HIDING HIS

tears as he stared out at the Pacific Ocean five miles down, avoiding the prying eyes of the Filipino couple sitting next to him. He was wearing his virus face mask, which made it difficult to be identified by someone who might have seen his face in the news, although it had been over six years since his incandescent burst of fame after the launch of *SwiftPad*. He had worked assid-uously ever since to blot out his face from worldwide media, with mixed results. Although he had been the driving force behind the social media mega app, he had mostly managed to avoid the public eye over the last four years, but occasionally stories about him did pop up. It seemed to him becoming "unfamous" was more difficult than becoming famous.

After Cornelius "Chubby" Welles (Kip's *nom de guerre*) snuck into Canada, he lay low for a few weeks in a tiny house at the end of a dirt road outside a little town 30 miles northwest of Toronto. Deciduous trees were in full autumn display. He knew it was time to get going and find GG (Cynthia Oglethorpe) before the fast-approaching US presidential election.

He had been in a dark-blue funk since he heard about Aldane on S-Plog from his Ishpeming contact. His contact had told him that Aldane was dead, along with a woman from Portland whom he might have met, but didn't remember. She had been working undercover against Cadez. He could find nothing else about her. Ishpeming was protecting their assets apparently. God damn it! Aldane!

Chubby kept looking out the window, down through the clouds at the Pacific Ocean. Tears streamed down his face like he was in a shower. He just kept sobbing, uncontrollably. He had cried when his dad died and probably, when he was ten, when he realized his mom was never coming back to Oregon. He couldn't remember if that was actually true though. His shirt was wet. He laughed, for some reason, at his weeping. But he couldn't stop. It would have been better for him to have stayed in Cape Girardeau, and faced whatever would have happened. Five colleagues, whom he hardly knew, but had trusted with his own life. And his oldest friend – other than Jim – Aldane!

The stakes are as high as it gets now. No going back now. Have to take it through to the end. As it likely will be. This is why they got me out, why they died. I am the one who has to go get G. And her newborn too. Either that, or I join Jim – and Aldane. Aldane, shot dead on the airstrip right next to the Illinois town of Kaskaskia. A little bit of Illinois on the west side of the Mississippi, where the river changed course.

Kaskaskia. Once the biggest city west of the Appalachian Mountains. Now, maybe 10 people live in the town of Kaskaskia, where the river of the same name flows into the Mississippi. He had read about it on his way to Vandalia, to meet Elwood, on the Kaskaskia River. The switching, meandering Mississippi had changed its course and left the once prosperous town flooded and stranded on the Missouri side, the west side of the river, in 1881. Illinois insisted that what was left of Kaskaskia stay in Illinois. Now the Kaskaskia River dumped out across the river from the town.

In the mid-1700s, before the American Revolution, when the French controlled the area, Kaskaskia had had over 7,000 people. At that time, the English settlers hadn't yet ventured into Kentucky. There was a huge Native American population in the area before the Europeans arrived. This wilderness metropolis was at the end of the river where Elwood had found the fungus. What had attracted so many people to this isolated place, this now near-abandoned place? It had actually been the capital of the Illinois Territory, before it had moved up to Vandalia. Now it was the last place Aldane and his crew would ever see.

He thought about all of these quaint details because he still couldn't wrap his mind around Aldane and this young woman from Portland dying in a shootout on that flatland, holding off the Missouri cops (Were they trying to make it to Illinois? Would that have even mattered?). But they got Hank out. It was big news all over the world and it had sent a message to everyone – we don't leave our comrades behind!

It was a long flight, and when he wasn't sleeping, that was all Kip could think about.

Now he had to go get his other comrade.

He felt the stiff blue passport still in his jacket pocket and took it out to stow away in his bag so he wouldn't lose it. He was using the same fake passport he had used last spring on his trek through the lost cities of Central Asia that Alexander had built and Genghis had blotted out. He had been blotted himself on the trip, drunk on vodka and stoned on Afghani hashish the whole way, wandering along aimlessly and haphazardly into the Republic of Georgia. He looked through his beautiful, travel-beaten blue booklet with its artfully smudged visa stamps carefully (and crookedly) crafted from all over the world, and then stuffed it in its special zipped pocket.

His "documents guy," Frank Kinsky, had also died. Sixty-something, lived by himself, maybe gay, with strange fetishes, probably tired of disappointment and loneliness. At least that was what he always projected to Kip when they met. He remembered looking through albums of drawings while waiting for Frank, to – do just about anything. Frank had been slow moving, slow talking, and slow to decide anything, from a price for his work to whether to stand or sit.

But Frank's drawings (his manga art under the pen name Owatatsumi) of teenage girls with big sad eyes, saddle shoes, and short plaid skirts were famous all over the world. No one suspected the artist was a little old gay American man. Hopelessly shy, celibate, and unerringly kind, Frank had come to hear Jean Katon because Kip, weeks earlier, had given him tickets. Then Kip talked him and several thousand others into marching out of the Jean Katon concert and blocking the Banfield to save the Insurgency that was in process on the other side of the river. The now famous demonstration was currently considered a master stroke of tactical urban warfare.

Chubby had rousted them out when he had barged onto the stage and galvanized the crowd into an energized weapon against the (V)ICE militia.

Frank had been shot dead on the Banfield while helping to block the highway – forming a human mass that kept (V)ICE reinforcements from reaching downtown Portland – what was it – twelve weeks ago? What is today, early October? The casualty lists from Portland popped up on an S-Plog – over 240 Portland civilians, 22 out-of-state volunteers, and 523 (V)ICE killed.

Since Chubby had been responsible for psyching the crowd into that very risky business, he knew that their deaths were on him. Frank and the many others who had only been expecting to enjoy a Haitian reggae music concert were shot down because he, Chubby Welles, had urged them to get out on the street to hem in and isolate the (V)ICE reinforcements headed for the city. He had promised them victory, but none had really expected to give it all. He had lied to them in a way, making it seem like it would be a heroic romp. Many were wounded too. A couple of quadriplegics and ten or twelve paraplegics, and some other horrible injuries, life-altering injuries, to go with it all. Chubby didn't have the stomach to lead the fight anymore, not after that. But he was too determined not to balk at risking himself. All of those people were on him too.

Frank had made the passport for his alter-ego, a slightly sleazy, dangerously noir, Portland-based private investigator. Ishpeming wanted to give him new documents, with a new ID, but he vetoed it. He wasn't sure if he was being sentimental, but on one level he was absolutely determined to keep Frank Kinsky's work alive, keep his brilliant forgeries in the game a little longer as a token of memory.

But the homage to his late forger aside, Kip thought it was actually smarter to go in again as Chubby Welles, using the same passport that he had used the previous spring. "Oh yeah, we've seen this guy before," he hoped the border patrol and security services would think, looking at their records. He was OK, they might think. He was hiding in plain sight again, a kind of steganography.

After all, nobody would try to sneak into Russia twice – not the same way anyway, using the same ID – right? He had returned from China and Russia – and Georgia – less than five months ago. Georgia on his mind. His deal to send Milana money on his return had fallen through the cracks after Portland. He had no idea what her situation was, only that she had been cheated out of what he had promised her. Another weight to hang around his conscience.

He got to frenetic Manila around midnight, and if that was midnight, how fucking crazy must it be in the daylight? He had six hours until his flight to Saigon, but he made it to the gate, took a piss, and sat in a half-wakeful netherworld with the ghosts of recently passed friends and neighbors. Everyone in the airport had a mask, in hopes that it would protect them from the raging virus.

A week and a half later, he traveled back up to the north, eight hours humping the fucking leg of a journey that had hardly even started, from Hanoi to Hiroshima. So sick of planes. The flight through Manila to Ho Chi Minh City had been a nightmare, standing room only, people squatting in the aisles, but with a pig in the middle seat next to him, a porcine for which the owner had apparently bought a ticket. No need for a seat belt, if they went down then he could finally say he knew that pigs could fly – or at least one anyway. After five days in Saigon, chilling in the heat and humidity, two nights on the train up to Hanoi (second class, sharing a cabin with three moody and taciturn Vietnamese men who spoke no English), three more days in an elegant little French-style bed and bistro in downtown Hanoi, and finally Ishpeming said go. Now on a flight back north up to Hiroshima, he was glad to see that there would be no more pigs flying or spraying gooey shit all over as they were landing.

This time-wasting disjointed schedule of international spycraft and misdirection had been one of many pieces of advice given to Kip by the team in Ishpeming. Kill time, get off the radar, shake any tails. He had been surprised how well his half-assed, insecurely obtained phony ID had worked. For all his flaunting of it in Portland, up to and during the all-out battle in Portland's Forest Park with Real-Prez's Immigration and Vagrancy militia, his attempt to create a new life as a seedy private eye had, on one level at least, worked.

The Insurgency security team in Ishpeming had massaged his old Cornelius Welles ID, creating a plausible backstory as an Oregon timber broker looking for partners in Siberia – Russia. It was a role he could easily play; he had been raised by a timber baron deep in the Oregon coast range and by osmosis if nothing else could easily assume the role of "timber broker." But it was not Siberian wood he was after.

The plan was to buy a 30-day tourist visa in Japan and take a ferry to Vladivostok. His "tourist" visa would help downplay his own importance, making him appear to be just another low-rent business hustler looking for pay dirt, because it would be clear to the border agent's eye that he wasn't in Siberia just to make pilgrimages to Czarist monasteries. The Russians would roll their eyes but (hopefully) just wave him through, maybe a question or two about his previous trip, which was just "business research," of course. From Vladivostok he would be on his own. He spoke good Russian, which he was determined not to show off until he really needed it.

He was extremely relieved when the cockpit announced, prematurely as it turned out, that they were getting ready to land. Kip hadn't slept at all during the last eighteen hours and two plane changes. The President of *SwiftPad* Inc. (Japan) was picking him up at the airport, and Kip was hoping he was alone. Arkie had assured him that his counterpart in Japan, Hanata Yokashita, completely understood the absolute necessity for secrecy, but experience had taught him to expect some kind of fuck-up.

The plane came around a third time, and finally the clouds cleared away and Kip looked down at the Ota River delta, at Hiroshima. He could see the iron skeleton of the dome that somehow had not been incinerated when the Enola Gay dropped "Little Boy." He found it disturbingly easy to imagine the city completely flattened, with only the bridges over the delta's rivulets left visible from the air. He couldn't wait to get out of the airport and take his face mask off.

Hanata met him at the gate, wearing a face mask. Kip slipped his back on. Hanata bowed a little, asked if he had checked any baggage ("no"), then led Kip to his car.

"So what are your plans, Kip?"

"I need to go to Sakaiminato. I was hoping we could talk on the way there."

"You can't stay? Are you sure? We have wonderful food and many other delights in our city."

"I have to stay in Sakaiminato, probably for a few days. I want to get my visa to Russia there and it might take some time."

"Why Sakaiminato?"

"It's where the ferry to Vladivostok leaves. I am possibly being tracked, so I am leaving clues that I am a disorganized traveler. Do you understand what I am saying?"

"Disorganized?"

"A fool. Unimportant. Not a threat. I will wait for my visa there. Stay in a cheap hotel while it is processed, then get the ferry. Maybe get drunk, get in an argument in the bar near the ferry or even stay with a prostitute. I want everyone to think I am a very unimportant, slightly disgusting, and foolish traveler. But it is important that you know this is for the future of the company. Or its lack of future, actually."

Hanata heard what he said, "lack of future." He waited a beat, but not hearing more, passed on asking what that meant exactly. "Yes. I remember that technique well. It's from the movie *The Spy Who Came In from the Cold*. I have seen it many times. Leamas, who was played by the marvelous actor Richard Burton, perhaps famous only because he married Elizabeth Taylor twice. Leamas got drunk, which Burton played to perfection, and started a fight in public to convince the East Germans that he was angry at his British employers in Whitehall."

Hanata's observation was funny but behind his chuckle, Chubby felt a cold shiver run through his body. Was he trying to be too clever? Russians read spy novels too. "Yeah. Well, maybe I shouldn't make a public display of it. I must have remembered that trick myself from seeing the movie a long time ago." He missed Jim and Arkie. They would have called out his obvious and lame plan. Jim used to tell him he was three parts idiot and one part genius.

"I am often surprised that new ideas are really old ideas that we have just forgotten."

"Yes." Kip looked at Hanata and they smiled at each other. They drove in silence for a while. "One of the reasons I am coming this way," said Kip, "and am meeting you here, Hanata, is to tell you to begin to prepare for a transition. We intend to destroy the *SwiftPad* app, to release a virus that will kill it, and keep it dead."

Hanata turned and looked at him with concern, then back at the road. He seemed to try to say something, but whatever it was caught in his throat.

"Another virus?"

"No – computer virus." Hanata seemed not surprised by the explanation, apparently his remark had been meant as a joke of some kind. "Cynthia has written microcode into the core of the app. It's undetectable, and immutable. The virus latches on to this code, and if it works – essentially – the app will delete itself. The virus will replicate and attack all instances of *SwiftPad*, both client and server."

Hanata looked at him again, but again, no sound came out of his mouth.

"We know you have built a wonderful company here in Japan and throughout Asia," Kip continued, "and have many bright young people who have been making amazing improvements to the product, making it saner, but fundamentally *SwiftPad* is destroying the United States. Destroying every society actually. Maybe not so much here, in your society, but in the US, it is chaos and crazy. Warping the meaning of human relationships. We can't control it."

"How can you 'destroy' software that is all over the world? I still don't understand how it will be technically possible."

"Well, actually, you are right, we can't actually do it yet. It is a bit theoretical. Apparently there is a missing key – a passcode, along with the exact procedures required to trigger the deletion."

"You really think it possible?"

"Arkie will be talking to you about that. We are not ready yet. It might be a while. But before the election would be the best time actually. Until we are ready, we will keep things going. Secrecy is paramount! I just wanted you to know it is coming, so you can start thinking about a post-*SwiftPad* strategy and hopefully figure out a way to keep some kind of business going that doesn't drive society crazy." Kip didn't tell him that GG had the key, and until he could find her and find the actual "trigger" lines of code, they didn't know how to do it.

"It is not so bad here."

Kip looked at him but didn't say anything.

"Well," Hanata smiled slyly, "it is not good either."

"We will destroy the app all at once, deleting all instances, on all servers, for good, by technical means. And if they restore and relaunch, the dormant virus will destroy it again. It also infects most known backup techniques, so most of the backups will be corrupted. The hope is the disruption will be enough to end the world's fascination. It will take a long time to discover the 'delete' triggers in the code, and by then – maybe the world will find they no longer need *SwiftPad*. But I beg you, please, tell no one! I owed it to you to tell you in person of our intention. We want to do it all at once, with no warning, worldwide – what we call – the 'nuclear' option."

Hanata flushed and then Chubby realized talking about a "nuclear option" in Hiroshima was not very polite, even if the option's victim was a software program.

"That will be very interesting," said Hanata, quickly retrieving his countenance and ignoring the embarrassing comparison. "I will look forward to working with Archimedes. Perhaps we can make lemonade out of it all, as you say."

"Yes. Maybe transition to another product or products. Figure out how to use the talent. We can probably salvage some features, but if we do, they need to be rewritten from the ground up. In any event, we will try and make sure the staff walks away whole, financially." Kip looked out the window of Hanata's Nissan at the vegetation, trying and failing to see if he could recognize any of the leftover effects from the bomb 75 years previously.

"What of the stockholders?"

"I am the principal owner; 85% of the company is still owned in-house. But for some of the smaller – investors – it will hurt, but, this is like war. Shit happens, as they say."

"Yes. We know about shit happening in Hiroshima. So you will take the ferry to Russia rather than fly?"

"Yes," Chubby looked at Hanata, who was about 45, and was an important man, one of the captains of Japan's high-tech sector, head of *SwiftPad* East, all of Asia reporting to him. He had spent over $6 billion over the last three years building up the Asian *SwiftPad* infrastructure, as well as hiring several thousand developers who localized the product. *SwiftPad* Japan, Korea, Vietnam, Taiwan, and the Philippines were still going gangbusters. They had met several times at company meetings in Portland, but back then, it had all been a blur for Kip. Arkie had set all this structure up. Now he was facing all of it just disappearing. A nuclear option. Chubby was hideously embarrassed at his own malapropism.

"Do you live in Hiroshima, Hanata?"

"No, Okayama. It's not far from the office. Closer to the airport really."

"You fly a lot." It was not a question, just an acknowledgment.

"Yes, all the time. Manila, Hanoi, Taipei, Singapore, Jakarta. We have so many teams, all doing good work. And no trouble." Hanata hesitated and looked over at Chubby, then back to the road, then back at Kip.

"We grew so fast," he continued. "It's one thing to create something, another to maintain and grow it. But Hiroshima is a small city, like Portland. Perhaps killing *SwiftPad* will allow us both to stay small. It is better that way."

Kip nodded. "Yes, there are advantages to being away from the spotlight. But since our trouble in Portland your team has been carrying us, in many ways. The business in the US is a mess. We are being challenged in court and we are being attacked over politics. I don't want to spend my time and energy dealing with that. For me, it is time to move on to something else. But first things first."

"Who will be your next President?"

"I don't know."

"Will you try and stop him?"

"Yes." Kip knew who he meant.

"So – this – 'nuclear option' –"

"Let's just call it 'pulling the plug' for now," said Kip.

"Pulling the plug –" Hanata laughed as he pulled up to a traffic light. "I was hoping you could come to the office. I know the team would be very honored to meet you."

Oh, shit, thought Kip, this is what he was afraid of. He looked at Hanata.

"But with the virus – not the computer virus, the real one – no one is actually in the office now. I have told no one you were coming. I understand, of course, your visit must remain totally secret. But I have some questions about – our relationship. Is Mr. Young still –"

"Heber is –" Chubby realized he had to be careful. Heber had been AWOL since the Battle of Portland. He had made it clear he was not comfortable with the direction they were on. Not that he thought Heber supported Real-Prez – or Temp-Prez for that matter. But maybe Cadez? Heber was a cipher. Kip had known him most of his life, but, did he really? He missed his father. "Heber is still with us, but you should take – you should work with Archimedes –"

"Well, we are getting some feedback from our government.

They are encouraging us to – be less entangled with companies that are not Japanese."

Shit, Kip thought. He wants to renegotiate. "Listen. I will support whatever arrangement – you suggest – that is fair. But not now. We have to get Cynthia back. That is all I care about. Figure out what you want. But please – please – don't tell anyone about the plan to delete *SwiftPad*. And remember – I am not here. I was not here. Tell no one you saw or talked to me. I mean no one. It is life or death – for Cynthia."

"Cynthia! Yes. We must not forget her! She is still alive? Are you..."

Kip waved his hand, indicating he didn't want to talk about it.

"I know you have much to worry about. You have my support! Completely. Thank you for coming personally to tell me! You are honorable. Nothing will leak! Nothing! No one knows and no one will!"

Chubby looked at him, struggling to project confidence.

"Not even my wife," said Hanata, "who I know would love to cook you dinner and invite you to our house."

"But you didn't tell her I was coming," Kip said, hesitantly.

"No, no."

"It is important that this remain a secret. I am traveling as Mr. Welles. Cornelius Welles. You must keep your guard up."

"Guard up?"

"Be careful. It is possible I am being tracked. Or kept track of somehow. I don't think so, but I can't be sure." Chubby looked over at Hanata.

"Mr. Welles – Kip –"

"Call me Chubby."

"Chubby – You must find Ms. Oglethorpe. That is all that matters. I will protect this secret, and cooperate completely. Archimedes will have all of our cooperation. As will you – in your –"

"Thank you." Kip turned away and looked out the window.

"We were all dreadfully sorry about Mr. Hunt's death and her kidnapping. She is such a wonderful young woman. I have only met her once. I was very –"

Kip nodded. He thought of his last moments with Jim Hunt, his best friend from childhood, and – Aldane.

"Her baby must have been born by now?"

"Yes," said Kip.

They smelled the sea before they got to Sakaiminato.

"Take me to a shitty cheap hotel. The smaller and cheaper the better."

Hanata looked at Chubby, nodded.

"I know a shitty-cheap one. I mean a bad one. But it is Japanese, so it will undoubtedly be clean. Is that OK?"

"Yeah. That will do."

~~~

Chubby didn't do any of the things he talked about with Hanata. He didn't get drunk in public, but he did finish a bottle of Korean sweet potato soju while lying in his room watching Japanese cartoons. He saw one that he thought was based on drawings that his passport forger Frank had drawn, but he couldn't be sure. In fact, he probably was just projecting.

He spent two days in Sakaiminato hardly leaving his clean little room. There was nothing to do; the place was desolate, a bleak little seaside town. When his 30-day Russian tourist visa arrived he bought his ticket for the ferry to Vladivostok. The ferry only ran once a week, so he had to wait a couple of days for the next one. He joined a tourist bus over to see some famous shrines near the harbor town of Mihonoseki on the mountainous Shimane Peninsula. As they were crossing the Sakaisuidoo Bridge, he looked back and saw a thin man wearing a blue Adidas tracksuit. He was Caucasian (the only other white person on the bus) with short salt-and-pepper hair. The man appeared relaxed and was alone, and never seemed to look at Kip, but he knew he had been watching him before. Kip noted his face, and decided to forget about him.

When they arrived in Mihonoseki, Kip followed a tour group. The guide was speaking only in Japanese, but he pointed out what to look at, and that was enough.

Kip's plan, as far as he had thought about it, was to slowly make his way over to St. Petersburg. Ishpeming was 75% sure she was there – somewhere. There was a whole other theory that she never left the States, that she was in an isolated subdivision guarded by Mormon goons outside Ogden, Utah. Chubby thought it possible too that somehow his father's long-time assistant, and the financial brains behind *SwiftPad*, Heber Young – a direct descendant of Brigham Young – long suffering under Chubby's father's cruel needling and bullying, might have somehow been behind it. Kip had known Heber all his life, but he had never met any of Heber's six (or seven?) kids who lived in rural Lane County 50 country miles from the compound where he had come to work every day. But his dad had never fired Heber, and Heber had never quit. Although it was a weird partnership, in the end – because of Kip meeting GG and starting *SwiftPad* – it paid off. Heber must easily be worth half a billion dollars himself. And that was just what he made legally. He could have stolen twice that and no one would know. But somehow, Kip was sure he had been scrupulously honest.

Of course if GG was in Utah, it stood to reason she was being controlled by some group in the computer programming business. Other than her vast fortune, her skills as a programmer were probably her greatest value – or in this case, liability. Naturally, the same was true if she was in Russia.

Looking out at the ocean from the windy peninsula was strangely relaxing. Then the weather turned shitty quickly, and he moved under the roof of a shrine to some water god. Normally he was an inquisitive traveler, but his mind was too busy to pay attention. There were pamphlets in English that explained the history and significance of the shrine, but he could not make himself read them.

He saw his fellow Caucasian, who had apparently befriended what looked like a young Japanese student who was speaking – French? This guy didn't look French, whatever a 35-year-old Frenchman would look like – certainly he would not be wearing an Adidas tracksuit. They were deep in discussion as they passed him, and again the man did not look up at him.

They got back to Sakaiminato just as the sun was going down. He had a rice bento bowl in the little café next to his hotel, and decided to have a drink in the tiny bar in the lobby of the hotel. The low moaning groans of the ferry boat horns were ubiquitous. He wondered where his friend with the salt and pepper hair was staying.

A young prostitute sat next to him. He bought her a drink, and they went up to his room. She spoke no English, but he discovered to no particular surprise that it wasn't required. Neither of them ever took their masks off, and they were able to avoid any face-to-face encounters through the whole experience. He tipped her well and she left, apparently happy with the exchange. He felt good for the first time in weeks and slept well.

He was always checking for tails, but if he was being followed, it was by professionals because he never saw them or his Adidas friend. With one more day until he left, he wandered around the docks looking at the boats. Chubby quickly saw Sakaiminato was not a rich man's moorage; almost all of the boats were working vessels. There were some private fishing boats, and he thought about finding a charter boat to go out fishing. But the rough weather put an end to that notion. Soon it started raining, so he ended up back in his tiny room, sleeping off and on, mindlessly watching TV while drinking soju, the Korean "fortified" sake (it actually wasn't "fortified" sake) that was quickly becoming his favorite alcoholic beverage. He dreamed about finding GG, but the GG of his dreams was not the same woman that he dreamed of (he was aware of all of this while dreaming), and the woman he dreamed of was not at all the woman who he was sure would be the real GG, who suddenly, he was certain, he would eventually find. Even before he woke up, he knew that he was having a good dream.

He was surprised his 30-day visa had arrived so quickly, having expected his paperwork would take at least a week as it went back and forth to Vladivostok. But there was a catch. He would have to take a physical upon arriving. If there was any sign he was sick – or suspected of being sick (and by what criteria? They were not specified) – he would need to be quarantined. But no matter, now he was on his way, on to the far eastern edge of Eurasia, where the virus was said to be especially virulent.

Chubby didn't think about it that much though, figuring if he got it – he got it. But he wore a mask, and continued his normal routine of avoiding people, mostly because it was the only thing anyone thought might be somehow preventative.

But the virus (if "virus" was what it was) seemed to Chubby like the least of his problems.

CHAPTER 20

ELWOOD AND PAULA GROW FUNGUS IN THE OREGON RAINFOREST

Mid-October

Strange events were occurring near the Ural Mountains in Russia. The virus hit Ekaterinburg, infecting over half the population in one week. All public buildings were converted to hospitals. But even that did not seem to suffice. The death toll was very high, nearly 50%. Those who recovered created a form of mass hysteria, going through the by then well-known stages of recovery: first ecstatic joy, then manic depression, followed by a flinty-eyed, hard-edged determination to end lies and corruption, with a willingness to join a life-or-death struggle against the government.

But in one place, at the Ganina Yama Monastery, an old woman made everyone a kind of mushroom soup. By the next day they were all fine. Among the recovered was a doctor, Vladimir Bulgakov, a grand-nephew of the famous writer Mikhail Bulgakov.

From *The Fall of It All – A History of the Big Dump*

PAULA SAID, "THE FUNGUS IS GROWING." SHE WAS ON her hands and knees looking at the fine white mycelium. "I thought you said it could only grow in cold weather."

"Well, I was 18 years old and freezing my ass off in the snow when we discovered it. So it made sense that it was the case."

"How long?"

"It still needs to go through its germination to reproduce. It should cover all of these trees. It's still hit or miss, but it is taking hold, now getting nutrients from the soil. When it releases its spores and connects on these cedar trees – sometime this fall – we'll see."

"It's already too late for me. I was without it for so long that I'm almost an old lady."

"Well, sorry it took so long," said Elwood. Paula looked at him, not sure if he was being sarcastic. But she caught a hint of a tear emerging from an eye. She put her head on his shoulder.

CHAPTER 21
THE MERCS PLAN THEIR ASSAULT

Mid-October

Never in the long history of this great country has so much been owed to a Few Good Men. Never forget what they did there, in that stinking Oregon city. The Persian virus started in a stinking rain forest, and we are going to rain down hell on them. We are going to do something very strong, that I can tell you.

Excerpted from a Real-Prez news conference

"I'M STILL BURNED ABOUT THAT PORTLAND OPERA-tion." Erick Duke stood up and walked around the suite. Just walked around, punching some on the shoulder, hugging others. He went into the master bedroom – his sanctuary. This operation was going to be a strain on Duke's laid-back off-duty discipline. "Some people should have been publicly shot – film it and make it viral, so people know that failure is not an option!"

"Starting with Temp-Prez!" said somebody.

Duke laughed. He had been mentioned in the online vlog "Mercs" as a possible replacement for Temp-Prez. He and Real-Prez were pretty close – his sister being the White House Chaplain, you saw her picture somewhere in every public White House event and in online magazines. He had split with his sister on religious issues, but they were still pretty close. He was Opus Dei himself and thought women had no business preaching, but he overlooked all of that when it came to politics.

"Everybody gather around," Erick said. "We got some scouts now. We know when the mistress of the house is out and about."

"So aren't we going to do an all-out assault? If we have a surprise, we can take them out fast."

"Their security is layered. They have the house and the barn, both well manned all the time and with round-the-clock surveillance. They have cameras hidden all over the place from every point of entry. They have radar; they know when choppers are in the vicinity."

"So what do we do?"

"We lure the queen bee out. Without the queen, the hive dies."

But up in the main part of the Compound, the intel team heard rumblings, and reported sightings from down in Newport and Lincoln City, of strange men filling up the motels, and meeting up on the beach, in groups of twenty or thirty, jogging together, in formation. They were no doubt the same ones who had been probing their perimeter. And, yeah, someone saw Erick Duke in town, always with about four or five thuggish looking brutes running interference for him.

They knew he was coming.

CHAPTER 22

THE HOUSE BY THE LAKE WASN'T WORTH IT

Mid-October

The Quantum Virus and Politics

The people in North America had become hyper-aware of the "Quantum Virus," as it was being called. Some were seeing terrifying visions of rapturous beauty, visions that answered the deep, personal, existential questions they had been too afraid to even consider. Some died, either in total harmony with the universe or in an existential hell, while others managed to pass through the worst phases of the disease, to tell of experiencing a whole lifetime in a few days of feverish delirium. Those who told of entering what they described as a "portal into a different world, which was both strange and familiar" were getting better.

What else was it doing? Epidemiologists were scrambling, but the more they learned, the more mysterious the origins and effects of the disease became with each passing day. How many were infected, how many of those were dying, what were the long-lasting effects, or even how it was spreading became more uncertain with each passing day.

It was being called the "Quantum Virus" because every time they tried to isolate it, it seemed to change its behavior and appearance. No one had successfully sequenced its RNA yet. It was fundamentally unlike anything anyone had ever seen before, and it was spreading everywhere fast. Masks were almost a fashion statement, because no one knew if the masks worked or even if they might not make the whole pandemic worse.

From *The Fall of It All – A History of the Big Dump*

SPENCE LAY IN HIS BED, TRYING TO WILL HIMSELF TO

get up. It was 6:30 AM, Friday, just one more day of work, and then he promised himself he would do something different, drive somewhere, get to a place where he could start making decisions about his life. He knew he had just been taking the course of least resistance, always the easiest decision – not just recently, but his whole life. From his disastrous first marriage, to then continuing to work at RDM after finding out that Gordy had been sleeping with Vickie while they were still married. And now, here he was continuing to work for Telly Haines, who stole the company after Gordy's murder. He said out loud, "He put a bag over my head and kidnapped me." He thought about it and it made him angry. How did he just go along with it?

He lived in a house by an artificial lake that was swarming with nasty horse flies. The lake had mysteriously started to dry up almost immediately after he moved in. It was an hour north of Dallas, but much closer to his office in Plano. The house was the "bonus" that Telly paid him after he agreed to continue working for RDM, which was now the Elect Cadez President committee. The lake was dried mud, except near his house and the little pier behind it, where a pool of muddy water, maybe a foot deep, remained. There was nothing in his bedroom, or anyplace else in the house, that would tell you anything about him. No books, no pictures; everything was generic. He got up and took a shower.

He had scored some excellent weed last night. It felt good to get stoned again; it had been at least a couple of months since he had smoked marijuana. After a long time without, even the morning "hangover" felt good. He got a gram of sativa (or so it was called) from a guy he had met at a blues bar near the Dallas Arboretum. They had a good happy hour barbecue menu, and he started up a conversation while waiting to pick up their orders. Following two or three comments about the weather, Spence, who picked up a vibe, or maybe just the odor of pot on the guy, said he hadn't smoked pot in a long time, wink wink (he actually said "wink wink"). The guy slipped him the bud, and refused to take money. The guy snubbed him immediately after giving him the weed, like he was a low-life beggar.

He was feeling a bit groggy, but relaxed. He looked at his fone and saw he was late, so he did not make coffee, or lounge around web surfing before leaving as he usually did, but got dressed and out the door within 20 minutes.

As he walked into SMIRK, the old EDS concrete bunkers in Plano, he was surprised to see Victor smiling at the security desk. Two other men were in the security cage with Victor, one sitting in a chair, the other sitting on the edge of the desk. They looked like cops or bagmen, in dark suits, dark short hair, and in their early forties, if that. The one sitting on the edge of Victor's desk glanced up briefly from his fone as Spence badged in, but the other guy ignored him. The air conditioning seemed colder than customary as he waited by the elevator. It took longer than usual to arrive, and even the ride down seemed to freeze time.

As he slowly made his way through the main server room, motion detectors lit up the row of racked pizza-box servers that hummed like mechanical bees. The dull mechanical drone and the sudden illumination of the bright fluorescent lights made Spence queasy. He pushed through the double doors and made it to his semi-private cubicle in the corner. He put his bag down and walked over to get some coffee, then insincerely smiled and said hi to Kayla, who looked up but barely nodded. Kayla, who had once been his boss at RDM, had quite a come-down since the Insurgency. She had come on board as Maybelle's assistant a few weeks ago, not long after Alison had left. He had not heard a word about Alison since then, and he hadn't asked anyone about her either.

Gupta wasn't in his cube. Somebody had left a printout of some code next to the coffee table, some of it highlighted in yellow, and he saw it was part of a Linux startup script – obviously Roy's. He wasn't around either, which was strange because Roy usually got in at least an hour earlier than everyone else.

Spence walked back to his desk, still a little out of it from the previous night's cannabis fog. He was feeling hemmed in and stuck, like moving through a vat of honey. He felt a bit paranoid; this cavernous, underground cyber den was a claustrophobe's nightmare. It's just because I got stoned last night, he thought. Toking up was a definite No-No in this organization, a firing offense. But he told himself to shake it off and stop worrying about it. He sat down at his desk and tried to log into his workstation. His password didn't work. He tried again, thinking he'd fat-fingered it. Nope. He leaned back, tried to breathe in and relax. His desk was situated so his back was to the wall and he had a view across the office. He was staring off, trying not to think about being locked out of his workstation, trying to pull himself together, when he saw the two men in suits from Victor's security desk casually walk in, smiling, saying hi to Kayla. She gave them a flirty smile back. One of them helped himself to a cup of coffee. Maybelle came in from the door on the other side and approached his desk.

"Spencer, you need to come with me. Something urgent has come up," she said.

"What's going on?"

The man without coffee slowly came up behind Maybelle, still wearing his friendly smile, and signaled with his hand for Spence to come along. They waited. The other guy made a face and put the partially drunk coffee on Roy's empty desk and walked over. The two guys from Victor's office looked at each other as if they were trying to decide something.

"Fine," Spence said. "Let's go." They walked back toward Maybelle's office. The campaign guy, Earl Walker, had an office behind hers. Spence had seen Walker giving interviews to the media. He was a former Texas state secretary of something or other, and seemed like an empty suit. Walker was just a mouthpiece for the Cadez campaign, right? Neither Earl "The Pearl," as Alison had called him (some basketball allusion apparently), nor Maybelle ever came through the main entrance where everybody came in, past where Victor sat. Spence knew there was another entrance, an "executive elevator" that was accessible from the parking garage.

Spence started to become very nervous as he was escorted to that elevator. Maybelle had peeled off and gone into her office, and he and the two guys from Victor's office got in the elevator. They went all the way down.

The doors opened, and things began to change. Spence felt hands on each of his elbows. The hallway was dull gray and the floor was bare concrete. They came to a steel door with a touchpad code above the knob; the guy in front entered a code and opened the door. When Spence hesitated to enter and sputtered an incoherent protest, he was pushed in.

It was a standard cop interrogation room, two hard-back metal chairs, a metal table, and a big mirror on the wall. They searched him, took his fone, and left without a word. The steel door closed behind him. He looked at the mirror and gave it the finger. The chairs were attached to the floor with short cables. He couldn't move them away from the table, which faced the mirror. Cameras stared down from opposite corners. He moved over against the wall, as far out of sight as possible, and slid down onto the floor with his back against the wall. He realized he was still a little groggy, and the thought came to him that this was about the pot he smoked last night. He started imagining that they knew he had gotten stoned and were turning on the third degree about it. But if that was it, why didn't they simply make him piss in a jar?

He had just dozed off when he heard the door open. The older of the two men and Kayla came in, not looking at him, carrying a laptop. The men, whom he vaguely recognized now, carried a couple of steaming paper cups and a paper bag. Spence smelled food – bacon fries, onions, odors that woke him. He was conscious that his mouth was watering. He had no idea how long he had been there, but he felt very stiff and disoriented as he slowly stood up. Then a guy in a wheelchair rolled in. He was about 30, short blond hair, and was followed a few seconds later by Telly Haines.

As the guy in the wheelchair turned and faced him, he saw a recent burn scar on the side of his face where it appeared his left eye was missing.

"Spence!" Telly had his oversized snow-white, capped, crocodile teeth set in what was supposed to be a smile. "You must be hungry. Come over, sit down, have something to eat."

"Can I use the bathroom?"

Telly looked at the older man who carried the food.

"Help him out, will you, Johnny?"

The man called Johnny signaled Spence and they went out and down a bit, to a basic bathroom – all concrete, no mirror, a toilet, toilet paper, a sink with liquid soap. Paper towels and a small cardboard box on the floor.

"I'm glad I don't have to wear a bag on my head anyway," Spence said. Johnny kept his deadpan look, put his hand on his shoulder, and gently pushed him toward the toilet.

Spence found himself looking and remembering everything since Portland, including Johnny at the airport with Alison. He remembered his too-brief time with Alison, the heavy canvas bag on his head, and his self-justification for working for them. It just all came to him at once, and he started crying. It was too late now, he realized.

He finished pissing, but now he had to take a shit. He dropped his pants and sat on the toilet, with his hands on his knees, fighting to make his mind blank. He didn't get up right away when he was finished. The guy in the wheelchair scared him. Johnny scared him; even Kayla scared him. Telly scared him. He sat there longer than he needed. Finally he heard knocking.

"Just a minute," he yelled.

He came out and Johnny was waiting. He flashed a smile and said, "Come on kid," as he ushered him ahead back to the interrogation room. "Did you wash your hands?"

"Yeah," said Spence dejectedly.

Spence went over without prompting and sat in front of the Styrofoam container with his breakfast. He looked up and Telly signaled for him to go ahead. Johnny stood at the door.

"Eat!" Telly and the wheelchair guy sat opposite Spence. "This is Kendal."

"Hey, Kendal." Spence tried to smile and nod, but he knew it came off as patronizing. Kendal just stared at him, without even a nod of acknowledgment.

"I suppose you are wondering what this is all about?"

Spence was pretty sure by now that it had nothing to do with him getting high the previous evening. "Yeah. I don't know what any of this is about. I don't like..."

"Spence. Spence. You were once one of the most successful media gurus in the country. You know what's going on. So you can't play innocent here."

"I am just a...I don't know, Telly. I don't know what you think I did. I..."

"You built *Reigny Deigh Media*. Everyone knows Gordon Lobetts was a putz. You know it too. You were a player, my friend. You kept it all afloat. A major player. You wrote TV shows. You wrote software, important software. You are a fucking genius.

You know it. Everyone in the business knows it. My question is: Why are you such a fucking loser? A weak nobody. Why? I have been watching you. You could rock the world – but I know you are slacking on us. I know and you know it too. We should have the C2B fully operational, and independently integrated with *SwiftPad*. But we are no closer than we were two months ago. You have let me down. Big time! It was just too –"

"I know – I know. What you are saying – it's so fucking true. But it's not me. I kept trying to get Gopesh to build a full proto-type, but he just kept pushing back. He –"

"Why didn't you get tough with him?"

"I don't know. I don't know how I got to this point. I lost connection with reality to be honest. I never bought into any of it before Real-Prez and I don't buy into any..."

"I don't buy into Real-Prez either, Spence." Telly smiled and shook his head as though admonishing a child. "On that we agree. That's why we need a younger, more rational leader – like Ben Cadez. I thought you understood that. But now I am not so sure."

"OK," Spence said.

"What's that supposed to mean?"

"OK, Cadez, yeah. I know." Spence put his plastic fork down, and stared as his fried egg–hash-brown ensemble coagulated before his eyes. "I mean me and Gopee are working on the C2B-*SwiftPad* interface. We know it's supposed to help Cadez. We should be done by now."

Telly Haines stared at Spence, and said nothing for a long time. Spence kept looking at him, then looking away, determined to not say anything. He sighed. He felt his heart beating.

Kendal kept his one good eye focused on Spence like a power drill.

"Where is Gupta?" Spence asked.

Telly turned to Kayla. "Let him listen to Roy's report."

She had been intently scribing their conversation, but now smiled at Telly, hit her mouse, and sat back to listen.

ROY: "Yeah, um, Maybelle, I don't know how to put this..."

MAYBELLE: "Yeah, what is it, Roy?"

ROY: "Well you know how Gopesh has been ordering up new Linux boxes...he has been provisioning them himself, putting his own security on..."

MAYBELLE: "Yeah."

ROY: "Well, I after I turned them over to him, you know, Spence was on my ass to hurry up, so I didn't get all the patches applied. So I logged into one of the boxes that Gopesh was building and he had changed the root password, which – I know, he claimed he had to, and we talked about how that was against the rules, I know, and he said you said it was OK."

MAYBELLE: "Yes, I remember him asking. But I said I would check on it. I never gave him permission."

ROY: "Well – somebody changed it – so I used a boot disk to get around it, and he still had not hard encrypted – which – you know freezes the file system, on the last box I gave him, so I thought, just to – cover my own ass – excuse me – follow procedures – so I tried to apply the patch on that one at least. So I cranked it up, and – well I was peeking around his home directory and found this text file."

MAYBELLE: "Go ahead and read it."

ROY: "Yeah – OK – 'The big dump is on. Interface irrelevant. Cadez set for B2Z. Overload – maybe only way,' and then – I think it was a copy of a message or something like that – 'Shred the works.'"

MAYBELLE: "What's that mean, Roy?"

ROY: "I don't know. Interface is the only thing – I suppose – since Spencer is working on the interface between *SwiftPad* and Gupta's brain machine –"

MAYBELLE: "Nothing else?"

ROY: "No, well – B – that could mean brain – right? The number 2 – if used like in C2B it is the connection like the word 'to.' You know – 'computer to brain'? But Z – I don't know Z. That is all just a guess."

MAYBELLE: "You found nothing else?"

ROY: "No – he encrypts his code as he works. I think he doesn't leave it unencrypted when he goes to the bathroom. Need to get the key from him, I guess."

"Well?" asked Telly.

Spence looked at Telly with real fear in his eyes. He put his hands out in a silent gesture of ignorance.

"What's 'overload'?

"I don't know."

"B2Z?"

"No, I – business – right? B? Z?"

"The big dump?"

Spence's stomach growled. He shook his head. I don't know. "Can I use the bathroom again?"

Telly chuckled, and shook his head. Johnny laughed too, and Kayla smiled. Nothing from Kendal. "When did you last see Alison Aykroyd?"

"When she was here, a month ago maybe."

"When did you last talk to her?"

"Then. When she was here!"

"No messages?"

Spence felt for his fone, but remembered they took it. "No."

Telly looked at Kendal, who pushed himself up against the

table and pulled a photo up on his fone. He held it up for Spence to look at.

Spence stared at it. It was the body of a woman, sprawled out, eyes half opened, her blouse torn, half opened, and darkly stained. Her blue bra exposed. He remembered the bra from that last night, that one and only time – her dark hair looked stiff and matted. He tried to speak but it came out as a guttural moan.

"You know this cunt?" Spence looked up and saw Kendal was speaking to him. "You familiar with this dead cunt?"

"Fuck you. Fuck you, gimp!"

"Oh my God," Kayla put her hand over her mouth. "That's – she used to work..."

"...OK, Kayla, I think we have enough," said Telly. "We can record the rest, if we need to. Just leave your laptop open; we have some more videos to show Mr. Stromborn here."

Kayla got up and walked out without a word or even a glance back. When the door closed Johnny came over and began to put shackles on Spence's arms. He tried to pull away, and Johnny punched him hard in the face three times. When he was done, Spence, completely restrained, tried to hide inside his pain. Telly pulled the laptop in front of Spence and started a video. Spence found himself looking at almost an identical scene to his, except Gopesh was in the chair he was in. The other guy from upstairs in Victor's office was there too, jackets and ties off, shirts opened at the throat. It could have been a live feed, but Spence suspected it had already occurred.

Gopesh's face was beaten so badly he was almost unrecognizable. There was a box on the table and wires going down Gopesh's torso. Spence heard Telly's voice. "Go ahead."

One of the guys pushed something on the box and then pulled a slide bar down. Gopesh appeared to start screaming. It was barely audible. But Gopesh looked like an animal in distress.

"Want to hear your buddy?" Telly turned up the volume. The screaming suddenly became loud enough to almost hurt Spence's eardrums. The man pushed the slide bar back up. The screaming stopped.

"What is the key to your file system?"

"I gave it to you," Gopesh gasped, trying to compose himself. "Didn't you try it?"

"Yes – it didn't work! It appeared to scramble the system even worse."

"Really? You had Mr. Roy..." Gopesh spat blood and stopped to get his breath. "...You had Roy run the key against it?"

"We ran it. It didn't work."

Gopesh smiled. "Maybe I gave you the wrong key? I am very sorry, but I think the key you want was deleted. It's gone, and there is no way I would remember 64 letters and numbers, even if I tried. So it doesn't matter now." He started screaming again. "It's gone, gone. Gone. You can't recover it. I only typed it once, and I am sure my subconscious can't remember it either."

"You're lying!"

Gopesh put his head down and seemed to stop responding.

The video ended.

"Do you have anything to say?" Telly asked. Kendal with the burnt face and broken spine continued to stare at him.

"Are you talking about his C2B development machine?"

"Yes," said Telly.

"Don't you have backups? Did you talk to Roy? He should have them."

Telly sat down. "What do you know about Gopesh's development? Did you talk to him about it?"

"He was having some trouble – we did a demo when..." Spence stopped. "Maybelle must have told you about that."

"We know that Gopesh – and you – deceived us. That it was much further along than you told us. And you were looking to pass it to the *SwiftPad* team in Oregon."

"Total bullshit. No."

"You talked about it with the dead cunt, didn't you?" Kendal wheeled his chair against Spence's leg, but he barely felt it.

"Maybelle experienced the same thing I did. I mean it was definitely something, but too unreliable. Just kind of euphoria, like being high."

"OK," said Kendal. "Let's come back to that, Telly." Kendal moved his wheelchair around and came up beside where Spence was shackled. "Let's bring in the 'crown.'"

"Go get the C2B headpiece, and the box. Maybelle knows where it is."

Johnny looked at Telly, then went out.

"We are going to hook you up to an ordinary C2B box, Mr. Stromborn. Turn on the juice, like you saw we did with Gopesh. Since you won't tell us about the Dot Head's enhancements, we are going to let you see what the commercial C2B feels like when the volume is turned all the way up. We'll just call it a product safety test," Telly said.

"Burn out your blub, fry your brain like an egg," said Kendal. "Then we'll shoot you up with the virus and turn you loose in one of our border migrant camps. After they finish fucking you in your little asshole for a week, maybe then you'll remember. But probably not. Probably – there will be no you. If you live. But – to be honest – we don't know what will happen. It's kind of an experiment."

"I don't know anything. I'll show you what I'd have done with the interface. I'll help try and recreate what Gopesh was working on. Maybe…"

"No," said Telly. ""It's too late, we'll never finish it and ship it in time now. We told you this was time sensitive. Time's up, bub."

"What? Honest! I will help you!"

"We'll see."

"Let's find out, Telly," said Kendal. "Give him one more chance. Who's Chubby? Spence – just tell us – who is Chubby?"

"What?"

"Chubby! Who is Chubby?"

"You mean fat? Who is fat? What do you mean?"

"Chubby Welles – who's Chubby Welles?"

"I don't know."

"Bullshit!"

"You mean Orson Welles? The movie director? What are you talking about?" Spence kept looking back and forth, between Telly and Kendal, like he was ready to flinch. They sat there saying nothing for a while.

"You never heard anyone called that?"

"No!"

"Did you fuck Alison?"

Spence looked at Telly. He opened his mouth but nothing came out.

"The dead cunt, dipshit!" Kendal screamed.

Spence put his head down and started sobbing.

"So – just for the record, how many times did you fuck her? Were you fucking her when you worked at Gordy's company? What did you guys plan to do?"

"No, we didn't – just – when she was here – just once…"

"Just once, huh," said Telly. "Yeah, I believe you. I believe you."

"Was she good?" Kendal raised his eyebrows. "Did she come?"

"I loved her." He started sobbing.

Kendal laughed.

"Let me ask you another question, Spence. What did you two talk about back in Portland? What did Gordy say about me?" Telly asked.

"We didn't want…"

"Want what? What, Spence?"

"We liked Gordy. I mean, he let us run things. We just thought he was a – I was afraid it would change…"

"Gordy fucked your first wife, didn't he?"

Spence looked up at Telly and felt bile rising in his throat. He leaped at Telly, but the shackles held.

"OK. So were you in touch with the opposition – the people planning to overthrow Real-Prez?"

"No."

"Gary Humpkin?"

"You mean the news guy – I've seen him on TV – but?"

"But..."

"But what?"

"Come on, Spence," said Kendal. "Don't play dumb. You worked for the Ishpeming Group."

"Who?"

Kendal and Telly looked at each other. "You know you were. We know you were. Come clean and tell us about it."

"I don't know! I don't know anything about that. Chubby? I just worked on the interface. I never heard of Chubby! That's all. I did – I had a crush – a thing for Alison. Yeah, it's true, but I was married. So – of course we talked, but only about helping Gordy. That's all."

Maybelle came in with Johnny. She was carrying the round headset with the electrodes and he was carrying the box.

"She insisted."

"That's OK, Johnny. Set it in front of him," Telly directed.

"I know how to work this headpiece, Mr. Haines. Let me put it on him. This creep played me." Maybelle looked down at Spence, shooting fire out of her eyes.

"OK. Cinch his arms down tight, Johnny. Then hold his head so Miss Maybelle can wire him up. Who knows? We burn enough of his brain, maybe what is left will remember."

"No, wait!"

"Gag him. I don't want to listen to him anymore," said Telly.

CHAPTER 23
ARKIE TEACHES SEQUOIA ABOUT HIS BRAINSTORM

Mid-October

The Saint Petersburg Flood Prevention Facility Complex (Ко́мплекс защи́тных сооруже́ний Санкт-Петербу́рга от наводне́ний, *kómpleks zashchítnykh sooruzhéniy Sankt-Peterbúrga ot navodnéniy*), unofficially the Saint Petersburg Dam, is a 25-km (16-mi) long complex of dams for flood control near Saint Petersburg, Russia....The complex is intended to protect Saint Petersburg from [Baltic] storm surges by separating the Neva Bay from the rest of the Gulf of Finland....The northern and southern parts of the dam act like two giant bridges, providing access from the mainland to Kotlin Island and Kronstadt.

Historically, storm surges from the gulf have caused over 300 floods of varying severity within the city, some with devastating effects. The dam has the capability to protect the city from water rising up to 5 m (16 ft).

From Wikipedia Article on the
Saint Petersburg Dam

SEQUOIA AND ARKIE WALKED OVER TO THE HOUSE.

Nate and Elwood were sitting at the kitchen table, in front of two glasses of white wine and a bottle that was almost empty. Two .22 pistols (a Walther and a Beretta) were also on the table.

"What are you guys doing?"

"Playing Russian roulette. Want in?"

"The last line of defense, huh?"

They both gave Arkie the finger as he and Sequoia went down the basement stairs.

"Actually, that is what we are going to do right now," said Arkie.

"Russian roulette?" Sequoia looked concerned.

"No. Design the last line of defense."

Only one person was working in the monitoring center. Usually there were at least four, but neither Arkie nor Sequoia was surprised everyone was topside. Alice was hosting a vegan barbecue, and it was nice fall weather. They sat in front of one of the stations and Arkie logged in.

"OK, let me do a little navigating." Arkie then pulled out a scribble he kept in his back pocket, filled with IP addresses and users and passwords. "Go ahead, write this down. Don't video it or even store it on your systems. I mean it, this is – of the highest possible importance. It has to remain secret!" It was a layered set of systems, about seven deep, meaning he had to pass through six portals, darkweb-type entry points, just to get to the starting point.

"OK."

"OK here – I was up all night looking up Siemens Switch command syntax. And researching hacks into the OS of the switches themselves."

"But – why?"

"Ever since 2011, the Russian city of St. Petersburg on the Neva River has been protected against the threat of high water from the Baltic by a dam and giant gate across the Neva Bay. There is a low pressure system in the Gulf of Bothnia, between Sweden and Finland. It might be nothing, or it could mean a

Baltic cyclone. They sometimes take a couple of weeks to form. There have been cases of it lasting a month or longer, before it breaks up or forms a storm."

"OK, so will the dam hold?"

"Ha!" Arkie smiled, and continued to test. "Probably. The dam is five meters above sea level. That is a lot. No, it is going to take a major off-the-charts storm to overflow that! Someday, sure, with climate change, and rising sea levels, but not yet. Unless..."

"Yeah..."

"Unless the gate on the dam doesn't close during a storm. Here is the piece that will be difficult. Check this out! I am into their control center. I came in through a server in the St. Petersburg City Admin building, so – the thought is – that their intrusion detection won't see me if I come in from one of their boxes. The Russians are good at attack, and sloppy on defense. Anyway, I have been working on this off and on for the last two months. We need to give Chubby some leverage when and if he tries to get GG out."

"So," said Sequoia, "What does that box control?"

"This is the Simatic PCS 7 system. I know this system. I helped some people with a simulation of an attack on process control systems years ago. It still looks pretty much the same. Command set is similar to Cisco's, turns systems off and on to activate, then steps down to lower levels to control those system functions. Of course the operators don't do it like this, they have a GUI they can mouse around. I know a guy who can crack it. He owes me."

"Who?"

"Well, I don't actually know him. I don't even know what country he lives in; I think he is in Europe somewhere. But he hates Siemens, the company. I don't know why. Maybe used to work there, or maybe something to do with the war, or maybe it is even more personal than that. Doesn't matter."

Arkie demonstrated how they could move around the system;

he was displaying and cutting and pasting the current settings of the devices it controlled – pumps for flooding and draining the lagoons, motors for lifting, and releasing the gates, etc.

"Here," he said. He looked over and saw Sequoia was mesmerized. "See, look – here is a map of St. Petersburg. See where the city is? It is all reclaimed marshland. Peter the Great built it during the 1700s and hundreds of thousands of workers died – froze, disease, the whole thing. It is hard to see how it was different from Stalin's worst atrocities. But the results speak for themselves. It is a waterway to Western Europe – the Baltic. Here – see this line across the bay? That is called the KZS – 16 miles of dams. Flood control. During storms it stops the flood surge and protects the city. The whole thing – the key point – is here. The S-1. On Russian maps it is "C-1" because C in Russian is pronounced like an S. This is a gate – 200 meters long – a floating gate that is almost always open – for shipping. But during a storm – it closes. It has only closed a couple of times since 2011."

"And the Siemens industrial control system controls it."

"Exactly. Well, there might be a storm coming; it might be nothing or it might be big. But there is an extremely low pressure polar vortex developing and if it moves south and hits the high-pressure hot air – bang! We have a massive Baltic cyclone that moves up into the funnel of the Neva Bay. So if we can take control of this system...before it hits...if it hits..."

"...Take control of the system and don't let them control the S-1! Right?"

"Exactly."

"Give us the girl, or we flood the city!" Sequoia said in a low, gravelly, hoodlum voice. Arkie laughed.

"As you can see we have breached the first layer of their defenses – we can get to the Simatic login prompt. Which means we can change things – but we need to understand the procedures they use to make it work. Their failsafe systems, etc."

Sequoia took over the controls and started maneuvering

around. She listed out the users, and their authorities. "We are just a guest user here. Go slow. We can look but not touch, right?"

"You are right. We will need to get super-user authority. Have to find a buffer overload sequence. I know we can do that – or my friend can – in fact he probably already has the steps for that. Hear, listen to this – 'The S-1 submersible storm surge barrier is 200 meters across and 16 meters deep. In the event of a flood warning the barrier's giant gates close shut. Each one can move freely, functioning like a submerging submarine.'"

Arkie and Sequoia spent about 14 hours straight working on penetrating the dam operation. Arkie's friend in Europe found a working version of the Simatic PCS 7 – including its virtualized panel – and allowed them to practice on it. He also gave them a technique to buffer overload the guest user and – voilà – super-user! Which meant they could lock out everybody else when the time came. His friend also gave him access into the classified section of Siemens databases, and found the full specs on the hydraulics and access points into the dam.

"The problem – well – the ultimate problem – we have a bunch of problems," Arkie shook his head.

"Let me get you some coffee; I need a cup myself," said Sequoia.

"The default setting – if you just let it float and open the valves – is for the S-1 gate to be closed. But they almost never close it. To keep it open they have to activate the hydraulic piston – and the motors that push it – there are two of them about five meters in diameter."

"Is there a manual override?"

"Of course," said Arkie. "Here, look at this schematic." Arkie pulled up a visual of the floor plan of the control room. "In order for this to be a surprise, we would have to activate the gate and lift it after the storm is surging. They will close it well before the surge arrives. So we will have to time locking it 'open' before they close it."

"Or figure out how to open it after it closes."

"Yeah. I hadn't thought of that. We will need to game both scenarios."

"We don't have time. We have to keep it from closing. Which means we have to sabotage it in a way they don't suspect until it is too late – for them. And of course have a way to fix it," said Sequoia, "to open it later."

"Right."

"The good news is that the dry dock where it sits when open will be flooded. The gates float out and close on their own. We just have to keep the dry dock 'dry' and keep people off it so they can't open the spigot manually – assuming we can shut it down with the process control."

"So if the hydraulics don't work – it will lift the gate up until it floats free, then the water pushes it closed. We can't let the gate float," said Arkie.

"It seems impossible. We have a long way to go..."

CHAPTER 24

CHUBBY TRAVELS WEST THROUGH SIBERIA

Mid-October

Three weeks before the election, panic was setting in. Humpkin was barnstorming the toss-up states, speaking in little towns across the Midwest. The crowds were enormous. But then a sharp-eyed reporter from Columbus, Ohio, noticed some men he didn't recognize handing out brand new masks with "Win with Humpkin" printed on the front. It struck him as strange, so he went through the line and collected one. He took it to a lab and had it analyzed. All of the masks, right out of the cellophane, were teeming with virus, a virtual petri dish of pathogens. The story hit the front pages of every blog and news organization. The photos of the men distributing it were identified as members of the Real-Prez advance team.

A week after the rally in Columbus more than two thousand people were stricken by the virus, and more than half died. Most were able to vote, however, as absentee ballots had been forwarded to them earlier. Real-Prez immediately went to court, suing, saying dead people can't vote, and tried to nullify all the Ohio absentee ballots.

From *The Fall of It All – A History of the Big Dump*

FTER A COUPLE OF DAYS IN THE HOTEL ISTOK, A grimy dump near the docks that rented flops by the hour, Chubby bribed his way out of quarantine in Vladivostok, got his passport chopped "no infection" ("nyet infekshuney" – нет инфекции), and then he was off heading west on the Trans-Siberian. He was feeling good, and pretty sure he was not infected. He bought a first-class ticket to Irkutsk, where he intended to bust any tails on him. He planned to lam it there for three days, and he studied maps the whole way.

When he got off the train, he started walking up to the cliff in front of the Irkutsk train station. The streets were winding, and after traveling for half an hour, he came upon a man approaching a late-model BMW. There was some rust showing on the hood, but otherwise the car looked in good repair, and the man, masked of course, appeared to be in his 40s. Kip approached him.

"My friend! I am an American! Drive me to the Lake."

Kip pulled out a hundred-dollar bill and held it out to the man, who leaned forward to look at the bill and at Chubby, then swiftly asked,

"Tourist?"

"Yes – I want to see the greatest lake in the world!"

"Да – садись в машину, быстро!" ("Yes – get in the car, quickly!")

"I am Igor," he said.

Igor opened his car door, put the money in his pocket, and they were off.

"Corny," said Chubby, pointing at himself.

"Corny – funny name! – OK!" They took the Academic Bridge (Академический мост) across the Angara River and headed east for Listvyanka, a small town 40 km away situated at the mouth of the Angara, on the largest body of fresh water in the world, Lake Baikal.

Igor was a good conversationalist. He must have figured that "Corny" was a mobster in some capacity, because he was careful not to pry and his questions were very innocent. As they left the city, he became nervous, and Kip did his best to put him at ease, said he was actually a businessman, and interested in timber, and wanted to see the lake. He said he intended to sleep by the lake and commune with its spirits. Did Igor think there was any truth to the rumor that Genghis Khan had been buried near the lake?

"Some say so, but no – it is not possible. He is buried south of here in Mongolia. The Mongols only say that because they want to claim the lake."

His new friend Igor understood Chubby's desire to commune with nature on the shores of the lake. "We have many legends about the lake. An entire Mongolian army supposedly broke through the ice, and disappeared in it. But the fish are dying now. Pollution. No mystery to that. The old ladies now have washing machines and the machine soap washes into the rivers."

It was more than old ladies' washing machines, but Chubby let it go without comment. Chubby's plan – to throw off tails, make "them" think maybe he stayed on the train instead of stopping in Irkutsk – gave him a focus, kept him alert, and of course put him in a place where he could think about what was happening.

But so far, he had no awareness of any tail, except for the Adidas tracksuit guy on his trip to Mihonoseki in Japan, whom he never saw after that.

He arrived late. He got out of Igor's car just outside of town, and immediately started walking north, past the edge of town, then down to the shoreline, along the lake, away from houses and buildings. He was sure no one was following him, and after walking until it was nearly dark, he set up a little campsite.

The weather was unusually warm. Although it was mid-October and this was Siberia, the evening temperature was nearly

27°C (80°F). With no rain in sight, Chubby set up on a cliff overlooking the lake. He had a little gas stove, and made rice with bouillon and dried seaweed. He finished his flask of Irish whiskey. OK – the air was so fresh, regardless of Igor's complaint of pollution. His sleeping bag was almost too warm, and he lay on it, with the flap unzipped. What's the plan?

Before he left Sakaiminato, he received a message – in the clear, but hidden in plain sight, in an obscure post where he knew to look – that GG was almost definitely living in St. Petersburg, that she was OK, and her baby, a girl, had been born.

She was living in the "Petrograd district," on the "Finland" side of the Neva, not far from the Peter-Paul fortress that sits across from the Hermitage. It took him three hours to decode the message, with his "One Time Pad" app.

Chubby had dreamed of visiting St. Petersburg ever since he started studying Russian in his many attempts to attend college – all aborted because some other shiny object in his life rose up and distracted him. According to the message he decoded from Arkie, GG was being held in the large enclosed campus where the Russian hackers worked. He was excited, but he knew he had to chill, go "stone cold," be sure to lose any trackers and take his time getting to Leningrad. Ishpeming Command was pushing for him to get there before the election. Why that mattered, he was not sure, but Alice's team at the Compound said it was "kind of an order."

Arkie, Elwood, and that psycho girl Elwood was living with had made it back to Oregon from Illinois. There must have been over a hundred people living at his old homestead. Alice was running it like she owned it. He shrugged. Let it go, he said to himself. Let it all go. Only one thing to think about now, one task. Find GG and get her out of Russia.

As night descended over Siberia, he listened to the gentle lapping of the water on the shore of Lake Baikal just below him. A magnificent place, he thought. You could spend five lifetimes exploring the lake and its surroundings.

The next day he got up early and walked back to Listvyanka, then talked his way onto an empty tour bus heading back to Irkutsk. The virus had killed the tourist business, but the driver seemed friendly and told him he could get him a woman for the night or the afternoon if he wanted. Chubby tipped him $10, and the driver was ecstatic. He found a plane leaving for Omsk that afternoon and took a cab in Irkutsk to the airport, arriving in Omsk that evening. No tail, nobody even noticed him, or looked up at his American-accented Russian. On the way to the airport he booked a room in the Mayak, which looked like a cheap but decent hotel (at least from his fone anyway) close to the river junction of the Irtysh and the Om in Omsk for that night.

The next morning he got up and decided to get out and walk around Omsk, find some place to eat, look at the sights. He walked up along the Om River and crossed over to the other side, which seemed like the older side of town. Omsk had been a "White City" during the Russian civil war after WWI, and the city felt somewhat "Czarist." Old-style Orthodox churches were everywhere. And over across the Om River from the Mayak, near the fortress where he spent 10 years in prison (and wrote *House of the Dead*) was a huge statue of Dostoyevsky. Chubby watched a parade of school kids carrying banners supporting the government. They looked happy just to be outside. It was really hot.

He stopped for a late breakfast at a little café. Mashed potatoes, a fried egg, grated carrots. Bad coffee, tasted instant, but gave him a nice buzz. He got up and asked where the bathroom was. Down the hall, past a closet, where he peeked in and saw a cot and a desk, and cleaning supplies. Chubby pissed. Maybe stay another night. Omsk had a nice feel. Beautiful murals on the walls, and statues everywhere, incredible artwork. He had seen an amazing Don Quixote mounted in front of a theater about to open a performance of Chekhov's *The Cherry Orchard*. The Spanish knight was made of various pieces of scrap iron, roughly welded together. He was hesitating, because he had no idea how to proceed. Now that he knew GG was in St. Petersburg, he felt stuck, because he didn't know what he would do when he got there, how he would get her out.

He got back to his table, and sat down to finish his coffee. He was thinking about having a piece of pastry. He was not quite satisfied. A piece of paper had been slid under his plate. Shit, he thought, they already gave me my bill. Maybe it was a sign for him to forget dessert. He picked it up and turned it over.

"Greetings from Nikoloz!"

He looked around. There was an older couple sitting next to the door. He walked over and asked them, "Did you see someone near my table just now?"

"Yes – a man in a tracksuit came in and left something there," said the old woman. The old man with her suddenly shook the table hard, rattling plates and condiment jars. "Stop!" he said. He shook his head at his wife, admonishing her for getting involved. Chubby stepped away and went back to his table, stared at the note, and finished his coffee. He left without ordering dessert.

CHAPTER 25
DISASTER AT THE REHAIN COMPOUND

Mid-October

Real-Prez had fired the chairman of the Joint Chiefs of Staff and announced he "was assuming direct command of all military assets" on October 3. Things suddenly got quiet.
From The Fall of It All – A History of the Big Dump

EIGHT MEN FROM ERICK DUKE'S ELITE SQUAD OF mercs had hiked up the Siletz River until they got to Skookum Creek, which was completely covered with thick impenetrable brush, mostly blackberry, but also goatsbeard, coyote bush, rhododendron, huckleberry, and azalea. Going was slow, but Gull led them through with a minimum of machete work, finding holes in the brush that were not at all obvious.

Erick himself was about 30 miles away, getting ready to take off in his own Airbus H160 chopper. He was piloting, and had a co-pilot to take over when they hit the ground with his troops.

It would be just starting to get light out when they arrived at the Rehain Compound.

"We are on the edge, prepare to drop, we've got the area covered," Erick said into the comm-mic. He considered himself a good chopper pilot, but he had never landed one under fire, and wanted to get into the action. They were going to drop off in the big gravel square. He looked down and saw the square was deserted. It didn't seem right somehow; there was usually some activity. Well, it will make the surprise more surprising, he thought. He heard some explosions over the comm and then a faint echo of them far to the north.

"Seahawk One to Gull, give me your ten?"

He received no answer. At this point he had to make a decision. He was sure he had lost the element of surprise. He had to assume Gull was out.

Then he heard "Still up." It was Gull in his headset. "Moving up to target." Nothing else. "OK, G team is still viable, we are going in, lock and load, gentlemen, we are taking these traitors out!"

It was planned to be a decapitation exercise. Land – get into the main house. Find Alice and kill her. Get into the underground command center, destroy all the computer systems, and kill as many as possible, then get out. They were packing ten kilos of C4. The goal was to disrupt *SwiftPad*. Erick didn't have to check with the Real President. His little sister Martha had been on TV only two days ago, and she was shilling for a "new" social media network, and calling for the destruction of *SwiftPad*. It was about the only media outlet that had still not bent to the Real-Prez. Erick had been told that by jamming the network's systems at the Rehain Compound he would be helping Real-Prez.

Gull had given him the layout. There were three entrances to the underground command center: from the cellar in the old house; a long tunnel from the hangar; and an exit off of the side of the hill north of the gravel square. Erick was leading ten men to take the house. Gull was coming up from the south through the woods to get to the hillside exit.

Erick checked the video from the drone they had sent out earlier. Nothing in the main yard. The hangar across the yard was closed. He had ten other guys, plus equipment, explosives, an RPG; everybody was completely decked out in the latest Waffen-Tech. They were all experienced, well-trained mercs.

"You go first," Gull said. The eight men were all geared up with a mélange of automatic rifles, AKs, MRs, Sig Sauers, laser scopes, grease paint on their faces, all with their own style of stealth. When they got into the hollow just below the border of the Rehain Compound, Gull heard through his earpiece that the chopper was about to move. They were behind schedule.

"Come on, let's go, we need to move!"

They moved up the hill from the creek bed that they walked in on. The brush was thick and it was slow going. Gull started cutting brush like a wild man. They came into a clearing.

In the command center, the microphones they had only last week strung out around possible access on the perimeter picked up the noise of Gull's team moving up the hill. One of the cameras caught one of the mercs in full view, and seeing him decked out with automatic rifles and camo was enough.

Maggie and a crew of five quickly went out the hillside exit and scrambled down to meet the mercs. They ran past Paula's hobbit house, and Nate came out.

Maggie laughed. It was an odd time to catch her former

boyfriend coming out of another woman's house in the early morning.

"What's up?" Nate tried to maintain a *sangfroid* countenance.

"We have mercs coming in up the north slope. We are going to surprise them."

"Hold on, I'm coming with you." Nate ran back into the hobbit hole, and then was back out carrying a gun.

"A pistol?"

"A Beretta 9 ain't just a pistol!"

There were only five of them, four with automatic rifles; they were outnumbered and outgunned. They were stalking toward the only practical route up the hill, a narrow path along a ledge over a deep depression. They set up along a line that had good cover and pretty clear visibility, and heard them coming just as they settled. Nate looked over at Maggie and she smiled and pointed to her fone. She pantomimed holding her hands over her ears. She and the others had on headphones that covered their ears. She touched the screen.

A series of concussion grenades went off. Nate held his hands over his ears. One two three.

Then the team moved down the hill. They found five of them unconscious, and one bleeding from the ears. All of them had strong vital signs, and so they zip-tied them like hogs.

"Leave 'em, we'll come back."

There was a shot. One of Maggie's men went down with a wound to the chest. Maggie returned fire. She killed one. Another shot. Nate went down.

Maggie, staying low, ran over to him.

He was dead.

"Fuck," Maggie got on her knees next to Nate. He was gone. "Oh, Nate! I'm sorry," she said. Tears came, but she fought them.

"Shit. Damn. I think one of them – I saw the bushes up over on that rise move," said Zane. "Only one though. We bagged six of 'em."

"Was it Gull?"

"I think so."

Maggie was nearly wailing out a sound that wasn't quite human. It echoed agony. She was shaking with her whole body. "Fuck," she finally said as she looked back at the neat efficient cuts through the brush. "Gull."

〰〰

Meanwhile Erick slowly guided his H160 chopper down into the center of the gravel square as his crew lay down automatic rifle fire. By now the Compound force was aware that they were under attack and had quickly moved into various positions around the square. Once the chopper was on the ground, there was a brief delay – five seconds with no noise or any movement. Then they began jumping out, one after the other, with minimal covering fire. After about five mercs had hit the ground and were running for cover by the trees next to the house, Elwood – taking advantage of his 20 years of hardball league pitching – stood and threw a strike with an M-67 US Army fragmentation grenade – the "baseball bomb." It covered about 30 meters across the square and went right into the door of the chopper, exploding and blowing out all of the windows. No more men came out.

Erick led the remainder of his men toward the house, firing on auto. They laid down a blistering barrage of bullets, killing a couple of people outright and wounding Jerry. Sequoia was just outside and shot two of the mercs, then hit Erick in the leg. He kneeled down behind a tree. His other two men were also pinned down. Six Compound members from the hangar came down and, running along the edge of the square, got in position to put the three remaining mercs in a crossfire. It wasn't going well for Erick's mercs.

Alice came to the back door of the house, stood there in the open, and told them to surrender. Erick stood and put his hands up. The firing stopped. But one of his men, still from behind cover, shot Alice and hit her in the head, killing her immediately.

With that the other two mercs' positions were quickly overrun, and they were shot as they begged for mercy.

Erick stood and put his hands up. Hester approached him with an AK aimed at his crotch. She told him to put his hands on his head. She got behind him like she was going to zip-tie his hands.

Instead, she pulled out her hunting knife and drew it across his throat. He fell to his knees, holding his throat with a look of abject fear as his life bled through his fingers. After a minute he was dead.

~~~

Gull had escaped Maggie's ambush and continued up the hill. He snuck past the Compound's warren of hobbit houses, resisting the temptation to break in and attack their occupants, and arrived at the hillside exit from the command center just as Erick's helicopter landed in the square. Gull waited to see how it would unfold. When he saw Elwood's grenade demolish the chopper, killing half the men, he knew it was over.

Gull had worked in the Compound for half his life. He was realizing that some of the Compound's defenses were new, like the cameras and mics on the perimeter. They had not trusted him. That pissed him off, but he wasn't surprised because they had shut him out almost as soon as Walt had died. He hated Kip, Walt's son, and blamed him for all of this. Kip was a typical son of a rich man, spoiled and self-centered, as well as lazy. Walt had built the place from nothing, and over the last five years he had watched it deteriorate into a summer camp for other kids with mommy or daddy issues.

He thought about what to do. He knew the Compound and the land around it intimately and could easily escape. He watched the gun battle up near the house from cover. Erick Duke was a stupid fuck, he realized. He just thought he could bull-rush the place.

While all the attention was on Duke in the trees by the house, Gull crab-walked along the side of the hill until he got to the steel plate door. The access point wasn't designed as an entrance, only an exit. He took his pack off and began to pull out his C4 when he heard the door creak. The bolt shifted and it opened. Arkie and two other men from the monitoring team, holding pistols, stood in the doorway. Mics had picked him up, Gull supposed.

Gull machine-gunned them where they stood and quickly made his way into the cavern.

The command center was cool, mostly due to the natural tendency for temperature to stay constant year round, but also owing to a big air conditioner blasting away. He locked the door from the house so he wouldn't be surprised while he set up the explosives. The computer systems were not especially organized, but they were placed all around the desks and giant screens that were used to manage *SwiftPad*. Two giant Juniper routers near the far entrance were both humming along with lights flashing by their interfaces. A big coil of orange fiber was connected there, and led out through a six-inch tunnel to a ditch that ran all the way down through the woods to a trans-Pacific cable that came ashore in Newport.

Gull started placing his C4. He knew explosives and had it all set with fuses attached to his electric igniter. He wasn't getting a fone signal down there, so he set the manual timer for five minutes.

In the meantime Maggie had come back up from below. She and Zane had brought Nate's body to Paula's burrow. Maggie didn't say anything and could see Paula was angry, but then Paula quickly became calm. The two women hugged each other, tears flowing like a waterfall, but no moaning or sobbing. It wasn't over yet. Gull's machine gun burst by the command center entrance sent Maggie running up toward the house. She approached the upper area close to the escape door from the command center and saw Arkie's body, and the others. Then she saw Gull start to come out. She laid down a barrage of fire that drove him back into the cavern.

"Hey, Maggie – it's Gull!"

"I know. You murdering fuck. Come on out."

"Maggie – I am coming out with my hands up, OK. Don't shoot!" She knew he was lying and set her sights on the entrance ready to fire when he showed himself. "You are going to shoot me, aren't you?" She didn't answer. Nobody moved for about a minute.

Then suddenly Gull charged out, shooting blindly. Maggie only needed one shot and he fell.

A tremendous explosion rocked the valley, and the blast out of the cavern was like a giant cannon firing.

CHAPTER 26

LAST TRAIN OUT OF OMSK

Mid-October

The assassination of Temp-Prez two weeks before the elections again sent redundant shockwaves across the nation. He was killed by one of his own secret service guards at the Capitol as he was coming out of the Senate chamber. Capitol police immediately arrested her. While she was in custody awaiting charges, a GoFundMe page set up for her legal defense collected $10 million in its first two hours.

From *The Fall of It All – A History of the Big Dump*

I T WAS FORECAST TO BE OVER 38° CELSIUS. HE DIDN'T plan to stay in Omsk too long, but he knew Dostoyevsky had been imprisoned there for 10 years and thought it might be cool to check out some of the museums around the prison where Fyodor had been held and walk along the rivers. In the back of his mind was GG. Omsk was a beautiful provincial city, and even though everyone was masked, he could feel smiles behind them.

His morning walk took him all around the town. He had started at 7:00 AM and got back to the hotel about 12:30 PM, having eaten a meager but tasty brunch at a café. He now knew for sure he was being followed by somebody who knew Nikoloz, Milana's half-brother, who he had thought was a GRU agent when he met him in a bar next to the Black Sea in the spring. As he walked into the hotel he planned on taking an afternoon nap during the heat of the day.

The Hotel Mayak (Маяк гостиница) was a collage of styles, two standard Soviet rectangular buildings not unlike their ubiquitous apartment buildings, four stories, each built along one of the rivers, and joined together facing the river's junction. The point of the "V" where the rectangles met was curved and mostly glass, with a bar on the top floor that overlooked the rivers. On the "inside" of the "V" stood a giant, globular replica of a Sputnik satellite, with a diameter of about ten meters, maybe ten times bigger than the original.

The young management team of the hotel, in sharp, tight suits or knee-length brightly colored skirts, was totally outnumbered by the robotniks. There were at least two cleaning ladies on each wing, who spent the afternoon sleeping or watching little TVs in the supply closets. The one restaurant, which never seemed to contain more than two customers, was served by an army of chefs, salad makers, bartenders, and waitstaff.

The hotel was in the process of being completely refurbished. The business office where the back office staff was located was being torn apart, the walls ripped down to the bare bones. The office staff sat out in the hall, their desks surrounding the door, with barely enough room to squeeze by. The workers laughed and mocked the managers as they moved back and forth, carrying buckets and tools, not particularly careful about where they spilled the plaster and paint. Kip slid past them to get to his room.

Kip was past the desks of the hotel apparatchiks when he saw, at the end of the hall, the salt-and-pepper–haired tracksuited guy from Sakaiminato. He was just standing there. Kip didn't know what to do. Tracksuit smiled at him and pointed behind Kip. Kip turned around and peered beyond the two people at their desks in the hallway to see three other guys coming down the hall toward him. They were looking at him and then he saw one holding a knife. He turned back, and saw the tracksuit guy from Sakaiminato signal him. He had no knife.

Kip ran toward the guy in the Adidas tracksuit. They guy signaled him on and they turned the corner. The stairs were blocked off, and to the right a whole section of the hotel, what looked like a hallway, was also barred. They were refurbishing a side entrance that normally would have led into the central courtyard and circular driveway. It had a plush waiting room, and waiting inside were two young men in buzz cuts and business casual, who looked at each other, then jumped up to chase after Kip and his new tour guide. They turned and ran five meters, where the guy in the tracksuit guided Chubby to another doorway, which led down some stairs. They ran down the stairs and into a tunnel. After running down the tunnel, the tracksuit guy led him up some steps to a door out to the circular driveway, where the engine of a Ford Fiesta was revving up and waiting. Kip hesitated.

He felt his pockets. He had his passport, wallet, and fone, but everything else – the backpack he bought in Vladivostok, the camping gear, his jacket, his – fuck, leave it, he thought, as he got in the front seat. No fucking idea what he was doing or why, but it just seemed like the best alternative.

Tracksuit jumped in too, and the car took off. The driver, a young blonde in a white blouse and blue skirt, with a mask that showed narrow, serious eyes, looked very intent but not scared. She drove away quickly but carefully, and did not appear to be in a hurry. Kip looked back and saw his pursuers standing out in the courtyard by the giant Sputnik, but he did not see any cars coming for them.

"You know Nikoloz? Did you leave the note in the café?"

"Of course! We met. You forget? At bar by Black Sea. I am Milana's cousin. Georgy."

"Oh." Maybe Kip remembered his face. He tried, then said fuck it. "Yeah, OK." There were a number of faces from that bar. "Who were those guys? Why were they after me?"

"I don't think they were after you. Maybe me they chase. But now..."

"What? So thanks to you – I am being chased?"

"Don't mention it." Georgy smiled.

"Where are we going?"

"Train station. First-class coach. I stay nearby. They not chase us in station. Here is ticket. We have five minutes. We go to Moscow!"

CHAPTER 27
REFUGEES FROM THE COMPOUND RETURN TO PORTLAND

Late October

At the Indianapolis funeral of Temp-Prez, Real-Prez announced that Turdashian would be his replacement running mate. Hours later, Cadez held a press conference that melted down into a total shitshow. He accused his own staff of betrayal and treason and blamed a wide range of enemies for his snubbing, including named and unnamed politicians, institutions and religious affiliations, D-list celebrities, financial cabals in New York, tech companies, and drug-fueled virus-spreading saboteurs. He begged Real-Prez to reconsider and make him the VP, saying he could bring a youthful "new leadership" to the country. He kicked over his lectern as he left his news conference.

From The Fall of It All – A History of the Big Dump

MAGGIE, JERRY, AND SEQUOIA CAME THROUGH THE Highway 26 tunnel and headed up 405 toward the old *SwiftPad* headquarters. They had come up the coast and cut across from north of Cannon Beach because the southern Willamette Valley was filled with roving gangs.

"I have to admit, it's good to be back in Portland," said Jerry. His arm was in a sling. He had taken a small caliber round in the shoulder, but it went through and did no damage to any bone or ligaments.

We're fucked, thought Maggie. We will never get GG out, Kip will be killed in Russia, and Real-Prez will be re-elected. She thought about her future. After the election, they would put a bounty on her head. She felt old. She had not heard from her daughter in a couple of weeks. After so much death, she had to put it out of her mind. They had lost almost everyone. Her husband Spence had never come out of SMIRK headquarters. Nor had Gupta. Spence's girlfriend Alison shot dead out off Highway 61, along with Aldane. Arkie was gone. All of his knowledge and his expertise – gone. We would never recover, especially since all of the systems had been destroyed. She looked over at Sequoia. Poor girl, so much on her shoulders. We're fucked.

And Nate. Maggie thought back to her salad days, when she was 20, 21, and what she and Nate would get up to, at all hours, night and day.

Losing Nate was worst of all for some reason. For some reason! You heartless bitch, it was your fault he's dead, she thought. Should not have let him come with you. He wasn't briefed, prepped, trained.

But she could never say no to him. Yeah, she had learned heartlessness up in those West Hills ahead. Kill or die: those were the choices in the night-time game of real-life Call of Duty. She had never played it before, but it was like playing "tag, you're it!" except it was really "tag, you're dead." She was done. Never picking up a gun again.

Nate! Her heart ached, and she couldn't escape it. When she was with Nate, almost 30 years ago, she could get tears in her eyes if a plant died. Few actually did die; she took care of plants like they were her children. Not like her real child, who couldn't stand to talk to her much less visit. It had been almost four years since she had seen her daughter, who never talked to her. Her daughter with Spence. Or maybe Nate, she was never really sure, and never even allowed herself to think about it.

Nate was really gone. He opened up the world for her, made a woman out of her. And he never held that over her head either, never tried to control her. Sometimes she wished he had. Some men, that is all they want, she knew that now. She was too young then to know how good she had it with Nate. She would not allow herself to cry anymore though. There would likely be more death. She would never know peace again, she thought.

They pulled up to the original *SwiftPad* headquarters and it was stunning! Almost unrecognizable! Completely rebuilt, painted, and from the looks of the neighborhood, the old Slabtown industrial district was humming, and much of it was *SwiftPad* Inc. All of the buildings within a three-block area had the same motif, without looking like a themed shopping mall. It was a rough exterior of reddish-white wood, painted with a translucent glaze that made it look like a couple of city blocks of giant jewels. They came around the back of the headquarters building (which was connected with overhead tunnels) and parked in the underground parking lot. It was all new.

They took the elevator up and arrived at the reception desk. Hadley was waiting for them.

She hugged everyone, and they went to a nearby meeting room.

"So who is still there?" asked Hadley.

"Paula is running things. Elwood is with her. We have lost so much. But – those two – the Golden Couple. Forever young, both so beautiful, so unassuming. They should have been together decades ago. But when you still look and feel like you are not 40 yet, yet – you're 70. They are 'shroom farmers now. They have a crop of Golden Fungus growing already. People said it couldn't grow up here in the Northwest," said Jerry. "But Elwood figured it out."

"Holy shit!"

"Yeah, pretty groovy, huh?" said Jerry.

Maggie looked at Jerry with distaste. "Groovy? My god! The place is trashed. And we lost Arkie, Alice, and Nate, and five others."

"And – they are investigating..."

Maggie looked at Jerry, who shook his head. They all decided they would not talk about what happened with anybody. The fact that stupid Hester cut Erick's throat while he was surrendering was not going to go down well with everybody who lived and worked there. Even though he had been shot in the shoulder, Jerry had sense enough to quickly retrieve Duke's own knife and substitute it for Hester's. Jerry pulled out Duke's knife and ran it through the throat wound, cleaned the handle, and put it in Duke's still-warm hand. Jerry knew forensics and said he didn't think they could prove that he didn't cut his own throat. Micro tears in the flesh might show evidence of a different blade, assuming they had the second blade to compare it to...but there were no nicks in Hester's blade, she was a ritual sharpener, to the point of some people thinking she was a bit of a psycho-nutjob, which now seemed likely.

Thinking fast, Jerry took her knife and made it disappear. Now Maggie knew why Arkie had put Jerry in charge of the Compound when he was away. Jerry had put it all together while Erick's wound was still fresh enough to cut again. And handled all of this while his own bullet wound was being patched up.

Since Erick had been the last one left alive (except for Gull's hog-tied crew almost a mile away), there was nobody to say otherwise even if none of the Feds believed it.

"The local sheriff is keeping the Feds out of the Compound for now," said Jerry. "Eventually some of the details will leak. The headline for now though is 'Erick Duke Killed While Leading Attack on Rehain Compound.'"

"Did you see that gaudy memorial service they had for him?" The crew all shook their heads in unison.

"My God," continued Hadley, "his sister Martha had on a red bodysuit that she said represented the blood of her brothers, Jesus Christ and Erick Duke. She was strutting up and down in front of the casket, wagging her skinny ass, vowing total revenge after the election. Absolute gibberish! Real-Prez was in the front row, clapping and nodding his fucking head."

No one had the energy to share Hadley's outrage. They all just nodded. After talking about the attack on the Compound a bit more, and remembering all of those killed and the damage to the systems, Sequoia spoke up.

"I don't know how to even start talking about this, but we lost something – maybe worse than everything else."

"You mean the St. Petersburg project," said Hadley.

Sequoia looked up, surprised. She started to speak, then stopped.

"We didn't lose anything. You didn't know? Wow," Hadley was overwhelmed by it all. "I am really happy to give you some good news." She smiled and wiped the tears away from her eyes, and moved close to Sequoia. "Arkie told me all about you. He was always thinking several moves ahead. It is all backed up. In fact we have been working round the clock on this project for the last week," said Hadley.

"How...?"

"Well," Hadley had a 30-second spell of crying at that point. It triggered Maggie too, and tears were flowing profusely all around. Even Jerry was moved to tears. Sequoia was crying too.

"Arkie and I had a – you know, some close encounters," Hadley said. "And just last week, we decided that we could not live apart anymore. I was planning on moving down there. I mean, I figured eventually I could convince him to move back to the city with me. Anyway – he told me all about your hack into the St.

Petersburg dam. And introduced me to your Siemens expert too. Guess what we got?"

"What?" asked Sequoia.

"A Simatic PCS 7 Process Controller! It's all set up over in the lab. Same model as on the dam. We were going to get some pumps and motors, but – we are getting close to turning into pumpkins, so – anyway. It's all yours, Sequoia. All your work, just like you left it. And – I think we have – uh, made some progress. Significant progress."

CHAPTER 28
BULGAKOV AT THE PONDS OF THE PATRIARCH

Late October

On October 12, meteorologists noticed that unusual conditions in the southern end of the Gulf of Bothnia were beginning to brew. Stockholm had a record 10 consecutive days of over 38 degrees Celsius (100 degrees Fahrenheit). In the Finnish Islands to the east the water temperature had risen to nearly 23 degrees Celsius, a record by nearly four degrees. The Baltic Fisheries Commission issued a warning that bacteria in herring had been detected and had sickened over 100 tourists on Gotland Island. At the same time an Arctic high-pressure mass was moving in from the north, setting up conditions for some ominous weather to come.

From *The Fall of It All – A History of the Big Dump*

A FTER CHUBBY GOT TO HIS FIRST-CLASS TRANS-Siberian cabin, he didn't see Georgy for the whole trip. It was possible he was nearby, because most of the first-class cabin doors remained shut. People bought first-class privacy to hide from the virus – fear of the virus was driving everyone into hiding, in order to stay alive...or sane.

So many trains, Kip remembered, had been open, social affairs. Strangers would chat in the corridor, share food, or vodka (well – not on Amtrak – Americans didn't go that far with their friendliness). Chubby left his cabin door open. He propped himself up and watched Siberia, through the doorway, and through the panoramic window in the corridor. They went through the Urals at night, and he slept, fitfully. And then they came to the Steppe. He had some music on his fone – Journey – Steve Perry belting out the lyrics...on and on and on and on.

They crossed the Volga at Kazan, the ancient outpost against the Tartars, which had been under siege almost continually for a hundred years ending in the mid-sixteenth century. Mother Volga...from the railroad bridge crossing it, you could see out across the Steppe forever.

When they pulled into Yaroslavsky station in Moscow, his plan was mapped out in his head. He caught a glimpse of someone he thought was Georgy, disguised with a blond wig and a long coat, looking like Bruce Willis at the end of *12 Monkeys*. If it was Georgy, he hurried away and disappeared into the crowd.

Kip's first task was to get some clothes. He had been wearing a long-sleeve t-shirt on top of a short-sleeve t-shirt. He walked out of the station and headed up the broad sidewalk on the Garden Ring boulevard. There were several clothing stores near the Pekin Hotel off Tverskaya not far from the train station, and he had no luggage, and was stir crazy from sitting on the train for nearly three days, so he walked. Cars on the boulevard but virtually no foot traffic. He found an athletic-wear kiosk, and said fuck it, good enough, bought some dark-blue sweat pants with a stripe on the side, a dull green Adidas jacket, a cheap nylon backpack, a pair of blindingly white Stan Smith tennis shoes (in memory of Aldane), some jock underwear, and three футболка "futbolka" (soccer) t-shirts. And a mariner's cap like Lenin wore. He bought a few hospital masks too, to fill out his flimsy backpack. Except for the high-class tennis shoes he looked like a wannabe Russian rapper.

The Pekin hotel was gloomy and foreboding, with blood-red heavy curtains on the windows, and Kip had a feeling that if he jacked off, it would end up as voyeur porn on Funcake. *SwiftPad*'s vlog app Funcake was GG's booboo. She designed it, and even invented some video manipulation techniques that at the time were pretty advanced. Called it "an adult sensuality app." Then – too long of a story to get into here – some of her developers went rogue and released it with no connection to its mother app.

He took a shower and changed into his new clothes and his black cap. Stalin had had a hand in designing the Pekin Hotel, and it was one of his big "triumphs" during the terror and deprivation of the times, when it opened just after the Second World War.

Kip studied himself in the long mirror in the bathroom (mirrors that were reputed to be two-way) as he put on his gopnik tracksuit. A total douchebag! In spite of wearing the Russian national gopnik costume (sans Stan Smith shoes), for some reason Chubby looked like a tourist. But he was only staying in Moscow one day, then on to St. Petersburg.

Somebody to meet soon. Georgy had told him to go to see Bulgakov's house first, then on to Lubyanka. "Sit on a bench in the little memorial park on the south end" of the infamous secret police headquarters, Georgy had told him.

Kip had already every intention of seeing Bulgakov's apartment, but wondered why Georgy told him to go. He was sure he hadn't mentioned his love for the Soviet-era author, who more than anyone (other than Anna Akhmatova) tweaked Stalin's nose.

He walked out of the Pekin Hotel into the morning sunshine, forecast to be another blisteringly hot day, and jaywalked across the Garden Ring street to visit Mikhail Bulgakov's apartment, which was almost directly across from the hotel.

Bulgakov's *The Master and Margarita* had been his touchstone, what he touted as his "specialty" when applying to the various Russian Language programs that he talked his way into during his many brief enrollments in a number of universities (including Harvard). The apartment was exactly as he pictured it. In fact (when he was living on a meager monthly stipend from his "trust fund") he had created almost the same atmosphere – an old building with a winding staircase, covered with graffiti, done in bizarre and quasi-obscene style, and definitely created by talented and skilled artists. It had a musty odor, and all kinds of rooms and alcoves with no regular size or shape, often connected with little hallways. The living room had been converted to a parlor with couches and chairs all facing the front. Here Bulgakov's friends would gather, and later, after his death, his worshipers all would come to hear secret recitations of his work and of other banned Russian authors, works called *samizdat* (самиздáт, "self-published"). It was here, Kip thought, in places like this that hope for mankind burned like a flickering candle. Little clusters of people who held onto the truth, even through the worst of times. He could feel their presence, even now. He could even feel their fear.

"You read Bulgakov?" A man, wearing a mask, in his sixties at least, confronted him. "You read Russian?"

Chubby realized he was the only tourist in the apartment. The virus had scared away most tourists.

"да," he said lamely.

"Here, I give you." He handed him a small paperback copy of *The Master and Margarita* in Russian.

"Спасибо!" (Spasibo – Thank you)

"Don't mention it." Where had he heard that recently? thought Kip.

"Here, one more thing. Take." It was a typed, stapled manuscript. "We go underground like before!"

"Political?" Kip nodded to the manuscript in his left hand.

"Not even a little bit. Well, yes of course all is political! I promise. It is scientific treatise on fungus. Common fungus – maybe – you find on trees, in forests in Georgia, near Black Sea. Ancient wisdom. Maybe Herotitus wrote about it,"

"Who is Herotitus?"

"I don't know, Greek maybe. You decide. No charge."

"What is it about?"

"Fungus may cause virus – and maybe cure virus – I give you."

"Why?"

"Go ask Alice," the man said. "Maybe she know."

"How –?" He let it go. It made sense, thought Kip. Of course – Jim's mom. Alice would know. She had been the closest thing to a mom he had ever known. But what did he mean?

The man turned, walked away, and seemed to disappear into the labyrinth of the Bulgakov apartment.

Chubby headed down the Garden Ring to Malaya Bronnaya Street, and came upon the Ponds of the Patriarch. The setting for the first chapter of Bulgakov's great novel was only a short walk from his home.

There was only one pond, although legend said there were once two. It had been a swampy hollow in the fifteenth century. The scene was exactly as Chubby saw it in his head: the graceful and ever watchful linden trees, the rectangular pond, approximately 100 meters by 60 meters. The pond was surrounded by a wide pea-gravel walkway. Benches were spaced all around the water, on both sides of the walkway. The grounds were immaculate.

It was right here that poor Berlioz, a literary magazine editor, and his young friend, a poet, met "the Professor," a foreigner who speaks perfect Russian. Sitting right here at the junction of Malaya Bronnaya and Yermolayevskiy, here is the bench! Probably the same bench. Except there are no tram rails on Yermolayevskiy Lane – that part is fiction. But next to a beautiful public park, the imaginary tram tracks are more believable than a guillotine.

The editor Berlioz had been criticizing a poem by the poet

that was not definitive enough or clear enough in expressing the historical fact that Jesus had never existed. The editor goes through a list of ancient writers whose statements about Jesus were later proved to be forgeries. This scholarly recitation conforms to Communist party atheistic standards, and also refers to some obscure but current (early 1930s) literary quarrels within the Moscow writing community. The Professor overhears their discussion and says that Jesus definitely did exist. They argue about the logical strength of Kant's philosophical proof of God's existence. Berlioz and the poet joke with each other about the appearance and accent of the Professor ("He must be German!") and attempt to tease him. But little by little they come to realize this guy is a heavyweight intellect, who might know more than they do. The Professor tells them what he says is the true story of the Passion of Christ – only the Christ he describes is a simpleton. He digs into Pilate's mind during the interrogation. Pilate knows something very world-shaking is occurring, yet he sloughs it off. We witness Pilate's slippery and deceitful negotiations with the Sanhedrin.

Berlioz says that scene is not in the Bible! But the Professor triumphantly points out that Berlioz had just said the Bible was not true! The Professor says he was there, he witnessed it, and the Poet and Berlioz mock him. Soon the Professor says he is moving into Berlioz's apartment and predicts that Berlioz would die (soon) from decapitation and it all turns out to be true (tram rails...) in a brutal, yet very funny way.

The Professor is the Devil, or maybe he really is Stalin. Anyway, as the novel proceeds, he takes over Moscow.

CHAPTER 29

CHUBBY MEETS NIKOLOZ AT LUBYANKA

Late October

"I continued down Bronnaya Street. It was so peaceful, fragrant, full of beautiful healthy linden trees, and very upscale. Tall and spectacularly beautiful women dressed in opulent Fifth Avenue style were escorted by short, balding men in too-tight dark suits. Still under the spell of the first chapter of *The Master and the Margarita*, walking in a trance, I snapped photographs in my mind's eye, pictures I can still recall and see in full color, each block, each store, each restaurant, just watching and consciously recording the scene in my memory. Beautiful cafés with beautiful waitresses, intriguing and very alluring alleyways, huge windows, half opened, hinting at great wealth and status inside spacious apartments. I felt friendly eyes where I least expected them.

"I had no idea that the stapled, smeared, half-typed, half-handwritten manuscript I carried in my flimsy back-pack was perhaps the most valuable treasure, the most important document in the world. It was the answer to so many prayers – and I remember, as I passed a rubbish bin, thinking – why do I need to lug this around? I almost threw it into the trash on Bronnaya Street."

From *The Fall of It All – A History of the Big Dump*

CHUBBY CONTINUED TOWARD THE CENTER OF Moscow, the Kremlin. He didn't go in to see the Apostolic Churches, but walked around to the side, through Red Square down to St. Basil's. There was a pretty big crowd there, with everyone wearing a hospital mask. Eyes, lots of eyes peering out of half-hidden faces, seemingly looking at him. He thought, this must be what it was like in the Seraglio – Mozart's Turkish harem. How seductive the eyes can be!

Chubby headed over to Lubyanka. It wasn't far. Georgy had told Chubby to expect company, that there would be people watching him. Chubby had a gut-level understanding of the danger he was in but understood the only way to fight it was to ignore it. He and Nikoloz (who bristled angrily after Kip called him Nicky) met in perhaps the most ominous (yet hopeful) place imaginable – on the southern end of Lubyanka, in the heart of Moscow. The giant secret police headquarters where tens of thousands of political prisoners were executed by the long line of Soviet henchmen was shrouded in a giant burlap covering in preparation for some renovations apparently, or perhaps it was only the sudden onset of shame, a desire to hide. He and Nikoloz sat on the pedestal of the Solovetsky Stone, the memorial to the victims of Stalin's Gulag, a simple large hunk of granite that had been hauled from a Siberian labor camp. The stone had recently replaced the statue of Felix Dzerzhinsky, Lenin's Interior Minister who founded what became the KGB (now the FSB).

"Moscow and St. Petersburg are ready to move against him. But unlike your Real-Prez, ours is a clever man. He clearly understands what people in the street have against him, and he creates hope and confusion to make them hesitate, make them somehow half-believe that he just might be a 'secret democrat.' They say, 'If only he can control the wolves who control him!'" Nikoloz looked out down to the park on Staraya Square. It was filled with young lovers cuddled on benches. A scene like that 50 years ago would have been informants meeting their handlers. "But he knows that his hold on power is dependent on Russians thinking that it is he who controls the White House! Once that illusion is broken, he is finished. The people here – in Moscow and in St. Petersburg – are ready for real democracy. But it all depends on America."

Kip had met Nikoloz before, in the spring, in Georgia, when he had romanced Nikoloz's half-sister Milana. When he had last seen Nikoloz – he had been certain he was on the other side. And in fact, he may be still.

"'Moscow rules' are obsolete," said Nikoloz, referring to le Carré's security procedures that agents follow when on enemy ground. "Technology has made so much useless, probably us most of all."

Chubby wondered about "us," but he remained silent.

"Walking around the city, be sure to stop and talk to people. Linger." Nikoloz looked back at the looming prison. It was once the site of one of the earliest churches in Moscow. Irony that thick is almost comedy. "See that window up there? Third floor – it was Beria's office, he used to look down here at the statue of his predecessor, the 'Iron Felix' who stood right here. Andropov used that office too."

"Maybe someone is looking down at us now?" said Chubby.

"Maybe. Doesn't matter. The only way to change the future is to ignore what the past says is supposed to happen. Envision the future we need to have. Join in with what you see. Follow the crowd. Join protest groups if you see them. They won't see you. They only see you if you hide. They are looking for the furtive, the side-eyeing man in the corner. Be open, and you are more likely just to walk in where you need. Russians are trusting, and they love the innocent idiot."

"How is Milana?"

"She can tell you herself. Allegro Hotel by Moscow Station, in Leningrad," Nikoloz's face gave nothing away. He put a burner fone on the stone and left.

CHAPTER 30
OPERATION FLOODGATES

October 27

The storm was slowly building. It started in the southern Baltic and was gradually gathering strength. Baltic polar-like cyclones, or Baltipolar cyclones, occur fairly frequently, with about 100 recorded between 1940 and 2010. Generally one or two polar-like systems per year form in the Baltic, usually in the Gulf of Bothnia.

But this one was scary. It already was being called the Katzenjammer because it was mischievous, not giving clues as to its intentions. Some trick was about to be played, but when, and how big of a trick would it be? The unusually warm weather was about to meet an inexorably forming polar vortex, but air mass fronts seemed to stall, then regroup even stronger. The potential for an explosive event was becoming more and more likely.

From *The Fall of It All – A History of the Big Dump*

Currently issuing advisories on Extratropical Depression Katzenjammer.

The waves should begin to emerge soon behind Katzenjammer. There's a small chance that it may develop next week. Models lately have backed away from rapid development, but models are changing hourly. Chances of formation...next 48 hours: near 0%...next 5 days: 50%.

From the ECMWF (European Centre for Medium-Range Weather Forecasts),
October 26, 2020

SEQUOIA RAN THE MEETING. JERRY HAD HIRED

twenty more techs, the best hackers in the business. Their exploits would be world famous, but you have never heard of them, because they are that good. "Five people can operate the pumps – they live here, here, and here. The security doors to the pump house are locked. The code to override – if the door opens – is here – we have to analyze it – tonight – and break it – find a hole. When we do, we will lock the pumps. If they try to start the pumps manually they will burn them out when there is no water to suck. Then the gate stays open, and St. Petersburg drowns. The Hermitage and all of the city will be underwater – including the Internet Research agency.

"Our hope is that this will not happen. But we must be prepared to do it."

CHAPTER 31

PLEASANT TRAIN RIDE LEADS TO A SHOCK FOR CHUBBY

October 29

Looking back on it all, the last three months before the election were a blur. Everything that happened in the United States seemed so consequential, and yet, all of it was just a series of shadow puppet plays, keeping the audience entranced, but not really informed. The myth that reality is played out in sequential chronology will come completely apart, and yet will only smudge the blur, because reality makes no sense if you are only able to follow it as it happens. Unfortunately, for most of us that means constantly looking back to see how it was done before, but history doesn't repeat, it only rhymes. Events unfold differently, at varied paces, and in different places. The real short strokes of the story started months later, far away, in the far northeast corner of Europe.

From *The Fall of It All – A History of the Big Dump*

THE TRAIN FROM MOSCOW TO ST. PETERSBURG WAS high-speed, clean, comfortable transport – all-around high-class travel. The seats were roomy and cushy and even had that new furniture fragrance. Chubby sat next to a retired professor at Moscow State College who had told him she was on her way to visit her brother, who had an apartment three blocks from the river Neva on Kazanskya Yulisa (Kazan Street). The lady seemed to want to practice her university English.

"It was very hot in Moscow, wasn't it? I hope it's cooler in St. Petersburg," Kip said.

"Yes it is very hot out, but – it is very comfortable traveling. The train is very cool, is it not?" The old lady seemed nervous. Kip was still dressed like a squatting gopnik in a cheap tracksuit, although he thought his Lenin-style Greek fishing boat captain's cap looked a little fey. He gave her his Hollywood smile, and it seemed to break the ice. He was polite and well spoken (for a foreigner, which his accent told her he obviously was), and she warmed up to him, even though he was dressed like a cheap hoodlum.

"There is a big storm coming," Kip said.

"I know. It is too bad. Your visit will be ruined, I am afraid. The museums will close, and the weather will be dreadful! My brother's apartment building is over 300 meters from the river, but still, during the big storm last winter, the Kotlin dam nearly overflowed and if the bay had not been frozen, it would have taken the Hermitage. The street was flooded, the canals were flooded, it was terrible."

"Nothing can stop water," Kip said. "It almost always wins the battle."

"I know. Is it true people in America don't believe the climate is changing? Let them come here! We know what is happening. We are only 800 km from the Arctic Circle. But – we believe in the dam. It is the President's greatest accomplishment. He is from St. Petersburg, you know."

"The most liberal city in Russia, and yet..."

"It is our national character, unfortunately. All nations have charms, and they all have their curses."

"That is very true," said Chubby. "Many nations are discovering – or perhaps rediscovering – their own curses even now."

She shrugged. "We held off the Nazis in 1943, but you are right – the sea is a different kind of enemy."

"It is a worldwide problem," Chubby said, mostly to keep the conversation light. The old lady looked at him. His Russian was good but heavily accented.

"Amerikanski?"

"Da."

"Will you remove your President next month?" She now spoke in clear, British English.

Kip shrugged.

"I hope so. If not," she looked around and lowered her voice, "we will never get rid of ours."

Kip smiled and nodded slightly.

They served a nice breakfast, and the view of the thick forests of northeastern Russia was broken by high-end dachas that seemed more western European than the wooden, unpainted single-story hooches huddled inside of stockades along the Trans-Siberian tracks. The dachas here looked like Aspen ski lodges. Kip wondered if being close to the railroad track enhanced or depressed their market value. After a pleasant five-hour trip, the train pulled into St. Petersburg's Moscow Station. The Russians built railway stations around the connecting points, rather than connect all the rail links to one central station. Finland Station, where it all started, was just across the river.

Chubby stepped onto the platform. The only thing he had in this cheap nylon rucksack was a typed manuscript, mostly in Russian, detailing the experiences of a group infected in the super-outbreak in Ekaterinburg. A small group in a monastery, all suffering, with no possibility of effective medical help (not that there was much that could be done). They all, almost in a religious frenzy (and that indeed seemed to be the point), ate some fungus soup brought in by a "mad man," a wandering holy man, a village idiot. Who called it a traditional Russian religious sacrament. There were some botanical illustrations of the fungus, and details that were meaningless to Chubby. But in any event they all got better – almost instantly, they all swore. The notebook was solemnly signed by about forty people, but most of the signatures were illegible. Chubby didn't know what he was going to do with it.

He walked out of the station, to where Nevsky Prospect meets Ligovsky at the obelisk monument to the Heroes of Leningrad during the World War II siege. It was a very hot muggy afternoon in mid-October. Normally the city was frozen half the year. By now, in late October, it should have started to get cold. But it was 36° Centigrade – the high 90s in Fahrenheit. He could not believe a cyclone would be here by tomorrow.

Kip looked down Nevsky Prospect, a two-mile-long boulevard to which long beautiful passages were written by Pushkin, Gogol, Dostoyevsky – and many others. This street, this glorious vision of what every progressive Russian ever wanted, a democratic thoroughfare where peasant, artist, writer, student, musician, shopkeeper, and aristocrat shared the sidewalk in daily promenades, even at the height of Czarist times. St. Petersburg was the crown jewel of Russian cities, the window gazing at Europe, and the wellspring of some of the greatest writing ever produced. As he looked down Nevsky Prospect, Chubby thought, here it was finally. I am here. But another voice was saying – this is where it goes down.

Milana's half-brother Nikoloz had given him a new fone in Moscow. Chubby turned it on now and pulled up a map to find his hotel. Nikoloz had told him it was close to the station. He crossed Ligovsky Avenue and turned left, walking down toward the Allegro Hotel.

The seamy street next to the railroad station advertised peep shows, astrological cafés, and pawnshops. The sweet smell of incense wafted out of coffee shops, whose darkened windows advertised in both Arabic and Cyrillic something more than coffee. Nigerians selling tour packages on the Neva seemed to be speaking in three languages at once. All of the many money-change kiosks claimed to have the best rates in the city. But now most the shops were being boarded up. They were more than a mile from the river but the wind could do much damage.

The hotel was back in a small alley. Chubby walked right by it by mistake though, and didn't realize it for a couple of blocks, but felt fortunate he did because he had a fear he was being followed. When he doubled back, he passed the woman he was sure was dogging him, but if so, she gave no hint of it. After half a minute, he stopped and turned and watched her, but she just continued walking ahead. If they had more than one person on him, he had bigger problems than someone looking for an easy mark. He decided he was in Russia, and there was very little he could do. Nikoloz had told him in Moscow that to avoid suspicion, just don't act suspicious. As stupid as that sounded, it actually made him less paranoid.

He entered the little alleyway and found the simple wooden door with a small white sign with black letters in both Russian and English – the Allegro – not the high-class Allegro Hotel on Moskovsky Prospect closer to the river – but just "The Allegro" across from Moscow Station on Ligovsky Avenue. He entered and found himself in a little hallway, where he came to a stairway, with another sign, this one handwritten, saying "Front Desk" again in both Russian and English. He walked up the stairs to the second floor and came into a very functional room that included a lobby, a laundry, and an intake table facing a dining area against the windows overlooking the station. They were setting up a simple and basic spread – a very appealing evening dinner buffet – that was included with the room.

A middle-aged Middle Eastern couple sat in the dining area, watching the staff bring the food out to the buffet counter. It was almost 5:00 PM.

"Yes sir, can I help you?"

"I uh, I think I have a reservation. Welles. Cornelius Welles."

"Double U? Yes – I see. 4th floor. Room D. You have a guest. She said you are expecting her? Is this true? If not we can give you another room. She – looked like a clean girl, but –"

"Fine."

"She has the key." The front desk clerk smiled. "Elevator is just behind me – or..." she gestured toward the stairs.

He walked up the stairs, slowly, not wanting to hurry, in fact, with a certain degree of dreadful anticipation. At the top of the stairs, the hallway formed a "T" in front of him. A and B were to his left and right. He walked to the top of the T, and D was to his left.

He knocked. There was stirring, and the lock tumbled.

"Kip!"

He didn't say anything for a couple of beats, staring, then, "Milana."

The room was only big enough for a bed, a dresser, a hard-backed wooden chair, and a small curtained bathroom. An uncovered window faced a brick wall a few feet away. Kip focused his eyes on Milana's, let them drift down to her belly.

"He's – ours. Yours."

Kip reached, but she pulled away.

"Did you get the money? I told my staff, but –"

"The money? That is what you asked me?"

"You never told me!"

"You didn't want to know."

"No," said Kip. "Yes! Of course, I –"

"So – Nikoloz says you here to find girlfriend, other girlfriend, the one who made you rich. She has baby too – already out. That one yours too?" Milana's eyes flashed with anger and she turned away in contempt. "Well – come in."

Kip took off his backpack and set it on the floor. Milana sat on the edge of the bed.

"You want sex now?"

Kip tried not to react to her. He sat on the chair. "Did you know you were pregnant when I left last spring?"

"I knew moment we finish making love." She began to laugh, first as a sputter, then more and more uncontrollably. She fell into his arms and her laughter slowly turned to sobs. They held each other and looked into each other's eyes. She smiled, and then Kip did. "Sit down. Here," she said. "Tell me everything. Then take me to dinner."

Chubby kept looking in her eyes.

"Dinner first then," she said. "I am eating for two. Tonight – I asked the cook – pierogies, chicken stew with carrots and shallots. Maybe a piece of cake?"

"I'm hungry too. Let's eat. Then I'll tell you everything."

CHAPTER 32
CHUBBY AND MILANA RECONNECT OVER A SIMPLE MEAL

October 30

Doug Turdashian, the ARRGH candidate for Vice President, died of the virus on October 30.
From *The Fall of It All – A History of the Big Dump*

HADLEY AND SEQUOIA HAD BEEN UP SINCE DAWN after working past 2:00 that morning. They had nearly perfected procedures for opening and holding open the S-1 gate. But they also needed to know they could close it. Communications with the Russians were critical. No one really wanted to flood one of the most beautiful cities in the world, so they had to know they could actually shut the gates.

"He's in St. Petersburg now," said Maggie, coming into the *SwiftPad* lab, a massive bank of open source systems chained together for maximum processing power. "And so is the cyclone. Are we ready?"

Sequoia shrugged. "As we'll ever be I guess."

"OK," Maggie said. "Let's get it started."

After dinner Milana told Kip that she had started her history PhD dissertation, and that no, she did not get his money; she never stopped believing that it was not his fault. She knew that the Insurgency had probably confused things, and anyway, she was perfectly able to get by on her own. She said she had been living a chaste and uneventful life while watching the United States torture itself. She had worried about him when she heard about the (V)ICE invasion of Portland. Kip listened to her as she burst out in a torrent, detailing for him the changes in Georgia and Russia over the last six months. He tried to check the web, looking for clues to her firehose blast of info with his Russian burner fone, seeing what he could do with it. Not much, as Nikoloz had it locked down pretty tightly. He put it down and kicked off his shoes and just listened to her.

"So it's true, pregnant women have sex. I always wondered about that."

"What? You are not that stupid – are you? Isn't that what – actually it is very good – I mean that is what I hear?" Milana smiled. "Especially for women."

"Uh huh."

"You want?"

"You wanted me to tell you everything," said Kip. "Let me tell you something first."

"You suddenly old man now, huh?"

"Maybe, it's been a while."

"Me too," said Milana. "Last time, with you."

"Yeah." They were lying next to each other on the narrow bed, faces inches apart. Suddenly they both relaxed. The tension was broken.

"Time enough for love," she said.

"Have you ever read it?"

"Of course. I read all science fiction, even in English. Heinlein speaks to us. A little, how you say –"

"Rabid rightwing? Sexist? Militaristic?"

"Please, Kip. You disappoint me sometimes with your fake idealism. You know better."

Kip laughed bitterly. They were quiet for a bit.

"You know we are having almost a revolution in the US. You hear about the Jean Katon concert in Portland?"

"Yes. You big hero, right?"

"No. Some of the people who listened to me died. They are heroes. I can tell you – what happened after – if you can wait for sex?"

"You make fun of me now. No sex for you! But tell me your story, I listen with hunger."

"OK, you heard about the Portland Insurgency?"

"Of course, it is all everyone talks about. A colleague at the Batumi State history department says that it portends the new rise of the city-state."

"Anyway, after that Aldane and I flew to Memphis. Memphis was really the center of the Resistance. There were fights, a few fatal shootings, but it was a stalemate, at least until after the coming election. And the Memphis Resistance had a leader, a charismatic Black man, a former Army colonel, Hassan Coleman, and they built a movement around him.

"I stayed in Memphis for nearly a month. I didn't see much of Aldane. I did have a brief flirtation – the wife of a big shot in the Resistance. Anyway, nothing happened, we just talked all night once in somebody's kitchen. It was hot and humid, and I was drinking and eating constantly. That is why I got heavy again. I was obsessed with finding GG. I thought about trying to connect with Nikoloz myself to find out how you were doing, and to see if he had a lead on GG, but he ignored all my attempts to contact him.

"I dumped a couple million in cash in Memphis and helped them negotiate a relationship with the Ishpeming people and with Portland. We had to coordinate our efforts or we would be separately taken apart by Real-Prez and his minions.

"Anyway – the woman – the Black woman I was flirting with asked me if I had ever heard of Nikoloz – she called him a 'Chechen who worked for the Russians, but who was feeding us information and connections to buy weapons, communication equipment, etc.' Described him down to a tee – smart, and he told her he knew me! The way we left things – well I wasn't sure what he was up to, but I see it now. He wanted to turn off *SwiftPad*! Anyway, he was right, even though at the time I didn't see it."

"I told Nikoloz you were not a bad man – for an American!"

"Well, I didn't know whose side Nikoloz was on – in some ways I still don't! But – my mind went through my experience in Georgia – with you, Milana, and with Nikoloz. I just assumed that Nikoloz was part of the Russian government, and that anyone from the Russian government would be helping Real-Prez.

"The Memphis intel was much better than what we had in Portland – which may have been because they were getting help from the Russians – that is what I thought then, but which Russians? That is the point – we all need help. We have to help each other, if we want to end this worldwide dictatorship of rich assholes!"

"Down with the kleptocrats!"

"Exactly. But I was certain of nothing, and even now, I am still not sure. Anyway, all that ended when Hassan Coleman was assassinated. I watched it happen. He was the real deal. This is how the rightwing in the US works – kill the leaders. So I joined the team that went hunting for his killers.

"We found the assassins a few hundred kilometers north, in Cape Girardeau, Missouri. And I was the guy to do it. To kill the assassins."

"Tell me! In Georgia, most think you intended to kill your President, during big funeral. But you missed, so you did this instead. I like stories of assassins. You know that is how we finally got rid of the Mongols in Georgia!"

"Do you want to tell me about your history dissertation now, Milana?"

"No, no – you tell! Much more interesting!"

The next morning, as Kip was taking a shower, Milana peeked in and told him that a message had been slid under the door. "I am afraid I will fall down if I bend to pick it up," she said.

Kip shook off most of the water, stepped out of the shower, and picked up the folded piece of paper on the floor by the door.

"10:00 AM, Akhmatova."

Well, at least it's not a titty bar, he thought. He checked his fone – about a kilometer down Nevsky Prospect to Vladimirsky – turn right.

He and Milana went to breakfast.

"So," he said.

"So," she said. "You are deciding what you want to do with me, aren't you?"

"How do you feel?"

"I am tired all the time. The baby is not due for another two months. I don't know how I will survive. Especially with the weather suddenly changing. Winter is coming."

It was chilly that morning and the wind was picking up outside. Milana had cleaned her plate of scrambled eggs and little fried potatoes almost before Chubby had started eating.

"Please bring some of those," she pointed at his waffles.

Kip walked over to the buffet table. There was a loud crack of thunder, not too far distant. He looked across the street and saw the Russian flag flying over Moscow Station fluttering wildly. The sky was dark and the wind was audible.

He brought the food back. "I don't know what is going to happen," he said. "I am going to be doing something that will probably be very dangerous. If I fail, then your plan is easy. Fly back to Tbilisi and have our baby."

"You are trying to get rid of me," Milana said.

"I want you to stay here and trust me."

"Trust you?"

"Yes. I will send for you or come back. I don't know yet what will happen. If I don't come back that will only mean that I can't – that something bad happened."

"What if you win your little game here?"

"What do you mean?"

"I mean," Milana looked around but there were no other people near their table, "what if you find your girlfriend and her baby? What happens?"

"We'll go back."

"Back?"

"To the United States."

"And then what? Who go back?"

"All of us. Cynthia, her baby...you."

"Maybe I don't want to go? Then what?"

Kip looked at Milana, then looked away. "Do you want anything else to eat?" Kip asked.

"No."

"Will you wait here?"

"Yes."

CHAPTER 33

ELWOOD BRINGS IN A FUNGUS CROP; WALLY POPS UP MOST OPPORTUNELY

Late October

Real-Prez announced a 30-year trade deal with Russia. When asked about the US President's announcement at a news conference, the Russian President quipped, "Sure, big trade deal, we all make money."

From *The Fall of It All – A History of the Big Dump*

I N PORTLAND, THE CITY HAD SLOWLY REOPENED. FOLlowing the fighting earlier in the summer, the city had pretty much shut down and retreated to the most basic of necessities: food, water, and shelter. The weather cooperated, so the million or so people who were living outside were reasonably comfortable. But as the weather cooled, shelter became a priority and the city united around taking care of everyone. The provisional government had taken over almost every public venue for beds: the Moda Center, hotels and motels, and even the Heathman Hotel on Broadway. The virus had burnt through the town and taken a frightening toll in the refugee camps. Many refugees died in agony and were quickly buried in mass grave sites around the city. But by October the worst seemed to be over.

The city was filled with ecstatic survivors of the plague who claimed that they had met God during their ordeal. Others claimed it was not God whom they had met but their real selves. As they recovered, researchers realized that their blood plasma lent a certain amount of immunity to others. They sold their plasma for thousands of dollars a pint, and the money went a long way toward getting their lives back together. Commercial blood retrieval centers were set up, and the lines of people wanting to get the plasma in order to keep from getting sick were much longer than the lines of survivors who wanted to sell their plasma. The exchange benefited all and helped the city's economy revive.

Back at the Compound, Elwood's new crop of Fungus was exploding with fecundity. It had a revitalizing effect on both Paula and himself, and they were out in the cedar grove below the hobbit houses from morning until night, spreading the spores to increase the growth of the Fungus, while also harvesting the mature ears. The Compound was quiet now; those who remained worked to repair the damage. Everyone killed defending the Compound received a green burial in various places in the woods they were known to visit, if possible. They planted trees on most of their graves to use the decaying flesh as nutrients. Others were cremated and buried at sea from fishing boats .

Elwood and Paula sat in a splash of sun that leaked through the canopy of cedar trees surrounding their Fungus grotto. All around them, the Fungus appeared quite different from the variety found along the Kaskaskia River in Illinois. Elwood had cloned the Kaskaskia mycelium and grafted it on the peridium of the apple-rust fungus common on cedar trees. The yellow, gelatinous fingers that oozed orange-yellow spore horns were plentiful and easy to gather, and when dried, had a bitter taste like a sour persimmon. The Fungus was not parasitic to the trees, and was so "fruitful" that the small grove below the hobbit dwellings produced nearly 200 lb of Fungus. And its spores spread naturally, staying almost exclusively on cedar and juniper trees. The Fungus was spreading on its own now, but, within the Compound anyway, the spores did not germinate beyond the border of the cedar grove. Elwood and Paula vowed to let nature decide the future of the Fungus.

Elwood discovered its effects were significantly milder than the Kaskaskia variety. It remained to be seen whether it had the same efficacy for retarding aging, but as far as Elwood could tell, the chemistry lined up. Still, you never knew with fungus.

Paula and Elwood continued to study the Fungus, both in the field, and in a little lab he set up in a cleaned-up portion of the tunnel that Gull had blown out. The telepathic qualities in Elwood's new strain seemed to have diminished from what they remembered of the original "wild" Fungus they had first discovered in Vandalia 50 years ago. They had sent several bags up to Portland, and all employees of *SwiftPad* were eating Fungus in sauces and salads, without knowing exactly what they were eating. But none were getting sick. And – tests done in the refugee camps in Portland showed the Fungus induced a remarkable recovery rate for the infected, and zero re-infections for those who ate about two grams a day.

The team members who remained at the Compound after the disastrous raid by Duke and his men were at first inconsolably sad, but soon began to recover. Almost all of them decided without any meetings or social pressure that they were done with fighting and carrying guns, and worrying about "perimeters" and rightwing invasions. The community was evolving into the kind of place that Alice had originally envisioned: a place of rest and reflection, a welcoming stopover for seekers of another way to live. More attention was devoted to cultivation, and the hangar barn above the main house was slowly being converted into a series of giant greenhouses. They got rid of all the guns and explosives and other weapons, and the former soldiers accepted a new challenge. They became itinerant distributors of the Fungus, Johnny Appleseed style, spreading it throughout the Northwest, while maintaining a strict vow to keep the source secret. It was Fungus after all, and raising it and making it do what you want it to do was hit or miss. Anyone was welcome to try to clone it, but Elwood's techniques were light years beyond what any other mycologists were attempting. Elwood had spent his life studying it, and even so, it still seemed like 60% magic to him.

Paula had aged quickly. By the fall, the 30-year-old woman of the previous spring had the metabolism of a woman in her mid-sixties. But then she started to stabilize. Meanwhile Elwood had stopped eating Fungus for a month or so while he approached Paula's apparent age. He developed some hip problems, which slowed him down some, but he was still fiftyish looking, and even handsome for the first time in his life. They then settled into a steady, simple life of trying new recipes of Fungus, in soups, in main courses, and in honey-flavored snacks, after taking short morning hikes around the compound.

Hester, as she had hinted earlier, could not stay with him if he got old, and she wasn't lying. She was never jealous of Paula, even though Elwood spent nearly all his time with her. She still aggressively initiated sex with him at least three times a week. But once Elwood started to slow down in that department and began to age, she was gone. The Northwest hadn't suited her anyway, so she headed off "back east" as they say, and was not heard from again. She did take a few pounds of the gelatinous Fungus, along with her bowie knife.

Elwood moved slowly, using trekking poles to hike around the Compound, and Paula had settled into a life centered around Fungus farming and cooking. She even got a bit pudgy, for the first time in her life.

"You ever think about Nate?" she asked Elwood, as they sat out in the fading afternoon.

"He made me laugh. Me and Wally were Curly and Larry, and he was Moe. To be honest, I got tired of being the butt of his jokes. Or being metaphysically slapped around all the time. He was smart, and it seemed like he tried to be a good guy, but didn't really know how to do it. Always left an out for himself – to be an asshole."

"I know," said Paula. "Tight pussy."

"What?"

"That is what he told me he liked, when we talked about getting old. He could be so – sensitive, but then – he always spoiled it. Don't know why he was like that. I was never sure he knew what he wanted in life."

"He always made me feel like something was wrong with me for not continually being up to chasing sex or getting outrageously drunk, or stoned, or pushing every situation to its limit."

"You were content, Elwood," Paula said. "That doesn't seem to be enough for some people, at least not when they are young. Like Nate – and me. But you – you found something to interest you your whole life. He just wanted the rush. You are the lucky one."

"Yeah," Elwood said, "I know."

"I did too. But now I don't. I miss it sure. But don't need it. Do you think – I mean – if he was still here – if he hadn't been killed – over there," she pointed in the direction of the hillside where he had been shot, "he might have been able to just sit here with us, peaceful, and happy. Because I am happy now. I thought, after he was shot, I would never be happy. But I am."

"Well, asshole though he was, I'm sure he would be happy to know that."

"Yeah, I think he would." Paula sat back and let the fleeting sun pass across her face.

Back in Portland, the network was quickly repaired, the command center was cleaned up, and a few systems were set up. Sequoia was in her element. She never seemed to sleep. She had a boyfriend she had trained to come over to her little corner cubicle at odd times – usually between 1 AM and 4 AM – and have rough hard sex. But that was it; she almost never left the Portland *SwiftPad* headquarters.

Maggie forced herself to leave *SwiftPad* headquarters every day for a few hours to keep her sanity. She rode her bike out to her and Spence's old house near Gresham off the Springwater Bikepath. It was still legally her house, but about 15 people were living there, and they weren't trashing it. The original occupants of the front yard had moved in and were keeping order. Maggie had dinner with them a couple of times and made everybody feel comfortable about being there. Then she rode back into town, where she was staying with her old Portland battle comrade Mosley, who was staying in a little house in the West Hills.

Hadley of course had seduced Jerry, but that wasn't serious.

They were all working long hours on remotely controlling the St. Petersburg floodgates, on the off chance that a storm would blow in. But beyond that, how it would all play out, they didn't even speculate to themselves.

It was on such a morning that Elwood popped up on a video call.

"Elwood? Can you hear me?" Maggie had taken over most administrative duties to allow Hadley a free hand to work on the "S-1" project.

"Yes," he said.

"Hear the news? Cadez brought an AR-15 full-auto gun into his SMIRK headquarters in Plano and killed almost everyone on his staff. Including Telly."

"What happened to Cadez?"

"He's in a psychiatric hospital in Dallas. I suppose that ends his run at the Presidency."

"Good riddance. Hated him from the get-go. His third party is still on the ballot though."

"Yeah – his followers were never that loyal. It's between Real-Prez and Humpkin now."

"I suppose we could help him out by getting him some of our new and improved natural Fungus," Elwood said. "You know it was that lab shit they grew at the Howard Hughes pharmaceutical company that made him nuts. But lately being nuts doesn't bar you from being President. Who knows how this is all going to turn out."

"Do whatever you want, Elwood," said Maggie, with a hint of disgusted resignation.

"Yeah," Elwood laughed, "I'm just kidding! Fuck him!"

"That's how I feel. Anyway, are you ready for a voice from the past? I am going to drop off. Elwood – Wally Cherry. I'll come back when you guys decide what to do."

"Fuck, Wally!"

"Hey, Elwood."

"Wally! Wow, where did the years go?"

Wally looked like a corpse. They had been close all through college, but after Elwood and Nate started publicizing their electroencephalographic sensory deprivation (and Fungus) mind-reading system, Wally dropped out of sight and eventually left the US decades earlier. At first he had been based in Hamburg, but after the fall of the Berlin Wall, he moved to Gdansk, Poland. Lately he had been moving around more, and apparently had business interests in a number of Baltic cities. He knew everybody, saints and sinners alike, and had enough money to buy most of them.

"You haven't changed much." Wally laughed at his own joke. "I hear we lost Nate."

"Yeah, shot. Dead before he hit the ground, probably. You heard about our fight with the Real-Prez mercs."

"Yeah, pretty wild. Did you get into it too?"

Elwood shrugged, and didn't mention it was his grenade that blew up the chopper and half the mercs before they got out.

Wally remembered him as an unathletic klutz. He would never believe Elwood could have made that throw. They were quiet for a few minutes. "So where are you?" Elwood asked.

"I am about to meet a mutual friend."

Elwood wasn't sure why Wally was being so mysterious. Was he being listened to; was he afraid we were bugged? The crew at *SwiftPad* was pretty good at securing communications. Maybe he didn't trust us, Elwood thought.

"We want to get GG back. We know she is over there," explained Elwood.

"So I understand. This is not as easy as it might sound. I am not sure what you have to trade for her."

"Oh." Elwood knew Arkie and Sequoia had been onto something, but had not paid attention to the details. He shrugged. "Well, we're working on that. Maybe you can introduce our friend to someone in a position to help. Any problem with that?"

"No. No, meetings are good. Bring it all out in the air. Speaking of air, the weather is suddenly pretty shitty here," Wally said. "We are about to have a Baltic blow – and up here near the Neva it is like a funnel, and it can be vicious. I mean flooding. I hope that doesn't fuck up any plans you might have?"

"Well," Elwood was almost unconsciously shaking his head, "help out if you can. For old times' sake."

"Yeah – OK."

"We'll be in touch soon with more info."

"Are you banging Paula now?" Wally asked.

Elwood laughed. Paula stuck her head in the frame. "Wally – I miss you. Come back after all this, OK?"

"We'll see," Wally said. "So is Elwood any good?"

"Compared to what? You? Hell yeah!"

"Me!?" Wally looked suddenly confused. "I wanted to but..."

"Don't you remember that snowstorm in Lawrence?"

"Shit. It's hell getting old," he said.

CHAPTER 34

AT AKHMATOVA MUSEUM, KIP AND WALTER COME TO TERMS

October 31

The Halloween mask was a white hospital mask.
From *The Fall of It All – A History of the Big Dump*

KIP BOUGHT A LONG KNOCK-OFF OF A NINE-teenth-century Russian military coat at a surplus store on Ligovsky Street just down from the hotel. The salesman told him it was vintage – very popular with the musicians and dissidents in 1970s Leningrad. It had round golden buttons, a wide collar you could turn up and cover your ears with, and was made of some kind of synthetic "light wool," military grade, created in KGB labs to keep their spies warm when on stakeouts. It was split in the back, like a tuxedo. But when he walked out in the rain, Kip found that it was waterproof too. He also traded his Lenin cap for a plain black wool longshoreman's hat, like British commandos used to wear. He thought he looked like David Niven, staying a step ahead of his Gestapo pursuers, all the while maintaining an air of *savoir faire*, but actually he looked like one of the kids who did the school shooting at Columbine.

He walked down Nevsky Prospect, staying on the left side, to shelter some from the south wind that was driving the rain almost sideways. It was suddenly colder too, after yesterday's sweltering, now under 10°C. It was odd, but in this nasty weather there seemed to be a lot of people in the street. At Vladimirsky Prospect Kip turned right and continued until he came to the home of Anna Akhmatova. It was 10:00 AM, and his coat was still keeping him dry.

He walked into the courtyard, which was a little urban park. The gusting wind was quickly stripping the few red leaves still on the majestic maple trees lining the gravel walkway toward the entrance to the Akhmatova building.

A cat was sitting on the bench by the entrance. A young woman was reading on a chair near the stairways. When she saw Kip, she got up and stood behind a card table that had a little cash box. The entrance fee was 100 rubles, a little over a dollar.

"You are lucky, there is only one other person up there. Enjoy."

Kip walked up the stairs and down the hall to where an opened door and a sign welcomed visitors to the Akhmatova Museum. He walked into the foyer, where a small settee, a table, two chairs, and two pictures of the poetess were on the wall. A skeletal bald man was staring at it with his back to Kip. He turned and smiled.

They walked to her study, where they found her desk. Her Olympia typewriter, with Cyrillic keys, sat in the center of the desk, surrounded by pictures of various people who must have been her friends and relatives.

"You know her work?" asked the bald man.

"Some," said Kip.

"You know before World War I she was already famous as the greatest poet of her generation. You can see she was beautiful. Maybe alluring is a better word. The world of St. Petersburg society was hers. She would have been queen of the émigrés, if she had left. But she stayed, all through the horrors of the '30s, and then the war. Stalin could not have her be captured or die during the German blockade where a million starved, so he sent her to Central Asia. But she returned after the blockade ended. She was probably the only one in the country who Stalin feared. You must be Kip. I am Walt, Walter."

"My dad's name was Walt."

"Oh, I didn't know that."

Kip nodded. They moved to the kitchen, passing under a storage shelf above the door where she stored her sled, and suitcases filled with manuscripts.

"She must have used the sled to shop during the winter."

"The city is too flat for downhill sledding. So, you want to meet the people who have the *SwiftPad* woman, right?"

"Yes. And see her if possible."

"I have a car downstairs. Let's go. After we finish the tour of course."

As they were leaving they passed out of the sitting room. "It was right here that one of the most famous meetings of the twentieth century took place. Isaiah Berlin, who grew up in Petersburg, came to see her after the war. They sat here and talked for hours. Berlin was then first secretary for the British Embassy in Moscow. His brilliance as a philosopher was acknowledged worldwide. He sat right in that chair. They talked all night. When Stalin heard of it, it drove him up a wall, and he demanded a transcript of their encounter, which he never received. She wrote one of her most enigmatic poems about Berlin later: 'Poem Without a Hero.' The encounter also left Akhmatova under heavy, intrusive surveillance by the KGB for years."

They left Akhmatova's apartment and headed out into the wind and the rain. They proceeded back toward Nevsky in Walt's Bimmer, then down past the Hermitage across the Anichkov Bridge.

"Look at the water!" The wind was whipping balls of water

out of the Neva onto the bridge. "It's moving in fast." The wind from the south was pushing the car to the right, and Walter was fighting with the steering wheel as they crossed the river. As they passed the middle of the bridge, the side of the car was smacked with a huge splash of water that sounded like a car crash.

"So we are on the Viborg side now."

"Russians sometimes call it the Finnish side of the Neva, although Viborg was actually a Swedish city. Well, they lost it in the early 1700s, but it still has a famous Swedish castle. Technically this is the Vasileostrovsky District. Anyway, everyone knows not to fuck with the Finns anymore." They turned south into the wind. "You hungry?"

"I could eat," said Kip.

"Well, maybe they will have a brunch for us. These guys are going to be watching you. I am not staying, so don't give away too much. They won't tell you anything, but we will see what they do. So you know...you might be putting her in danger. They are not going to let her go for nothing. Afterwards, meet me at the Café Rasputin, on the other side of Palace Square."

They parked on the street, and entered what looked like a second-tier office building. Walt waved as they passed a guard who stared back blankly, and they went into a darkened doorway. Another guard was sitting there reading his fone.

A young man, well dressed, but not too well dressed, came over and hugged Walter.

"Rodin, this is Cornelius Welles. Cornelius – Rodin Smersky. An old friend of mine asked me to introduce him to you, Rodin, but beyond that – well, I don't need to be here," said Walter. "I don't exactly know what Mr. Welles has in mind."

"You look familiar, Mr. Welles."

"Well, this is the first time I have ever met Mr. Welles," said Walter. He looked at Chubby, who nodded sagely. "Have we ever met before today, Cornelius?"

"No," said Kip. Walter shrugged, smiled, and held his hands

out in a 'there you go' gesture. "So, I am going to leave, Rodin. Sorry to run, but this does not concern me. When you conclude your discussions, can you get him a taxi or a car to take him back to his hotel?"

"Sure, Walter. No problem. We'll be talking." Rodin and Walt went in to kiss each other's cheek and Walt put up his hand. They stepped back and laughed at themselves, and Walt left.

"Mr. Welles, please, sit down. Have some tea?"

"Thank you. Your English is excellent, much better than my Russian I am afraid."

"Говорить?" ("Gavroite? – You speak?")

"Немного." ("Nemnogo – a little.")

"Well I am sure you speak fine, but since I need the practice, I will be glad to try and use my limited English. Where are you from, Mr. Welles?"

"Oregon – it is in the Northwest of the United States."

"Oh, I know it well! So what do you think of the riots and revolution in your city there – Pot-land, right?"

Kip smiled and waggled his head.

"We know about revolution here in Peter, as I am sure you know."

"Well, things got out of hand, but – anyway, I am in Russia trying to line up some joint ventures about Siberian timber. My family was in logging – mostly Douglas fir."

"Well, that is interesting. I don't know if Walter told you, but we are a small software firm."

"Oh," said Kip. "What kind of software?"

Rodin looked down, "We specialize – not popular, we make products other companies use to make their products – security-related mostly."

"I see," said Kip.

Rodin looked at Kip for several seconds, and smiled.

"I don't mean to be rude, Mr. Smersky, but…"

"Please – call me Rodin!"

"Oh, well – call me Chubby then," said Kip.

"Chubby! Yes! You seem very fit! Strong!"

Kip laughed and patted his belly. "Thank you. Rodin – I am looking for a woman. She possibly has a young child with her."

"An American woman?"

"Yes?"

"And you think she is here? That we – might know where she is?"

"I think she is in St. Petersburg."

"I see," Rodin sipped his tea, not taking his eyes from Kip. "This woman – she is – is – do you have some claim on her or on the child?"

"Some claim?"

"Is she running away from you with your child?"

"No," Kip shook his head and smiled. "But the child's father... was a very close friend of mine."

"Was?"

"Yes. He was killed. Murdered."

"Oh," Rodin nodded his head. "I see."

They sat quietly for almost a minute.

"Well," Rodin said. "Walter and I have done much business together and he is – a trusted friend. So I will make a very – strong – no – not strong – your President uses that word to describe everything. I don't believe it's a good word to use all the time, is it?"

Kip shrugged. He watched Rodin placidly. "I will make a determined –" he looked up and saw Kip nod ever so slightly, "a determined effort to find her. Can you describe her?"

"Brown hair, not tall, 165 centimeters, very deep, dark eyes. Slight build, small bosom."

"Pretty?"

"Yes. But too intelligent looking to be extremely pretty. She doesn't care what people think about her looks."

"And the baby?"

"Very young, maybe two, no more than three months old."

"Well, I assume you don't want to involve the authorities. Perhaps…"

"Rodin – I think you know who I am talking about. You can find her description in a million magazines, books, or video blogs. I am talking about Cynthia Oglethorpe. The creator of *SwiftPad*."

Rodin looked slightly shocked, but then smiled and shook his head. "Oh! Well, as I said. We will keep an eye out for her." Rodin stood up. "Can I get you a car?"

Looks like no brunch, thought Kip. "No, I need the exercise. I want to walk over the Neva, and see the Hermitage."

"The weather is dreadful!"

"I am well dressed."

"Yes I see that, where did you get that coat? It – a famous piece of clothing – it is called the 'Leningrad frock.' All our Russian rock bands wore it during the '70s. It is warm, no? Practical yet elegant. The frock is made right here in Peter, of course. Or was. I have not seen one in years." Rodin rubbed the material of Kip's coat between his fingers. "Your feet will get wet though. Petruskavich, get him some rubber overshoes to wear."

"Thank you," said Kip.

"I don't understand your insistence on walking. We have driver with nothing to do. You are going to Hermitage? To see the paintings? I tell you secret – the State Museum in the park behind Hermitage is much better. Not so much Greek – but all of the great Russian artists are there. Let him at least drive you there, no?"

"I do appreciate it but – as I said," he patted his tummy, "I need the exercise. By the way, you don't think there will be a flood, do you?"

"Maybe a long time ago. Petersburg is protected now by the Kotlin Island dam."

"I was just wondering – you are pretty close to the river over here."

"Yes, not far. It is beautiful on a nice day to walk down to the river. But not today. Please let our driver…"

"No, thank you. You are very kind to insist, but I must insist. To tell you a secret, I love storms, I love to feel cold rain in my face. It is – an affliction of some kind."

"No, I understand, it is not an affliction. It is almost a Russian thing to do." Rodin looked at Kip with an increasing curiosity.

"I would hate to see your Institute over here flooded. You don't have any of your software business systems in the basement here, do you?"

Rodin didn't say anything, but looked at Kip with even greater intensity.

"Give Walter a call if you hear anything about Ms. Oglethorpe. Thank you for the tea."

It was about a mile to the Anichkov Bridge. Kip walked along the Neva, the wind at his back. The river was visibly reversed, flowing fast upstream. It was also even higher than when they had crossed. Along the embankment, the water was even with the top of the bank.

He walked past the Hermitage and across Palace Square and headed for the Café Rasputin.

CHAPTER 35
FLOODWATERS RISING

November 1

Churches filled up on the Sunday before the U.S. election. "We have never had a Sunday like this," said a Lutheran pastor who asked not to be identified.

From *The Fall of It All – A History of the Big Dump*

"DIMITRY, THE CHIEF IS ON THE FONE." SVETLANA had only been working on Kotlin Island for three months. She felt the severe tension from all of her colleagues, and she was scared. The S-1 gate had not needed to be closed since 2011. Three months after the dam opened, a Baltic storm arrived and they closed the S-1. Svetlana had been in middle school then, and no one knew if the dam and the gate would work and prevent flooding then. The water still rose to 1.3 meters above sea level, but there was no major damage to the city. The dam; Russia's President, a native of the city, who pushed it through, even in times of austerity; and to a smaller degree the staff here operating the dam had all been lauded as heroes.

"Dimitry, the level gauge at the Mining Institute is at 130 centimeters and rising. The storm is getting worse. The boss wants to know why you have not yet closed the gate," the chief asked.

"Yes, well," Dimitry hesitated, thinking carefully about what to say next. "We are having difficulty starting the pumps to release the booms."

There was silence at the end.

"We have dispatched a crew, a good crew, they know their business. It appears when we started the pumps, we locked them instead."

"What?"

"There was – a malfunction in the process control. We are reviewing the steps, and are almost sure that there was no mistake. There is a fail-safe mechanism – to prevent the pumps from overheating, it is related to the thermal sensors, but there is nothing wrong with the sensors, so – it must be something else."

"When was the last maintenance?"

"Oh, every year on the first of September, we run a full check – two months ago – clean everything, stop and start the pumps, begin the process and bring it back. We run the drill to ensure all the systems are..."

"So the computers have failed..."

"It's not the computers it's the – process control."

"You mean that German shit! Siemens! I knew that was a mistake. My grandmother died of starvation when those Nazi fucks blockaded the city."

"It is acting like it has been...several functions are not working as – they are supposed to..."

"So go to manual procedures!"

"We are!! We are bringing in the auxiliary pumps on trucks. They are parked in Lomonosov. It is going to take – maybe two hours to get them over the causeway to Kotlin."

"The flood is..."

"Yes – we estimate it will be at 1.65 meters then – that is..."

"I know what that is, Dimitry. That is five centimeters of

water on the Palace Embankment. Lapping at the Hermitage. How many men can I send you?"

"That won't help. We are working diligently. We can handle this, chief. Please."

His chief hung up. Dimitry stared off, thinking. The fone buzzed again.

"Dimitry – the power is out," said Bruno, his first engineer.

"How is this possible?"

"It is all in the process control."

Dimitry put his face in his hands. He finger punched his fone. "Svetlana, get me the Internet Research Institute!"

"Sir, I have Rodin Smersky on line 4."

"Rodin, it's Dimi. Have you noticed any activity with hackers? We are having trouble with the process controllers over here on Kotlin."

Sequoia went through the procedures again. Turning off the controls was easy. Now she was hoping they could turn them on again and do it quickly, but only when told.

"I figure we have a fifteen-minute window," said Jerry, his feet up on the desk, barely keeping his eyes open. "When did we start?"

"3:00 AM – yesterday," said Hadley. She had her head in her arms and on the desk, but was apparently still awake.

"No pressure, kids. If we blow it, Kip and GG die, a great city will be destroyed, and we will probably be at war. Either that or the 101st Airborne will come storming into our office shooting. I am sure the Russian President has a direct line into the White House."

Sequoia pushed down the urge to say "I wish Arkie was here" – first off, it was morbid and useless, and second, Hadley would go off on a crying jag again and would be worse than useless. "We have to release the lock on the electric motors first."

"Right," said Hadley. "If we don't, and they try to start them, they will burn out and then it's major fucko." That was the one hole in their procedure. They didn't have the electric motors to test each step. "I think this will work," said Hadley. It was a command line toggle – on or off. Easy enough. Does it work?

"I was thinking," said Sequoia, "rather than turn it on for them – why don't we just directly release the pontoons ourselves. Rather than have them do it?"

"But – we don't know all of the possible problems," said Jerry. "Every structure varies from the specs. No, I think that is a bad idea."

"OK," Hadley said, with the enthusiasm that sometimes comes to those who are in desperate need of sleep. "So turn on the power, unlock the motor, open the platform doors, and reload their process control OS with the original commands."

"What if they are doing the same thing," said Jerry. "What if they are reloading their process controller from their backup at the same time? We could hose it up bad."

"Well that's not going to be a problem," said Sequoia. "They figured out our intrusion. We no longer have connection with the dam controls."

"Fuck – they will burn out their motors now if they restart!" Hadley looked as though she was going to cry again.

"We need to talk to them."

CHAPTER 36
CHUBBY HINTS AT A SWAP; FROM FINLAND STATION

November 1

The world is fortunate that the one and only time Real-Prez missed a call from the Russian President, he was under anesthesia. He had lost about a third of his comb-over when his Slovak wife "accidentally" pulled it out in what was described later as "a moment of passion." There are doubts as to the nature of the passion, however. A White House household staff member reported that there was screaming coming from the second floor and that several Secret Service agents were seen with their guns drawn.

Since he was giving his final speech before the election to the nation the next evening, fixing his hair was a matter of great national emergency. Because the Office of VP was currently not filled, the message was never delivered or acted on, and the fighter-bombers that the Russian President demanded attack the *SwiftPad* Headquarters were never dispatched. The St. Petersburg Dam Hack progressed.

From *The Fall of It All – A History of the Big Dump*

"SO WHAT DID RODIN SAY WHEN YOU ASKED HIM about the flood?" Walt asked.

"Nothing, but then again, it seemed to spark something. Can't tell. This meat and cream sauce is delicious! What do they call it?

"Beef stroganoff."

"You're shitting me?"

"No."

"Wow." Chubby was chewing like he was having an orgasm. "This isn't anything like..."

"I know." Walter's fone played the opening bars of Wagner's *Parsifal*. He looked at it, made a face at Chubby, and answered.

"Yes, Rodin. Yes, he is here. Do you want to speak to him?" He listened for a few seconds, making a sarcastically shocked face. "Rodin, I know nothing about any of that. Do you? Yes, OK." Walter handed his fone to Kip. "I think he wants to talk to you."

"Mr. Smersky. I didn't expect to be hearing from you so soon." Kip listened. "I see. Well, maybe I can help. I was wondering..." He listened for a whole minute. "No, no. I don't think so." More listening. "I'm not the one wasting time." "No." "No. Money doesn't interest us." "Wow. Rodin, you should see this. I am eating in this nice restaurant and we are right near one of the canals – not sure which one – but – the water is almost starting to lap into the street." "Oh, I agree it would be tragic." "I understand." "Yes of course. Hold on – could you hold please?"

Kip was getting a message. It took him two minutes to unencrypt it with his OTP app. "Need to contact directly! Urgent!" He showed it to Walter.

"Alright, Rodin. I'll get a signal to them. I think they will need a direct line to your staff." "Yes – I know time is short. Let them help you, Rodin! Of course. But you will work on that other thing, won't you? That really needs to be done." "Good. I will have them call you at this number." "You too, Rodin."

Kip looked at Walt, waiting.

"They figured out the incursion and cut off *SwiftPad* to their dam. Which means that your guys can't fix whatever it is they broke...You know – if this doesn't work – we are all dead. They will kill us. In fact, they might kill us anyway," Walt admitted.

"Well, that is out of our hands now," said Chubby, who continued to eat. "Your guy at Izvestia News Corp – he can get it on the air?"

"Number one in local news in the Leningrad Oblast!"

"OK, let's go pick up Milana."

Jerry, Sequoia, and Hadley looked back at Maggie. Maggie knew next to nothing about hacking, or Internet attack and defense techniques. Her old day job – teaching basic psychology to undergraduates at Portland State, was pretty far removed from the problem at hand, but by some silently-arrived-at consent, she was driving the decisions.

"Jerry, you talk to them."

"Yes, go ahead," said Jerry.

"Am I speaking to the criminals who have illegally attacked the St. Petersburg dam?"

"I can confirm that we did have control of your facility, until you shut off the connection. Now we have no idea what your situation is. With whom am I speaking?"

"Call me R, and you are?"

"J."

"Like Jay Leno? He is stupid comedian, never funny."

"I agree, R. He is not funny. I implore you. Do not attempt to start those motors yet. Have you tried yet?"

"Why did you sabotage them? Is this some kind of trick?"

"Yes, R, we sabotaged them. But we want to help you fix them!"

"Why should I believe?"

"R – have you ever seen the movie *Fail Safe*?" Jerry was unconsciously doing a Henry Fonda impression, reaching as far as he could to impart some level of credibility to his voice. He waited, for what seemed like a long time, for an answer.

"Yes, I know movie. It ends with the destruction of Moscow, after criminal attack by Americans. Why do you bring up such horrible film?"

"Actually the end is when New York is destroyed."

"By same criminals who destroy Moscow. Is that what you are suggesting? That you destroy St. Petersburg and then destroy some unimportant place like Pot-land?"

Jerry looked over at Maggie. She rolled her chair over to the microphone. "R. I am in charge. My name is Margaret Stromborn. We have taken over your dam in order to convince you to release Cynthia Oglethorpe, whom we know you are holding. Will you release her?"

"Margaret. OK. Good. I would rather speak to you, a woman – in charge, as you say. I am wearing sweater and jeans, and will soon put on boots, as the water is rising rapidly here in this most beautiful city."

"And I am wearing a very thin layer of patience. Will you release the girl, or will you have to put on a life preserver as well?"

There was a delay. The team looked at Maggie. She could feel that they thought she had pushed him too far. She took a deep breath through her nose and stared straight ahead.

"We agree, we will deliver the woman and her child to Mr. Welles."

"We will do preliminary work to close the gate, and complete the procedures when you have done your part. But we will need to contact your staff directly. We need you to allow us back into your network."

"Oh, I see now. Fail Safe. I will complete arrangements with Mr. Welles. Or rather Mr. Rehain. You think we are stupid? We know who he is and we know who you are, and we know where you are. We complete this successfully, fine. Otherwise..."

"We have no wish to harm your beautiful city, Mr. Smersky."

"Ha, we know each other. I believe you wish correctly. However Ни пу́ха, ни пера́. – К чёрту!"

"What does that mean?"

"When you wish for success you jinx it. Close our gate and save our city or we will never end our search for you until – help us please."

"We will, Mr. Smersky."

"Yes, Rodin. You must have talked to our people?" "Good. That was quick. Are we OK?" "I see." "Simple. There is a train leaving for Helsinki in two hours. Have her at Finland Station in a half hour." "45 minutes – that will work, but no later." "No – no – it will just work like normal." "Can I guarantee it? Well – I can't guarantee your technical staff knows how to work the bloody floodgate, but if they do..."

"Dimitry, nice to meet you," said Hadley.

"And you, Hadley."

"So Mr. Rodin told us you have not started the motors. We have a list of steps you need to take to recover your process control. It would be easier if we could connect directly and help you?"

"Nyet. We want to do it. How long will it take if you step us through?"

"Half hour. OK. Are you ready?"

"Yes, I have all my team on the line."

"Good. First there are three daemons that are running in the background on station, host name Gogol, UDP port 2203, internal IP address, 10.10.151.23. Do you see it?"

"Yes!"

"OK, let's start the kill sequence…"

Kip stood over on the sidewalk next to Finland Station, under the awning, visible. Walter's BMW pulled up right in front of him with Milana. She looked beautiful. She got out and ran through the rain to him as he stood on the sidewalk. She hugged him and kissed him and radiantly stood next to him as they waited under the canopy.

Kip looked out at the parking lot toward the spot where Lenin had spoken after arriving here, right here, in 1917, sent in the sealed train by the Germans to undermine the Russian war effort. The picture was iconic, and menacing. Lenin haranguing the crowd had happened right there, 20 meters in front of him.

The rain was blowing sideways and the wind was terrifying. Walter got out of the car and ran over. "Is this necessary? Can't we wait in the car?"

"I love it! The wind feels wonderful!" said Milana. "It has been so hot until today."

"I want them to see me," said Kip.

"Look!"

A van pulled up. Rodin leaned out and waved but stayed put. He had a fone to his ear.

"OK." Kip's fone rang. It was Maggie. "Alright, we are down to the last sequence."

"Are you controlling it?"

"We are waiting. We have one more system to unlock. We are refusing to give them the sequence until you say it is OK."

Kip looked at Walt, who spoke into his fone. Rodin turned and signaled someone. A woman got out of the passenger side holding an umbrella. The back door slid open. The woman with the umbrella reached in and he saw a hand reach out and grab hers.

Then suddenly the very pregnant Milana waddled out in the rain, without an umbrella, her dark hair streaming down her face. She leaned forward into the wind toward the van. Finally Kip saw Cynthia, holding a tightly wrapped bundle. Milana arrived, completely soaked, took the umbrella from the woman, and she and Cynthia started walking together toward Kip.

"OK, Maggie. We have her. Go ahead. We'll manage."

Rodin was on the fone, intently listening when suddenly, from Botkinskaya Ulitsa Street, a white van with red and blue stripes like the Russian flag driving very fast pulled up. It had a satellite dish on its roof, and the words Известия – Izvestia – the news agency – painted across the side.

From across the parking lot, Rodin, listening and nodding, watched as the door opened and a camera crew began to pull their equipment out.

"What is this?" Rodin was shouting into his fone at Walter. "This was not part of agreement – you wait!" He was leaning out the door of his van and pointing at GG. Walter walked over and began shaking hands with the journalist who was sitting in the front seat. He was laughing at a joke. His camera crew was just finishing setting up in front of Kip, GG, and Milana.

Kip barely noticed any of this though. His eyes were planted on Cynthia – GG.

They stared at each other, and then GG showed Kip her baby.

"Meet Alice," she said. Kip touched her cheek, saw Jim almost immediately. It was the eyes, the same eyes. He looked at Milana, who was crying as she struggled to hold the umbrella. Kip took it.

"Are we OK, Rodin?" said Walter.

Rodin saw the second Izvestia reporter approaching his van. His eyes flared, but then he smiled. He had to get out of here.

"Yes," he yelled into his fone. "But not a word! IF you embarrass us..." He let the threat hang in the air.

Kip smiled. He had no intention of revealing anything about the hack. "Let's get out of the rain!" Kip walked between the two women and they entered Finland Station, followed by the Izvestia crew and Walter. They continued the interview inside, and were watched by nervous Russian police from a distance. Although there had been reports already in the local Petersburg press about the rising water, and even some mention in blogs about the oddity of the gate remaining opened for so long, it was never mentioned by the reporter, nor of course did Kip bring it up. But Kip dispensed with his ruse of being "Chubby" Welles – he identified himself as Kipling Rehain, President of *SwiftPad*, and Cynthia too was openly identified. She played the part naturally, waving and saying she could not yet discuss her "kidnapping and imprisonment," but thanked the Russian security services for their wonderful work saving her and her daughter. The camera kept on them for almost twenty minutes until Walter pulled them away, saying they had a train to catch. At the entrance to the tunnel down to the platform, they stopped.

"You can come, you know," said Kip.

"Naw, I live here," said Walt. "Things are good. I do have a girlfriend, so maybe I'll bring her over to the US to visit."

"Thanks, I don't know what else to say? If you need anything..."

"Say hi to Woody and Paula for me, will you?" He took one more peek at the baby, stared at GG, and kissed Milana. "You," he said to Kip, hugging him one last time, "have your hands full!" He was laughing as he walked away.

The train ride through the forests was quiet, peaceful. Even though they were still in Russia, Kip was unconcerned. Everybody won. GG was nursing little Alice. Milana and Kip sat next to each other holding hands.

When they came to the Finnish border, the Finnish border cop came on, checking their passports, smiling. He took their temperature, and gave them a virus test recently developed in Denmark. Swab of the tongue, and ten minutes later the Finnish border guard came back and stamped their passports, "No infection."

"Give me your fone, Kip. I have not played with my software since they grabbed me."

"Really?"

"Come on! I'm still just a nerd at heart."

Kip continued to use his Cornelius Welles documents to be stamped "Exit" to match his entrance into Russia at Vladivostok. It all occurred without incident. Maggie had his Rehain passport overnighted to the hotel in Helsinki for his trip home.

They checked into the Hotel Kämp in Helsinki. GG eyed him as he ordered adjoining suites. They had no luggage, other than the strange document the man had given Kip at the Bulgakov apartment. With all her free time, Milana had read it and told them that the fungus referred to in the document was from Georgia, near the cabin she had shared with Kip eight months ago. In fact, she had used them in a dish she had prepared for him and Paula during their brief "ménage à trois" in the woods overlooking the Black Sea.

"It will be interesting to see what happens as the fungus spreads through Europe. It will stop the virus, but what about the side effects?"

Kip was still in a daze. So much had happened, but he got GG. He couldn't have done it alone, and that was what made it so sweet. Kip was drinking champagne, next to Milana. He had a goofy grin on his face, and was determined to finish the bottle himself, being as he had no one else to share it with. GG sat at the end of the bed, and was busy changing Alice into some diapers that Hotel Kämp had sent up. Alice giggled and laughed, something she had never done before when being changed.

"Halloween was yesterday," GG said. "It was my favorite holiday. Did you tell Milana what I used to be called when you met me?"

Kip looked over at Milana, and patted her tummy. "She was called by every hacker and cybercriminal in Portland 'The Goth Girl.' Dressed all in dark clothes, heavy make-up around her eyes, hair dyed black. Everyone was scared of her."

"We don't have Halloween in Georgia, but I know what it is."

"Shit – one more thing – G – we have to destroy it. Pull the plug."

"You mean *SwiftPad*? As usual I am way ahead of you, Kipster. Look at your fone. Try to log into your *SwiftPad* account."

Kip hit his SP icon. It came back with a picture of the Fool from a deck of tarot cards.

"I sent the sequence to Hadley as soon as we passed into Finland. It's gone, never to return. The worm is loose, and will stay loose for years. And when someone tries to restore a *SwiftPad* server, or any app cloned out of its code, it will spike the CPU and burn out the box. Hence no more *SwiftPad*."

"You mean...?"

"No more *SwiftPad*. It's gone. Everybody's fone in the world is free. Just like me."

www.ingramcontent.com/pod-product-compliance
Lightning Source LLC
Chambersburg PA
CBHW071137100726
47908CB00008B/2629